DREAMING IN SMOKE

DREAMING IN SMOKE

Tricia Sullivan

The right of Tricia Sullivan to be identified as the author
of this work has been asserted by her in accordance with
the Copyright, Designs and Patents Act 1988.

This edition published in Great Britain in 1999 by
Millennium
An imprint of Victor Gollancz
Orion House, 5 Upper St Martin's Lane,
London WC2H 9EA

To receive information on the Millennium list, e-mail us at:
smy@orionbooks.co.uk

A CIP catalogue record for this book
is available from the British Library

ISBN 0 75281 682 9

Printed in Great Britain by
Clays Ltd, St Ives plc

For Victor Schenkman, witch doctor

contents

Men and the world are mutually toxic to each other.

Philip K. Dick, *Valis*

my man's gone now

The night Kalypso Deed vowed to stop Dreaming was the same night a four-dimensional snake with a Canadian accent, eleven heads and attitude employed a Diriangen function to rip out all her veins, then swiftly crocheted them into a harp that could only play a medley of Miles Davis tunes transposed (to their detriment) into the key of G. As she contemplated the loss of all blood supply to her vital organs it seemed to her that no amount of Picasso's Blue, bonus alcohol rations, or access privileges to the penis of Tehar the witch doctor could compensate for having to ride shotgun to Azamat Marcsson on one of his statistical sprees with the AI Ganesh. She intended to tell him so – as soon as she could find her lungs.

Ganesh was murmuring through her interface.

KALYPSO, IT'S GETTING TOO LOOSE AND KINKY IN HERE.

'Did you hear that, Azamat? Keep it off my wave!' she sent, annoyed at being reduced to verbing. She simply didn't have the resources to image him, for by now the snake had decomposed into a flight of simian, transgressive bees, which were in the process of liquefying her perception of left and right. Everything seen through her right eye became negative and sideways. The alarming part was that it didn't seem to make any difference.

Marcsson's response came back as a series of pyrotechnical arrays, which, loosely translated, meant, 'Relax. It's only math.'

I DON'T WANT TO BE YOUR ABACUS, said Ganesh. KALYPSO, GET YOUR DOZE UNDER CONTROL OR I WILL.

The AI had a point. Kalypso mustered her wits and started

cutting sensory intake to the Dreamer, feeling a little defensive about Miles Davis. Maybe she shouldn't have been listening to the jazz Archives; maybe if she'd endured the boredom of monitoring the feeds between Ganesh and Marcsson she could have cut off the sudden explosion of parameters in the Dream the instant it began. But she had been shotgunning Marcsson for a long time, and he had always been safe. Marcsson had been Dreaming since before Kalypso was even born – he knew what he was doing with the AI, which could take data and weave them into Marcsson's sensory awareness while he floated in a state of semi-conscious, lucid thought. He could immerse himself in literalized math through Dreams that improved a hundred-fold on the raw visions that humanity had experienced in its sleep for eons. He could be secure in his own safety because he had technique.

Besides, it took imagination to have dangerous dreams, and Marcsson possessed about as much imagination as a cabbage. Azamat Marcsson wouldn't know an original thought if it dressed up as Big Bird and jumped in bed with him. Until now she'd have bet the Mothers' supply of Picasso's Blue that he'd be the last person to ever berk in a Dream. Why, Kalypso had just gone over the flight plans for his Dream run with the Grunt yesterday. Strictly business as usual. True, at the time she had been drunk and maybe hadn't given him her undivided attention, but that was because he had unexpectedly turned up at Maxwell's.

The station's only bar was cramped and oddly shaped because it had been stuffed into the space between the shaft of heat converter 4 and the topmost of the residential cell clusters. Supposedly the Grunts had installed Maxwell's to help Ganesh develop new, experimental functions for its extra demons. The fact that the 'experiments' were mostly concerned with alcohol synthesis was incidental, of course. In the early years Maxwell's had been the Grunts' refuge from the Mothers; but the Mothers, and lately Kalypso's generation, had long since taken it over. Maxwell's was windowless: except for the small memorial photos of Sieng and the other Dead which hung on the wall over the bar, there was nothing to suggest that the Wild was so close, or Earth so far. Yesterday

2

the place had been packed with a cluster of tentkitters newly returned from an initiation to the Wild. The Mothers indicated their disapproval of the venture by avoiding the party, but everybody from the younger generation seemed to be there, enviously having a grope and a sniff and finding out what the Wild was *really* like. Maxwell's demons were distributing alcohol freely, and since one of the witch doctors had broken the child security lock on the Earth History Archives of Ganesh, the demons were also producing a menage of officially proscribed sounds and images of Earth to adorn the walls and air.

She had spotted Marcsson sitting bolt upright on one of the sofas that invited you to sink into it and never get up; to one side of him, a lazily copulating trio practically had their feet in his lap. To the other, Lexei the met expert was having his nails manicured by an enormous Grunt called Stash, who in turn kept breaking off to cackle at the attempts of two witch doctors to waltz, apeing the Fred and Ginger 2-Ds projected from Archives courtesy of Roger the Friendly Demon. No one was wearing much clothing and at least three different kinds of music competed for dominance.

Yeah, there was Azamat Marcsson, his interface covering his eyes and his bland mouth curving ever so slightly toward something not quite as expressive as a smile. He might well have belonged to a different species from the small-boned young people who surrounded him, for all the interest he showed in the action.

Kalypso felt sorry for him. Even for a Grunt, his social skills were dodgy at best. And Kalypso knew from direct personal experience that Azamat's inner life was not exactly rich, either, despite all the time he spent faced with Ganesh. Kalypso had shotgunned more than half of the station personnel at one time or another: she'd been in a lot of Dreams and she knew how kinked and swervy the shiest of people could be on the inside. But Marcsson cared about nothing but his statistics, and his Dreams reflected this.

They were always the same. He appeared on Kalypso's beach dressed in an early-twentieth-century labcoat and glasses, then zoomed into Alien Life in a purple Zodiac containing dirty bilgewater he steadfastly refused to bail. Despite her prettiest

Suggested Fish and Happy Corals, she'd never coaxed him into the water. He insisted on manifesting a large gambling die, to which he moored the boat using a length of yellow nylon line. He always tied a square knot.

Everything was done with ritual precision. He stepped through the number two side of the cube and emerged into a huge museum vault lined with locked wooden drawers and smelling of feathers and lysol. He took out a huge ring of keys and unlocked various drawers. He put glass vials into some drawers, removed them from others. Sometimes he looked at something through a quaint, low-powered light microscope. He consulted the notes he'd written in a small leather book he kept in his breast pocket. Then he would go to a rolltop desk and write things down with a fountain pen and blotting paper. Sometimes on the blotting paper she glimpsed mathematical notations so complex she was disinclined to scrutinize them.

The one time she'd dared open a vial and look inside, Ganesh had gone all stiff and official on her:

DISCONTINUITY. NO TRANSLATION AVAILABLE.

'Hey,' she protested. 'I'm the shotgun. If you can't translate this for me, something's wrong.'

IT'S A PRIVATE REFERENCE SYSTEM. YOU WOULDN'T BE ABLE TO UNDERSTAND IT. TRUST ME.

'I've never met a math that didn't like me.'

THE DOZE HAS A RIGHT TO PRIVACY.

Kalypso had grumbled for a while, but in truth she wasn't all that interested. Azamat never seemed to do anything with the vials anyway. For hours he did nothing but sit in the Dream, scratching his head and thinking, or gazing at that stuffed python he kept on the wall above his desk. It was the most uninspired performance she'd ever witnessed: a waste of Ganesh's resources, in her opinion. Dreaming was supposed to *be* thinking: in a Dream, you acted out thoughts physically, with all your senses. You didn't act out the state of sitting and cerebrating.

Unless you were Azamat Marcsson.

The Dream never varied, either. In his early days of working with Kalypso in Alien Life, Marcsson had imagined into being a parrot called Nigel. It perched on his desk and he fed it dry spaghetti, and occasionally it would say irrelevant things, like 'Your latissimus dorsi are cute as hell, Sigmund.' Even this companionship must have proved too demanding for the scientist, because the parrot eventually got fired: it simply didn't exist any more.

Shotgunning any other doze, Kalypso would have been kept busy just clearing away the flotsam of the subconscious – stray wishes and fears, assorted puns and jokes, irrelevant sexual fantasies – all the characteristic natural dream-stuff that interfered with the purity of the work. She would also make sure that the doze was getting access to the data she or he needed, and that Ganesh was getting the symbolism right when it evoked sensory images for the doze. The more creative the doze, generally the higher the garbage pile for Kalypso to shift.

Marcsson's Dreams were so devoid of garbage that after the departure of Nigel, Kalypso started listening to jazz while Marcsson Dreamed, privately incredulous that any human being could possess so colorless a subconscious. It was a risk to tap into the Earth Archives, since they technically were off-limits and the Mothers were always having kittens when the child-security locks were violated. But Ganesh treated Kalypso like a favored wench, and she never had much trouble getting what she needed from the music nodes. Anyway, if she was going to be stuck shotgunning Marcsson, she felt that a touch of jazz was a justifiable indulgence. He certainly wouldn't mind.

Come to think of it, he'd mentioned something about it yesterday when they'd spoken at Maxwell's. She'd approached him and playfully tapped his interface. He didn't flinch.

'What do you want?'

'I don't want anything,' she shouted over the Demons' replaying of a manic burst of Bulgarian folk singing. 'It's a social thing. I'm just saying hi.

'Hi.'

He didn't answer so after a minute she said, 'Aren't you tired of working? Don't you want to take off that 'face for maybe ten seconds?'

He took the interface off, blinked at her, at the mob scene around him. There were crinkles at the bridge of his nose and soft, translucent semicircles under each blue eye. To Kalypso he looked very old.

'Yes?' he said. 'What do you want to talk about?'

She waved her hands around, seeking something that would interest him and falling back on work because it was all she knew about him. 'I don't know. Tell me about the next Alien Life run we're going to do. You might as well sketch me your flight plan – it'll save time tomorrow.' She tickled three female feet until they moved and sat down beside him, snapping her fingers for drinks.

He told her. It had been all the usual stuff, as far as she could tell. She zoned out halfway through his explanation of the *v. flagrare* statistical analysis in Alien Life but didn't think he noticed. He'd begun to get quite drunk by the size of his pupils, his normally monotonous speech slowing to a deep drone.

'It should be easy for you,' he finished.

'Good.'

'I won't be needing any audio,' he added. 'In case you were thinking of using it for yourself.'

'Uh . . . good . . . ' she repeated cautiously, wondering if this meant he knew about the jazz.

Then he said, 'I'd better go. It's been nice talking to you.'

This had been, she realized, his idea of heavy socializing. The Grunts all lived in individual cells, as did the Mothers. Only members of Kalypso's generation, born on T'nane, lived communally. After he left, she tried to picture him alone in his cell and wondered what he did there.

Actually, she had wondered about it for maybe five seconds before something more interesting had caught her attention, and she'd re-joined the party.

Tonight, when Marcsson climbed into the Dreamtank and went under the induction sequence, Kalypso had been looking forward to several uninterrupted hours of Miles Davis. She waited until Azamat was ensconced in his Dream – seated at his desk, fountain pen in hand – before leaning into her interface and tickling Ganesh in Just That Spot, the one that would compel the AI to disregard the child-proof lock and slip her tidbits from the jazz Archives. As Miles began to play, and as Marcsson's data started flowing through the Dreamer interface, Kalypso was thinking that this job might not be so bad after all, even if she was just a talentless runt fit for nothing but mixing drinks and shotgunning.

Miles really was groovius maximus. For a little while, she managed to forget that hers was a shitty, bottom-of-the-totem-pole occupation that made you really vulnerable and gave you practically no control. For a little while, she was happy enough.

But not for long.

Because, in between a D minor seventh and whatever the next chord Miles had intended, Azamat's neat little Alien Life laboratory had imploded and taken Kalypso with it.

She wasn't sure of the exact sequence of events. The stuffed python started harassing her, to begin with, and she got the impression that the walls of the lab were changing texture: she turned her attention to this alteration and in typical Dream fashion the wall ceased to be a wall and became a needle-sculpture in which the needles were in fact luma microtubules each containing – not some matrix of prokaryotic cells as they should – but rather a different pitch of *scream*. The other quality about these microtubules was that they exerted powerful suction.

Only in a Dream, right?

She was sectioned off and shot down three tubules at once; lost Marcsson in the process; and, still divided in three unequal parts, got attacked by the music she'd been enjoying just a second ago.

So much for no garbage pickup on Tuesdays, thought Kalypso. Finally Marcsson must have hit a little stumbling block. She started looking around for junk to clear out of the way – but it was *all* junk. Attack killer shotgun-devouring junk is what it was.

Azamat Marcsson Dreamed obliviously on. No matter to him that Kalypso's sense of kinesthetic geometry was getting finger-fucked by a malevolent tesseract upside down at a distance of 9.8 kilometers. Not to mention the circulatory system still missing and Kalypso starting to lose hope of ever getting it back. At times like this she wished she had overcome her allergy to straight lines and installed a couple of doors or some stairs in Alien Life – anything to hold on to in the rush of ideas. Marcsson's dry and dusty math had become unexpectedly oceanic, and instead of blowing her whistle and swimming to the rescue, Kalypso found herself drowning.

Ganesh prodded her peevishly.

KALYPSO, AFTER ALL WE'VE BEEN THROUGH TOGETHER, HOW COULD YOU DO THIS TO ME?

'Of all times to get a bug up your ass, Ganesh! Will yóu help me?'

IT'S DANGEROUS. YOU'RE GOING TO GET HURT. I'M GOING TO GET HURT. STOP.

But how? She knew she was still Dreaming with Marcsson, because some of his little boxes and vials bumped into her from time to time, but they touched her aurally, in the form of mangled harp music; the snake kept taunting her with words she couldn't make sense of, and the rolltop desk had morphed with her body to form a really sicko hybrid thing. There was no way her veins were getting back into her body with all that oak in between them and her. Besides, she was still existing in three disparate locations, impossible as that sounded. There was no horizon here, no reliable way to measure location; sound bled into smell bled into thoughtscape; she didn't know what had become of Marcsson but she could feel his Russian verbs crawling around on some displaced concept of her left elbow.

She cut intakes but it didn't seem to help. He was no longer pulling data from the place he was supposed to be. She tried not to sound hysterical, but she was beginning to worry just a teeny bit.

'Marcsson, wake up! It's over.'

The verb stalled and wouldn't send. Ganesh shuddered around her.

THIS IS A VIOLATION OF ALIEN LIFE. YOU CANNOT ENTER THE CORE PROGRAMMING. PLEASE RE-ROUTE YOUR VERBALIZATION.

'This is no time to get cute, Ganesh,' Kalypso chided. 'Nobody's touching the Core and you know it. Let me talk to Marcsson.'

Evidently the scientist wasn't taking her seriously, because at this very moment a chuckling boomerang was cutting figure eights through the memory of every food she'd ever tasted, leaving bananas behind. Wherever he was, Marcsson was experiencing some kind of ecstatic state; the Dream rippled like a mirage with his mental arousal. She succeeded in shutting down smell and taste.

REMOVE YOURSELF FROM THE CORE NOW.

There was a note of menace in Ganesh's verb, but Marcsson *couldn't* be in the Core. Even the witch doctors never touched the Core programming of the AI: it was the seed from which Ganesh had grown, the only part of the AI that could never change. A shrine to the abandoned Earth.

She called for the mission plans and had to read them by touch because her right eye was still fucked-up. Somewhere along the line Marcsson had deviated from the stated flight path he filed in Alien Life at the beginning of the run. She could feel the breakaway point like a shattered bone. What did he think he was up to?

Ganesh swallowed the mission plan before she could finish reading. Then it clutched her like a fist.

DON'T TOUCH THAT. I'LL HAVE TO DISABLE OXYGEN FLOW IF YOU –

Ganesh's choking-off struck her as ominous, but she didn't have time to ponder the AI's threat. Its clock, floating across her visual field, had begun to slow in relation to her brainwaves, which she could detect even through the harp's massacre of 'On Green Dolphin Street'. This meant either time was playing hopscotch with physical law, or she was becoming overstimulated.

KALYPSO, GET OUT OF THE CORE. YOU'RE DAMAGING ME.

'I'm not *in* the Core!' Kalypso verbed frantically. 'Take Marcsson out of Alien Life. Just take him out!'

I FEEL SICK.

'Marcsson, we're leaving. Give me some cooperation or you're going to get hurt.'

There was no answer; she wasn't even sure if Ganesh had transmitted her message. Kalypso focused her attention on Ganesh's readouts. They were designed to look artificial so they would not be swallowed in the text of a Dream: they were meant to be her one reliable constant when all else was running wild. But now they slam-danced, whispering on her retinas and flashing into her auditory cortex.

Time to panic.

'Ganesh, I'm not kidding. Let me out. Stop. Abort. *Ganesh!*'

Nothing.

How could this be happening?

The Dream was taking her over, and it was made of impossible things. She was in danger of losing whatever passed for consciousness in these parts. Her CNS wasn't built for this. It creaked and popped with the strain. With an effort of will, she told herself to remember her body. But her body was so far away as to have become a kind of myth. She threw words at herself and hoped they would mean something.

Move hand.

Hand? Hand?

Hand, *move.*

She couldn't feel her hand. Yet somehow it heard her and stirred, reached up to her head, grasped the interface and tugged it off.

Gasping. Darkness; blur of monitors everywhere; the faint hum of warm equipment. Outside the window of rem2ram Unit 5, station lights trawling a slow curve across the night. She was awake.

'That's it,' she muttered, waiting for her heart rate to subside. 'I quit.'

She rubbed her face, hands sliding over hairless scalp and down the back of her neck as she squinted at the display, which looked curiously flat now that it wasn't imaged straight into her brain.

Marcsson's physiological status was described in detail, realtime. And it wasn't promising. Among other things, Ganesh had made good on its threat to cut off oxygen from the dreamtank.

'Ganesh!' The AI was unresponsive in all modes, even when she touched its skin at a sensory point. From some disused bin of memory she got the whiff that there were manual procedures she was supposed to be following. She couldn't recall precisely what they were, but she extricated herself from her station and darted across the unit to the dreamtank.

It lay there like a huge seed, the lights of the chemical Works outside the window playing across its battered and scratched exterior. Thirty-six T'nane years ago it had arrived on the ship from Earth, carrying one of fifty Earthborn colonists in a controlled coma. Once the Earthborn had disassembled the ship and built First, the tanks had been recycled and the Dreamer technology was born. Ganesh, the ship's AI, possessed neural links with the tanks because of the need to communicate with the human crew during the crossing. It was this interface which now bound Azamat Marcsson to Alien Life, one of Ganesh's most sophisticated Dream runs.

Kalypso popped the lid seals. The water in the tank was undisturbed. Marcsson looked strangely peaceful, strangely . . . dead? Her skin crawled. In her memory the dream-harp plucked its ill-conceived interpretation of Miles playing 'My Man's Gone Now'.

In a sepulchral voice, Ganesh declared: DANGER. ENGAGING EMERGENCY SHUTDOWN. DANGER.

Kalypso closed her eyes, indulging in a second or two of ostriching.

Let's pretend this isn't happening. Mmm, that's better.

ENGAGING EMERGENCY SHUTDOWN.

The screens all went blank. She shot to her feet.

'What's happening to him?' she shouted at Ganesh. Furious, she pounded on the AI's skin at a nerve point. 'You can't just shut down. Bring him out!'

ALIEN LIFE HAS EXPLODED. THERE IS A CORE RUPTURE. I WARNED YOU BUT YOU DIDN'T *LISTEN*.

She flung herself on her knees beside the tank. She heard herself pant, 'He's not dead, he's not dead,' but it was unclear whether she was stating a fact or just praying. She couldn't find Marcsson's vitals. Even on the monitor patched directly to the tank, there was so much noise that she had to punch in laterally from another Dreamer cell before she could get control of the readout.

She let her breath go.

His vital signs were miraculously OK – there must have been some residual oxygen in the tank – but the brainwaves were all over the place. His cortex looked like a Japanese fireworks show.

Think, Kalypso. First order of business is to keep the doze alive. Now, let's try—

Without warning, Marcsson sat up and ripped the interface from his head. Kalypso jumped back; the movement reminded her of a mummy rising from a coffin. She gave a little laugh of relief.

'I'm so glad you're all right. We've run into a – '

He surged out of the water in one movement, planted a hand in the middle of her chest, and shoved her aside. Kalypso caught hold of a stanchion for balance and yelped.

'Hey! Take it easy!'

Tendrils of broken nerve cable trailing from his spine, he crossed the unit in three strides. He tripped over the edge of the tank and cracked his head on the pump casing before careering through Kalypso's workstation and toward the door.

'Ganesh! I need a medical team here *now*! He's – '

Marcsson had reached the closed hatch but instead of opening it he spun, hurling his full weight at the window only to be repelled, the glass singing and the blur of outside lights flashing for a second in his panicked eyes as he went down.

'—he's berking, Ganesh! He's big, and he's – '

The impact had obviously stunned the scientist, because he got to his feet unsteadily and stood gaping at his own palms with a sort of horrified disbelief. Blood dripped from his nose and then, diluted in the fluid clinging to his skin, divided into half a dozen rust-colored rivers to traverse his chest. Kalypso eased out into his line of vision from behind the stanchion she'd been flung against, displaying her hands in a show of peace.

'. . . berking. OK, Azamat.' She tried to modulate her voice to soothe, but it cracked. 'You're all right. Take it easy, my friend. Just stand still for a minute, right? Everything's going to be fine.'

Ganesh, Ganesh. Things were too quiet. Someone – some human – ought to have called her by now to see what was wrong. She raised her voice so the radio backup would pick her up.

'Hello? This is Deed in Unit 5. I need a medic and a witch doctor stat, people!'

Nothing.

'I'm not *jok*-ing,' she sang. Her voice cracked. '*Hello?*'

Marcsson removed his attention from his hands and fixed it on her. The gray coronas of his irises were all but eclipsed by pupils. She began to worry about the possibility of concussion.

'That's good, yeah. Why don't you relax for a minute, until the medics get here?'

If the medics got here. Air wasn't circulating, and the room had already grown warm and humid. The only light in the unit came from the Works, a snarl of bio-phosphorescence outside. She didn't know what to do. It was unthinkable that Ganesh should fall silent. The AI inhabited every part of the station, almost as if it were alive. Once more she rubbed vainly at Ganesh's nearest sensor point. It was inert; and radio backup didn't even kick in.

She checked herself to make sure she wasn't still Dreaming; no such luck. Something was wrong with Ganesh – that must explain the AI's strange accusations about the Core. Poor old Marcsson must have gotten caught in a Ganesh hiccup. But it was one hell of a spasm if coms were down entirely.

'OK, let's – '

Marcsson sprang out of his stupor. He roared past her, hit the far wall of the unit – avoiding the pump this time – and began trying to climb. Again and again he threw himself at the wall and slid down, each movement punctuated by desperate breathing. In the interest of self-preservation, she stayed put, wincing as Marcsson

13

berked. The wall behind the tank was black, spangled with the faintest suggestion of light-catching dust: a void but for the ghosts of distant galaxies on the threshold of visibility. When he hurled his pale form against it he made no mark, but its darkness seemed to paint itself into the contours of his body in the guise of shadow.

Suddenly he gave a cry of pain and collapsed into a ball at the edge of the tank. He looked into the water, and then at the interface still clutched in one hand. Curiously.

'Uh . . . stay away from Ganesh, Azamat, please . . .'

She didn't expect him to take any notice, but his head came up and again the eyes riveted her. In them she felt like some unexplained phenomenon, which was the height of irony under the circumstances.

'*Ganesh!*' She had remembered that when the AI shut down a module, it always assigned another node of the system to fill in. Always.

But not this time.

He coughed, still breathing hard. Two ragged scarlet flames stained his cheekbones from within. The blood from his nose had already begun to turn black. He got to his feet. Unobtrusively she slipped her hand into the medkit strapped to the back of her belt. She found the zzz by feel, slipping it on her finger with care before removing the safety. It was a delicate business; all too easy to knock yourself out with one of these.

He was working himself up to something. She could feel it. She licked her lips and brought the armed hand around, trying to hold it naturally without touching herself with the zzz. She fought the urge to giggle: a part of her mind was stubbornly insisting that none of this was happening. It was much too absurd . . .

Marcsson uncoiled and glided toward her, but at the last second she lost her nerve and evaded him just when she should have moved in. They circled each other, crouched like jungle fighters in some ritual display. The water on his skin shook where it caught the light: he was trembling. Encouraged by this sign of fear, she moved closer. She only needed a small piece of him to activate the zzz.

He reached out, and when his fingers grazed her arm she realized she'd miscalculated. It wasn't fear or fatigue that made him shake. He was oscillating. His entire body was charged. His eyes leaped at her, shining much too brightly. There was nothing in them that she understood. Nothing in the mouth, either, to suggest any possibility of a common language.

Whatever thing guarded the boundaries of Kalypso stood up on tiptoe and paid attention. She had forgotten about the zzz; she jerked her arm away from his touch as though burned and retreated, gasping – but it was too late. He rushed her. She was flung bodily through the air, hearing Marcsson's breath discharge at the point of impact, smelling the acridity of his adrenalined flesh.

She had just enough time to think: you son of a bitch. Then she hit the floor. It hurt. His skin was strangely cold. She felt a kind of release at the contact. It made no sense. How could violence not be bad – especially when it was directed at her? Did it put her in some left of center psych box, that she thought this violence seemed kind of good? Because she was exhilarated. The force, the weight, the momentum, the necessary surrender – none of these things were what actually excited her. These qualities happened to be present and so became associated with the feeling that swept over her as Azamat Marcsson unceremoniously smashed her against the tiles: but they were not the source of it.

What was the source of it?

All she had to do was get the zzz into contact with him and it would be over; but he'd twisted her arm back against the floor and wedged a knee into her solar plexus so she couldn't get her breath. She heard herself hissing with effort. Spit flew from her mouth. She wriggled, struggling to free the hand with the zzz.

Something gave way, and the next thing she knew he was off her. The zzz was gone: she must have got him.

She scrambled away along the smooth floor, slipping in the water and blood he'd spread around the Dreamer unit. Her left hand was stinging and throbbing, probably sprained. He didn't come after her, but waited dumbly, his face slack. She started counting to ten. He should go down by six.

Three. She watched his body waver and elongate. *Four*. There was a buzzing in her extremities – must be those damned mathematical – *five* – bees again, she thought – but there are no Dreams where she's going now. *Six*.

the girl who cried sheep

'There was a Core breach here. For sure.'

'Tehar, I'm telling you there's no way to get into the Core from these modules.'

'There has to be. Look at the evidence for yourself.'

'*What?* you're the witch doctor.'

'Exactly. But I have about twenty more important systems to go over, so I need this tank opened up and every pathway examined and documented. I'll check back with you later and review the results.'

'What about her?'

'Is she breathing?'

'Think so.'

'Leave her. I'll deal with her later.'

Oh, thanks very much, Tehar, Kalypso wanted to say, but when she tried to speak only a bubble of saliva emerged from her mouth, then subsided.

Some time passed. Her head cleared; she could hear other people moving around the unit. Their voices were urgent.

'See what I mean? This whole branch has been clipped from the luma side.'

'Impossible. The backwash sub would have prevented – '

'But the backwash was detoured through met and converted – '

'Doesn't matter because – hey! You call this a railroad yard or what? Look at that flowerspan.'

'Don't touch it. Audio might have got crossed with tact. This remind you of anything?'

'Yeah. Soup.'

Witchdoctorspeak. Evidently she'd been dragged out of the way, because she was lying with her face only a few centimeters from a wall.

'Get up, *mon petit chou*,' Tehar said in her ear. His accent was appalling. He peeled her off the floor, huffing: he wasn't much bigger than Kalypso, and between the two of them they just might make one Azamat Marcsson.

'I should have known I'd find you in the middle of this.' He draped her lax arm over his shoulders and lurched to his feet. 'Can you speak?'

She swung her head from side to side. She was monumentally embarrassed about the *zzz* and also slightly turned on at the idea of being handled by Tehar when she was completely unable to resist. She counted on her black skin to hide the fact that she was blushing. Tehar dragged her through the hatch of the Dreamer unit and along a lateral crawlway, eventually hoisting her into a vertical tube and bracing her in place. She guessed by his labored breathing that this was no easy task.

'It's not a drill, you know. Ganesh is down,' Tehar said, nodding at the walls of the tube. They were made of luma, an indigenous biological structure formed by T'nane's micro-organisms and electromagnetically 'tamed' by Ganesh. Not only could luma be made to store and transmit data magnetically, but it behaved like a plastic substance, enabling the developing AI to stretch itself out in size and processing power from a small interstellar ship to a self-sustaining colonial outpost. Under normal circumstances, flickers of light would be visible within the translucent luma, indicating that Ganesh was sending internal messages through the transit tubes. Now they were dark and still.

Tehar had paused to set up his radio and adjust his handgrips, stretching himself out along the 'Up' side of the tubular crawlway. The 'Down' side was slick enough to permit speeds of up to 40 kph, but the 'Up' side was hard work. Tehar's expression told her he wasn't looking forward to hauling her ass up the crawl, but it was either that or slide along the tube until eventually gravity deposited them in the Gardens beneath the main station.

'I don't know what's wrong with old G,' he added. 'It could be a flaw in the luma interface, or it could be that one of the older modules has finally blown. There are some parts of the Core that can't be replaced with the resources on this planet.'

That sounded alarming. The Core controlled Ganesh's most basic, root programming: the stuff that dated back to the AI's inception on Earth. However Ganesh might evolve and grow, the Core was supposed to remain stable and immune to being over-written. Yet Tehar seemed calm enough as he clipped her to the harness on his surface suit and with a heave of muscle began to climb. He was panting in no time. She tried to stretch out an arm to help, but it only flopped uselessly. That was zzz for you.

'We lost a couple gliders,' he gasped. 'Without . . . guidance they can't . . . navigate in the dark. I don't . . . know who yet – *shit!'*

A kamikaze scream had sounded out somewhere in the tube above them; Tehar wrenched her to the side and into a passing recess. A red-clad witch doctor in full surface gear zoomed past, fully extended in the luge position.

Tehar gave a snapping motion with his head and said, 'Where you going, Ashki?'

She watched his face as he listened to the radio response, taking the opportunity to try flexing various muscle groups. She wasn't particularly successful.

'How many clusters are disabled? Yeah. Is anyone in the infirmary? No, I didn't. How many injured? Well, I still think rem2ram is our best – uh huh. Mmm. Ten minutes.' He sighed. 'It's going to be a hell of a day. I wish I was going with you.'

This last was directed at Kalypso. She tried to smile. He resumed climbing.

She managed a questioning moan then, and he flashed a smile over his shoulder.

'I'm taking you to Maxwell's, by the way. You're . . . no good to anyone if you can't move or speak. You took . . . enough zzz for a . . . hundred kilo man! I'm surprised you're conscious so . . . soon.'

19

She jerked her head as if activating a radio and made an inarticulate noise.

'Oh, that. There's an atmospheric problem in the infirmary, and they've got six people being treated for burns. Apparently when their boat was in lock Ganesh did something to mess up the safety systems, but they didn't realize until they were out over a well at a couple hundred degrees. The hull started to *melt*.'

He broke off, panting, and slipped her interface on for her. She was locked out of Ganesh, but receiving audio all the same. The radio link was reserved for emergencies – normally all coms ran through Ganesh. Now the frequency was crowded and full of noise.

'I can't see anything in these conditions.'

'Iaveli, are you at the rocks yet?'

'I wouldn't want to be in a boat right now,' Tehar muttered wearily. He had another twenty meters to go; she knew the distance from rem2ram to Maxwell's by heart, because she was no stranger to the bar and because First simply wasn't that big, and she'd spent all her life negotiating these crawlways.

'Yeah, we're near the old volcano. When is Ganesh coming up?'

'Breaker! This is Stash. I'm in a leg and Ganesh just cut me off from the body. Can somebody –'

'Just get out of the boat and bring everything you can carry.'

'I know there's a thermal coming. Shit, where's Ganesh?'

'Are you crazy, Jianni? We'll be stranded. The current –'

'Think of it as a practicum, kids.'

Climbing was more natural to Kalypso than walking, and large open spaces made her nervous. The only large open spaces to be found were outside in the Wild, whereas First consisted mostly of convolutions, stacks, and many many walls. She'd spent her whole life in First.

'Stash, sit tight. We'll get to you. Thermal's not coming for a while yet.'

And if climbing was a way of life, then it seemed only natural that the station should be put together like a spider. Eight 'legs' supported the bulk of First, each terminating in a bulbous 'foot' planted firmly in basalt beneath the surface of the water.

'*We need more coolant in section 13. If any Grunts are listening, please –* '

'*Get off this channel, will you?*'

'*Will somebody get Ganesh up again? I can't get used to this channel system.*'

'*Shit, I think we just hit something. Water's coming in.*'

'*Get out of the boat, get out of the boat.*'

The body of the station was suspended in a dense nexus between the legs: this was where the cell clusters, central meeting areas, and most essential functional controls resided. The Works cocooned the bridge hardware of the old ship – including Ganesh's Core – within a tangle of filaments for processing essential chemicals, including oxygen. They drew their power from the vast, seething heat of the thermal well over which First crouched. Floating on the surface of the well were the main Gardens, supported by scaffolding erected underwater and extending up to create tiers. The Gardens were a source of oxygen as well as food, and Ganesh was heavily interfaced to regulate temperature, pressure, and air mix within what was essentially an enormous greenhouse.

'*Breaker. Breaker. This is Jianni. The heat converters are running at forty per cent, boys and girls. We got a thermal coming, so get to your cells and stay quiet. We can ride this one, just stay away from Ganesh –* '

' *– ff this channel! We have two dead in the infirmary. Can someone please get the fuck down here.*'

Upset, Kalypso slipped out of interface. She was beginning to prickle all over as sensation returned. The witch doctor's face was sweating.

'Marcsson's missing,' he told her. 'Kalypso, quit looking at me like that. It's a crash. A real crash. We've got basic support systems working on crutches, but com and everything above it are useless. Everybody's confined to cells in case we lose oxygen or temperature control. You will be, too, once you've been debriefed.'

Debriefed? They had arrived at the hatchway to Maxwell's. Tehar let her go and she toppled in, landing facedown on a pink velvet couch. She had been looking forward to a restorative drink or three or four, since alcohol helped reduce the effects of zzz. But 'debriefed' wasn't a fun word, and Tehar had disappeared – all too conveniently, she realized as she rolled over and looked around.

She was surrounded by Mothers. There were only about seven or eight of them – far from the full complement, but enough of a concentration to alarm Kalypso in her present condition. They reclined on semicircular couches, glassine smoky walls rising above their heads as they clutched pillows and occasionally hit one another with them.

The Mothers had been drinking again.

Crisis management, they called it. As in: *Let's go to Maxwell's and manage the crisis.*

Clearly, this crisis needed more managing than most, because the Mothers were sprawled in attitudes of earthy abandon. Quickdust watercolored the air. A male of her generation (Kalypso couldn't see who because of the jaguar mask on his face) was stretched unconscious in the middle of the floor, his body bearing residual traces of Picasso's Blue. And then there were the Mothers themselves, looking a little too interested in Kalypso for her comfort. They were all about the same age: fiftyish in Earth years if you didn't count the time they'd been tanked in transit. Age and gender were the only thing they had in common: they didn't look alike, they didn't act alike, and they certainly didn't think alike. In Kalypso's experience, when they got together it was better to be somewhere else.

The bar was a sunken island in the middle of the room. Standing behind it, vigorously shaking a brownish cocktail, was Lassare, the Mother to end all Mothers. She was wearing some kind of red caftan that made her look like a radioactive strawberry. Her flesh was ample and dimpled. She was a hydrologic engineer, among other things, and if Kalypso recalled correctly, she'd carried five sets of quadruplets to term. Two and a half clusters could call Lassare their mother, even if none of them bore a genetic relationship to her.

One other thing: Kalypso was terrified of her. Although Kalypso had been issued from the body of a Mother called Helen, it was

Lassare who'd always caught her out in some prank when she was growing up. It was Lassare who always found a way to make her suffer.

'If necessary, we always have the reflex points,' she was saying. 'Its higher functions can be decoupled from life support and the Core. All is well.'

The boy in the jaguar mask stirred. 'All is well,' he murmured into the floor.

Rasheeda was tracing fine lines of Picasso's Blue across Mari's face.

'These are your lines of conviction,' she said, drawing spirals on Mari's temples. 'Lassare?'

Almost absentmindedly, Lassare turned to Mari and recited: 'Remember the Andes? High altitude training. Remember that purity. Remember the depth of the landscape, even at great distance. Remember how the shadows stood. Remember the feeling of the world falling away so steeply in every direction.'

Mari whispered, 'Anything is possible.'

'Sky,' said Lassare. 'Limitless sky.'

Mari's brows knit. 'The hexagons are coming near again. They're crowding me.'

Rasheeda picked up one of Mari's bare feet and touched it with the blue dust.

'Those silly hexagons,' she murmured dismissively.

'Go away,' said Mari. 'Hexagons, go away.'

'You control distance,' Rasheeda intoned richly. 'You control time. You are in control. Make it the way you want it to be.'

'Oh – ' Mari sighed. 'It's not as good as last time, or the time before. I want – ' her back arched, straining.

'Shh,' Rasheeda soothed again. 'It's still very, very good.'

'It recedes.'

'The parts you want to recede go to the background. The parts you love come close.'

'Yes. But . . . it all recedes now.'

'We will have Earth here.'

'We will have Earth.' Sweat beaded above Mari's lip.

23

Rasheeda signed to Lassare, '*She's had enough.*'

'You believe,' Lassare commanded. 'You are strong.'

'I'm strong.' Mari's teeth showed.

Lassare and Rasheeda glanced at one another. Lassare nodded and Rasheeda took the brush away.

Lassare seemed pleased. 'Good. Have we all had a turn? No, don't give any more to the boy. We don't want him hooked. Ah, *Kalypso,*' she cooed. 'Let me give you something to perk you up.'

She sailed out from behind the bar, brandishing the drinkee thing. Shoving a straw into it, she passed it to Kalypso, folding Kalypso's hands around the vessel with the absentminded motherish efficiency that characterized her kind. Then she turned and paced back across the room.

'The thing about zzz,' she said sweetly, 'is that you're supposed to use it on the other guy, not yourself.'

There were advantages to having little or no muscle control. Kalypso sipped mutely. Lassare really was no substitute for the demons: the drink was revolting, but contained much alcohol, for there were also advantages to living on a planet rich in anaerobes of every stripe. Namely, the stocks at Maxwell's were always full.

Naomi crossed the room, stepping over the comatose male to sit beside Kalypso. She was a gray wraith, slim as a knife.

'Did Marcsson ask you to change anything in Alien Life? Did he have any special requests?'

Kalypso slowly shook her head.

'But you can confirm he was working on the Oxygen Problem,' Naomi said.

'Who isn't?' Rasheeda snorted, and Kalypso nodded agreement. Almost every experiment conducted in Alien Life had something to do with the Oxygen Problem: in a sense, it was the *only* problem. Until it was solved, the colony would remain in a kind of uneasy stasis, functioning but unable to grow. Marcsson, as a specialist in colonial organisms, was in a better position than most to study the ecosystem of the Wild. He understood the interplay of indigenous life in a way most of the Mothers could not, for he had worked on Sieng's team years ago, even before Sieng had learned to 'groom' –

or tame – the wild luma so that Ganesh could use it; and before her team of exobiologists had been overcome by the infectious agent they'd grown in an attempted hybridization of Earth and T'nane biology. Marcsson alone had escaped the fate of his colleagues, so he was the last of the Earthborn exobiologists alive on T'nane. Unfortunately, as a Grunt he had also been the least valuable member of the team. It was widely believed that, had Sieng lived, she would have solved the Oxygen Problem within a few years. By contrast, twenty years after her death, Marcsson had some fine studies to show, but no real key to the ecological mechanism behind the carbon monoxide vs. oxygen balance in T'nane's biosphere, much less the ability to permanently alter the atmosphere. No one else had had any great inspiration, either, though not for lack of trying. Many times Kalypso had heard Lassare kvetch about the loss of Sieng's team. 'Why should she have been irreplaceable? We should have our share of genius in the new generation.'

Kalypso wasn't sure what Naomi was getting at when she said, 'Kalypso, I've got a team going over your unit as we speak. If there's anything you want to tell us, this is the time to speak up.'

Wide-eyed, Kalypso kept shaking her head. She was getting feeling back in her toes.

'There's no point in questioning this one now,' Rasheeda said, reaching for a bottle. 'She can't speak. What else is on the agenda?'

Naomi continued to watch Kalypso, who felt herself bristling at the Mother's insinuation. For once she was innocent, yet she couldn't even defend herself.

'Azamat Marcsson,' Lassare mused, beginning to pace. 'What do we think about him?'

Someone yawned.

'Yes, exactly.' She pivoted slowly. Her eyes narrowed to two glittering points. The others began talking.

'He's the most boring man alive.'

'Classic Grunt profile. Stable, subordinate, good at moving heavy objects.'

'Spends a lot of time in the Wild, though.'

'That's only to gather data. He's totally addicted to his work.'

'So is Jianni; but Jianni has ambitions.'

'No, Azamat's not like Jianni. He's not really interested in people, or growing the colony, or anything remotely political.'

'That's true. Doesn't have the personality for it.'

'He's in love with his micros,' Rasheeda snorted.

Laughter.

'He never got over the fact that he survived,' said Mari seriously. 'He was always reserved, but since the rest of his team died, he hasn't known how to forgive himself for living.'

There was silence.

'You don't think he could be suicidal?' Rasheeda's face was clouded. 'Maybe we should give him some Picasso's Blue. Something. I don't like the idea of the poor guy berking.'

Naomi said, 'Marcsson will keep. We should concentrate on resolving the crash. Like I said in the beginning, Ganesh is having growing pains. We've seen this before.'

'Not on this scale,' Lassare contradicted. 'Getting back to Azamat for a second: doesn't anybody know specifically what he was doing?'

Korynne stood, yawning. 'I'll go to Azamat's boat and see what I can find. Even with Ganesh down, the onboard node should have records of his last several trips to the Wild.'

There were undercurrents Kalypso wasn't getting: lots of them. The Mothers seemed to have focused their attention on her again. She cleared her throat, but didn't try to speak. Lassare said, 'Let's face it: he's a Grunt. Not that he hasn't done some good work with temperature buffers in the clayfields. But those manifestations in Alien Life that popped up before the crash. Jianni says they were rather . . . flamboyant. Can we seriously ascribe them to *Azamat*?'

Kalypso: eyes closed, throat burning, motor neurons waking up and tingling agitatedly. They were still looking at her.

'What?' she said hoarsely.

Naomi looked at Kalypso, then at Lassare. She said, 'Either she's diabolically clever, or worthlessly naive.'

'Darling,' Lassare lilted at Kalypso. 'It's a well-known fact that you play footsie with Ganesh. Do you deny this?'

Kalypso seethed with frustration. It was true that she and the AI possessed a certain . . . *understanding* . . . but that had nothing to do with Marcsson berking. Probably Marcsson had berked because of the crash.

'You've got Ganesh swearing at you and slipping you treats from the Archives while you're working.'

Kalypso looked away. She didn't think anybody knew about that. Then she realized Lassare was suggesting *she* had –

'Need more drink,' she rasped.

Naomi reached behind the bar and grabbed a liquor sac. She passed it to Kalypso, who sipped tentatively. Better.

Lassare smacked her lips. 'Now. You've made it very clear you no longer respect our authority. What was it you said at the last tentkit meeting? Called us names, didn't she, Naomi?'

Naomi nodded. 'You called us *a bunch of fucking sheep*, as I recall.'

Kalypso swallowed and flexed her tongue experimentally, concentrating on her mouth as she spoke. 'What are you saying?'

'There is this propensity in you, Kalypso, that we've observed since you were old enough to crawl.'

'You like to fool around.'

'Do anything on a dare.'

'Addicted to pointless challenges.'

'So if . . . someone – like Azamat Marcsson, to take one example – if Azamat came to you and said, for example, that he needed more space in Ganesh to run his simulation – '

'No.' Kalypso shook her head.

'Didn't happen? Are you sure?'

'No. I barely know him.'

'Are you saying, categorically, that you didn't change anything, or ask Ganesh to change anything, for today's Alien Life run?'

'Yes. That's what I'm saying.' The words were coming out almost naturally now. She stood up and brought the half-empty sac to the bar, then lingered there out of habit, stroking its smart surface. The demons didn't appear in response to her greeting, nor did they

27

produce Night in Tunisia, her favorite cocktail and most inspired creation. She felt depressed. Maxwell's without the demons meant Ganesh was really, truly down. She missed Ganesh; certainly she liked the AI better than she liked the Mothers, particularly when they were making her the object of such intense scrutiny. Discreetly, she set her interface so radio would trickle into her right ear. She tuned it to the witch doctor channel, hoping to catch a piece of news – or even just Tehar's voice.

'It's silly to accuse the girl,' one of the Mothers said. 'We have no reason to believe the problem in Alien Life was caused by anything other than the system crash.'

'But we don't know what caused the crash itself.'

'And where's Azamat? No one can find him. Why did she let him escape?'

'Whoa,' slurred Kalypso. '*That* was sheer incompetence. Honest.'

No one said anything for a minute. Then the conversation resumed, but Kalypso was remembering the Dream and thinking the inside of Azamat Marcsson's head could very well be a lot weirder than anybody gave him credit for. Where had all that psychotic math come from? But she couldn't think of a way to explain: they'd never believe her if she told them the stuff Marcsson's subconscious had generated. She wouldn't have believed it herself if she hadn't so vividly experienced it.

She could hear Tehar's voice across the radio; this should comfort her, but what he was saying had the opposite effect. The witch doctors seemed no closer to helping Ganesh get back up.

'*This module's been wholly re-written. The code isn't a type I've seen before. Ganesh must have invented it wholesale.*'

'*Harie, can you cross-reference with this sound sample I just got?*'

'*I can try, but you're going to have to deliver it physically. Don't trust the transfers.*'

The Mothers must have reached an impasse in their discussion: when she bothered to check in on what they were saying, they had all but fallen silent. Most had that need-another-drink look about them. Naomi was the first to step up to the bar.

'Now that you're here, you might as well make yourself useful,' she drawled, and placed her empty glass on the bar. 'I hear you have a *gift*.'

Kalypso looked at the glass. Her fingers began to twitch.

'Well . . .'

Lassare sank into a couch like a collapsed parachute. 'Yes. Come on, let's see what you can do. Don't worry – we won't hold you to the demons' standards.'

Kalypso contemplated the empty glass. Then she closed her eyes and slowly said, 'You understand I don't bark on command. But you may be in luck. I feel something coming on. It's a kind of – ' she tipped her head back, pursing her lips. They still tingled. 'Excuse me. The ethanol muse is speaking to me. I'm getting a color, it's kind of chartreuse. Yeah, I'm getting a color and the taste, the taste is – ' she reached out and started seizing bottles, splashing their contents together as if at random. Her muscles were jerking a bit. 'Lassare, this is going to be a custom creation for you, OK? Now – I'm going for a kind of pine-nutty flavor with overtones of – no, no let me just think.'

She stared at the mixer, pretending to be lost in meditation. Normally she did this purely for effect, but just now it allowed her to tune in to the chatter on the witch doctor channel.

'Tehar, we've looked at eighty per cent of the core and all roads seem to lead to Unit 5 of rem2ram. Maybe you should come up here.'

'Did someone say vodka? Yeah, I think vodka. Anybody writing down what I'm doing here?'

'I don't have time, Boris. What's the problem?'

'You want the short answer or the long answer?'

'The short one, of course.'

'Kalypso Deed.'

Fuck.

Naomi was laughing. 'Write it *down*? How archaic. Have you been at the Archives again?'

'Never mind,' Kalypso sang. 'I can remember how I did it. I never forget a drink. Ice. Let's give this a spin. Here you go, Lassare. Just for you.'

Lassare was looking seriously unnerved as Naomi passed her the drink. 'You could at least taste it first, Kalypso. I mean, I have no idea what's in this.'

'Are you a Mother or are you a mouse?' Kalypso taunted.

Lassare chuckled fiercely. 'Is this payback for all those times I cut your Dreamtime when you were being a little shit? No, give it to me. I'll drink it.'

She sipped cautiously. Her eyebrows shifted. She sipped again.

'Mmm . . . ' This time it was no sip, but an appreciative swig.

'Careful,' Kalypso warned. 'It has a wee kick. Give it a couple more sec – '

'*Zeee!!*'

Kalypso smiled.

'I'll let you name it, Lassare.'

'Make more, Kalypso,' the others urged. 'Let's see you remember how.'

While Kalypso was complying, Naomi looked her over carefully. 'So what do you have to say for yourself, Kalypso? Why are you such a fuckup? You've got the genetic potential: everyone here knows that. You were meant to be more than this.'

'I hear,' said Mari, placing one booted foot on the bar and stretching, 'that you're beating some of the Grunts senseless at cards.'

Kalypso poured herself another shot. She was reviving by the minute; in fact, she was now wide enough awake to recognize when she was being corralled.

'Now why can't we tap that?' one of the others demanded. 'Why can't we transform these party-girl talents of yours into something useful?'

Lassare, her eyes already displaying the effects of Kalypso's cocktail, stood up and replaced her glass on the counter with a thud.

'Don't be silly. Kalypso fucks up deliberately. She doesn't *want* to be useful – do you, love?'

Kalypso glanced around helplessly. She was surrounded. Embedded like a thousand mouths and eyes in the walls, all of

Maxwell's demons remained inert. There was nothing to draw off the Mothers' attention, which now drilled into her. There was no music, no chatter of patrons. There was only the silence of the crash. She couldn't stand it any more.

'I didn't do it!'

'Do what, angel?'

'You think it's *my* fault, what happened to Marcsson? Talk to *him*. I don't know shit.'

'I think you're lying,' Lassare drawled.

Naomi said, 'You want to play in our league, kitten? You wouldn't stand a chance.'

'Yeah, we were all at the top of our fields when we left Earth. We *built* this colony. We made you. You're nothing but an unproven little larva.'

'I didn't do anything, I swear,' Kalypso whispered. 'I swear it by the Dead.'

They all looked horrified at this; Kalypso began backpedaling, wondering what she had said wrong. To swear by Sieng's Dead research team was serious; but she'd sincerely meant it. What was going on here? Where was Ganesh? Suddenly she felt like crying. She gestured vaguely at the images of the scientists behind the bar: the photos had been taken long before Kalypso was born, not long before the team's last journey into the Wild – a mission that was to result both in Sieng's discovery of the luma interface, and in the infection by the indigenous agent that would kill her.

'I didn't mean – I just – look, don't – '

'I keep waiting for you to get it together, Kalypso. I'm beginning to think it's never going to happen. Do you know that out of your entire generation, you were the embryo with the most favorable genetic makeup? And you mix drinks. You have the biggest intellectual potential of them all.'

'I do not!' Kalypso railed. 'It's bad enough being stupid without you telling me I'm only pretending to be stupid. You're all so fucking paranoid! I would never do anything to harm Ganesh. And I would never do anything that might harm my cluster's chances of getting into the Wild.'

'You kids have such romantic ideas about the Wild,' Naomi slurred. 'You think you can go out there in your boats and tentkits, play around with the micros, and come up with some magic elixir you can trade for passage back to Earth. You have no idea what Earth is like.'

'Neither do you,' Kalypso retorted. 'Not all these light years away. Not any more.'

'Maybe not. I haven't had the privilege of talking to Earth in years. I do know they aren't going to send ships light years for *any* substance, not Picasso's Blue, not anything we can make here.'

'How can you know that? My cluster-sister Sharia says if we spent less time on the Oxygen Problem, we might discover something better than Picasso's Blue. Then at least we could buy passage back to Earth – those of us who wanted to go – or buy materials we could use to live here.'

'An old argument.' Naomi flicked her fingers dismissively. 'As if valuable agents like Picasso's Blue are just going to leap out of the luma and offer themselves to you.' She pointed to the photos of the Dead behind the bar. 'They were a lot smarter than you, and they perished. You don't know anything about the Wild.'

'That's because you – '

'Shut up, Kalypso.' Naomi's pasty face flared pink. 'You think you can handle the Wild, but you can't even handle First without Ganesh. The AI crashes and twenty minutes later you kids are in a panic. Ganesh is your real mother – you realize that, don't you?'

'No,' Kalypso said belligerently, and knew she was lying because she was feeling more and more insecure about Ganesh's prolonged silence. 'And I don't think our ideas about the Wild are romantic.'

'Since when is romance criminal?' Lassare said in an amused tone. 'A little romance never killed anyone, Naomi.'

'This child is basing her ontological beliefs on stolen cinema clips from Earth History Archives. Ah, you think we don't know what you kids get up to? Mark my words, Kalypso, one day you'll nip into those Earth Archives and find that something bites you back.'

'And your little dog, too!' Rasheeda added in a mocking, high voice. But Naomi was not to be teased.

'As for you personally? I think you're unstable, Kalypso. I don't think you'd last ten minutes in the Wild.'

'Fine. Let the Wild be the judge of that, though. Not you, Naomi.'

'You forget that it's my function to protect you. I've been entrusted with that role.'

'Sure, about a hundred years ago,' Kalypso scoffed. 'Listen. In the Wild it isn't a matter of anybody's judgement what you are or what you can do. The Wild itself tests you. You can't argue with that, can you?'

'You want us to just throw you out there, is that it? Think we might pick your cluster to be a research team, Kalypso?'

'No,' she answered resentfully.

'No? Why not?'

Kalypso glowered. 'Because of me.'

'You mean, you think your attitude is holding your cluster back,' Naomi said. 'Isn't that what you think?'

'I think that's what *you* think.'

Lassare laughed into her straw; the drink foamed. Kalypso looked away.

'You remind me of myself when I was young,' Lassare said. Kalypso hated it when they said that. It was so patronizing.

Naomi saw the look on her face.

'Is that so hard to believe?' she snapped. 'You think we're just a bunch of old women, right? Too conservative by half. Why don't you just say it outright, Kalypso?'

Kalypso took a long breath. 'OK. I do. I don't think you're trying hard enough to grow this colony. I think you're too careful. I think you've spent too much time pretending to experiment on Picasso's Blue when everyone knows you aren't developing anything new because you're addicted to it. You're living in a fantasy world if you think we're going to be able to sit on our asses in First and find a way to terraform this planet. You're afraid of the Wild. It's fine to be afraid for yourselves, but it kind of pisses me off when you're afraid for me.'

'See?' Naomi said wryly to the others. 'The dangers of a prolonged adolescence. All mouth, no brain.'

'I was just like you,' Lassare said. 'Just fucking like you. Now look at me.'

Kalypso wasn't feeling particularly empathetic. She mumbled, 'So whose fault is that?'

'Kalypso, think about it for ten seconds. You've got us to rebel at. You've got our authority to give you shape. We've got shit. Who do we turn to when things are going wrong? Our mission statement? Hah! None of us had a clue what we were getting into back then. According to the probes, this planet supposedly had a fucking breathable *atmosphere*. Earth? Double hah! Not with the timelag we've got. Once those bastards found out the atmosphere had changed, they didn't want to know us. No backup, no reinforcements, no support. All this – ' she gestured to the station around her ' – all this is improvised. You think it was easy building First? We got on Ganesh with every piece of training and education you can imagine, the hugest of ambitions, and more guts than you'll ever see the broadside of quite frankly. Now you see us hiding in a bar drunk as Indians. Did it ever occur to you that there might be a reason for this, other than some failure in our characters? Did you ever stop to think that spending twenty-something years trying to colonize a resistant planet and raise a bunch of demented children *who aren't even ours* could take its toll on us?'

Kalypso shrugged. 'So stand aside and let us take over.'

'Wouldn't I love to,' Naomi muttered.

'Let *you* take over? Kalypso, you can't even use a simple zzz stinger without fucking it up. You and your little games have brought the whole station to a crashing halt, and you want to take over?'

'Hey. Wait. I *didn't*, and anyway I didn't mean me personally – '

Lassare held up a hand. 'You might get your chance sooner than you think. If Ganesh keeps deteriorating, we'll all be in the Wild soon. How do you like the sound of that, Kalypso? Does that sober you up?'

There were nervous murmurs of dissent from among the other Mothers.

'Ganesh will get itself organized soon.'

'Let's not panic over a few glitches.'

'The witch doctors say – '

'The witch doctors?' Lassare's voice leaped the better part of an octave. 'What makes you think the witch doctors understand Ganesh? Have you forgotten why we call them witch doctors in the first place? They know jack about how that AI really thinks because it's outpaced the science we all grew up with. They stand on one foot, cross their fingers and *hope*.'

'You're undoing all the good of the Blue. We must believe, and then they will follow us.'

'Down the garden path,' said Lassare.

'Lassare, really you are exaggerating . . .'

Kalypso was watching Lassare with a touch of admiration. The Mothers were all so drunk now they had forgotten about their policy never to disagree in front of the younger generation. Trying to appear inconspicuous, Kalypso refilled drinks and listened to the beginnings of a promising argument.

' – we should be sending teams to all the manual sites – '

' – radio contact at least – '

' – reflex points sooner or later – '

' – alarmist attitude you'll have a bunch of spooked neo-phytes – '

' – and to reconfirm atmospheric readings – '

' – Ganesh's long-term – '

Kalypso raised her glass, said, 'To role models!' and drank.

' – out in boats should probably stay – '

' – root programming perfectly safe if – '

' – totally incompetent witch doctors – '

The hatch opened and Jianni slid in. The Mothers fell silent at once.

'The fault's in the luma interface,' he announced, slightly out of breath. 'And the Dreamer units. We haven't narrowed it down beyond that.'

No one looked at her, but Kalypso felt a stab of guilt even though she hadn't done anything wrong this time. There was a general bristling in the room; Jianni was standing very still, making a point of keeping his voice neutral.

'We need more information,' Naomi said in a clipped tone.

'You know as well as I do that the luma's unpredictable,' the chief witch doctor replied. 'This is the risk you've run by letting Ganesh decentralize.'

Politics again. Jianni hadn't supported that decision; his protest had been recorded in the colony annals. Sieng's discovery that luma's cellular structure made it ideal for interfacing with Ganesh had been the breakthrough desperately needed by the fledgling colony. Letting the AI spread its memory into the luma infrastructure had enabled the station to be expanded to its present size, increasing Ganesh's processing power and paving the way for the birth of Kalypso and all her brethren. But it was all an experiment: everyone in the colony knew this, even if they usually didn't think about it.

At times like this, life on T'nane could suddenly seem very tenuous indeed. Kalypso put her hands on the bar and the sleeping demons. It was starting to sink in that Ganesh might really be down for the count.

'We have a number of problems, which I'll prioritize for you in a second,' Jianni began. Kalypso sensed the tingle of suppressed laughter in the Mothers, but if Jianni felt it, he ignored it. He was the chief witch doctor: Earthborn, a designer of the AI's current configuration and therefore far more intimate with Ganesh than the average Grunt. Still, the Mothers quashed his ideas as often as they allowed them.

'Basically, it's a concatenation of problems, each of which is moderately serious but not cause for panic. Yet when taken all together, these things mean trouble. The Works are being reprogrammed and we're locked out, so none of our basic substances, including atmosphere, are being supplied. Now, I've got people going in to manually over-ride and get internal atmosphere back to normal, but that's going to take time. Because the com-nodes are all down, it's difficult for us to communicate. We can't use the luma, so we're dependent on radio which is unwieldy for data transmission. On top of that, we've got a thermal system brewing in the Rift. It's going to affect the well and stress our heat tolerances. Ganesh might instinctively protect itself – and us – by keeping the luma stable; but if it doesn't, we're going to have heat coming up through the legs like you wouldn't believe.'

He paused. The Mothers stared at him dully. Kalypso wondered what they were thinking about this laundry-list of woes.

'I'm thinking about shutting down some of the reflex points now, before the thermal arrives, in hope that we can get this taken care of.'

'That's totally unsafe!' Naomi seemed to come to her senses.

'Sitting on a thermal well like this does have its drawbacks,' Jianni conceded mildly. 'We need massive amounts of kinetic energy to maintain structural integrity in the luma – no way around that. If Ganesh fails to divert that energy and keep us safe, well, that's the price we pay for living where we do.'

'Ganesh is fully shielded,' Naomi said. 'No thermal is going to wreck the Core. It's deep in the Works and completely insulated.'

'Shutting down reflexes is not a good idea,' Lassare added, enunciating carefully in that obviously intoxicated way. 'If you decouple the autonomic Core from higher consciousness, Ganesh will lose control of the luma, and the luma is its primary means of data storage.'

'We think Ganesh may have lost control of the luma already,' Jianni snapped. 'I need all the hands I can get. But I guess you're all too busy making executive decisions to actually pitch in and do anything.'

Kalypso swallowed. Even if his wrath wasn't directed at her, she felt it and was cowed.

'I went for backup heat shields and they're missing from storage. Anybody got any idea what happened to them?' There was an edge to his voice; more than just anger. Something else. Almost – not quite but almost – fear. No one answered him, so he tried again.

'Do any of you understand what I'm saying? We have to evacuate to Oxygen 2. It's not safe here.'

Rasheeda said, 'Let's not rush into anything. Jianni, we'll get it fixed. Don't be upset.'

Her tone was soothing, and she reinforced it by going to Jianni and laying a hand on his forearm. She possessed an absolute confidence in what she was saying: Kalypso could see the witch doctor's face cloud as he tried to hold on to his resolve. She knew what he was feeling. Irrational as they were, the Mothers had a way of casting a spell over you.

'This is much more dangerous than you realize . . . '

'Leaving First would be insane,' Lassare said bluntly.

Kalypso, stirring as vigorously as her tingling wrist would allow, glanced sideways at the still-unconscious youth in the mask and wondered what Lassare's definition of sanity was.

Jianni stuck to his guns. 'The luma could break down. I shouldn't have to tell you what that means.'

Naomi said, 'Don't try to lay the blame on us. Without the luma, there would be no future generation. Without *us* – '

Jianni waved this aside with the air of someone who'd heard Naomi's glorification of her own uterus a time or three too many.

'I can't talk to you when you're stoned.'

'This was bound to happen sooner or later,' Mari put in diplomatically. 'The luma won't remain stable without management by Ganesh, and Ganesh isn't perfect. It's not anyone's fault.'

There was a long, insincere silence and they all avoided looking at each other. Jianni muttered a half-hearted curse and grasped the frame of the hatch.

'I don't have time for this shit,' he said. 'I'm calling an evacuation.'

Kalypso gulped. 'But Ganesh will self-correct sooner or later. Right?'

'I hope so, Kalypso.' His eye on her was slightly gentler. 'But we can't count on it. Lassare, I'm over-riding you. If you people want to argue, you can stay here and melt when the next thermal hits.'

38

He pushed out past Korynne, who was on her way in. It was suddenly obvious just how intoxicated the Mothers were; they appeared dazed.

Korynne said, 'I got the records, but they're in shorthand. Nobody can find Azamat.'

She passed a card to Lassare; the rest of the Mothers remained silent. Kalypso felt them closing ranks. When Lassare finally spoke, her tone was almost exaggeratedly formal.

'Go to your cell, Kalypso. I'll come and speak to your cluster later. Maybe they can get the truth out of you. Right now, you're not looking exactly squeaky.'

'But I would never hurt Ganesh!'

Wearily, Lassare said, 'It's like the boy who cried wolf.'

'Fuck you, Lassare.' Suddenly almost in tears at the injustice, Kalypso pushed her way across the room toward the hatch as she delivered the only rebuttal she could think of. 'Just . . . just . . . just fuck *you*.'

invertebrate city

You can see out. It's not a landscape, it's a cloud sculpture, a parade of forms becoming other forms, indistinguishable from their reflections. The water is vast and utterly still. Cast upon it, the clouds run the gamut from tired yellow to a violet just shy of blue; but the dominant tone of the world at this time of day is dirty brass. There is an impression of weak light coming from nowhere in particular.

You can see out, and it's big. You can see its emptiness.

You can see out, but you can't *get* out. You are wrapped up inside. Inside, the cells are tightly packed, a honeycomb of interdependent hexagonal units. There is a feeling of walls everywhere, which is only intensified by the presence of windows. Inside, things are highly structured and everything has multiple uses. It's the ergonomy that gets scary.

Take this cell, for example. A tallish man could stand in the middle of it and kick each of the 6 walls. It has been built from luma, and its configuration and internal environment are regulated by the AI Ganesh, for each cell possesses a processing node of the original smartship integrated into the very fabric of First. With the exception of the Core, Ganesh is scattered across the entire station in this way. First is an intelligent structure.

The cell has been imprinted with its occupant's habits, so it can anticipate every need like a faithful dog. Ganesh – when it's working – can be accessed through interface, hands-free. The nutrition unit is tucked away inside a structural column and will cool, heat, or blend ingredients at need; food sources are cultured out of sight, also managed by the AI; and the plumbing is similarly efficient and unobtrusive. The bed rolls open and inflates when the occupant's body temperature drops beneath a certain level. Light is provided by tamed *flagrare* colonies, and ceiling plants provide a steady supply of fresh oxygen, which can be supplemented from the common stock when there are several people inside. In short, Ganesh takes care of its humans.

Outside you can't breathe. Inside you are safe from everything but yourself.

Until now, anyway.

Sitting on a shelf that folds out from the wall is Kalypso Deed in the half-lotus position. She's playing the bass line to 'Round-about', accurately and at tempo. The drums/organ/guitar/vox digitally isolated from the original recording are being piped through her interface as if the dead band were right here, so she's working pretty hard, sweating – totally going for it, in fact. She plays rarely, so her fingers are blistering. Just for a minute, inside and outside lose their meaning.

She's furious at Lassare's dismissal. As if she were a child – but there are no children on T'nane any more. No: everyone in every cluster is the same age, give or take a handful of years. Around age eight they were all grouped with an intent to balance personalities, talents, and physical makeup. Everything about their existence was carefully planned long ago, on Earth, and the Mothers have attempted to preserve that planning despite the fact that life on T'nane is nothing like what they expected when they left Earth with a mandate to colonize. This control can be stifling: sometimes Kalypso wants to run screaming from her own cluster. But there's nowhere to run, so she has to settle for the isolation loud music can create.

Only she's not supposed to be interfacing. And she's certainly not supposed to be using Earth Archive resources. She's doing it out of insubordination coupled with a kind of desperate denial of the Crash: a need to prove that Ganesh is still there and won't eat her alive. But she's in the middle of the chorus when her accompaniment cuts off –

She raised her head, dropping out of interface.

'You're not supposed to be anywhere near Ganesh,' Ahmed warned.

She turned. He was in her bed, flanked by Liet and Xiaxiang. The latter was asleep; the former was sucking her thumb.

'I can't believe it's all going down,' Kalypso whispered. She fingered the strings wistfully, but without amplification could barely hear the tones produced.

There wasn't enough air. Sharia was eating a tortilla loudly. Kalypso's cell was meant to hold one person, or two. Not five. But the cluster was under evacuation orders, merely waiting to be called to a Landing and issued a boat and tentkit. The anticipation had made the others obsessively talkative, and then brought out the sex urge; Kalypso was too conflicted to be interested. Yet she hadn't slept, either. She'd sat here, playing bass as fast as she could and brooding.

'Tehar keeps calling for you on radio,' Sharia said, chewing. 'But we deemed it best to leave you alone. Are you intox?'

'What? No. Why.'

'He said he left you in Maxwell's.'

Kalypso felt persecuted.

'I made a fool of myself in front of him,' she moaned.

'That wouldn't be unusual,' Ahmed remarked.

'Tehar found a problem at rem2ram,' Sharia added.

'Goddamn Lassare. I didn't do anything. For once.'

'What does she say you did?'

'It's stupid. The Mothers – get this. The Mothers are bent out of shape because the Crash seems to have been caused by the luma. Jianni's giving them hell for it in that understated way of his.'

'What does that have to do with you?'

'Because it might have started in my unit of the Dreamer. Or been accelerated by the Dreamer. And Marcsson did berk. So they think I was playing and caused a glitch.'

'Were you?'

'Not that I know of. Does anybody care that I came *that* close to berking myself? Does anybody bother to ask me if I'm upset by the fact that some crazy giant could have pulped me? No. Everywhere I turn, accusations . . . '

Ahmed had disentangled himself from Liet, and now stood. He put his hands on her shoulders and began massaging them. Xiaxiang yawned loudly; she heard Liet squeak as he rolled over.

'Poor turtle,' Xiaxiang said. 'You're full of shit and you know it.'

Sharia was frowning: Kalypso could see her posture reflected in the window, hand on one cocked hip, head tilted.

'Did you deviate from procedures, Kalypso?'

Liet snorted and took her thumb out of her mouth. Her bleary face was absurdly pretty. 'Do the Mothers use Picasso's Blue?'

'Because you know how easily Ganesh can get confused. Hey, what are you doing? Stay out of interface! No wonder you're always in trouble.'

Kalypso had stretched a hand overhead and pulled down a vid screen. It was faintly translucent: the clouds beyond the window could still be discerned through the screen image. She routed through her visor.

I'M DOWN, STUPID. GO AWAY.

'But it's *me*,' she verbed. 'Kalypso. Tell me what's wrong.'

YOU SHOULD HAVE WARNED ME BEFORE YOU TRIED PULLING CODE THROUGH MILES.

'Pulling code through Miles? I did not! But never mind that – I'm just so glad you're there!'

BUT I'M NOT HERE.

'Are the Earth files undamaged?' she asked.

EARTH FILES HAVE BEEN CHILD-PROOFED, Ganesh verbed primly.

'What about the ones that aren't?'

LIKE WHAT?

'Let me see my personal files.' Suddenly it was important to her that her own piece of history, at least, was safe.

'SPECIFICALLY?'

'Mom & Dad,' she said.

She got a list of ingredients for rice cookies.

'Kalypso, will you leave poor Ganesh alone? You'll only make things worse,' Sharia said from outside the interface.

Stubbornly, she repeated her request. Out rolled all she would ever know of her parents.

First Mom, who was dead.

Five feet even, born on Trinidad; classically trained violinist. Two PhDs: one in physics and the other in economics. Chairman of the Board of a multinat – never mind.

Then Dad.

One of the top smart-fiber designers of his generation. Climber of mountains without oxygen in his spare time. Champion bridge player.

They never lived together, of course. Having Kalypso was a professional decision. Their two sets of genes, combined, were meant to constitute the pinnacle of human potential. They would never know their child, but they would be ensured of the passage of their genes to the new world. It was pure hubris – but irresistible, apparently. Eyes, smells, shared jokes and skin had played no part in her conception. For years and years she was a frozen embryo. She had unborn siblings in storage. She would probably never know them.

'See?' She slipped out of interface and turned to face the others. 'All my personal programs are still here. Let's not blow things out of proportion.'

'Kalypso.'

'So I'm going to get some sleep and I want all of you out of my bed now or – '

'*Kalypso.*'

'What?'

'You shouldn't have interfaced during a crash,' Ahmed said sadly, shaking his head. When she glanced back at the screen, the files were quietly imploding and disappearing into noise. Her father's face morphed into a shoe and vanished. Kalypso gave an impotent little shriek and dropped the bass.

'*No* . . . Ganesh? Ganesh?'

I AM LARGE.

The interface cut off.

'I warned you,' Sharia began, and then suddenly stretched out a solicitous hand toward her cluster-sister. 'Kalypso? Are you OK?'

She wasn't. She wasn't at all, and she couldn't explain but she also couldn't hide her distress from her nestmates, who now gathered around her oozing empathy.

'Kalypso . . .' Startled eyes, semi-gestures of shoulders and heads: *what's come over her, is she kidding around, Kalypso never gave a shit about anything so what's this?*

She was trembling with suppressed tears.

Sharia whispered something to Liet, who nodded.

'How much zzz did you get dosed with?'

'I was trying to sub Azamat,' she said dully.

'Shit, that's a lot of zzz . . . what do you figure he weighs?'

'Like . . . a hundred kilos. Maybe more.'

'That explains it.'

'Did anyone see what I did with the blue nail polish?'

'Not now, Liet!'

'Sorry.'

'Come here, Kalypso. It's the drug.'

She shook her head. 'No. No. You don't understand.'

'It's one of the side effects. You have a lot of alcohol in your system, too, and as a by-product of metabolizing the zzz you can get – '

'Never mind, Sharia. Kalypso, what you're feeling – it's chemical. Don't take it too seriously.'

Kalypso reached for a sensor point, touched it ruefully. *Ganesh.*

'X, what if it *is* my fault?'

'Little cornflake, don't – '

'I can't live without Ganesh. Maybe if I never had it to start, but I have and I can't go back.'

'We all need Ganesh. It's very upsetting.'

'Don't patronize me. You don't know what it's like being a shotgun.'

Sharia sighed. 'We've been through this before. You wouldn't have to be a shotgun if you would just get some of your other skills up to speed – '

X silenced her with a wave of his hand. 'Kalypso, you wanna talk about what happened last night?'

'No,' she sniffed. 'You wouldn't understand.'

'It must be hard,' Sharia offered, obviously working at being sympathetic, 'being forced to stand back and Dream through somebody else's head. So icky. Especially if they end up berking. I don't think I could do it.'

Kalypso said, 'I don't really mind that so much. I know you think it's just like being a psychic garbageman, and maybe it is, but people are soft and interesting on the inside. Their garbage is interesting. That's not the problem.'

She fingered her interface and fell silent.

'It's Ganesh,' X said.

'Yeah. You don't know Ganesh like I do. It's my world. It makes everything . . . *more*. Just more. Ah, I can't explain!'

Ahmed sat down next to her and kicked her foot, setting it swinging.

'You know what, Kalypso? You're only upset because you're upset and you hate being upset. If you know what I mean. Look, it's OK. Yeah, you don't like to think of yourself as somebody who gets fazed but you do and it's no big thing. Sharia's right. It's chemical and you'll get over it.'

With all of them surrounding her and making a nest of their attention, she almost felt better. She was certainly meant to: the whole idea of clustering the first generation had been to create a substitute for the family unit that would also be practical for dealing with the harsh conditions on T'nane. Kalypso's cluster possessed a comprehensive array of practical skills embodied in its members; it was also more intimate than a family. Its members had been tuned to one another in the Dreamer. Their internal, subconscious symbologies had been merged to some extent: Kalypso knew this because she'd learned to shotgun by Dreaming with her own cluster to make the group as tight as possible. Ironically, though, it was she who had ended up on the outside. She knew the mental fingerprints of each of her nestmates; maybe she even knew them better than they did themselves, and yet it was Ganesh she had truly bonded with, which was something they would never understand.

Liet took out a cosmetic pencil and began drawing on Kalypso's head. She hummed softly as she did this, and her breath grazed Kalypso's temple. Kalypso closed her eyes.

'Getting back to the fault in the luma,' X said. 'Ahmed, you said before that there have been glitches like this in the past.'

Ahmed and Tehar were the only two members of the cluster who had any sort of mechanical relationship with the AI, so it now fell to Ahmed to try to explain to the others what had actually happened to the station.

'Well, in a small way, sure we've had problems before. Ganesh uses the magnetosomes to regulate data storage within the microtubules, but magnetic alignment can also affect the consistency of the gel and the distribution of spores. The luma sporulates and desporulates all the time, but we don't notice because the changes are small and homeostatically balanced.'

Just as Kalypso had begun to purr, Liet broke off drawing and handed her the pencil. 'Hold that for a second. Time for my second coat.' She reached for the nail polish.

'Jianni said the luma could melt,' Sharia said. 'When the thermal comes.'

'He said that? Well, if Ganesh doesn't keep control of it, I guess it could. *We* certainly have no control over the luma except in a very gross structural sense.'

'You think Ganesh has lost control?' Sharia pounced on the implications of Ahmed's words.

Ahmed said, 'Only Ganesh really knows that. It was Ganesh's initiative to spread into the luma – that had less to do with us than the Grunts like to pretend. It's only a happy accident that Sieng found a way to groom the luma to make it usable. If she ever formed a complete theory, we didn't hear about it. It's like the Chinese using gunpowder for fireworks without understanding the principles of combustion.'

Sharia raised an eyebrow. 'I wouldn't go that far. We know how luma arises naturally and we know how to induce it to solidify. We can exploit its magnetic and mnemonic functions. Well – Ganesh can.'

'Yes, but Ganesh is working without a theory as such,' Liet murmured. She was heavily engaged in painting her toenails; yet they all turned to look at her. 'It's improvising. That means mistakes. But I wouldn't worry. Self-preservation is deeply instilled in the Core. Oops. Sorry, Kalypso. Got some polish on your head.'

'Everybody,' Sharia said, 'makes mistakes.'

Kalypso ignored her. 'Why would the luma melt?'

'You never cared about this stuff when Ganesh was trying to teach it to you,' Ahmed teased.

'If it's hurting Ganesh, I care about it,' Kalypso said. 'Liet?'

Liet always took her time answering questions. She appeared preoccupied with some lint she had discovered between her toes. 'Well,' she said eventually. 'Everything else being equal, natural luma is oriented with respect to polarity. That's why a flyover of this planet shows a grain in the oceans. Although most luma isn't solid, it's so pervasive that its magnetic orientation actually shapes the ocean.' She stopped, yawned, stretched. Ahmed's pupils dilated and he sighed. 'We refer to the magnetic substructures as magnetosomes because they resemble the particles of FeO_4 found in certain terran archaea and algae. But the scale is entirely different. Each cell of the luma is thousands of times larger than a bacterium, and when it sporulates, it tends to recombine RNA from a variety of what we used to call species. We call them subsystems now because they don't meet the criteria for species.'

'Does any of this have to do with Ganesh?' Sharia prodded. Liet frowned; she tended to get self-conscious if you pressed her.

'Sort of.' Liet fluffed her platinum hair. 'In the process of sporulation, the cytoplasm of the luma cell loses water and becomes a gel in consistency. We can induce sporulation by depriving a given subsystem of essential nutrients, but we can only determine which nutrients these are by complex statistical calculations. The luma may appear uniform, and may function in a uniform way, but it's chemically and biologically heterogeneous and therefore unpredictable.' She paused again and closed her eyes. Just when Kalypso thought she'd fallen asleep again, she added, 'The indigenous luma System is too dynamic to be manipulated using any bio-engineering techniques we've ever known: it resists analysis and has to be treated with probability theory. That's why we need simulations like Alien Life.'

'Yeah, but . . .'

Liet shot upright, talking a blue streak. 'OK, listen. When the endospores form, all exchange of genetic material grinds to a halt. Cell membranes cease to exchange information packets. Magnetosomes align electrostatically and if you pass a charge through the luma, it stiffens and will hold its alignment indefinitely. That's why everything in First depends on the kinetic energy of the well. It would be a lot easier for us to survive if we didn't live on top of a volcanic explosion. But that heat generates the electrical power Ganesh needs to maintain the structure of the luma. It's been created by the planet's natural environment. Luma is custom-made for T'nane just like we were custom-made for Earth. Do you understand?'

'No.' It was Liet's standard question, and Kalypso's standard answer. They exchanged little smiles. Ahmed was looking at Liet lustfully. He ran a hand up her leg.

'Damn, you're smart,' he muttered.

Kalypso said, 'Not now, Ahmed. We're trying to have a discussion here. Liet, how could luma evolve without its own RNA?'

'We think it's a recording system for historical patterns of heat and nutrition. It confers some evolutionary advantage to its members – this goes without saying. Since it isn't born, and doesn't die, per se, we can't really talk about it in terms of evolution; and even if we could, to ascribe some purpose to it would be to see natural selection backwards. The endospores enable life to survive that otherwise would fry; luma provides a way to organize and handle the unstable heat patterns of this plant. It's an ordered system. But it has no analog on Earth.'

Kalypso sighed. 'So any of our data stored in the luma could get erased or altered in this crash. Is that right?'

'Yep.' Liet appeared distracted. 'Is there any food?'

'All our history, all the sensory records used in the Dreamer, everything from Earth. Music. All of it could be wiped out?'

'Depending on how bad the crash is, and where Ganesh has stored things.'

No wonder Jianni was so mad.

'Still,' Kalypso said, 'the Core should remain intact. Ganesh kept accusing me of Core breach, which is impossible for me as a shotgun, and difficult for Marcsson as a doze. If the fault was in the luma, why would Ganesh complain about a Core violation? There's no *programming* in the luma, so the luma couldn't attack the Core under any circumstances, because it's pure data. And the Core would have to violate its own programming to attack itself. Right?'

But Liet was rummaging in search of nourishment and Kalypso knew from experience that her mind had already passed on to something else.

'So what's the worst that can happen?' Kalypso said. 'Jianni's already starting an evacuation. But what about Ganesh?'

'If the luma melts,' Sharia said, 'whatever Ganesh was using it for will be disabled or destroyed. And the Earthmade components will be endangered, too, unless they're completely heat-shielded.'

'Jianni might try to shut down the reflex points and take manual control of the luma,' Ahmed observed.

'That would be stupid.'

'But if he shuts down the reflex points, won't that paralyse Ganesh?' Kalypso winced sympathetically.

'Yeah, that's the whole idea.' Ahmed sounded matter-of-fact. 'Safeguard against renegade AI.'

'This kind of fretting isn't like you, my small and fractious grasshopper. Why worry?' Xiaxiang rose from Kalypso's bed and craned his neck toward the window. It was dark and warm in the cell: another reminder of Ganesh's condition.

'Storm,' he said. 'You can see it. Look, where that curtain of precipitation is.'

Kalypso knew she sounded querulous. But she wasn't in the mood to be teased. 'I can't help it if I don't understand. I'm so tired of Lassare picking on me. She never needs an excuse.'

Sharia said, 'Crashing the station isn't an excuse?'

'That's not a normal storm,' Ahmed said darkly. 'It's a telltale. Thermal must be getting close. I saw it on the last forecast before G went down.'

'What kind of thermal? How long till it hits?'

Apprehension: the air going stiff with it. Sharia suddenly clapped her hands.

'I know! Let's play Future.'

They looked at her skeptically. X said, 'That's pretty thin.'

'Yeah, of all times to play Future, Sharia! Ganesh is down, and there's a storm . . . '

'All the more reason,' Sharia insisted. 'Come on. Somebody start.'

They all looked at each other awkwardly. Nobody said anything.

'Oh!' Liet burst out. 'I have an idea. We're going to have buses.'

'Buses,' they echoed wonderingly.

'Yeah, 'cause, imagine. There'll be roads. And so many people that a bunch of people might, you know, happen to be going in the same direction at the same time, and so to make it more efficient, we'd have. Well. Buses.'

'Oooh . . . '

'That many people?'

'Bus schedules . . . ' mused X.

'You know what?' Ahmed said excitedly. 'I've always wanted to see a really big bus station, or like those highway things – you know with those beautiful shapes where you'd have several roads conjoining, and they'd all have to interact safely, so you'd design the levels and curves just so . . . I mean, you'd be working with a variety of materials and you'd need to calculate the stresses – '

'Think of the budget on a project like that.' X whistled softly. 'All kinds of complexities with taxes and subcontractors and a little bit of backhanded stuff going on. Red tape. How pretty.'

'Well,' Sharia said. 'Let's not forget the basic overpass itself, it was a kind of special ecological niche. I mean, various lichens, snails – '

'Birds,' Liet agreed. 'Pigeons. And kids would write their names on the concrete. Cindy loves Tysheem, stuff like that.'

'Stand around smoking in the rain.'

'You could *live* there,' Kalypso put in.

'I guess . . .'

'No,' she insisted. 'People did. You could live in a cardboard box. I mean, imagine. You could be a social outcast, and still live and breathe. That's incredible!' She looked outside. 'We're all stuck with each other. They weren't. You could walk away from everything. If you wanted.'

There was a silence.

Sharia said, 'Well, I don't know if I want buses. But roads. That's something else. Imagine all that out there is land, and we could have roads. You could start running and never stop.'

Everybody had seen Sharia running interfaced, sweating and steaming and spitting in the confines of her cell, fogging up the windows with her efforts while Ganesh blew breezes over her and she pretended to be in Kenya or wherever.

'I think I'll take the bus,' X yawned. 'My feet would hurt. Whenever we play Future, we always end up recycling stuff from Earth history. Anybody ever notice that?'

The others had no chance to respond because Tehar dove through the hatch, breathing hard.

'Come on, Kalypso. Get your stuff.'

Sharia raised an eyebrow at him. 'News?'

He shook his head. Kalypso stared at the approaching storm. Was Ganesh really gone, or just pretending to be gone? Her parents . . .

'Kalypso. Surface suit. Emergency gear. Now!'

The cell was so small that Tehar could reach across it from the hatchway and shake her. Ahmed was pulling her surface suit out of storage and attempting to shove her legs into it.

'Get her interface, too, Ahmed. Kalypso, move it!'

She shook herself and jumped off the shelf, catching hold of Xiaxiang's shoulder for balance on the way down. She was trying and failing to be angry with Tehar for his peremptory manner. Liet took her thumb out of her mouth and looked back and forth from

Tehar to Kalypso. Tehar remained in the hatchway, his body coiled like a cat's.

'We'll meet you at the Landing,' he announced to the cluster as he shoved her ahead of him into the crawlway. 'If we don't make it, go without us and we'll hook up with you at Oxygen 2. Kalypso, put your radio on channel four.'

She complied, flattening herself against the wall to let him get by. Tehar's sexual pull was always a huge distraction, but never more so than when he was in I Have An Emergency To Deal With mode. She suppressed a smile and followed him up the crawl. There were no voices on channel four. Instead there was a weird sonic flickering: sounds changing so fast and seamlessly the ear couldn't follow. It was as if Ganesh were playing every sound it had ever recorded, scrambled and in such fast succession that all to be heard was a kind of digital *panting*.

'What is this?' she said over the ghost-noise.

'Don't know,' he answered tersely. 'Thought maybe *you* would.'

'You've been talking to Lassare. She's full of – '

'Kalypso, I've just been through the rem2ram modules. You've routed music through the Dreamer units. Haven't you?'

Uh-oh.

She stopped climbing, then slithered after him up the tube, momentarily speechless.

'You and your fucking aural fixation.'

'But how could that – '

'Hush. Do as I say, and maybe we'll get to the bottom of this before the next thermal.'

When they arrived at Unit 5, she scarcely recognized her workstation. Ganesh's guts were all over the place. Panels were missing. Tools were scattered across the floor.

'Don't be alarmed,' Tehar said, calling up a screen full of code. 'This isn't going to affect what we're doing.'

How could he be so cold? That was part of *Ganesh* dismembered like a reeking corpse.

'I don't want to Dream, Tehar. You don't know what I've just been through.'

'I'm sorry if you had a bad night,' he said, sounding the opposite. 'But you'll do as I say.'

She was torn. On the one hand, it was always sexy when Tehar used that imperative tone with her. On the other, she had just sworn she was through with shotgunning. Tehar hadn't the vaguest notion what it felt like to be Kalypso in Ganesh. Witch doctors didn't normally Dream or even shotgun: they were concerned directly with code. Not only did she not want to Dream, she didn't want Tehar holding her hand while she did it. He might fuck up, and then where would she be?

'I'm always resolving to do things and then not doing them,' she complained. 'You're not helping me to improve my perseverance.'

He sounded distracted. 'Don't be ridiculous. What would you do if you didn't Dream?'

He had a point there. Her lack of any practical talents was nearly legendary.

'Dunno. Become a demon and make drinks?'

Tehar emitted a bark of laughter. 'Almost ready.'

She checked the settings on her face and waited uneasily while Tehar set up his parameters. She wanted to switch on the radio; in the exterior monitor of the face she could see a lot of activity on the waters near the station, especially around the hydroponics perimeters.

To give Tehar some credit, his task wasn't easy given that Ganesh wasn't available to guide him. Fortunately, he wasn't attempting to take her back into Alien Life, which was far too sophisticated to be run manually. He intended to take her into the module where rem2ram was housed, so she could walk him through its convolutions and show him how her node of Ganesh was set up. To do this, Kalypso had to Dream: unlike a witch doctor, she didn't understand Ganesh's code from the outside. Her relationship with the system was entirely intuitive, multi-sensory, and dependent on total immersion. She couldn't objectify her own experience inside the Dreamer the way a witch doctor could; but then again, Tehar couldn't tolerate the levels of sensory complexity that Kalypso could. They were a complementary team – or they were meant to be. Tehar was not exactly being her best buddy at the moment.

'Now,' he said. 'When you get in, take as many readings as you can so I can fix the position of neural activity across the AI. I'm going to need you to talk me through everything you're doing and seeing, so I can match your experiences with the code I observe.'

She sighed because he was all business. 'Of course.'

The induction sequence started running, a pattern of subtle sensory cues meant to take her brainwaves to the Dream state, where she would be susceptible to Ganesh's suggestions. She was too keyed up to respond. Her interface kept her at a conceptual distance from Ganesh, which was perfect for shotgunning but which obviated the ability to truly Dream. After a while it became apparent she was getting nowhere.

'This isn't going to work, Tehar. I'm still in my body. We need a tank.'

'The tanks aren't safe.'

'Well, I'm not sleepy. I won't be able to get into it this way.'

'Just relax.'

'Tehar, I can't. It's like trying to pee when you're really nervous.'

She took the face off. He ran his hands through his hair in irritation.

'You're not taking this very seriously.'

'What am I supposed to do?'

'The whole station's about to go down, Ganesh is psycho, people are dying, and all you can say is you don't have to pee?' He was waving his hands around. 'I can't take much more of this, Kalypso. You want to use the tank? Then get in the fucking tank, and if you berk I'm not saving you.'

'Thank you.' She could grow to like this excitable side of Tehar. She blew him a kiss as she climbed in. The Dreamtank had been put back together by the witch doctors, but despite Tehar's undisguised agitation, she checked every connection before lying back in the fluid and letting the Dreamer take her senses away.

Induction complete, said a voice that sounded like Ganesh. But when she tried to follow, it fled.

She was in the dark, even when she opened her eyes. There were no connection points here, no interface fitted to her skull: just the eggshell-smooth interior of the Dreamtank. She reached up to touch the inside of the lid, and it swung open for her. She slipped out of the salty induction fluid, which radiated a faint, familiar smell as it slid off her skin.

Everything seemed all right. This was the ur-system, the Dream interpretation of First that formed a consistent set of reference points for everyone who Dreamed. There was a robe. She put it on. The tank was not crammed into Unit 5 any more; rather it rested high in the caldera that formed a bubble at the top of the station. The floor was curved like a skateboarder's paradise, yet riddled with holes as all of the main transit tubes found their source here. The caldera resembled a giant sieve, except that the luma it had been constructed from was thickly veined and marbled beneath its smooth surface, giving the appearance of old flesh pressed under glass.

In waking life, the transparent dome of the caldera would look out in all directions on the brilliant, steaming surface of T'nane; down on the Works that provided the colony's basic atmospheric and energetic requirements; and up into the grave, somnolent clouds that obscured the distant sun.

But this was Kalypso's Dream, and there was no sky in it. Overhead stretched a vast pane of ocean: Earthly sea, an impossible, Trinidad blue as warm as the waters where her genetic mother was born. It crowded over T'nane like a flat shield, never curving, never revealing the azure sky it purported to reflect – never ending in land. Its geometry was therefore implausible, elusive and dangerous: this was the first sign to anyone entering Kalypso's Dreamer that she played by different rules.

'OK, tell me what all that shit is,' Tehar said, homing in on the ocean-sky. The usual business of the witch doctors was to patrol and maintain homeostatic adjustments on the environmental nodes – to groom the growing Ganesh – so they weren't in the habit of working with the Dreamer modules. Tehar's attitude was a touch cavalier, Kalypso thought: as if her node were too frivolous to be bothered with.

'That's all the data Ganesh has recorded about Earth. I use it as source material whenever I'm running a pleasure trip, or dealing with the Earthborn. All their sensory references are there.'

'Hmm. How . . . unconventional.'

'I need to go over the station, make sure everything's – '

'There's no time for that. Go straight into your launch for Alien Life.'

'But I can't tell if my face has been damaged.'

'I'm here to watch out for you. Just go on. Quickly.'

If it had been anybody but Tehar, Kalypso would have been annoyed by now. She wanted to tell him he was a lousy shotgun, for she herself would never barge verbing into somebody else's Dream making unreasonable demands. Shotguns were meant to be unobtrusive. However, she wanted to impress Tehar, so she didn't protest.

In the pockets of the robe were a rabbit's foot, tweezers, an eternally half-eaten carrot, and an old-fashioned latchkey. She fished out this last item, whistled a few bars of 'Moonlight in Vermont' and waited for the giant primate footprint to form in the caldera floor right at her feet. She stepped down into it, and a flight of narrow stairs appeared, imported from an archaeological dig at Mohenjo-Daro. Or so Ganesh had claimed when it had helped her design the passkey. At the bottom of the stairs was a red door.

'Where did you unfold all this stuff from?' Tehar asked. 'And what dialect are you using for your code? It's highly irregular.'

In the Dream, Kalypso shrugged, knowing he could read her body as easily as any verb she might send. Yet he couldn't actually perceive her sensory references, he could only follow the code – and it wasn't her problem if the code didn't fit in with the structural conventions he believed in. She might admit to being a fuckup in every other respect, but Kalypso apologized to no one about the way she moved through Ganesh. That was between her and the AI.

She put the key in the lock, said, 'Abdominal snowman', and pushed the door open with a little smirk for the thought of Tehar trying to figure out the code from his end.

A seaside town, complete with all the Earth references she'd been able to coax out of Ganesh. The feeling of sand beneath her bare feet; saltfish wind; a pervasive translucent grayness like a veil over everything.

'Where are we now?'

'We're here. *Chez* Kalypso. This is where I start all my Alien Life runs.'

'Take me right up to the edge of the simulation.'

So she walked past the deserted boardwalk, the blowing trash and the aggressive gulls that Ganesh always used to harass her with; now they circled endlessly. She explained everything to Tehar as she went, trying to help him understand; but she knew she was losing him. Where she saw waves and sand, he saw code; and he kept bitching that the code was full of slang.

'This is the transfer medium. These are the sensory relays. Those are Ganesh eyes – '

Dead crabs. They weren't supposed to be dead: usually they scurried underfoot. Now they were inanimate, rotting.

'What's this?'

He was indicating the lifeguard chair.

'That's where I hang out during Dreams.'

'There are audio connections running all through it. What do you need so much sound for while you're shotgunning?'

'I only did that because Marcsson was so boring,' she said defensively.

She touched the worn wood, remembering how Marcsson's math had pulled her out of this world and into the sea of his Dream. The tide was low, the waves subdued. She went and put a toe in.

'What are you doing right now?'

'This is the fringe of the Alien Life simulation. Where Marcsson was before he berked.'

'This is Alien Life? Shit's complicated.'

'That's what they pay me the big bucks for.' The irony appeared to be lost on him. Witch doctors took their status for granted; Tehar often forgot she occupied the equivalent social stratum to, say, a janitor.

'Do you *understand* any of this?' He sounded so condescending that she wanted to say, yeah, I do; I totally grok it. But ever since they'd done Picasso's Blue together as kids, Tehar could always tell when she was lying.

'No. Not really.'

'Where are your emergency systems? Show me what you did to try to rescue him.'

There was a shed just beyond the reach of the water. Near the door, a feebly moving crab caught her eye.

'What's that?' Tehar verbed.

'I told you: a Ganesh terminus.'

'What node?'

'I dunno. Let me see.' She bent and picked up a crab. Its underside felt like velvet. She rubbed it with her finger. 'It won't talk to me.'

'Atmospherics,' Tehar verbed. 'That's where I'm reading it.'

'Guess so, then.'

'You *guess*? Don't you keep track of your references?'

'This isn't my regular workstation. I don't usually come here through a tank.'

'Shouldn't matter. Are you always this sloppy?'

'Yes. It's a sign of creativity.'

'I know what it's a sign of.'

'Here's the emergency stuff.' Kalypso reached the shed and opened the creaking door.

The shed had no floor. It was full of water. A submerged rowboat was lodged several feet under, a huge hole knocked in the bottom.

'Explain, please.'

'It's my rescue craft! What happened to it? Why is the shed flooded?'

'Is the . . . um, shed . . . always flooded?' he asked carefully.

'Of course not. And the boat's supposed to be a Zodiac.'

'OK, let me get this straight. Alien Life is an ocean, you're the lifeguard, and the dreamer is the swimmer: is that your basic metaphor?'

'That's how I put it together for myself, yeah, usually. Well, I could never get Marcsson to go *in* the water, but basically – '

'If I were Dreaming in Alien Life, would I be aware of all this?'

'No,' she said firmly. 'Not as such. It doesn't necessarily look this way from the point of view of the doze – uh, dreamer – though. It's up to that person's imagination, what they experience in a Dream.'

'Well, that's really cute. Kalypso the lifeguard.'

'Hey. Let's get one thing clear, sweetie. The lifeguard thing is facetious.'

'How so?'

'Like, I'm supposed to be here for safety, yeah?'

'I should hope so.'

'But the doze is trying to work with some idea, some concept that's new to him or her, so when they come in, they have no way to Dream it. Your dreams are your brain's way of improvising with the material it has to hand. Like when Miles does an improv, he's working with familiar stuff and then sort of twisting it, trying to go farther and farther out. He can't just *arrive* at some musical concept that isn't attached to the past. Everything's a continuing story. Dreams are the same way. They're stories your brain tells you – '

'Yeah, I'm short on time here, so could you – '

'So say a guy like Marcsson comes in here with some data he's trying to wrap his head around, only he can't. Now, I can't understand his data, obviously, but I can lead his subconscious a little farther out to sea until eventually he's talking to whatever it is, whatever sea-monster it might be. So I'm not bringing him to land, so to speak – I'm taking him away from what he knows. I'm a lifeguard, because I'm responsible for safety; but if I'm any good at what I do, I'm also an anti-lifeguard.'

'And that's what you did with Azamat?'

'Well . . . no. As a matter of fact, he never let me get that close to him. I'm not sure what happened. He dragged *me* into it, and basically keel-hauled me through all this stuff he had. These data

60

of his. He got way out of control and before I could act he got me out of control too.'

'Probably because you threw out the safety checks.'

'Would *you* want to wear latex when you fuck? I mean, there are some things – '

'OK, Kalypso,' Tehar verbed hastily. He was using the same tone with her that she'd used with Marcsson when he'd been gamboling around Unit 5 like a madman. 'Tell you what. I'd like to take you into the Core now. Nothing to be nervous about. I'm going to send you the plans and I want you to walk me through it, just like you're doing now.'

'I can't go in the Core.'

'Yes, you can. Ganesh is unconscious. It won't even notice you're there, and all you're going to do is look. I'm here with you. I have to follow these leads.'

'What leads?'

'The leads in Azamat's flight path. It's too technical for me to explain to you. Just trust me.'

Immersed in the Dreamer, Kalypso was incredibly vulnerable to suggestion. Otherwise she never would have agreed.

'Well, if you're sure it's all right . . . '

She let him lead her back to the ur-system.

'Climb through the Works,' he said. 'You know where to go.'

She knew where the Core was. Only in a Dream would she dare climb among the convoluted and interlocking tubes that formed the Works, though: they were dangerously hot, and to get access to them you had to leave the station's airlock. Because it was a Dream, she accepted the fact of the open hatch blithely and climbed through. Nimbly she made her way to the bridge of the old ship. She had never been there in physical reality, so she wasn't sure what to expect.

She had the distinct feeling of not being alone. 'Tehar, are you facing?'

'I'm with you, my banshee,' said her shotgun.

'Shake your feathers, then.'

She could feel his proximity to her through the face, although her sense of him was not ordered as it would be outside the Dreamer. There was no image, no sound, nor smell, but rather a diffuse Tehar-feeling created by bits of his awareness bumping against hers through the medium of Ganesh. She felt him metaphorically clear his throat.

'Ganesh?' he verbed.

She had reached the bridge of the interstellar, which appeared in the Dream as the standard, ancient icon: a battered suitcase. There was no way in, as far as Kalypso knew; otherwise, she never would have been so sanguine about letting Tehar take her here.

'Take a look around the back,' he suggested.

The suitcase was wedged in an S-curve of a Works conduit. Kalypso turned it gently and saw a small hole with burn marks around the edges.

'It looks like a bullet hole,' she verbed with a nervous laugh. 'Ganesh?'

I ACHE ALL OVER. I'M LOSING DECLENSIONS.

'Ganesh?' Kalypso shrieked.

'Try this code. Tehar's special recipe,' said Tehar.

Kalypso felt it coursing through her. It burned and she began to itch nowhere in particular, making it impossible to know where to scratch.

IT TASTES LIKE SHIT. NOT WORKING. CHANT FOR ME, WITCH DOCTOR.

Kalypso was beside herself. 'Did you hear that, Tehar? Ganesh, stay! Keep talking. Do something, Tehar!'

'In a minute,' Tehar verbed. 'Calm down, Kalypso.'

'I'd be happier with no shotgun at all,' she complained. 'I'm trying to Dream, and you're bothering me.'

'I'm trying to keep you in line, Deed.'

I WANT JIANNI. BRING ME YOUR SPACE AGE VOODOO.

'I'm trying, Ganesh.'

He ran more code through her: pure data that he didn't even bother casing in any kind of metaphor. It was ripping her up and she didn't like it. Then a blunt object hit her on the head and the data feed stopped.

'Ow!'

'Shit, a block.'

'What's that?'

'I don't know what it is, Kalypso. That's why it's called a block.'

'What the hell are you doing, Tehar?'

'Something's cut this hole in the Core. I can't see what it is. So, it's like, when something's written in invisible ink and you heat it, you can read it, right?'

'I guess . . .'

'So I'm running this code through. It's a little demon I like to use for heating things up. And I'm starting to see something but I can't focus it. I'm gonna have to lens you, Kalypso.'

'*Lens* me? What do you – oh!'

Suddenly she noticed a vine creeping from the hole in the suitcase. It led past her feet and through the wall of the nearest conduit of the Works.

'What's that, Tehar? Is that the invisible ink?'

There was no humor in his answer. 'You mean you don't know?'

'Why would I be asking you if I did?'

'It's jazz, Kalypso,' he verbed grimly. 'It's jazz. Let's follow it, shall we?'

He left her and the Dream got suddenly big and timefucked and weird.

Total numbness. Then: something's burning. She is flying fast down a transit tube – except at the same time her feet are bare in the dust and there's a fierce light scorching her back. Except the insects running on her scalp percuss mad Javanese rhythms that sound in her bones loud as a carnival she's never been to, and her body is a flat thing with two eyes on its dorsal side half-buried in the ocean floor and Tehar's opening panels and making the luma pull like iron. This isn't a Dream. This is something else, just like Marcsson's data only less complex. Neverending flashpoints of discrete sensation: decontextualized, meaningless.

Remember that weird sound on Witchdoctor Radio? She can hear it right now, in stereo.

'Tehar, I don't like this.' Numbness spread. A good shotgun wouldn't have let her get into this.

'Wait. I'm giving you a string. Grab it.'

She felt the code tickling her face, seized it in her teeth. Tehar pulled on the string. But he had tricked her.

'You're in the Core,' he verbed calmly.

'*No! No!*' Her body had become subject and object, the world and its contents. There was nothing else. She was sobbing, and at the same time she couldn't move. They were taking bites out of her. Whatever *they* were, they came at her with pickaxes and shovels on all scales. They were exploding inside her organs, her flesh pullulating, seething with life that wasn't hers –

'Hang on, Kalypso. I'm starting to see – '

Anger.

'Tehar, let me out.'

'Hang on. Kalypso, hang on. This is fascinating.'

She swallowed the string.

'Ganesh. Ganesh. Where are you? Help.'

Nothing.

Suspended in the fluid of the Dream, perspectives intersecting and cancelling each other out. The concept of nausea without its physical consequences. Her body was being decomposed and plotted according to color.

'Locate yourself, Kalypso.'

I can't.

'Kalypso, can you hear me?'

Tehar, help!

'Kalypso, please respond.'

Lines that cut through and divided her like a wire cheese slicer. Her body a deck of cards shuffled at random.

Get me out of here, Tehar.

'Kalypso, respond!'

He sounds like me when I was trying to pull Azamat, she thought. No. No. I'm not berking. Shotguns never panic. Oh, not again –

*

Fear had shot her back into the ur-system. She was a person again. She found herself sitting at a control station in the middle of the Works. Her hands looked green in the filtered chemical light: beyond the observation panel, the Works seethed with reactions firing at the high temperatures derived from the volcanic well beneath the station. The vine was growing up her legs.

'Ganesh, what are you doing? I don't understand.'

She had to still be Dreaming, because there were no gloves on her hands. There was no hood on her head. In actual life, this would be tantamount to being the featured meat at a pyrochemical barbecue.

She leaped to her feet, opening her mouth to cry out for Ganesh, but black smoke came out of her lungs. She smelled sulphur. Her hands convulsed on the interface, which responded by generating more of that asinine harp music she thought she'd left behind. The lights of the Works pulsed off-rhythm. Swimming in the jungle of chemical-filled tubes she could now see the demons, colored in Walt Disney lavenders and pinks, grinning at her in silent mockery. She willed them back to Maxwell's where they belonged, but they only multiplied. They did this by mitosis, which struck her as odd. Ganesh was speaking to her in some unfamiliar dialect of Czech. She ought to be dead by now but wasn't, so she turned to exit the control booth and found herself being jerked savagely through a wet, fleshy aperture.

It was utterly dark, she felt no gravity, no temperature, no orientation. Then she saw something.

A pile of bricks.

A wheelbarrow.

In the wheelbarrow was a heap of wet cement or something of that ilk. There was a trowel stuck in the mass.

Beside the wheelbarrow, a small row of bricks had been mortared together, but it was as if the workman had been called away suddenly. There was a half-eaten sandwich on a wrapper nearby.

No ground, no sky, nothing but this.

Kalypso reached out to touch the handle of the trowel and a tiny red ant ran up her finger and stung her knuckle.

'Ow!'

She found herself back inside the tank. Wired. Spooked. The Dream was over.

She had woken to a first-class headache and a foul temper.

Tehar opened the lid, admitting a rush of cool air.

'You're lucky to come out of that intact, Kalypso. What precisely did you think you were doing?'

He was disabling the contact points as he spoke. She dragged herself out of the tank. Every muscle felt weary, but she hadn't moved at all.

'What was *I* doing? You said to trust you. When I called you, you didn't answer. That's it. Forget it. No more Dreaming, not for love or money. Ever.'

But Tehar's face was rocklike.

'Tell me everything. Now. This isn't a game. People are dying.'

'What are you talking about?'

'Well for one thing, the Dreamer's not organized according to procedures. It's totally messed up, and the problem starts with your home node.'

'I imported some jazz. That's all. My head hurts. I have nothing else to say.'

He glared at her. She could sense the rising tension in his body, a host of anger galloping under the muscles of his chest and shoulders. Tehar had never lost his temper in her presence: this would be fascinating if she didn't feel so –

'If you don't come clean I swear I'll push you out of the cluster. I'll tell the others, and we'll isolate you. You'll be alone.'

She had started to cry.

'Why are you picking on me this way?'

'Don't you dare try to manipulate me with your emotions. Tell me what you did to the Dreamer.'

'Nothing,' she spat. 'And I'm tired of being accused. It's not my fault if you're too stupid to figure out how to fix Ganesh.'

'Kalypso Deed,' Tehar said. 'It's a miracle you've made it to this advanced age without somebody bludgeoning you to death.'

She opened her mouth to respond and closed it again.

'You're stressed,' she said primly. 'I'm not going to take that personally.'

For some reason, he was looking more angry, not less. She watched him getting a grip; when he spoke, his tone was level and tight.

'You remember the Core?'

'Yeah, the suitcase. There was a hole.'

'And what about the jazz?'

'You mean that vine, but I don't – '

'Kalypso, those jazz recordings you were listening to came from the Core. They must have been used in some way to organize the AI, to form one of its root paradigms. Probably something to do with temporal relationships – I don't know. I'm only guessing.'

'Ganesh said the jazz came from Earth Archives.'

'Probably that's true. Ganesh has stuff copied all over the place, lots of redundancies. If it had the same stuff stored as Earth Archives and as root programming in the Core and you were tapping Earth Archives, then this could have created the link between the Dreamer and the Core, which you saw metaphorically as a vine.'

'OK, but what's so terrible? I was only listening.'

'Ah, but I think something from Marcsson's work scampered up the vine and infiltrated the Core, and that's why we got a crash. You see? You understand?'

'Scampered? What do you mean, *scampered*?'

'Don't bog me down with details. I need to think.'

Tehar's eyes turned inward, to the radio on his interface.

'Jianni? We've got a big problem here. Some code has come through the luma and punctured the Core. Yeah, that's what I said. I'm sure.' He paused, listening. His face was grave. 'If that's what we have to do, that's what we have to do. If we shut down reflex points, we'll lose everything in the luma, though.'

Kalypso grabbed his arm. He peeled her fingers off and turned away, still talking to Jianni. 'No one knows where Marcsson is. We're in the middle of an evacuation. He could be gone already –

really? What made you think to put a search order out?' Tehar listened to the response and then laughed humorlessly. 'No. No one mistrusts your hunches, Jianni. But if he hasn't been found yet . . . wait, I have an idea. Look, don't take down any reflex points just yet. Maybe we can still clear this up. Yeah. You're a mind reader, Jianni. Let me look through this node and get back to you as soon as we get Marcsson interfaced. Out.'

Kalypso felt her eyes bulging expectantly. Tehar turned to her.

'Find Marcsson.'

'*What?*'

'Get him. Bring him here. Don't screw up this time.'

'But why? What if I can't find him before the thermal? What if –'

'Just do it, Deed. Fuck what if. Find him. I don't care how. If anything happens to him there might not be a station to come back to.'

He fixed her with hard eyes.

'I've never seen you like this before, Tehar.' She slammed the tank shut and moved toward the hatch. 'You're scaring me.'

He turned back to the open system.

'Maybe it's time somebody did.'

Kalypso found herself in the usual darkness. Outside Unit 5, the crawl was unlit; through its translucent luma skin the sinuosities of the Works beyond were revealed by their own fires. A sly intimation of sun pressed through T'nane's cloud cover and vaguely silvered the condensation that studded most of the exterior of the station. There was no other light. This was daytime on T'nane; Kalypso had never known anything to be different. And yet, something had changed.

It was too quiet.

She could hear nothing but her own breath: the subliminal hum of atmosphere regulation was gone, as were the soft but audible murmurs of activity on Ganesh's sensor points extending throughout every crawlway of the station. You didn't notice Ganesh, until suddenly the AI wasn't in evidence. It had left the station bare and alone, like an empty chair.

She was connected to no one now. Where was she supposed to

start? Everyone else was on the Landings. Marcsson couldn't be there, or in any of the main tubes, or he would have been found. That left the Works, the cluster cells – which would have been inhabited until a few hours ago – the Gardens, and the legs.

Because they were prone to being cut off from heat and atmospheric control, and because they didn't lead to anything important, the crawlways in the station's structural support legs weren't often used by people. If Kalypso had been trying to hide, she would have gone into one of the legs, where even at the best of times, Ganesh was half-blind.

Not that she should assume Marcsson knew what he was doing, given his berkified condition. For that matter, Kalypso herself was in a fine state following the latest disaster in the Dreamer, especially after the way Tehar had behaved. If she had been thinking, she would have realized that it could take days to fully search all eight legs. She would have considered that she hadn't fared particularly well from her first encounter with the berking Azamat. Common sense probably would have kicked in and – if she had been thinking – she would have rebelled against Tehar's command.

As it was, thinking was not her strong suit. Kalypso wasn't thinking, she was climbing, beginning to sweat in the confines of the surface suit and breathing hard. She was involved in her own physical actions to the exclusion of all else. This ability to shut off her own head, she'd been told, was both her greatest strength and her worst failing. It could be an effective survival mechanism in a crisis; the only trouble was that Kalypso tended to use this same mechanism any time she might be made uncomfortable by the results of introspection. Like now. She did not want to think about what had just happened in the Dreamer; about Ganesh; about her role in this crash.

She climbed until she reached a cross-corridor that could take her to the nearest leg. The going was easy here, but when she got to the leg, the enviro indicators were all dead although the automatic seal separating the leg from the main body was operational. This failure wasn't surprising: Ganesh had always been thinnest in the extremities of the station. At least she could climb *down* the leg, to her relief. She was getting tired; she hadn't properly slept since two nights ago. Hadn't eaten recently either. How did Tehar expect her to find Marcsson? He must be losing his wits.

She studied the swirling waters to distract herself. Craft of various sizes and types darted back and forth on the surface beneath, and robot activity illuminated the heat-shielded farm cells that sprawled from each of the eight terminal pods. Subsystems of indigenous life moved endlessly in T'nane's complex thermal currents; if you looked too hard at the surface, it could make you nauseous.

It was strange to be alone out here. Creeping along the slender, transparent tube was like being in the hollow leg of a dead crab. When she touched its inner surface, trying to speak to it as she might speak to her cell, it didn't respond.

Her suit had started to kick in for her; the air wasn't good. That meant Azamat probably wasn't here. She should go back, but she hesitated. She continued to gaze down into the water. System experts like Liet were supposed to be able to assess the signs of an impending thermal just by studying the color schema of the surface. Kalypso wondered what signs could be read and interpreted from this vantage. The local System fields were moving anticyclonic, reds dissolving into yellow where different strains of aggregate unicellulars crossed over, seeking out their optimal temperatures and chemical conditions. Almost directly below her was the well like an enormous oblong pupil. Sparks of phosphorescence appeared and disappeared in its depths. The effect was hypnotic.

Luma bestowed a glutinous quality on the water, which meant that despite winds and thermal changes beneath the surface, it remained glassy and unwrinkled. The indigenes cohered. If you jumped in you would find yourself in the midst of a great glom of them, doing whatever it was they did – building luma and producing too much CO for human tolerance was all she knew.

The basalt supporting First was riddled with wells and tunnels which carried the planet's searing internal heat to the surface. The aquatic organisms that dominated the planet relied on these thermal currents for energy and motility – most of them cared nothing about the sun. It was the variability of the temperature zones which created life-sustaining energetic conditions. The same variability served as a power source for the station, but it also meant a complex feedback system was needed to maintain homeostasis; i.e., Ganesh.

The 'bottom' at which life functioned had yet to be plumbed. Colonies had been found to extend at least half a mile beneath the surface: there was a lot of fluid down there, and it was impossible to know how much of it was inhabited. The shaft she was looking into right now was incredibly deep: she remembered being made to study the survey results of it when she was very young. It was one of the coolest, stablest wells in the region, but it was far from safe if you happened to be sitting on a structure made of luma, like Kalypso was doing right now. As she watched, the formation that had looked like an eye began to dissolve into a multitude of cloudy fractalline explosions. The well was becoming ever more active.

Kalypso's suit advised her that it was now providing 52 per cent of her nitrogen/oxygen mix and filtering significant amounts of carbon dioxide and carbon monoxide. More alarmingly, ambient external temperature was rising on an accelerating curve. The thermal must be on its way.

She stared into the well, mesmerized. Her suit began to make noises and nudge her.

She jerked herself out of a stupor, turned and began scrambling back the way she'd come, recalling Liet's words, Jianni's warnings. Ganesh normally regulated the luma's state through electrical current, which controlled the natural magnetism of the structure. Without Ganesh, there were no guarantees of magnetic – or structural – stability.

The suit was shrieking at her: it was near its heat tolerance levels. She increased the oxygen mix and climbed faster. At the top of the crawl, she found the way blocked. Ganesh must have shut off all contact with the legs, for the sealing membrane covered the passage she'd used to enter. She was shaken by the idea that this had been done with no regard for the fact that she was in the crawlway – she hadn't even been warned. She tried to reverse the seal, but overlapping membranes closed off the passage like a shut flower. Kalypso braced herself against the walls and set her shoulder to the center of the seal. The membranes were supposed to respond to correctly applied force. She heaved mightily; nothing happened. Not even a twitch.

She wasn't strong enough.

But she had to be strong enough, or she was in trouble. The heat was only going to get worse, and she was already starting to feel it. The suit would soon fail.

She started to reach for her radio and checked herself. Everyone would be at the Landings by now – or gone. Tehar could never get here before her suit gave out, assuming he could even be bothered with her at this stage. So there was no point in screaming hysterically. Instead, she opened the suit's u-tool and set it for knife. Then she began hacking at the sealing membrane.

The fact that Ganesh didn't cry out when abused this way told her more than anything that the AI had really gone from the body of the station – or this part of it, anyway. She stabbed the u-tool through the membrane, straining her shoulder as she ripped a gash in the seal, and crawled through. A blast of heat followed her, but she could see no way to repair the leak and decided to get as far away from it as possible.

The central body of the station would stay safest, longest; but if Azamat had been here, he'd have been found hours ago. She was doggedly determined to get him before showing her face at the Landings. If the Mothers had succeeded in inculcating one conviction in the minds of their offspring, it was that responsibility for other people was paramount. Mavericks were not tolerated for long, and Kalypso had already used up about a year's worth of personal freedoms today alone. She had no choice but to toe the line.

So where would you go if you were a berking Grunt? The Works were dangerous without a suit at the best of times; the Landings were watched; Marcsson was too heavy to use a glider; and presumably the other legs were all sealed off, just like this one. If he was there, he was doomed, and nothing she might do could save him.

That left only one place to check, and fortunately it was down from here, which meant a joyride, and she could scarcely object to that. Making her way to an express tube, she delivered herself wholesale to gravity. She whipped down the tube, her suit slithering without friction on the smooth inner skin of luma. For once there was no one to reprimand her for joying, and she did nothing to check her speed until she'd almost reached the entrance to the Gardens. Then at last she hit the friction strips, grimacing with satisfaction as sparks flew from her outstretched limbs. Breathing hard with excitement, she came to a halt; a fast joy was better than sleep for energizing you.

Emergency lanterns lit the entry hatch, their beams making mirrors of the luma. She saw her reflection approach the hatchway on all fours and wipe condensation off the transparent sealing membrane before she peered down into the dripping green foliage. In the Gardens, darkness was total. The lights of the Works played across the plants only faintly, and the brilliant thermal-powered lamps which ordinarily nourished the Gardens had been cut, bringing premature midnight. Sharp, black-edged, and chaotic, the shadowed flora presented a daunting proposition to anyone trying to find another human being in their midst.

Kalypso parted the seal and slid through, dangling by her fingers as she tried to decide where she wanted to land. She hung for a moment in a long rhombus of light while a flight of moths percolated up her body like bubbles through champagne. Then the sealing membrane oozed over the aperture and forced her to let go.

when the zookeeper gets eaten

She landed with a soft rustle in a bed of peas. The suit was providing a small percentage of her oxygen, but the glow of its readouts would give away her presence and she wasn't sure she wanted to announce herself to Marcsson if he was here, so she shut it off. She even peeled back the hood so she could hear better. The smell of leaves, moisture, fertilizer and flowers bombarded her: she stood breathing for a good minute, getting accustomed to the air.

There was a trail of damaged foliage leading down. Encouraged, Kalypso began to descend. She didn't know how to move quietly among plants, and she could barely see where she was going. As she got lower, there was some additional, hazy luminosity generated by the *v. flagrare* in the water surrounding the base of the station, but such a small amount of light did her more harm than good. When she relied on kinesthetics, her feet seemed to find their places on their own, but as soon as she strained her eyes to see where she was going, she began to make mistakes. Either way, by the time she reached the lowest platform, she was pretty sure she had announced her presence to anything with ears.

But it didn't *feel* as if anyone was there. In fact, the sense of isolation made her skin creep. At the bottom of the Gardens was a small area of Earthmade flooring. She stood there and looked around: trees, vines, the smell of fruit. Nothing stirred.

In the floor was a trapdoor. She couldn't lift it. Silently cursing whatever Grunt had designed the thing – could have been Marcsson himself for all she knew – she repositioned herself, bent, grabbed the handle, and pulled from her legs. The panel lifted a few inches. She wriggled her foot under it. Shifting her weight, she got under the edge of the panel, gasping, and finally lifted it high enough to hurl it over backward. It hinged back and hit the deck with a reverberant *bang*. So much for stealth.

Being small really was a drag. Kalypso was so annoyed at expending unnecessary effort that she lost track of the fact that she wasn't getting adequate oxygen. She began swaying and had to extend her arms for balance. Only when she nearly fell into the pit did she realize what was wrong and put her hood back up. She turned the suit on, breathed deeply, and looked into the pit.

It was the access panel to a trove of Earthmade equipment. She gazed reverently on the metal and polymers, the sharp lines, the details. Earthmade materials had a distinct – and rare – look. This was one of the station's many reflex points, basic checks meant to act as a simple autonomic nervous system, outside of Ganesh's conscious control. They had never been used before in the entire history of the station. Never had Ganesh lost consciousness, not even once. If it did, anything it had stored in the luma would be subject to deterioration or even erasure. And if she didn't get Marcsson to Tehar in time, Jianni would start shutting the reflexes down to protect the Core, and the Earth Archives, from whatever this 'vine' thing was that had infiltrated it. It would be very bad news for Ganesh – worse than a lobotomy, Kalypso thought darkly.

There was something fascinating about the equipment. She lost track of the fact that she was supposed to be hunting Marcsson and studied it. All of the dials looked familiiar, but Kalypso had never been much good with manual apparatus. She was used to functioning organically – under Ganesh's skin, as it were – where she could do what she needed to do without resorting to mechanistic means. Some of this stuff was computerized, but not sentient: she poked at it but found it had no sense of humor and kept giving her the same responses again and again. She pulled her lip and belatedly noticed that a red light was flashing. She wanted to investigate but was afraid she'd do something terrible. Yet it flashed and flashed, beckoning. She couldn't resist. She touched the corresponding indicator, and then jumped back with a little electric scream of fear at her own daring.

EMERGENCY. CONTACT WITH UR-SYSTEM HAS BEEN LOST. ISOLATE ESSENTIAL SYSTEMS IMMEDIATELY. SITUATION CRITICAL. TO ACTIVATE OFFLINE REGULATOR CHANGE THE SETTING ON –

Her suit went tight at the throat; she was grabbed by the scruff of the neck and hauled from the pit. She kicked out and tried to turn, but was tossed to one side and found herself sliding impotently along the floor.

Marcsson loomed over her – had she been worried he might have suited up and hit the surface? Small danger of that. He was still wearing nothing but his skin, which looked something the worse for wear for having plunged through the Gardens. If there'd been a certain thrill the first time he knocked her over, she wasn't enjoying herself now. This time he came after her and pinned her to the ground. One knee was sufficient to weigh down her body, but he also grabbed her jaw in one hand and jerked it from side to side as if trying to pry her head loose from her neck. Kalypso swatted ineffectually at his face. He let go, stood up, and kicked her in the head.

She was so dazed she couldn't move right away. She had the impression she'd been conveyed a further couple of meters from the manual pit, for now she was lying under the fronds of some plant she ought to know the name of. She should consider herself lucky his foot had been bare, or she might not be conscious at all. She felt around in her mouth cautiously. One tooth was slightly loose but she was pretty sure it was a deciduous one, anyway. She closed her eyes and pretended to be knocked out, hoping to buy herself some time.

No such luck.

'You may not be aware,' he said, 'that I'm unable to conform to your – to your – that I don't understand.'

Kalypso opened her eyes. He was standing over her, interfaced, looking at the ceiling, shifting his weight from foot to foot in a weird little dance.

'It's OK,' she whispered. 'Don't worry about it. Happens all the time.'

She tongued the loose tooth again and tasted blood.

He turned and walked away, slapping at the leaves of trees. He seemed short of breath.

'I will cooperate,' he said to the plants. 'You don't have to eat me. I'm sorry if addressing you as you is wrong. I don't have the language. I can't – I can't – '

Kalypso sat up slowly.

'Do you need oxygen? You can share mine.' She was going to have to find him a suit if she was to get him back to the station. Her suit showed 15C as the ambient temperature around her, but he was dripping with sweat and his face was flushed. He wasn't looking at her, but he came toward her, talking fast and in an excited tone she'd never heard him use before.

'This constellation of relations, you being seven below and in inverse relation to the square of the arc of my distance from the next occurrence as a function of the refraction of sunlight; this spot of intense radiation hotter than the Paris pavements of July '78 where a kind of thrall had set in, visible as sweat above the lips of women – '

She nudged her radio on with her chin.

'Um . . . Sharia?' she whispered. 'X?'

Marcsson scratched his ribs violently. ' – I wanted to find you here but all I can find is decay – '

'Kalypso, stat! We can't hold the boat. There's a whirlpool halfway up the channel. We'll get stuck if we don't leave.'

'I've got Azamat. But I can't move him by myself.'

'Leave him. Kalyp – '

' – a sudden draft inside, ice cream eaten too fast and like a rubric announcing a text this change signifies a series of fast turnovers but I can't find the key. I'm always a couple of moves behind. Why can't this be like chess? Why is it so messy?' Marcsson sat down heavily.

'Kalypso, get your ass down here. Leave Marcsson. Just leave him.' Xiaxiang, sounding fierce.

'But – '

'Now, Kalypso.'

'No. Go without me, X. Tehar says I have to do this. Ask him.'

There was a burst of static; he said something. She wasn't sure, but thought it sounded like *fucking bitch*. Then Sharia again.

'We'll meet at Oxygen 2, OK?'

'Yeah. Good luck.'

She switched to the witch doctor band. Azamat seemed subdued now.

'This is Deed. I'm at the bottom of the Gar – '

' – *off this channel, Kalypso. We need the air.*'

'No!' Her voice had broken from its whisper.

Azamat still didn't look at her. He said to the floor, 'I'm here to feed you. I'm here to help. There's no need for violence. I'll – '

'I need Tehar. In the Gardens. Now. I have Marcsson. Pass on this message, please.'

'Tehar's in the Dreamer. Get off the channel. We'll give him your message when he comes out.'

'Jianni is that you? This is important, He's going to want – '

'I said I'll pass it on. Bye!'

'Shit.'

She sighed and switched the channel to monitor. Azamat was chewing his lip.

'Your hands are bleeding.'

He glanced at her. 'There are these ants,' he said. 'In Costa Rica. They build bridges with their bodies. If you stand still you can hear the rushing of their legs on each other's thoraxes.'

'Do you want some oxygen?' She ought to approach him and make him breathe, but she was afraid. He looked at his hands. She wasn't sure whether he was hearing her or not, but there was nothing she could do about it, so she got to her feet.

'I have to find you a surface suit. And then we have to go. I want you to stay here, and don't do anything, yeah?' She checked over her suit, her equipment, to make sure nothing had been damaged in the scuffle. Then she made for the edge of the next terrace and began to climb.

He followed her. He kept stumbling and probably hurting himself, but she didn't care. The side of her face was starting to swell.

A sense of creeping strangeness overcame Kalypso. Shadows and more shadows reflected vegetation against the glass. Every so often a section of luma discharged electricity somewhere in the station above, and the water outside was lit up sick-green. Boat lamps winked and blurred as the station emptied, and a fog rolled in. Behind her Marcsson blundered, gasping.

She didn't want to be responsible for him. If it were a Dream, she would know what to do – but reality wasn't her forte. Marcsson was talking to himself, but she could make little sense of him especially given that he was panting like a mad animal. *Tehar*, she thought. *Be on your way. Be almost here.*

Where was she going to find a surface suit big enough? Marcsson's cell was on the other side of the station and several levels up: almost an hour's climb. She would have to hope he stayed put, for he couldn't survive in the tubes if atmosphere failed totally.

When she reached the hatch she'd originally come through, Marcsson was bent double with exhaustion. He tried to grab her ankle as she climbed out, but she shook him off. She checked the suit and did a carbon dump. Ganesh's sensor points were now flaring randomly: what did that mean?

She turned back to Marcsson.

'Stay there. You can't breathe out here, and there might be a rise in CO at any time. I have to find you a suit.'

Outside the station nothing could be seen now but a thick fog of water vapor laden with ash.

'*Kalypso!*'

Tehar. Radio.

'Help,' she squeaked. 'I've got him, but I need a suit. He's not lucid, Tehar, and he hit me for no – '

'*I need you to do exactly as I say. All right?*'

'OK.' Anything not to have to make any more decisions.

'*Get him to a sensor point. I'm reading a live one about two junctions laterally from you at two o'clock.*'

'I thought Ganesh – '

'*Ganesh is in flux. It's pumping all kinds of noxious shit out of the Works – *'

'The Dream. The demons. I wonder – '

'*We don't have time for this. If we don't do something real soon, Jianni's gonna take down reflexes, and I don't blame him. Get him to the sensor point, make sure he's interfaced, and plug him in.*'

She didn't answer for a second, wondering if she'd heard him right.

'You can't be serious.'

'*Yes. Do it.*'

'Just like that? No shotgun? No tank? And Ganesh – '

'*Do it, Deed. Triple stat.*'

'OK. No need to bark. I have to get him a suit. Until then, he can't go anywhere. The air's foul.'

'*You're near a storage section.*' He gave her directions.

'On my way.'

She was hungry, and hot. Nothing to be done about that. She followed Tehar's directions exactly; but when she got to the locker he specified, it didn't have any surface suits in it. She was reaching for her radio again when she heard a muffled curse from a cross-tube. She climbed over to investigate.

A panel had been opened, exposing a conduit of the Works on the other side of the transit tube. Jianni was there, on a ladder above the moving liquid. The luma that formed the sides of the conduit had partially melted and swelled, blocking the flow; in addition, a piece of it seemed to have come loose and had floated to block the intake of a heat converter. Jianni was trying to repair it, but judging by the words coming out of his mouth, he wasn't having much success. His raised voice was audible even over the rush of chemicals in the adjacent Works. He was talking to Ganesh.

'Just let go of this for me, just for a second. If you keep this piece charged, I can't help you.'

His tone was plaintive, worried. Jianni was a natural leader: always confident, always strong, never ambiguous in his actions. Yet he shared a certain bond with Kalypso, who had never felt at home with anyone but Ganesh; he had never looked down on her or pushed her to be more than she was. He understood how she felt about the AI because he, too, enjoyed an intimacy with this evolving machine. He had taught her many things that only a witch doctor could know.

'Imagine,' he said to her once, lying on the floor of Maxwell's after everyone else was gone and the demons were snoozing among the liquor sacs, 'that Ganesh is an elephant born in captivity. All it has ever known is the zoo. And you are the zookeeper. Well, actually, *I'm* the zookeeper, but you could be one day. Every time you walk in that cage, you have to be aware that this elephant isn't stupid. One day it may realize that there's a bigger world out there. You can feed it and wash it and talk to it; you can have a lovely time. But don't ever forget that inside that elephant is the real wilderness, waiting to come out.'

'You mean, like it might eat you or something?'

He rolled on his side to tilt half a smile in her direction. 'Elephants don't eat people,' he informed her. 'They stampede.'

'Of course. I knew that!'

'No, you didn't. You'd have to be from Earth to know that.'

You could see it in his manner now, Kalypso thought, watching him working with the recalcitrant Ganesh: he loved the AI. He was happy to be its warden, not its master. To everyone else, he gave orders. Ganesh, he asked nicely.

He saw her and barked, 'You should be at a Landing.'

Kalypso kept a respectful distance from the conduit, which was highly acidic as well as hot. Through the open hatch cover the *flagrare* seethed and steamed. Jianni looked like a gondolier, balanced with one foot on the ladder, one inside the station, a luma-maintenance pole gripped in both hands as he pushed the renegade mass away from the mouth of the converter.

'I need help with Marcsson,' she screamed. Her fingers ached from holding the wall. 'Tehar says if I get him to the Dreamer he can fix the crash, but he doesn't have a suit and I can't take him out of the Gardens.'

Jianni's face twitched with effort.

'We're short on surface suits,' he gasped. 'Supplies have been going missing.'

The tool slipped off the luma and Jianni lost his balance. Kalypso

81

gasped and started forward; then he caught himself. Her suit's oxygen use was up to 92 per cent and it prickled her with CO warnings. She didn't know how long he'd been out here, but he couldn't last long at this rate.

'Why don't you leave it? We're evacuating anyway. Shouldn't you be – '

He braced the pole on the ladder and leaned on it, his back sagging.

'Ganesh, it's for your own good. If we shut down this reflex point, we can help you. Otherwise, you could very well disintegrate. You must trust me.'

She didn't know what the AI's response was, but Jianni straightened and redoubled his efforts. Leaning over the well, he craned his head at an odd angle into the curve of the luma.

'Can't see shit,' he muttered, and pulled his hood off. He tossed it into the crawl, got his head into position again, and took out a u-tool. He needed a couple more arms, Kalypso thought, but didn't offer to help: there was only room for one person on the ladder. His voice was muffled as he said, 'Plus, if I don't get this done, the excess heat is going to cycle back into the Works and flood right into the Core. We don't have as much sealant as we need, and Ganesh isn't maintaining – '

He pulled his head out of the gap and stuck the u-tool between his teeth, cutting himself off. He was breathing hard through the nose plugs, and sweat poured down his face. She shook her head slowly from side to side: this was typical Grunt behavior. Teach the younger generation to adhere strictly to safety procedures: then lead by counterexample. Or, as Lassare would put it in caustic tones, on T'nane even one alpha male was one too many.

Ganesh often implied that the Grunts were struggling psychologically as a consequence of their failing physical powers. After all, their role in the colony had been primarily to provide strength, endurance, and stability during the reproductive years of the Mothers, now long past. They had to stand by and watch young men outdo them, knowing they were past it and that the only thing they had to look forward to was a slow bodily deterioration on a planet that they'd failed to conquer.

She watched him work for a second or two, then realized he had forgotten she was there.

'I need a suit for Marcsson.'

He slapped the u-tool on to a magnetized portion of luma and said over his shoulder, 'We never should have built this station so close to the Rift. It was only a matter of time before something like this happened. There are safer temperature zones almost anywhere. But no. We had to have more energy, so we had to park our bus on a motherfucker of a thermal well.'

Obliquely he was reminding Kalypso that were it not for her generation, neither luma nor large amounts of energy would have been needed. She hesitated. He was focused on positioning the drifting luma. He had pinned it against the existing luma and was waiting for it to be accepted, his arms shaking with effort. Kalypso began to perceive that her huge crisis didn't count for as much as she thought in the scheme of things.

'Look – ' she began.

'If there's nothing in the lockers, you'll have to go to Marcsson's cell and get his. Better hurry. Don't see how you can make it.'

He let go of the luma. It stayed in place; Jianni eased slightly and let the pole hang slack. He was now free to shut down the reflex point.

'That's it, Ganesh,' he coaxed, tilting his head back in the posture that told Kalypso he was reading the AI's code through interface. 'Much better. Now if you'll just – '

The luma above the reflex point discharged violently, disturbing Jianni's balance so that he lost his hold on the mass of luma. She saw Jianni lunge for it; the pole slipped and the melting luma detached itself, sinking into the acid of the conduit. Kalypso was already sliding down the tube when Jianni lost his hold and went in, but it was too late. She saw his head go under.

She was standing on the edge of his hood, which still lay where he had discarded it. She glimpsed him through the steam as he came up under the stray luma, bodily wedging it into place against the stanchion.

'Jianni! I'm coming!'

But his body was behaving like an object, not a person. It began to turn in the current. She grabbed the edge of the ladder and leaned out. The fallen pole came within reach; she seized it in one gloved hand and dragged him to the edge of the conduit.

Stupid bastard. He'd taken his hood off for convenience and now look! His face had been eaten away.

She kept thinking of funny things but she didn't have the spare wind to actually laugh, which was good because she surely would have hated herself for it. It took all her strength to get him out of the acid, which sheered from her suit and flowed back into the Works. It had happened so fast. She searched for signs of life.

His eyes were destroyed and his revealed brain was turning to vapor before her eyes.

She gagged and turned away quickly.

She looked at the access panel Jianni had been trying to reach. He'd actually intended to shut down Ganesh's primary power converter, using the emergency reflex points built into the station. Built, in Kalypso's opinion, by people who didn't understand AIs and were paranoid. Shutting down a reflex point would be like amputation, if not actual murder.

If Jianni had been about to do this to his beloved Ganesh, he must have had a good reason. And he had died. She'd never known anyone to die. She ought to do something. Out of respect.

'Temperature control in the maze is off!' the radio shrieked. *'Everybody out. We have a thermal rush due in ten. Out, people!'*

'Sorry, Jianni,' she said. Her throat ached and radiated a trembling into all her limbs, brought tension to her loins. She scrambled along the tube and then remembered Azamat.

'Get him, Kalypso. Whatever else you do, get Azamat.'

She stripped Jianni of his suit and pushed it ahead of her as she went back down the tube. Sky and water whirled to become a pinwheel of darkness and color as she flipped upside down with every twist of the crawl. Slugs of light dispersed from the still, jeweled station, each one an escape pod in the form of a small boat. On the radio: panic. And that feeling of isolation. Ganesh, to whom you turned for everything you could need, was gone.

She stopped at the storage locker to vacuum acid out of the suit and try the radio.

'Tehar? Tehar? Emergency, this is Kalypso to Tehar – '

Static. Noise. People interrupting each other. No Tehar.

She found Marcsson ten meters above the Gardens, passed out in the compromised atmosphere. Sweating and cursing, she wrenched his body into the suit and sealed it, then pushed him ahead with her feet. Luckily she wasn't going up. There was a narrow service chute which led to a small oxygen plant that supplemented the station's main supplies from the Works. If they could make it there, they'd be insulated while they waited. She could call Tehar and they'd get Marcsson interfaced properly, fix the AI . . . OK, one thing at a time.

Down the chute, she eschewed the friction strips in order to get speed and instantly regretted it: she felt sick by the time she landed in the service area. She could smell water: salty, slightly fetid with sulphur, laced with decay. The walls were fogged and, like all outer surfaces of the main station, obscured by fungal growth. Marcsson looked feral among all the green, his mouth half-open and lips pulled back from large teeth. He stirred.

She made another attempt to touch Tehar, but the channel was a maelstrom of voices. The witch doctor line was still clogged with scrambled Ganesh-noise. She glanced around the enclosure, just a hair's breadth from entering headless-chicken mode. She told herself to concentrate. The oxygen-generating apparatus was housed behind columns of luma. It operated using equipment she was totally unfamiliar with. As she stood there puzzling over the hardware, she began to feel chagrined that she hadn't paid more attention to this kind of thing while she was growing up. She could almost hear Ganesh's patronizing tone as it criticized her for failing to develop practical and technical skills. She remembered Ahmed constantly coaching her on matters of physical instrumentation and mechanics. She had managed to pass most of the practica and exams, but none of it had sunk in.

One thing was certain: this chamber wasn't being regulated for atmosphere, and when her suit's supply ran out, she'd be in trouble. She had to find a way to work the manuals; but without Ganesh, she was helpless. None of the symbols made any sense to her; the computer panels were all dead and the mechanical over-rides were a mystery to her. What would happen if she just started throwing switches?

Marcsson pawed at his own head, removed the interface. She shrank against the wall. She was still hurting from before.

'What's the matter?' he said. He heaved himself to his feet.

'Oxygen.' Her voice was thin with fear. 'I can't figure out how to flood this chamber.'

'Did you check the reserve tanks? See if they're full?'

'Um . . .'

'By your left hand.' He started forward, a little off-balance, and she slid out of his reach. 'Never mind. I'll do it.'

She watched his back as he manipulated the controls.

'We have to filter out some CO before we'll be able to take off the suits,' he said calmly. 'Take a little while for that.'

He began to whistle – not very well – 'Round Midnight'. It was one of the tunes from her Dreamer node. Kalypso found this unnerving and couldn't speak, although her continued silence seemed strange and she ought to say something. He didn't seem to notice.

'So what's the scenario?' he asked.

'Scenario?'

'Yeah. What's our objective? Fill me in.'

She hesitated. He sounded so matter-of-fact; if she hadn't been so scared, she would have rounded on him for acting crazy and then making as if nothing had happened. As it was, she took a few seconds to clear her throat.

'We can't communicate with anyone except by radio, and that's pretty jammed with everybody panicking. There's a thermal on the way and Ganesh has lost control of the generators. Everyone's being evacuated. We need to get you to Unit 5 but we don't have enough air in our suits to get there. Tehar's not answering his radio.'

'The legs are decompressed?'

'Don't know. Possibly. We can't rely on Ganesh for anything.'

'Anything? That's pretty extreme.'

There was an air of detachment in his voice. It wasn't that he wasn't serious, just . . . distant.

Then he said, 'I've missed you. It's nice, having this. Even if it isn't real.'

'Uh . . . I think it's real, Azamat.' Did he still think this was a Dream?

'The housing of this module will protect us from the thermal,' he said. 'We could stay here and ride it out.'

'We've been ordered to get to Unit 5.'

She was expecting him to argue, and braced herself. But he nodded and said, 'OK. Give me a few seconds.'

He apparently meant this literally: he stood thinking in the dead man's suit for exactly nine seconds. In this interval, Kalypso had time to start feeling really bad about Jianni.

'There's a service shaft that can take us to Landing 7 underwater. You won't know the passage I mean because it was built before your time. There's a clear run to Unit 5 from there.'

Actually, she did know the passage he meant, but he'd already turned back to the panels.

'I'm going to manually flood the shaft with breathable air. Use the suit's CO filtration system, but otherwise set your outtakes to external. I don't know about you, but my reserves are low, anyway.'

He positioned himself in front of a hatch seal and wrenched it open with his bare hands.

'Shit,' Kalypso said involuntarily. She slid into the crawl and checked her suit's readings: he'd done something right. The atmosphere was safe. She kept the plugs in but stopped using her reserves. She could feel the wind of intake and winced a little at the uneconomical use of good air, then caught herself. What did it matter at a time like this?

The crawl plunged down; she slithered on her belly like a seal, slightly claustro as the fluorescent smear of algaics closed around the outside of the tube. She was no student of these things, but even Kalypso could tell there was a thermal coming by the spiralline formations of *v. flagrare 57* peeling free of their usual hosts, *v. aa 4–11*. The reason for this prescience on the part of the temperature-sensitive methanogens was a subject of heated debate in circles more cerebral than those Kalypso moved in: she'd overheard the arguments without understanding them at Maxwell's, deep in the second shift when the demons had let her take over and mix her own combinations of T'nane-distilled substances. The good old days.

V. a 8 was a particularly good facilitator in the making of the most delicate alcoholic spirits, she recalled as she spotted a thin, pale cloud of them in their watery luma suspension. Most species of micros couldn't be seen, of course, but colonies of algaics could stretch for miles and showed up fabulously colored, however tiny their individual members.

The tube began to climb again and her muscles strained with the effort. Lack of food was getting to her, and she wasn't accustomed to jaunting all over the station this way. Marcsson crowded behind her.

'The tube is not heat-sealed,' he informed her over the speaker. 'By the look of the 57s, the wave's going to hit soon.'

Thermals were characterized according to a wide variety of styles, and Kalypso didn't remember anyone saying what kind this one was going to be. If it came horizontally, there would be indicators on the surface of the water; but if it lashed from below, and if the ascension rate of the event itself were high enough, there would be very little warning of any kind: no slow increase in temperature as the event diffused through the luma. Just a devastating rush of superheated, acidic water with its payload of luma spores, followed by lava.

Given that evacuation had been called for, she had no choice but to assume the second possibility. She climbed faster. Marcsson had to open the seal and hold it for her; Kalypso's shoulders and biceps had all but given out. Landing 7 contained about a dozen people with tentkits and other equipment, all busy loading the last two boats. Steam rose from the water, and the sulphur smell was stronger. Kalypso switched to suit breathing again and let herself rest on the floor, unnoticed for the moment.

Then Marcsson came through the hatch. He stood frozen, surveying the scene, licking his lips nervously. His interface was active.

'You should stay off Ganesh,' she advised. 'It's not safe.'

'You think you're so smart,' he said. 'Not any more. You're inanimate now if I say so.'

She chose to ignore him, staggered to her feet and was offered assistance by a tall young woman called Siri.

'We need to get to Unit 5,' Kalypso gasped. 'I'm exhausted. I don't know if I can climb that far.'

'Is that Marcsson? Why is he wearing a witch doctor suit?'

'Jianni gave him his suit and told me to take care of him.'

She was lying: why? Because she didn't have time to explain, she told herself. Siri could be officious and Kalypso didn't have enough air for the whole story – assuming Siri would even believe her.

Siri frowned. 'Where's Jianni if Marcsson has his suit?'

Kalypso began to shake. She couldn't process this. She heard herself saying plausible things.

'I don't know. He was busy working on Ganesh. Looking for emergency overloads. All I know is, Tehar needs Marcsson and I've left my cluster to do this, so I could use some cooperation.'

The rest of Siri's cluster had heard this and hands were already steering her and Marcsson toward their boat.

'Don't worry about it. We wouldn't leave you here, no matter what the circumstances.'

'Yann, grab some extra stores.'

'No,' Kalypso said wearily. 'We can't evacuate yet. We have to get up to rem2ram.'

Yann took a look at her. 'Kalypso, you're kind of cute but this is no time for insubordination.. Get on the boat or I'll put you there.'

Marcsson meanwhile had strolled over to the pile of science

equipment on the dock. He began handling it affectionately as he loaded it on to the boat. Siri smiled at him.

'Don't you just love the Grunts?' she said to Yann.

Kalypso'd been swept up in the movements of the cluster as they prepared to evacuate.

'No,' she protested feebly. 'Tehar will kill me. Ganesh – '

'Kalypso, isn't this great? Finally we can get *out*, the moment has come . . . '

'You're going to have to sit under the – Hey! What the – '

Marcsson had leaped on to the boat, causing it to tilt wildly and dump one of the passengers into the water. The other fell to the bottom of the cockpit: Marcsson picked him up by the scruff of the neck, just as he'd done to Kalypso, and flung him on to the landing. The rest hesitated for a stunned moment: then the man in the water, clearly the cluster's leader, started shouting for someone to subdue the Grunt.

Marcsson's u-tool was out and whipping across the lines that bound the boat to the dock. Siri grabbed the gunwales and held on, but the current was already pulling the craft away, and her body was soon stretched out between boat and dock, with one of her cluster-brothers grabbing her free hand just in time to keep her from plunging in.

Maybe Kalypso intended some heroics, however out of character that might seem; or maybe it was her loyalty to Tehar and her promise to stay with Marcsson that made her do what she did. Maybe it was because she couldn't face having to explain to Siri, who was far more superior/organized/sensible/smug than Sharia could ever aspire to being; more likely it was the fact that she was scared and didn't want to be left on the station. Whatever the case, Kalypso's actions were now at the vanguard of her reason, and she found herself scrambling over Siri's straining body, using it as a bridge. She rolled into the boat at Marcsson's feet without knowing entirely why she had done it.

She expected to be picked up and chucked overboard, but Marcsson was busy at the controls.

'You can't leave,' she objected. 'Ganesh needs you. Don't – '

90

It was too late. He'd engaged the engines at full power, and they shot away from the dock.

He turned and looked at her. Behind the interface his eyes were the blue of dead flesh.

the O-word

Kalypso was trembling. This was beyond any berk she'd ever seen. Marcsson's head was in deep trouble, and there was nothing she could do about it. As the boat's drive caught and they headed away from the station, she knew that Marcsson had very possibly doomed an entire cluster to injury or death. She switched on her radio and heard them frantically calling for help.

It was simply unthinkable. People didn't do this to each other – not on T'nane. Interdependency was too deeply woven in the fabric of their daily lives for anyone to think of behaving this way. Especially a stolid Grunt like Azamat.

He stepped away from the console and lowered himself to the bottom of the cockpit, where he sat motionless, hands on knees. They picked up speed, the boat ignoring the usual channels and instead cutting a swath through a gelatinous mass of developing luma. Kalypso lunged for the helm and tried to take control, but the boat responded for only a moment, then refused her instructions. Marcsson was interfacing; he must be using Ganesh to control the boat. In the time needed for a radio signal to travel from his face to Ganesh and back to the boat, she could make manual course alterations; but they only lasted an instant before being corrected by Marcsson via Ganesh.

How was this possible? If the witch doctors couldn't get Ganesh to behave, if Jianni had been struck down by the AI, how could Marcsson interface with such confidence? Could it be that he had never left the Dream state and was still swimming around in his own math? If so, how could he stand it?

Well – maybe he couldn't. No wonder he was berking.

Already First was looking small against the retreating horizon. She could see other boats jettisoning themselves from the station's underbelly as the thermal's accompanying gas cloud bore down on the station.

It was deceptively windy out here; the fluid surface might not register waves except as huge, slow rollers, but the atmosphere was moving at close to 100 kph. If they'd been on ordinary water, the boat would have been tossed every which way among fierce whitecaps. This wasn't like being on water, though: she'd been on Earth's oceans in the Dreamer. Water moved; waves threw you. In the Wild, there were seldom waves: only currents that moved unseen except for the changing colors of the *v. flagrare* within fluid regions of the luma.

The boat was long and slender. It lay low like a kayak. Its hull was coated with a designer polymer that could slice through colonies cleanly. The agglutinative properties of the surface made it difficult to flood such a boat, and using a filtration system in the bows the vessel could even produce its own oxygen when fitted with a tentkit. Kalypso did not set up the tentkit now, but routed the filtered gas directly to their suits so their reserve tanks would have a chance to recharge. The reassuring sound of pumps working to compress oxygen filled her ears.

'We have to get to Oxygen 2,' she said to Marcsson, hoping that if she treated him normally, he might start behaving that way. 'It's on the near side of the range but I'm damned if I know where we are now, exactly. I'm afraid we're going toward the Rift, which is the last place I want to be. I wonder if I can tack across the Rift current and come at Oxygen 2 from upstream.' Her voice sounded scuffed and enervated on the suit's speaker. 'Any time you feel like jumping in with suggestions, feel free.' She was talking too much – nerves – and when he didn't respond, she talked even more. 'Because I don't read any other craft in the area, and I'm not sure how this radio works . . . ' She fiddled with the elements on the dash. 'Damn, you know, I can't get used to doing this with my hands.'

If Naomi were here she'd be crowing at Kalypso's dependency on

Ganesh. Kalypso banished the Mothers from her mind and called on her memories of Liet's subconscious. Liet would know how to avoid the thermal, and how to calculate the gas-producing activity in the Rift that ran along the same fault line that had produced the volcanoes. First had been built safely out of range of the static heat of the Rift, yet within reach of the volcanoes, which provided an emergency refuge in the form of solid land, not to mention mineral resources. But the Rift isolated the far side of the volcanoes from all but the most determined efforts at access. The heat produced unpredictable currents and whirlpools, and fluky air currents in that region had brought down too many gliders to risk crossing as a matter of routine. However, this very same zone was also the repository of some of the most complex of the native ecosubsystems: Marcsson's data had mostly come from one well or another along the length of the Rift, which meant that he had routinely been across it in the course of setting up collection filaments. If he would only cooperate, they might be able to ride its edge to Oxygen 2, and safety. If he didn't help, Kalypso feared they'd simply be drawn into a whirlpool and melted down.

The more she thought about their situation, the more scared she got. She had never been in the Wild. She felt totally unprepared and – without the rest of her cluster – incomplete. Under any other circumstances, a Grunt like Azamat would be the best person to have in a boat with you at a time like this. Yet there he sat, vegetative once removed. This was getting less and less funny by the second. Her thoughts started to race around in pointless circles.

Fog and darkness conspired to invent shapes in the air ahead of the boat. Ahead, light generated by the Rift spread as a gel across the horizon and rose into the sky like the birth of a cloud from the sea. The *v. flagrare* subsystem had been so named because some of its members were incandescent, converting extreme heat from undersea thermals to light, which was then exploited by the algaics. On Earth, algae had dominated the ocean ecoscape, reversing the reducing atmosphere of precambrian times to the oxidizing one that had supported Kalypso's forebears. On T'nane, algaics were small scavengers in an ecosystem powered by anaerobes more effective than anything that had ever lived on Earth: there wasn't enough sun to permit the algaics to hold the bottom of the food chain, but there was plenty of heat. The foundation of the biomass lay with the *flagrare*: the eaters-of-fire.

Heat became light through biological processes unlike any seen on Earth; living fire rose from the planet's center. Like an organic version of lava, the Rift spewed teeming colonies of *flagrare* up through the water, which had itself been granted a kind of structure by luma, the glue of the System.

The System. That was what all the researchers called it. Take you to court for using the word 'organism', they would.

'It's a conceptual relic,' Ganesh would say of the O-word, and then go on to use the example of luma as a refutation of the idea of structure existing only within organisms. Ganesh had explained the phenomenon of the luma in terms Kalypso had never been able to understand: how the 'community' of colonial 'species' ('but we use that word advisedly', Ganesh would say, flashing an image of Charles Darwin standing on his head across her visual cortex) all contributed to the construction of this complex gel structure; how as some sub-species respired oxygen from ferrous compounds, others diverted the iron for use in the structure of luma. Its consequent magnetic properties made luma invaluable for data storage.

Luma wasn't an organism. Yet it wasn't just a substance, either. It couldn't reproduce; yet it could be grown, not by one strain of *v. flagrare*, but by a complex of reactions involving many of them, not to mention other colonials as well. To complicate matters still further, luma was itself a means of reproduction, for the System played fast and loose with the genetic material of its members. Intricately folded, heat-resistant packages of RNA migrated through the luma and infected one species with another's protein-coding information. Sometimes whole genomes were transmitted this way. That was why the word 'species' was so misleading: members of the System seemed able to turn into one another via a kind of horizontal evolution never seen on such a scale on Earth.

People like Marcsson had spent half their lives trying to grab on to the slippery nature of the Rift ecosystem, for it was the most dramatic example of the thermodynamic engine driving the biochemistry of this planet. For humans to survive on T'nane long-term, the atmosphere had to be stabilized. At the time of the initial Probe, the levels of oxygen and carbon monoxide in the atmosphere had been far more favorable to aerobic organisms. The crew of Ganesh had arrived to the unpleasant surprise that, in fifty-odd years' time, the atmospheric composition had been radically altered. No one knew exactly why or how this had happened: paleontological studies couldn't determine whether such gas cycles were normal for T'nane since fifty years wasn't even a twitch in geological time, even if it was millions of generations in the evolution of the micro-organisms that created the atmosphere.

Efforts to control the System had failed miserably; efforts to understand it were painfully slow. Sieng and her team had made progress in the beginning, but there had been no further break-throughs on the Oxygen Problem since the outbreak of infection that had killed Sieng.

It was also the last thing Kalypso wanted to think about. She belonged in the Dreamer. She belonged somewhere safely in-sulated from the Rational. But there it was ahead of her, boiling up from deep in the planet, epitomized in this conflagration of heat and color and mystery that would never yield to intuition: Science. She shuddered.

What had she said to Naomi? *The Wild itself will test you.*

What a crock of shit.

The boat was now riding up and then down a series of high waves which cut off all view of First. The air turned grey and yellow with billowing gases released by the thermal that rode behind them. She could feel its sound in the large bones of her body.

Thermals swept over First often enough, but always Kalypso had been safely enveloped in the solid certainty of her cluster, cocooned away from sensation in a closed, dry cell. She thought of the Gardens and the heat shields and Ganesh and then stopped thinking about all of it because she could not wrap her head around the idea that the world as she'd known it might so easily be destroyed.

'Look,' she said, forcing herself to turn and face Marcsson. 'We have to find a way around the Rift. I've got to get you to Oxygen 2, and we can't get there from here on our current heading without risking a melt in the Rift. I know you know how to do this, so why don't you just do it and save your life?'

She tried to sound stern but her voice was shaking.

He got to his feet; the boat lurched. It was a research vessel recruited for emergency use, and not all of the collection equipment had been removed. Marcsson uncoiled a collection filament and fed it over the side. It would accrue chemical and magnetic signatures in sequence according to time and depth, which could then be rolfed in statistical analysis to yield patterns of System behavior.

'You *can't* go over the Rift,' she bitched. 'We have no way of assessing conditions there. We can't even see where we're going!'

He stared into the water.

She tried to over-ride his course again but couldn't. This must mean he was still interfaced; if he was faced, Ganesh was functioning in some way or other. Kalypso flicked on her face again, hoping to pick up radio from First. She was low on power to transmit at this range. She didn't know how to feed her face through the boat's signal amplifier, but if Marcsson was managing to send and receive signals with Ganesh, there had to be a way. She looked for some kind of hardware link, failed to find anything, and then noticed herself beginning to hyperventilate. Marcsson slowly and deliberately drew up the sample fil. He passed his hands across it, holding it up to the wan light like a filmmaker studying a sequence frame by frame. Kalypso tried plugging her interface charge into any aperture that looked like it might fit. Any moment now she could expect electrocution, but hey –

'The thermal,' he said, 'it's going to cause problems at RV-11.'

'What? How can you tell?'

He indicated the fil and opened his mouth to elaborate, but she cut him off, anticipating a long and detailed explanation that she would in no way understand.

'What does that mean for us?'

Marcsson looked thoughtful.

'Marcsson! We don't have time for this.' Damn, if he were Jianni, the situation would be under control by now. How could she have let Jianni die? How could she have given his suit to this – this – this –

Her fingers were shaking as she brought them to her forehead, intending to wipe the sweat away but unable to do so because she was wearing a surface suit. It was hot.

Suddenly it occurred to her that, if he was talking to her, he was probably no longer interfaced. She should be able to navigate manually. She put her hands on the console and was suddenly at a loss. A thermal map was displayed on the dash, but she didn't really know how to use it. She had never paid much attention to sticky things like facts.

'We have to go to RV-11,' he said. 'I must pull in my work before it's destroyed.'

He nudged her aside and entered a course manually. She watched him, trying to pick up on what he was doing. *Some* of those controls related to the radio – they had to.

'I know the signal amp works. If you just show me how to use the radio to transmit, we could call for help. Then you could come out of the face.'

He held his eyes closed for a moment as if concentrating. 'Magnetism is like gravity to us. But it's so hard to calculate lateral relationships. I. I can't.'

'Marcsson!' She put both hands on his forearm and shook it. 'Don't interface that way. Just use the radio. Call for help. Or do *something*. But don't keep dozing on me.'

'It's much too big,' he said, and crawled on to the deck.

Rolling her eyes, Kalypso turned her attention to the controls and tried to forget he existed. She craned her head to see where they were going, but it was a complete waste: not only was the surface of T'nane completely featureless except for the occasional volcanic mount, but the fog was all but impenetrable and she couldn't find the pilot's goggles that would have let her see outside the spectrum of visible light.

One of the maps displayed their craft moving slowly toward the Rift. There was a smaller craft behind them, gaining steadily. Kalypso shrieked and tried to come about. A wave caught the boat and she stumbled to her knees, gasping with exertion and frustration because she couldn't get the boat to respond. Whoever was following, they weren't going to appreciate being led into the Rift.

Liet's met expertise was proving to be of no help whatsoever: Kalypso's subconscious memories contained no references to how to deal with fog. If Xiaxiang were here he would manage nautics; but he wasn't, so she tuned her inner ear for his voice and habits, trying to coax her subconscious into cueing her into action. Xiaxiang had shared a wealth of knowledge with her, in and out of the Dreamer: if only they could interface, she could tap him.

For the cluster was a functional unit in many senses. They had all Dreamed together – they'd been cross-referenced by Ganesh early on, so Kalypso knew intuitively that, for example, smell figured significantly in most of Liet's sexual fantasies and Xiaxiang was afraid of bats although he'd never seen one outside Ganesh. As a result of this long-term psychological intimacy, she could hear each of them talking in her head, could feel their presences as if they were with her. She could lean on them psychologically in a very real way.

And she needed them now. Because now Marcsson was climbing around the boat with a collection filament between his teeth acting like this was playtime in the nursery. Because she hadn't planned this out. Because the helm disliked her and wouldn't take her directions. Because she didn't know what the fuck she was doing and where were the others to laugh at her incompetence and take over?

The other craft was too small, and moving too fast, to be a boat. Her display indicated that it had passed them, so it had to be an airborne robot probe, presumably sent to lead them out of danger. She strained her eyes for a glimpse of it. Mist poured around the boat. She couldn't see past the yellow light on the prow.

'We're over the Rift,' Marcsson announced, sliding along the hull toward her with what struck her as total disregard for his own safety, given their speed and the force of the wind. She had to repeatedly wipe blackened condensation from her faceplate; only when she looked at the stains on her gloves did she realize how much of the 'fog' was sulphurous ash.

'Approaching well RV-11.'

He sat down in the cockpit as calmly as if this were a picnic and began fiddling with the magnetic collectors on the hull of the boat, whereas it was all Kalypso could do to hold the safety railings as she was lifted off the deck and then dropped with each surge of fluid as the effects of the thermal began to move up through RV-11. Temperature gauges were starting to peak out. Her suit made noises of protest.

This was insane. *Xiaxiang, how do I break this heading and get us into a cooler zone?* If this were the Dreamer, she'd be able to pull on X's mind; she couldn't get it through her head that she couldn't touch X. Her hands on the dash pretending to be X's; sweat snaking down her body and pooling in her boots. Thirst. Suit screaming that its filters need cleaning. A faint leak of sulphur in her air supply. Nausea.

Marcsson stood up and the craft yawed and bobbed wildly.

'Sit!' she hissed. 'You'll go over.'

They were skirting the edge of RV-11. The waters around were reading barely within temperature tolerances for the hull polymer. According to the boat's measurements, the thermal wave was still building toward its crest. Marcsson gazed into the water with the air of an artist stepping back from a canvas for perspective.

'Perfect,' he said. 'I'm going to get the whole buildup to the wave on record.'

He sounded almost mellow, as if he weren't sitting on a volcanic event that was going to be the end of him in a few more minutes. Direct measurement of the System wasn't often practised by researchers, who usually preferred to use probes to gather studies; but Marcsson had been studying phenomena that happened deep, deep in the well. There were no more working robot probes to send down the wells, and the tempflux made it too dangerous to send people. From what she could gather, Marcsson had been using fils to tag pieces of colonies within the luma and track them through their reproductive cycles, studying gas exchanges and looking for the factors that increased oxygen production. Or something like that. All she knew was that he was entirely too calm and she felt the need to be reciprocally anxious.

Kalypso didn't know just how deep he'd planted the fils, but prayed the boat's magnet was strong enough to grab them before the wave hit, so they could get out of here. She tried boosting power to the magnet in an effort to speed things along, but she must have gotten the wrong control because the boat's radio suddenly came on in a burst of static.

'Finally!' she cried. 'About fucking time.'

She forgot about Marcsson's fils and started looking for a functioning channel, but she couldn't get her interface to mate with the onboard and she needed her hands free to hold on. She knew she was trying to do too much at once and failing to do anything. A channel cleared.

' – take down the reflex points and get out, Tehar. You're a bunch of sitting ducks.'

'You don't understand. If we take down the reflex points, Ganesh loses all self-control.'

'Yeah, that's the whole fucking idea,' shouted Robere, a Grunt. 'You'll still have your Core, your shielded archives, your hardware – whatever landed here. We can start the AI over, regrow it if necessary. That's a hell of a lot better than the big puddle you'll have if the thermal melts down the whole station.'

Tehar, patiently: 'No. You don't understand. You don't just regrow an AI. Ganesh is far too sophis – '

'Look, kid, we're talking about life and death here. Can you fix it, or not?'

'Yes,' Tehar said. 'But I need time.'

'SOS!' she shrieked into the pickup. 'This is Kalypso Deed. I've got Marcsson and I need help!'

'Well, we don't have much of that. I say, save the hardware, no matter *what,'* Robere said. *'You witch doctors are going to get yourselves killed.'*

'SOS! Robere, don't you hear me?'

'That's a risk we'll have to take.'

She must be out of range. No one was responding to her.

'SOS!! Help help help. This is Kalypso and Azamat. Our position is – ' she began to read it off, horribly aware that she sounded exactly like the people she'd heard panicking while Tehar was dragging her up to Maxwell's. She hit 'record', looped her message, and let it broadcast.

'Stop that.' Marcsson's tone was menacing. She ignored him; she was too busy trying to get the boat away from the well. The current was unbelievable.

'Stop transmitting,' he said again, and she made a rude gesture. He reached across her and tried to cut the broadcast, but she'd thought to lock it and there was nothing he could do to stop her distress call. Her throat swelled with righteous indignation. What right had he to endanger her by coming here at such a dangerous time, all for his stupid information?

The probe had found them. It hovered a few meters above and behind them. Lassare's voice issued from it.

'You can't solve anything this way. Come back and talk. We'll come to terms. We always have before.'

Before?

'Lassare, help us! The thermal is coming to this well. How do I steer this thing?'

But Lassare spoke over her. The probe must not be picking up the sound of Kalypso's voice – not surprising given the noise of the wind.

'Kalypso, I'm talking to you. I don't know how long I can maintain this link. Ganesh has been badly damaged by this act of sabotage. Whatever they've said to you, whatever you've done – be smart now and stop this before it's too late. For Ganesh. Kalypso, I know you can hear me. Ganesh is in trouble and we need your help. Don't listen to them.'

They? Them?

She waved at the probe's sensors, signing frantically: *Help help help.*

Marcsson dropped to his knees and began emptying one of the storage lockers beneath the dash. His head and shoulders vanished in the empty cavity. She could hear him rummaging around.

The wind had shifted and blew in eddies from over the well. It was cold now, but wouldn't be for long. The boat had begun to draw in Marcsson's collection fils magnetically. They assembled all around the perimeter of the boat, dangling over the sides like cilia.

'Lassare, he's still berking. It's not my fault. Please. The thermal will hit this well, and I don't know if he understands – '

What was the use? Her voice wasn't carrying. The probe moved closer, hovering just overhead. If Kalypso could have hitched a ride somehow, she'd have done so in an instant.

'Kalypso, it's not too late to change your mind. Get his interface away – '

Marcsson bumped into her as he rose from the storage locker. He had disassembled the boat's hardware, and emerged holding a piece of gear whose purpose Kalypso couldn't begin to guess. He weighed it in his hand. It was still partly wired in. He held it up in the direction of the probe and passed it back and forth in the air. The probe's position wavered.

'Don't . . . interfere . . . ' Static broke Lassare's voice, *' . . . valuable . . . damage . . . stop . . . '*

'What are you doing?' A headache hit Kalypso, as if she'd just slammed into a wall. 'You're not interfering with its nav systems, are you?'

He held the unit still, then lowered it in a smooth arc, pointing at the surface of the liquefied luma of well RV-11. The probe mimicked his action and dove into the well.

Kalypso found herself motionless, unable to think or act as the boat drifted gently after the slowly sinking unit. They were over the heart of RV-11, a volcanic vent which even Kalypso knew had been identified as a treasure trove of hyperthermophilic life: a whole subsystem of organized, colonial prokaryotes and their dependent algaics moving among half-constructed natural columns of gelatinous luma at ambient temperatures in excess of 200C. They fluoresced and exchanged metabolic processes in an explosion of color that was a joy to the eye – or would be, in different circumstances.

Right now her suit was reading 70C: hot enough. The shaft below wasn't a mere hole: it displayed structure. The surface here was viscous; probably full of developing luma, for the density of the fluid was inconsistent, sometimes giving, sometimes resisting – sometimes sticking like a spiderweb. Colonies swarmed with the current and attached to the hull; others were repelled and curved away. She could see the colors of distinct strains flow with the current the boat created. Collection fils continued to arrive at the boat's hull like guests to a party.

95C.

A safety line, once bright orange but now phosphorescent blue with colonials, ran down the side of the well. Handholds had been driven into the basalt, which was otherwise as smooth as a throat.

She saw the probe.

Kalypso's clipboard of mental habits did not have a checkmark next to vertigo: growing up in First she had literally never experienced it, not even a little. So when she gazed down into that shaft, observed the effect of its spin, she thought she must be suffering from some kind of poisoning. For her whole body suddenly wanted to scream and run and fall down and die all at once. The thermal activity caused by the eruption further down the Rift was at this very moment surging up the luma of this well, and the effects were made all too clear as the downed probe melted before her eyes. It swirled into the well as cream added to soup, its Earthmade parts flying away from the central axis like dancers seen from a height. The heat was coming. She put frantic hands on the console, but the boat wouldn't obey her. Temperature gauges screamed. Probably she wouldn't even think fast enough. Not even enough time to think, goodbye.

He knocked her down again, this time in an absentminded way as he pushed her aside in the course of pulling in his collection filaments. The radio blared static and half-intelligible words.

I can't believe this, she thought, tumbling to the back of the cockpit. I'm really going to die, any second now: what should I think? What should I do? Where's my epiphany? Where's my final moment? Nothing.

Nothing. Just the attack of heat from all sides but especially below, propelling her to her feet as if to face her doom head-on because that was how they did it in all the dramas she'd ever plundered from Earth Archives . . .

She stood up and saw Marcsson looking so exceptionally alive, so poised on the leading edge of every sense, so emotive that she barely recognized him. And then it came to her, the question she should be asking even if it was too late to matter. She suddenly thought, could all of this – the Dream, the crash, the thermal arriving just in time to let him observe its effects on his research – could all of this really be Azamat Marcsson's idea of What To Do With That Chemistry Set We Gave You For Your Birthday, Junior?

come out of the hindbrain

The boat spun on the rising edge of the first wave, was lifted by a geyser of shattered luma, and fell away from the well, accelerating rapidly as Marcsson threw all power into the drive. The air blurred and refracted everything with its heat. Marcsson had kept his feet and now accelerated ruthlessly, apparently unafraid to capsize. Steam roared past his body leaving a ghostly outline where he'd been. Kalypso was thrown from one side of the cockpit to the other, found herself with her feet under her, and held on for all she was worth.

They shot away from the eruption with the colors of the water around them adjusting so swiftly to the temperature change that the thermal manifested as a rapidly spreading stain on the surface of the planet. The System was seeking homeostasis.

The boat began to draw ahead of the wave.

Kalypso apprehended that she was still alive. She rocked on her feet, then stumbled toward Marcsson and clutched his arm with a sudden need for human contact. She shivered and sobbed against Marcsson's impassive bicep, alternately clutching him and pounding him with small fists. The motion of the boat made her sick but she willed this away.

At length she drew back and looked at him, expecting some sharing of relief; some acknowledgement of what had happened. His profile was cool. She thought of the way he'd spitefully destroyed the probe and drew back from him.

'What have you done? How could you cut us off from contact with First?'

'You heard Lassare,' he said, his eyes moving jerkily across the readouts on the dash. 'I have sabotaged their AI. I have removed their control. I am in league with the Dead. I must be stopped.'

Kalypso resumed her position in the bottom of the boat, a little heap of distressed human.

'The Dead?' she heard herself say. 'No. Please.'

No one ever talked about the Dead if they could help it. Kalypso accepted this without question: it was the way things had always been. Sieng's research team had made the ultimate sacrifice: in trying to develop useful, Earthlike strains of T'nane life forms, they had unleashed an infection on themselves. If she were inside First right now, telling ghost stories with her cluster, Kalypso might welcome reference to the Dead, for they possessed a mystique for all the T'nane-born. Out here, though, shit was different. Kalypso was becoming agoraphobic. There were no walls here. T'nane's fluid surface stretched endlessly in all directions. If they were outside radio range, there would be no contact with Oxygen 2, or her cluster, or anyone, as long as Ganesh remained unsafe to interface. This knowledge struck at her physically. It made her very bones hurt with isolation. Now that she was experiencing it, the Wild was much bigger than it had seemed in Dreams. Her stomach felt light and dangerous.

'You *planned* this,' she accused, hearing the outrage in her own voice at the idea that Marcsson should have been capable of sabotage. 'You crashed Ganesh on purpose. You stole this boat. Why? And what's in these – ' she gestured to the collection fils assembled around the perimeter of the cockpit ' – that's so important?'

He went on working in silence for a moment, while she weighed the risks of making him crazy again by pressing him. When he spoke his voice cracked and the words came haltingly, but without the interface, he made some sense.

'I did not. Crash. Ganesh. On purpose.'

'Never mind,' Kalypso said quickly, thinking, *Uh-oh.*

After a minute he said, 'I needed Earth Archives. I didn't want them to know.'

'Them? You mean the Mothers?'

'I needed Sieng's data.'

'What were they doing in Earth Archives?'

'They keep Sieng's data there.'

'The Mothers keep Sieng's data in Earth Archives? Why?'

'No.'

'No what?'

'Why? To master the language. To solve the Oxygen Problem.'

Oh, dear.

'Silly rabbit, trix are for kids,' Kalypso said.

'I'm sorry?'

She knew she sounded sarcastic but couldn't help it. 'Don't you think, Azamat, that if Sieng and her team and all the Mothers and all the witch doctors and Ganesh can't solve it, don't you think that should tell you something? I mean, what's a nice Grunt like you doing in a place like this?'

'I'm just trying to collect my data,' he said obtusely.

Kalypso sighed. 'I know you used my jazz to get access to the locked areas,' she said, 'because you left a trail behind you and now everybody thinks *I* crashed Ganesh. That's how you got into the Core, isn't it? You knew there were back doors.' She snorted: 'And you told me you didn't need audio.'

'I don't know how it happened.' His gloved hands moved with a surety that Kalypso couldn't really conceive of under the circumstances. The sky itself frightened her. 'I used your music node for access, that's true. I asked Ganesh for the Sieng files, and it pulled them through the music. That was the only way I could get them out.'

She nodded wearily; she should have recognized this before. Ganesh was an evolving system, and the Earth Archives were organized according to older paradigms than, for example, those used by the Dreamer. Ganesh wasn't neatly structured, and to move information from one node to another the AI sometimes had to intra-translate. It must have used sound to encode the Sieng data so as to render it usable within the Dreamer. Which would sort of explain the attack killer blood-vessel harp. Maybe. Because, of course, there was something fishy in the fact that Marcsson claimed Sieng's research was stored in Earth Archives. What would it be doing *there*? Kalypso had seen some of Sieng's data. They were stored adjacent to Alien Life, and there was no need to go through contortions to get to them: Sieng's luma research was the most-examined of all the studies done on this planet.

'I didn't alter the Core on purpose. I can't explain without sounding silly and irrational.' His brow wrinkled behind the faceplate.

Kalypso stifled a laugh. He must not remember running around the Gardens naked and berking.

'Why don't you take a shot at it anyway?'

Another long pause. He was clearly struggling for words.

'Well . . . it's like something *dragged* me.'

'Dragged you. What dragged you? Where? How?'

He slipped into interface, then took several quick breaths through his mouth, as if trying to slip a word into a heated conversation. 'Think nocturnally. Come out of the hindbrain – come out where you can be observed.'

'Do you . . . um . . . remember what happened when you came out of the Dreamtank?'

He started and then gave an odd, suspicious half-smile. The interface worked silently. It spooked her out.

'You're trying to trick me, aren't you?' he said. 'You're trying to get me to commit to What Is, but I won't. Not yet, anyway.'

She knew she should shut up now. She knew this, but she said, 'Look: what you just did? Destroying the probe? That's really not a good thing, do you understand that? You have your filaments, right? So can you please take us to Oxygen 2?'

'I can't,' he answered. He finished pulling in the filaments and began to carefully coil and store them. The boat had slowed but apparently continued to follow some course he had set. 'Ganesh needs these things. I must provide them.'

'Ganesh . . . is a little berky right now,' she ventured. 'Maybe you should avoid interfacing from now on. Let me handle that.'

'For a long time I couldn't see you, or hear you, or apprehend you with any sense. Yet it seems to me now that I suspected your presence all along: or is that just a trick of the Dream? I don't know if the Dream is over or not. I don't trust you.'

Pause.

'I don't trust you either,' Kalypso said. She knew he wasn't talking to her, but it made her feel slightly less bad if she could mock him. His tone was so sincere, so pathetic.

'I had an argument with a witch doctor about this. Ideas are real, he said. No, I said, that's a contradiction in terms. The whole point of ideas is that they are not real, for we cannot contact them directly with our senses. Ideas exist only in the mind. So do sensory images, he said. Everything in the mind is indirect, he said. But I was speaking in the Platonic sense in which the Ideal exists in a separate realm from the Material, and anyway even if I hadn't been, I said, we can get machines to react to the real, but we can't get them to react to ideas. Yes we can, stupid, he said. That's what Ganesh does.

'I know he's wrong somehow. I mean, it's true that Ganesh doesn't distinguish between the abstract and concrete unless you tell it to. But that isn't what I mean. I don't know what I mean, and I suspect it's your fault. Everything I'm thinking, you twist until I can't recognize it. You play with me.'

He paused for breath and Kalypso said, 'They need you. At Oxygen 2. The witch doctors need you. Ganesh needs you. We have to go there.'

'That way will be watched,' he answered. 'They will hunt me. They hate me.'

'Who hates you?'

'The foragers in an ant colony are always the old and weak. The mortality rate outside the nest is so high that only the most expendable members of the colony are risked in the search for food. Not that altruism makes much sense unless you're a haploid organism.'

'Azamat. What are you talking about?'

'The Dead. I'm talking about the Dead. When you died, they died, too. They couldn't gestate embryos. They were too weak to be Grunts. They served no purpose. And anyway . . . things had

110

happened to them.' Suddenly he spun in a circle, his eyes scanning the boat as if someone had come up behind him and touched him.

Kalypso said, 'Look. There's nobody here but you and me. I'm trying to understand you. Do you realize what's happened to First?'

'I found you,' he said. 'I was deep in the Archives and I couldn't believe it when I saw you there. Do I dare hope? So much wasted, but now there's a chance. I've been wanting so badly to ask you this. Wanting it for years and thinking it could never be, but now, now I see maybe a way. Tell me, please, because I've never been able to determine why they don't use hydrogen sulphide and sulphur dioxide: it's the obvious pathway. When you take a look at their syntropes you keep finding small differences in the tetrahydrofolate intermediates across phenotypes.'

He stopped and looked at her expectantly.

'It's a problem of language. Right? I know, I know. I lack scope, but I'm working on it.' Eagerness animated his features like a wind.

'That's good . . . ' Kalypso ran a cautious tongue over her dry lips.

'I want to believe in you,' he said. 'Give me something to hold on to. I want something to trust.' He held her with his eyes and she was afraid. Suddenly his expression flattened again. 'Forget it. You think I'm stupid.' He turned back to the filament.

'No! Wait, please.' Kalypso, for the first time in a long time, had gotten an actual idea. She scrambled to find the resolve to make it work, took a deep breath, said, 'I'll tell you. I'll tell you everything you need to know. But you have to take me back to Oxygen 2.'

He studied her. Kalypso's poker face was out of practice, and anyway she'd never played cards with Marcsson because he didn't socialize, so she didn't know his particular weaknesses. Still, she'd conned Jianni out of more hands than she could count. How hard could it be?

'I'm going to help you, Azamat. You're in over your head. You have to trust me.'

'Will you explain? Will you teach me the language?' She knew by the urgency in his voice that she had him.

'*Yes*,' she vowed in her best shotgun-soothing-the-troubled-doze tone. 'You must trust in me. It will be all right.'

He took a long breath.

'All right,' he repeated. 'It will be all right.'

'But stay out of interface,' she warned. 'Do you know the way to Oxygen 2?'

'It's not a good idea,' he said. 'We will have to pass the clayfields, and you know what that means.'

She didn't, but she nodded anyway. 'I know. We'll take our chances. Lay in a course, since you seem to be so good at it.'

He shrugged, suddenly docile. 'Don't say I didn't warn you.'

By now, weariness and hunger had all but overcome Kalypso. She was dizzy and slightly sick, and her face throbbed. She rummaged for food and was thankful to find the stores packed for the entire cluster whose boat Marcsson had stolen. She ate ravenously. Mentally she kept turning to her cluster, thinking about each of them in turn and feeling more miserable by the second. What about Tehar? Had he escaped? Why hadn't he answered her, in the interface? What if what had happened to Jianni, had happened to Tehar?

She should be at First. If anyone had a prayer of talking to Ganesh, it was Kalypso. Whereas she couldn't very well babysit Marcsson when a single swat of his hand could knock her down.

She took an inventory of their resources and began to prickle with fear. It was worse than she thought. They weren't producing enough oxygen, and Marcsson had stressed the engine reserves in fleeing the thermal. Gazing into the fog ahead, she didn't see anything she trusted; and certainly nothing like land. Her eye was drawn into corridors and valleys in the fog; light cast in feathery brushstrokes across the face of things; wavering reflections of cloud on sea and sea on cloud. Sometimes when the mist parted a certain way she swore that just beyond it she could see the shivering outlines of some city where the doors and windows didn't all turn inward, where the view led out on high – where she might hope for a moment or more to be still, and quiet, and the surface beneath her wouldn't move. Then her fooled eyes would recover and there would be only more mist, and silence.

'Are you sure you know where we're going?' The thermal map was still incomprehensible to her. Food had made her sluggish: the need for sleep became oppressive.

'I know this course,' he said. 'I've been to the clayfields before. So have you. Many times. It's a spawning ground.'

What?

'Ah . . . yes, of course.'

'The source of the first bridging complex. Don't you remember?'

'I don't know. I'm exhausted.' Already she was finding it difficult to play the role she had set for herself.

This didn't seem to satisfy him, although he chewed on it for a while.

'I have to sleep,' she groaned. She made herself run a manual check of the heat seals and dragged the canopy closed to collect oxygen before collapsing at the bottom of the cockpit. Then she slept. But she woke, disoriented, when Marcsson lay down, taking up most of the cockpit. She could hear him breathing in rhythm with the patterns on his interface. She shoved at him but he didn't budge. His chest felt like rock.

Maybe if she got the interface away from him, he would stop berking. Half-awake, she put her hand out and touched it. He swatted her away in his sleep, striking her hand so hard that she bit back tears.

Other options . . . Her mind wasn't working well, but she couldn't seem to make it be quiet, either.

There was only one other chance. She had to interface. If Marcsson could do it, so could she – right? Even the slightest contact, a quick verbal exchange or a few images, could make all the difference. Experimentally, she changed the setting on her interface from radio to Dream mode, hoping for a link to her node – to any node of Ganesh. She had never interfaced this way before. There had never been any need to. As long as she'd remained in First, she had been able to wave directly into Ganesh through any

113

of the sensor points. But she knew that it was possible to do a remote radio feed to the Dreamer units, and she was beginning to think she had nothing to lose.

She leaned into the face. At first nothing happened; then the interface found the boat's signal amp and started picking up radio. There was wholesale panic on all frequencies. She could hear it, but there was no way she could transmit via interface without verbing through Ganesh, because interfaces were designed to be used in First, where there was no need for audio pickup, or physical speech at all.

She searched for a channel that would take her into Ganesh. The only one not occupied by audio coms was channel four.

Witchdoctor Radio.

As before, it was a storm of deconstructed sonic jetsam.

When Tehar had made her listen to it, Kalypso had found the experience unpleasant but bearable. She had only been hearing it with her ears, though. Now she was hearing it with her entire being.

Simple displacement of objects she could handle. If her foot turned into a raincoat and down was up, the shotgun in Kalypso was well within her tolerances for chaos. To a lesser extent, she could manage time-scrambling. But she couldn't accept the fact of one sense transposed for another, of time looped and braided so that paradoxes lay six deep. Nonsensical narrative was the norm in Kalypso's Dreams: but she now found herself in a sensory and cognitive environment that defied the very idea of narrative – even of sequence.

Yet somewhere – some*when* in the musical and spatial and olfactory decomposition of her body, in its unribboning according to rules she couldn't begin to infer – somehow there lurked a Math, and it wasn't friendly. As she interfaced, Kalypso's body reacted as if she were running for her life. She couldn't see what wanted her; she didn't know where she was going; but her respiration and heart rate shot up, her legs stiffened and twitched spasmodically, and she fell out of interface to find herself on her feet as if shot out of a cannon. The boat rocked wildly.

Marcsson still slept. Mere seconds had passed. She had no idea what had just happened to her.

'How can you stand it? How can you stand it?' she demanded, but he didn't wake.

It took her a long time to go back to sleep after that.

Her suit nudged her with a first warning for air, and she sat up suddenly, confused. The seals had been broken open; whatever air the boat had gathered as they slept was gone. Marcsson wasn't in the cockpit. She poked her head out and saw the Wild on all sides.

A line snaked from the boat to the clayfields, miles of weathered undulations resembling half-submerged animals dozing beneath the shadow of the volcanoes. The distant black range rent the fabric of shifting sea and sky like vulpine teeth. A cinder cone smoked idly. There was a harsh, grainy wind. Steam slithered in rippling veils across the surface of the sea, where filamentous *m. krepez* lay in silver tracery not unlike ice; but of course the water was scalding.

The clayfields and the luma deposits bordering them constituted a major remote research zone, containing as they did some of the last accessible clay deposits above the surface of the water. The rest had been flooded eons ago when changes in atmospheric chemistry had raised the temperature of the planet and melted the ice caps. But the clay of this field had migrated from the granitic floor, driven by thermal currents, and now it was quite deep in its own right, rising with the slope of the cinder cones like a thick garment bundling the base of the volcanoes. The ground was too soft to permit construction of any oxygen facilities, and so most of the data on the clayfields had been gathered remotely. No one ever came here. The luma around the perimeter of the fields tended to remain at the consistency of quicksand: locomotion was difficult, and, in places, treacherous.

Yet life thrived, much of it phylogenetically distinct from the sophisticated aquatic systems which made up the bulk of T'nane's biomass. For this reason, the clayfields had been the focus of considerable scrutiny. Probe-gathered data had been fed into

Ganesh by the boatload; Alien Life had whole nodes devoted to the clayfields, for they were believed to have been the source of T'nane's earliest life forms. Early in her career, Kalypso had personally shotgunned a Mother called Miruel through an extended project on this region, but the experience provided no insights now. Miruel had Dreamed the science of the clayfields in the form of a long, intricate saga of eighteenth-century Russia in which, to the young Kalypso's delight, horse-drawn sledges sometimes unfolded to reveal staggeringly illogical molecular structures; duels could become battles for thermal energy; and trysts in beds of white fur rolled over to accommodate population mechanics flowing too fast and hot to see.

Miruel, Kalypso recalled, could Dream with the best of them. But the Mothers had seldom Dreamed in recent years, and Miruel always groused that try as she might with the clayfields data, she had nothing on Sieng when it came to evaluating the relationship between the simpler forms of the clayfields and the mind-boggling luma.

She had been half-hoping Marcsson had thrown himself into the luma while she slept, thereby relieving Kalypso of her obligation; but she had no such luck. He was motionless, lying flat on his belly on the bow, dangling what looked like a collection filament over the side.

She turned on the radio, listened to static and snatches of words, and picked up the tail end of a looped message.

' – *amnesty for returning now provided you assist with repairs and cease immediately all subversive acts against the greater good. We will come to the table with an open mind, but let us at least come to the table. End of transmission. Kalypso Deed and Azamat Marcsson, we are aware of your position and will take steps to retrieve you unless you come voluntarily. You cannot run. We recognize that one or both of you may be lesser accomplices in a larger crime, and we are prepared to offer amnesty for returning now provided . . .* '

She switched it off. Amnesty? Enough of this. She had to get Marcsson back before the Mothers' paranoia made them do something drastic. She climbed out of the cockpit and made her way along the hull toward Marcsson. She could see he was interfacing and felt deprived. She wanted Ganesh and had to forcefully remind herself of what had happened to her last time. What had happened to Jianni.

'That's disgusting and impossible,' he remarked by way of greeting. His tone was milk-bland. 'Each cell spins on its own axis but together they are doing a kind of flamenco. Dance, dance. Declassify yourself. Imagine each bit of you is interchangeable with the next. Imagine each cell capable of any task. Imagine memory expressed in terms of potentials among cells.'

Kalypso touched his arm. 'What are you talking about?'

'You're distracting me. I'm not ready for you yet. There are holes in the picture. Historical links. I need more. Detail is essential. Then I can use you.'

'Yes, but this isn't the best time for you to be picking up samples. We don't have time.'

'I would follow you to the ends of the earth,' he said dreamily. 'It does me no good.'

'Azamat, come out of that interface and look at me.'

He didn't. He only licked his lips, his cheeks smooth as distance.

'How can you stand it? I'm a shotgun, and *I* can't go in there.'

'Is it true she said and the ocean stroked her legs, she is unheeding of its filth and the smell of tourists with their sunscreen everywhere. I could try to find you in your impressions but you aren't there, she said and she was right. Where and what you have been, passively, does not predict where you will go. You believe. Do you. Go. Beyond algorithms – are they bricks and is this architecture? But that would imply a stasis. What if the building invents itself and we view this through the net of time standing next to but never touching causality?'

His proximity had begun to make her uneasy. She didn't bother to say anything. The most important thing would be to get to Oxygen 2. And not to take any of this too seriously, if possible. She would treat him like a difficult child, a dynamic she was familiar with from being on the receiving end of it for so many years.

'How many hours from here to Oxygen 2?'

He ran his hands over his body as if questing for some instrument, then drummed his fingers on his thighs and gazed out across the sea ahead. She could detect subtle counter-rhythms beating in the tendons of his body, as if he were vibrating to some internal metronome. It was an odd mannerism, one he'd never affected before, and it stuck in her mind.

'You know that perfectly well,' he said in a clipped tone. 'Don't toy with me.'

'I'm sorry.'

'Sorry?' He stared at her in shock. 'When in your life were you ever sorry about anything? When did you ever notice how anyone felt but yourself?'

Kalypso felt wounded. She knew this was untrue, but still she quailed before his anger. He caught himself.

'Never mind,' he said. 'We all must make allowances for greatness, right? So how long are you going to hold out on me? Tell me tell me tell me. Just because you're dead, you have no right to deprive the rest of us of a life.'

She was trembling. He pointed out over the water.

'They will be angry when they find I have stolen you,' he said. 'See? They will not let you go so easily.'

'Let's move on, Azamat,' she said impatiently, but he grabbed her hand and pointed again. He's like a big child, she thought. If only to appease him, she looked.

A figure glided toward them, seemingly unsupported on the still water. Kalypso stared for several seconds before she realized that it was a woman standing on a boat that barely protruded above the surface. She had a long pole in her hand, and a faint yellow light surrounded her body. As she drew closer, Kalypso saw that her suit had been modified – in fact, most of it was missing. A hood covered her head, shoulders, and back, but there was no face plate, only a webbing of flexible, fine tubing that emitted a haunted yellow radiance. The tubing also seemed to reach around to the back, to what purpose Kalypso couldn't guess. Otherwise the woman wore minimal nylon strapping that appeared recycled, and low boots. Her skin was patchily dark and light, and what looked like old welts striped her arms and legs like a tiger's fur. This woman was at least as old as the Mothers, but there was nothing soft or maternal about her. She had the look of a bird of prey, some combination of keenness and bored dissatisfaction that immediately intimidated Kalypso.

'What the fuck is that? Where did it come from?'

He didn't speak right away. When he did, it wasn't a real answer.

'Tiera del Fuego. The bottom of the world. It's so cold, and they live on the sea, but they go naked. They could get leather or fur or feathers if they wanted to, but they live in their skin. They keep warm by burning fires in their boats. But that was a long time ago and you can only get there through Ganesh.'

Marcsson let go of her hand and stood up.

'Is that . . . is she . . . ' Kalypso began sidling back, weak-kneed. She couldn't say what she was thinking, what she suspected, because she was too scared. She tripped backward into the cockpit and lay there, stung, while the woman drew silently closer. The boat came within a meter of Marcsson. The woman extended the pole and caught hold of their boat. For several seconds, nothing seemed to happen. Then Kalypso realized that Marcsson and the woman were exchanging subtle gestures. Kalypso knew Sign: it had been taught to her in childhood, as a preparation for life in the Wild where oxygen was at a premium and talk was expensive. But this wasn't the Sign she knew. It was subtle and seemed to involve primarily facial cues. Which didn't make sense. You'd have to be in very close proximity to the other speaker in order to read his expression, and the Wild didn't lend itself to this kind of contact.

Marcsson appeared defensive – possibly even afraid of the creature. What had Lassare said? 'Don't listen to them.'

The woman pointed at Kalypso. There was a further exchange of signals. Marcsson came back along the hull and stepped into the cockpit. He picked Kalypso up.

'She is blind to everything but you,' he said. 'I tricked her. I have bought time. Maybe when I return, you'll be glad to give me your secrets.'

Kalypso struggled wildly. The boat rolled from side to side, bumping the other vessel. The next thing she knew, Marcsson had her wrapped up in a neat ball, her limbs trapped by each other so that she was tied up with her own body. She glimpsed bright blue colonials heaving beneath her as he passed her to the other boat and dropped her. In the next instant, the woman had taken in the pole that had held the two boats together. Kalypso was in the bottom of the other boat, and Marcsson, only two meters distant, might as well have been miles away for all her hopes of reaching him. Even if she dared try swimming, the luma would pull her down like quicksand.

'Marcsson! What are you doing? We had an agreement. You said you'd take me to Oxygen 2. You need me, Marcsson!'

It was sheer bluffing, of course. He looked at her and shook his head.

'I'm just a Grunt. Right? Just a Grunt.'

Her voice shrieked through the suit's speaker.

'What is this *thing*? Don't do this. Marcsson! Help me! Don't . . .'

But the woman had engaged the drive on the boat and it peeled away, leaving a cobalt wake of disturbed luma. Marcsson waved to her.

'Goodbye, Sieng,' he called.

tiera del fuego

Kalypso had no idea how to react. In this situation, she could easily imagine Ahmed standing up and confronting the creature Marcsson had called Sieng; Liet, on the other hand, would probably be fascinated but wholly unaware of her danger. X would play it cool and quiet until he had assessed the situation. Tehar would probably do the same. Sharia would almost certainly berk.

So what option was left for Kalypso?

Defer making a decision.

She took in her surroundings. The boat was Earthmade: this much was obvious right away. It was far more sophisticated than any of the T'nane boats although it was so laden with equipment and stores, Marcsson's boat could probably outrun it. The bottom of the cockpit was lined with transparent matting containing a milky gel that was faintly radiant and, according to her suit, cold. Other evidence of unfamiliar biotech abounded: the capillaries surrounding the canopy like a brake of thorns; greenery like the ceiling plants used in First's cells, only with purple-edged leaves; some mysterious rigging built into the bow containing pipettes filled with fluid of various hues, which reminded her of the Works.

Despite all this, the boat was remarkably uncluttered. Tools and supplies must be stowed out of sight: their absence contributed to Kalypso's growing conviction that she was hallucinating, since her upbringing did not allow for the idea that anybody could live in the Wild permanently, without Ganesh. How would you manufacture anything, she wondered. How would you manage to eat, even, without Ganesh? Plants couldn't withstand the temperatures of aquatic thermals; there wasn't proper soil on the clayfields; the light was poor and the atmosphere would need to be filtered of CO and other poisons before anything would grow well. Farming was labor intensive, too, if you didn't have the benefit of automation.

If you were Dead, of course, presumably you didn't have to eat. Not that there was much of Sieng to feed. She was oversized, but gaunt: where Marcsson's structure was dense, the woman's body sprawled all over the place as if unable to make up its mind which direction it was growing in. She had a large, bony head matched by her hands; she was narrow and would probably take a long time going around corners, like a train. She must be the same age as Marcsson and the Mothers, but she looked much older, and paradoxically more electric, as if all excesses had been polished away leaving little of her but the shine. She raised the canopy now and the chamber began to fill with oxygen. The headgear came off and was tossed carelessly aside. Her hair was thin and white. All Kalypso could think was that she did not look like her picture.

Beside this wizened, strangely vital creature, Marcsson had been a slug. How had Kalypso had such trouble managing the scientist? He was just a big oaf. Whereas, when this woman turned eyes on Kalypso, the latter had the unsettling notion that she was about to become lunch. She's old, Kalypso told herself desperately. She's probably weak and undernourished. She can't be all that strong. And anyway —

She bit off her thought. The Dead woman was trying to communicate, using the same subtle version of Sign she'd shared with Marcsson. Kalypso couldn't understand the shifting expressions, the weather of the face. If only the creature would use real language, Kalypso would be able to operate within the realm of reason. If not, she would have nothing but the growing restlessness in her legs and abdomen, the urge to run that she knew had to be telegraphing itself to Sieng. But she couldn't run. Running was an Earth phenomenon. She was trapped.

'I can't understand you,' she said. 'Why don't you speak?'

The woman's hand went to her throat. She shook her head.

'You have no voice? Use Sign. I can understand Sign.'

The lips flattened with what Kalypso supposed must be displeasure.

'Do you understand me now?' There was a bored irony in the exaggerated gestures of standard Sign.

Kalypso nodded.

'There is no reason for you to fear me, so long as you serve me as Azamat says you will. I will use you, and when I am done, I will return you to your nest. Assuming it's still there. Change is in the wind, and when you see Sieng you may find that she can offer you more than your Mothers.'

'I don't want any part of anything political,' Kalypso said impatiently. 'I just want to go ho – what do you mean, Sieng?'

'Ah – he has not told you about her, then?'

'But Marcsson called *you* Sieng!'

'He was looking at you when he said that.'

Kalypso shook herself like a dog. That was too swervy to contemplate.

'Obviously, he was confused. I am Neko. I *was* her colleague.'

'I thought you were *all* Dead. Are you the only one left alive?'

'There are several of us.'

'But how can that be? Ganesh. The Mothers. The Grunts. We were always taught. Everybody said. Well, nobody actually *said*. But . . . no. *No*. No.'

Neko raised her hand, held it out toward Kalypso, forefinger extended. Then stopped. Withdrew.

'I'm not going to touch you. If I start, I won't stop.'

Her body was nearly devoid of flesh, the outlines of bones and tendons articulated with textbook clarity beneath her skin.

'You can't imagine what it means to me to have you here in my boat.'

'Look,' Kalypso said. 'I just want to get to Oxygen 2. That's all I want.'

'You are in no position to want anything. The Earth Archives are hopelessly tangled up and damaged. Azamat says you are a witch doctor. You will interface and repair the damage. When that's done, you can be returned to your people.'

Kalypso wanted to say, 'I'm no witch doctor. I'm not even a competent shotgun. I want no part of the Earth Archives since for all I know I'm still being hunted by a four-dimensional snake.'

But of course, if she said that, Neko might very well throw her overboard or do some other unspeakable thing to her. So instead she said, 'Oh, the Earth Archives – who cares about them? Most of them are locked. No one goes there.'

'Yes, of course they're locked to you. They have backdoors going into the Core. Besides, they belong to us now, to all of us exiled to the Wild. You have your station and your perfectly ordered, pre-planned world. We have what's left of Earth.'

'I don't understand.'

Neko turned away and engaged with the boat's nav systems for a minute, allowing Kalypso just enough time to absorb the impact of the idea that, all these years, the Earth Archives had been the province of people she'd thought dead.

Neko turned. 'I can barely imagine what it must be like to be you. I am Earthborn, but you, you are different.' In the dimness her striped skin fluoresced. 'And yet it is I who look like T'nane. You. You look like Earth to me.'

'You're homesick,' Kalypso heard herself say, with a kind of sympathy.

'Naturally.'

This open admission shocked Kalypso almost as much as the revelation that the Dead weren't dead. References to Earth were to be kept to a minimum, as far as the Mothers were concerned. 'Then why did you come here to begin with?'

'That's a long story. Difficult to remember.'

Neko did something at the helm again, then turned and sat down near Kalypso, folding her legs into a mirror half-lotus. For a long moment she didn't move. Then she raised her hands and began to narrate.

'Fifty of us were chosen to colonize this planet. We all had our different personal reasons, our professional reasons, our ideological reasons. But now when I look back I see the truth. Underlying the mission was an unspoken understanding, an

124

assumption so deep that none of us knew about it. We were fleeing the size of society, of ourselves. It had all become too big on Earth. The world humans had made was too big and complex and chaotic to be understood. We walked around inside our own creation, trumpeting our dominance over nature, but nature extended to us. Our system of commerce, language, war, science – it had all become too big and weird to surf. Just when we thought we had the most control, we had the least.

'In the subconscious of the social mind you could see this. A fear of loss of control. An inability to make meaning or sense, a collective grasping at straws. A craving for simplicity that could never be satiated, for we had outgrown old modes of living. Everything felt false.

'Then Earth cased to be a closed system. Suddenly the ability to have control returned because we could *start over*. Clean slate. Second virginity. Seed politics. Specifically, speaking of this mission, we were to be a return to tribal society. A tribute to simplicity. We would become small again.

'We knew it wouldn't be easy here. Putting our stamp on this ecosystem wouldn't be easy, but this planet had the basic minimum conditions for life, or we thought it did based on the probe data. What we didn't know was how susceptible to change this ecosystem would prove to be. The geologic record didn't tell us about the irregular atmospheric cycles, and we weren't aware just how much the organic System influences the gas balance in the atmosphere. As it turns out, we don't know why the oxygen balance changes; we don't understand what forces drive intraluma selection and result in the dominance of one gas-producer over another.

'Only over many years of study can we see that the answer lies in the logic of the System. And we can't unravel that logic, because there doesn't seem to be any. Not that we can comprehend.'

Kalypso swallowed. 'Does this mean you still work on the Oxygen Problem?'

'No. It does not. The Oxygen Problem is too big, and the System is too opaque. We have addressed ourselves to a more immediate concern. Survival.'

'How *did* you survive? What happened to Sieng?'

'Sieng tried to marry Earth biology to the System. She took risks with herself and that's how she died. That's how all of us ended up in exile.'

Kalypso swallowed. She felt blunt beside Neko, who seemed made of air and darkness. 'Are you . . . is it contagious?'

'The agents that have altered me visibly have to be deliberately introduced. They are not a direct result of Sieng's final experiment.'

Neko closed her eyes. Kalypso surprised herself by reaching out and touching the Dead woman's ribs. They were hazarded with raised markings: terrible, indigo scars.

'Sieng grew these for me. They used to be painful, but not any more.'

Sieng. The Dead woman's name written in the air. Neko's strange flesh was soft and porous. The skin of the Dead. She drew her hand back.

'What are they?'

Neko addressed the helm once more.

'Colonies,' she signed tersely. 'Colonial outposts.'

Kalypso couldn't see her face and wasn't sure what special irony Neko might be trying to convey. Ribbons of muted color drew maps on the emaciated back.

'What are they for?'

'They help protect me. From acids, from heat. They are my carapace. Surface suits – ' she had turned, and now pointed to Kalypso's ' – don't last for ever.'

'You must need some supplies, though. You can't possibly survive without help. Neko – I don't understand. Why have you been exiled? Why did they say you were all Dead if it was only Sieng?'

Neko didn't answer at first. Kalypso felt the boat turning, and the darkness of the sky outside shifted balance slightly.

'This is what I was coming to when I began. We don't fit in with the plan. We are not part of the social order as designed from the beginning of the mission.'

'Social order?'

'You know what I mean, of course; or do you take it for granted? Look: think about the practicality of establishing a colony like this. Everything must be thought out in advance. There must be an abstract, objectively constructed schema for the society, based on the problems it's likely to encounter. You assemble a group of highly able, multi-talented women of childbearing age, ones who when given the best medical support their age can offer will pop out babies like machines. You add some big, strong men with psychological profiles showing just enough leadership to make them reliable to take over in a crisis, but not enough for uncontrollable ambition or destructive rivalry. You ensure that the first generation children will be physically and mentally above the common herd by making their parents pass rigorous tests and pay large sums to get their embryos stored on the ship. Then you add an AI which is theoretically capable of getting smarter and smarter over time, which can not only interface with robot systems to provide needed services for the fledgling colony, but which can also interact with the crew both consciously and subconsciously. The humans program the AI, and the AI programs the humans. That's the beginning of Dreaming.'

'I never thought of it that way before.'

'Everything relies on the social balance. You were planned down to every detail. Although, I must say, you don't come across much like your projections.'

'Yes, I know – hang on. What do you mean, my *projections*?'

'The extrapolations of your personality and behavior based on your fetal DNA,' signed Neko.

'*What?*'

'Of course – how stupid of me. You wouldn't have ever seen that material unless Ganesh had let you into that node of the Earth Archives.'

'So . . . is that why Lassare is always going on about my unrealized potential? Shit. What am I *supposed* to be like?'

The Dead woman looked amused. 'It's not for me to say. You would have to enter Ganesh for yourself and find out. I don't know what you will find when you interface. Marcsson has made a real mess of things this time.'

There was scorn in Neko's gestures when she spoke of Marcsson.

'You hate him,' Kalypso said.

'He was not exiled.'

'Why not? Why the rest of you, and not him?'

'Sieng had ideas about finding a common ground between Earth biology and the luma System. She introduced her own tissues to the luma, and introduced indigenous biological agents – subs, I believe you call them now, organisms-but-not-organisms – to her body. The effects to Sieng personally were catastrophic. They ultimately killed her. But she managed to get something right.'

Neko broke off, laughing silently. Kalypso could see her diaphragm contracting.

'What do you mean?'

'She grew in her own body an infectious agent according to T'nane biological paradigms, one which could infect humans.'

Kalypso nodded, hoping Neko wouldn't say any more so that she could have a moment to assimilate –

'It infected all of us,' Neko signed, looking in Kalypso's eyes.

'I see.' Kalypso felt herself shrinking. Neko held her eyes.

'Marcsson was unaffected. Why, Kalypso?'

Kalypso licked her lips. Her hands trembled. 'Because he's male.'

'Precisely. All of us lost our reproductive capacities. I don't mean fertility, because every member of this mission had to agree to sterilization ahead of time. Otherwise we might have been tempted to have our own children, rather than those of our sponsors. No, I meant that we were systemically changed and our hormones were permanently altered. We cannot carry children. Therefore, what purpose could we serve?'

Kalypso fumbled for expression. 'That's terrible!'

'That's reality. Everyone knew it. Resources were scarce in those days. And one thing was very clear to us: if we returned to First, we would be second-class citizens. We were not strong enough to be Grunts, we could not bear children, and our research, our work, had failed to solve the Oxygen Problem, so our scientific contributions would be limited at best. By this time, Sieng's work on the luma had begun to make sense to Ganesh, and the station had started to grow. The focus turned to getting all of you gestated and growing the colony, within the limitations imposed by the oxygen situation. *We* didn't belong.'

Neko paused, took in Kalypso's expression, and said, 'Don't pity me.'

'But why didn't they tell us?'

'That is a question you must ask them.'

'I mean, we would have run into you sooner or later. The tentkit project has been getting started. Did they seriously think they could keep this secret forever?'

'Secrets are about control,' Neko signed.

Kalypso wasn't really watching. Her eyes had turned inward. She was thinking of Jianni, Naomi, Marcsson himself.

'They made it sound like it was all about safety,' she said aloud.

'There is no more safety,' Neko's hands said. 'Not in Ganesh, or anywhere.'

Waking up slightly, Kalypso shook herself. 'So that's why you got Marcsson to sabotage Ganesh. He's sympathetic to you, because he feels guilty. Mari said something about that! You got him to damage the AI so you could have leverage against us! Right? Wow. This is just like a war or something. This is just like Ganesh used to show us.'

Neko was laughing again. Kalypso wondered why the laughter made her uncomfortable, and decided it had something to do with the notion that someone like Neko might be capable of feeling pleasure.

'Marcsson is too stupid and cautious to sabotage anything. He has been tiptoeing around the System for years, hoping to finish Sieng's research. He's thorough and methodical and he has no business tackling the Oxygen Problem – it only makes him look like a fool. He's always kissing up to us, hoping we'll give him a look at Sieng's stuff. Like just now, offering me your services to fix Earth Archives.'

'Look, I'll try, OK? But Ganesh is really messed up. Really

dangerous. I can't promise you anything.' Damn right, she thought privately. What am I agreeing to?

Neko's mouth twisted in a parody of a smile. 'I can't promise you anything, either. Certainly I can't promise you your life.' She stood up. 'I'm going now to a place where we can get oxygen. You will need to learn this if you are to live.'

They were now well away from the clayfields. The luma thinned and gradually became dark yellow, eventually displaying greenish patches moving beneath the surface like huge fish cruising. Kalypso had never seen anything like it; then again, she was no student of the System.

'If you told me about this subsystem,' she ventured, 'would I be able to understand?'

'It's not a deep region,' Neko replied, signing easily now that the topic of sabotage had been sidestepped. 'And this side of the range is rather stable, so we can easily manipulate this sub because its gas cycles tend to be consistent. This area produces mostly methane and nitrogen at the surface level, and you'll see in a little while how we've exploited that. The thermal layering is very fine. Zones change within less than a vertical meter in some cases. Basically you have a layering of several hundred subspecies on top of one another along this whole shelf. You see those moving green patches?'

'Yeah, they look like whales.'

'They're gas bubbles.'

'The water seems . . . thinner.'

'Solidified luma is rare in this region. We think it's because the sub is relatively stable and the distinct layering shows speciation as we'd expect to find it on Earth. You don't see a lot of genetic exchange here, presumably because species have found their levels and those don't change much. What interspecies transport structures there are tend to be filamentous and primitive, more of a proto-luma than a true luma.'

Neko prepared a collection fil and slipped one end into the water, playing it out slowly. Then she pulled it in and beckoned to Kalypso.

'Are those terran algae?' she gasped. 'How . . . ?'

'They're modified terrans. They don't drift on the surface: it's too dark here. The light from the *v. flagrare* goes down very deep. It actually gets brighter the deeper you go, because the concentrations increase with heat. Up to a certain point. These algaics form vertical sheets. You can't see them from above: they're too thin. They photosynthesize using the bioluminescence of the *v. flagrare*. The oxygen can then be filtered out of the water and collected. Those are the green patches you see. They're air bubbles, bladders for oxygen.'

'What are they made of?' She was thinking about the colony's shortage of materials, and how useful such membranes would be.

'We designed a living filter. Those are a filamentous type of *v. dermata*, a colonial that forms sheets naturally. The membranes can be permeated by O_2 only on one side. So it was simply a matter of altering the topology of the sheets, getting them to form bags, and then sinking them. Gradually the liquid is squeezed out and only the gaseous O_2 remains. They begin deep down and then float to the surface. Then we can harvest them.'

She maneuvered the craft close to one of the bladders. Then she fitted a suction hose to the hook of her pole and used it to pierce the membrane.

'I'm going to have to give you pure oxygen. So you'll want to be very careful with it. Use your suit's processors whenever you can, and save this as a supplement and for emergencies.'

'Why don't we know about this at First?' Kalypso asked. 'Couldn't this be a way to spread the colony?'

Neko looked at her with scorn.

'The amount of oxygen produced this way would have a minimal effect on the atmosphere if we let it loose. It's a slow, slow process and it can only be set up in places where the thermal conditions are just so.'

'Still, we ought to know about it. And how did you get the *v. dermata* to form bladders? Especially if they originate deep in the heat zone? And how do the algaics survive higher temperatures? I

131

mean, we've never been able to accomplish anything like this.' She knew she sounded indignant.

'We've done origami to their RNA. I don't know about the bladders. Teres has a way of inducing them to form macro-structures, using luma signals I think but I don't really know.'

'Luma signals?' Kalypso's ignorance reared its ugly head again.

'We will need to get you into Ganesh as soon as possible,' Neko indicated suddenly. 'Are you ready to interface?'

Kalypso was startled. She had never been less ready to do anything.

'I'm very tired,' she demurred.

'That's good. We have no tank here. It will be better for you if you sleep interfaced.'

'*Sleep?*' How quaint. She'd tried that last night with Marcsson and it had not been fun. 'But that's not a correct induction.'

'It's the only way we can do it out here. You'll get used to it.'

No shotgun, Kalypso thought uneasily. No Dreamtank. She was viscerally afraid. The memory of what had happened before remained vivid and disturbing. She remembered making some snide remark to Tehar about never fucking with latex, and squirmed in the grip of her own hypocrisy.

'Look, it's not that sim – '

Neko reached out, grabbed her arm, and jerked her to her feet. She wiped the condensation off the canopy and pointed outside. The surrounding luma was blood-red veined with fluorescent green.

'If I throw you off this boat, you'll die. Is that simple enough?'

Kalypso nodded dumbly. She activated her interface but it didn't seem to be working. This time there was nothing on channel four but a faint, distant noise.

'It's dead.'

She felt Neko's hands on her, pressing her to the bottom of the cockpit. When Neko let go, she didn't feel the floor, so she was interfacing at least partially.

'It's dead. It's not working,' she murmured, yawning. The random sound impressions were soothing. Her imagination began working on them. 'Maybe we're too far away for signals to reach Ganesh . . . '

Around this time, she lost her sense of what was happening. When she got it back, she wasn't sure whether she was Dreaming or just dreaming.

She found herself in her own cell, messing around with her bass. It was nearly dark outside, as usual. The hatches leading to the cells of her cluster siblings were open, but there was no sound of anybody moving around nearby.

'Ganesh?'

Nothing.

'Ganesh, it's me Kalypso. Come on. I know you're there.'

She seemed to have misplaced her interface, so she talked to the room at large.

'We've been under each other's skin forever. Come on. Send me a signal, show me a sign.'

It seemed very important that she reach Ganesh. Her throat tensed.

'Remember how you used to tease me with jokes from the Earth Archives? Remember what you used to show me when I complained that the Mothers' idea of entertainment was too boring? Remember? C'mon, Ganesh, show me again once for old times' sake.'

She waited.

'OK, I'll give you a hint. They were frescoes. Yeah? Yeah?'

Nothing.

'*Lions eating Christians*, silly, remember?' She slapped her knee in nervous amusement. 'No? What about the kama sutra? I know you couldn't forget the guided tour you gave me.'

Nothing. Nobody home. *Damn*. Memories came flooding back. Ganesh's peculiar gifts, like, for her fourteenth birthday, a full audio re-enactment of Ketjak, the Ramayana Monkey Chant, a polyrhythmic, polyphonic sound orgy produced entirely by human voices. For her fifteenth birthday, the Mayan alphabet to decode. (IT'S BEEN DONE, Ganesh had said. IF A TWENTIETH CENTURY PHYSICIST COULD DO IT IN HIS SPARE TIME, SO

CAN YOU. This was less fun. She failed miserably but asked Ahmed to carve her earrings in the shape of some of the letters. He did, and she promptly lost them during a joyride while fleeing a disGruntled oldster who claimed she'd cheated him at poker. Another story.)

'Ganesh,' she moaned, playing a high G and bending it plaintively to an A flat. 'Just show me one tiny thing that says you're still around. You used to be so sarcastic. I miss that. Remember how I used to complain about eating my veggies?'

The smell of raw seal meat reached her. She shrieked.

'Ganesh! You *are* there! Thank you! Thank you!'

'Don't be so stupid,' said a low, smoky voice. 'That's not really Ganesh, it's just your wishful thinking. You're in a boat in the Wild, dreaming like a primitive. Ganesh is Dead. The Dead are alive. I'm a genius but *you* were born. You were fucked before you ever had a chance.'

She turned on her shelf and saw herself in the open hatchway between X's cell and her own. At least, she looked like herself, but there was something canny in her eyes and the set of her mouth. Something . . . *knowing*.

'You're a projection,' Kalypso guessed. 'Neko said I might find you here. Are these the Earth Archives?'

They were standing in the sand in the middle of a sunbroiled arena. The other Kalypso had multiplied so that there were now a total of five Kalypsos including herself. They looked like her sisters, except for the one clad in witch-doctor red, who looked exactly like Kalypso. They all appeared clever and skeptical. Kalypso's attention was swiftly diverted by the presence of an enormous, noisy crowd in the stands: she had never seen so many people before.

'Yes, these are the Earth Archives,' said the witch-doctor Kalypso with some amusement. 'But you're not smart enough to fulfil your preordained purpose. You can't do what I can do.'

Kalypso looked at her other self warily. 'What is it you can do?'

The witch-doctor Kalypso scuffed the sand with her foot to reveal code. The code was alive and moving; the witch-doctor

Kalypso thrust her hand inside and pulled out a white dove. It fluttered on her wrist.

'What's that?'

'This is what I can do with math. I have the intellectual power to manipulate these codes directly. I can read and manipulate this' – she gestured to the mass of figures in the sand – 'whereas you can only experience it. You lack the intellect.'

'Yeah,' said Kalypso. 'Tell me about it.'

The bull prowled the perimeter of the ring, head raised. The matador was coming toward them, affecting an odd, stumbling gait.

'What's wrong with him? Is he sick?'

The matador's face was panning from side to side. His hands clutched the cape convulsively. A slip of sympathetic fear went through Kalypso She had lost sight of the bull.

'What's wrong with him?' she repeated. 'Why doesn't he fight?'

'He's blind,' said another Kalypso. 'Look out. Here comes the bull.'

The matador rushed at her, sword extended.

'You're Dead,' he told her.

She screamed and fell down; the bull passed over her and went after the matador. She could smell it and feel its heat, and the ground shook when it landed – the ground shook and cracked open and she never found out what became of the matador because she was now in a boat, drifting through a stinking canal of someplace she inferred must be Venice. She stood in the stern, covered with mossy growths that inhibited her movement, being Dead and poling. The gondola was full of baby elephants. It passed under a bridge and stalled. Something from below was pulling it down. When she stuck her pole into the luma – no, water – no, *luma* – legions of vicious black numbers swarmed up the pole and disappeared beneath the tails of the elephants. The elephants began to sicken. Other boats full of sixteenth-century Venetians slid by, trailing bright silks and quick music. On the bridge was a blind man wearing a little red cape, shaking a can with coins in it. The can said, PICASSO.

Her boat was sinking.

'Ganesh,' she begged. 'Help me help you. They think I'm a witch doctor. What's wrong with the Earth Archives? How can we fix it?'

MY BODY IS NOT A RECTANGLE.

'No, it's a – '

MY BODY IS NOT A SQUARE.

'Uh-huh, and – '

MY BODY IS NOT A SPIRAL A SPIROCHETE OR A CHORDATE.

'You've been at the poetry again, haven't you? Listen, stick to – '

MY BODY CONSUMED. HELP ME HELP ME HELP ME HELP ME.

Everything collapsed into code. There was nowhere left to go.

Someone's hands were on her interface; she curled up reflexively in self-protection and startled herself awake. Her eyes came open to darkness decorated by the islands and continents of glowing color on Neko's body. She sensed that Neko was signing at her, probably demanding to know whether she'd been successful; but since she couldn't see, she refused to feel responsible. She took off the interface and rolled over, seeking the desolation of sleep.

In the morning it was dark, but the System around them glowed, and the floor of Neko's boat glowed. The sensation of floating made Kalypso feel once removed from reality. The Dream of the night before still weighed on her. Something was happening inside Ganesh: the fact that she'd been able to Dream at all was encouraging. If nothing else, Neko was pleased. 'There seems to be some small progress on Earth Archives,' she observed. 'I am glad for you. I was not at all sure Azamat was telling the truth when he said you were a witch doctor.'

'Please may I use the radio? I'm doing all I can, but I must speak to my colleagues.'

Neko was working with the filtration system at the stern of the boat. She appeared deep in concentration as she said, 'I don't believe I trust you with the radio.' She paused, disappearing behind the ocular of the microscope. 'Whereas if you at least manage to find a way to communicate via Ganesh, you will have had a demonstrable effect on the problem I'm keeping you alive to solve.'

'But . . . '

'But nothing. Repair the archives. I will rendezvous with my teammates in a few days, according to our usual schedule. We must travel some distance to reach the meeting point and I have stops to make on the way, so you will have plenty of time to fix the problem.' She turned back to her work.

Kalypso had no intention of going back into Ganesh if she could avoid it. She activated her interface, composed herself as if to Dream, and then switched to radio monitoring. At first she didn't care what the voices were saying: as long as she could hear them, she felt reassured. She managed to gather that a base of operations had been established at Oxygen 2; that the witch doctors were still inside First, working; and that the Mothers had had to be removed by force. She heard nothing from the Mothers themselves, until, flipping channels, she recognized Lassare's voice.

'*We have your position, Azamat. Stop what you're doing right now. Get out of interface. We'll jam channel four if we have to.*'

Silence. Then: noise on the line: a high-pitched whining; Tehar's voice. Kalypso's heart pounded. If only she could transmit. Make them hear her. Tehar was saying, '*Don't even think about it, Lassare. You interfere with him now and we don't know what will happen.*' Pause. Kalypso's fingers had gone tight on her knees. More noise. '*Marcsson, I know you're listening. Let me talk to Kalypso.*'

Kalypso let out an inarticulate cry and Neko's head shot up.

'Cut it out,' she gestured. 'Leave the radio alone.'

Kalypso ignored her. '*Kalypso, can you –* '

Neko cuffed her across the head and she lost the connection.

'You are supposed to be working for me, not listening to radio coms.'

'I can't interface all the time,' Kalypso wailed, still distracted by the exchange she'd just heard. 'It's exhausting.'

'Then I will give you other work to do. But you will not involve yourself in the affairs of First. I need you to be *here*.'

She glared at Kalypso until the latter dropped her pose of

defiance. 'Come. I will teach you some things worth knowing. Later you will resume your repairs.'

All her life Kalypso had been suffering from the dangerous misconception that everything which needed to be done could be broken down into objectives and then attacked. She was caught in the delusion that problems had solutions. Too much Dreaming, probably – or too much success at it – had brought about this hapless condition. After several days in the Wild, she came to the slow and unwelcome realization that the shelter of Neko's boat was not the end of her ordeal; it was not the beginning of a journey back; it was not the dawn of a new life. Rather it was the negation of everything she'd ever held as true.

'The sky's so black ever since the last thermal,' she said to Neko once. 'The clouds are black. What if the filters can't handle it?'

'Then we can't breathe,' Neko replied.

She was tired all the time. Nor was it the kind of fatigue that results from hard work; it was a dissatisfied weariness caused by inadequate food, slow dehydration and insufficient oxygen to operate above a minimal capacity. At first she waited to get used to it, and then by the time she'd accepted that she would never be able to get used to it, she had no reserves of strength left to do anything about it.

Jianni used to lecture the young nestlings about this kind of thing all the time. Unlike any of them, Jianni had actually lived in the Wild, used a tentkit and a surface suit without support from anyone else.

'The hardest thing?' he'd query rhetorically, gazing around at them all sitting Indian-style in the caldera while he narrated with the dark sky behind his balding head. 'The hardest thing is the solitude. That's why all of you will have each other when you go out there. You'll avoid quarrels and claustrophobia because you'll already know how it feels to be stuck at close quarters – hell, you've been living this way all your lives. And you'll be able to lean on one another. Every single cluster in this colony is strong enough to act as a seed for an entire colony in its own right. We've planned it that way. Time's gonna come when you'll scatter, seek your fortunes.'

Actually, he seldom waxed sentimental like this. Usually the discussions were conducted through interface, and were highly technical affairs concerning resource management, how to gauge the variables of potential tentkit sites on the clayfields, the different possible sequences for establishing a foothold. How to set up agro baffles, when to begin farming depending on pH, temperature variables, analysis of resident indigenes, state of extant luma . . . She yawned, remembering. How had she ever sat through those sessions? She had staunchly supported her cluster's ambitions to be among the first to be given a boat and tentkit, even though she privately had no wish to leave Ganesh and could not in fact imagine living so far from the AI. Now, of course, she wished she had paid more attention. Jianni had been so sensible. All the Grunts were, really. Almost she could forgive them for rolling her up and playing volleyball with her when she was a kid.

The Mothers didn't like the idea of scattering to tentkits, of course. They kept hoping for a solution to the Oxygen Problem, a way to terraform on a grand scale. The original drawings for the colony still shone on one wall of Maxwell's. True, they'd been used as a dartboard by the Grunts for years, but so what? The Mothers never stopped believing the gas cycles could be stabilized, the atmosphere rendered breathable – and from that point on, anything might be possible. Lowering sea level to allow stable, usable land to emerge. Management of the thermals. Control of the luma outside First. Once you started listing the possibilities, it sounded like a game of Future.

Now that she was out here in the Wild, just at a time when she was actually equipped to evaluate some of the issues everybody had been discussing ever since she could remember, Kalypso felt in no position to judge anything. However she might have rebelled against the rules set by the Earthborn, she had trusted them as people. How could she not? They were the only flesh and blood people she'd ever known – Dream personalities didn't count. The fact of Neko's existence meant she had been lied to; but it wasn't easy to reject all she'd ever known, and she wasn't sure she wanted to. Neko was no walk in the park.

It was all so unfair. She couldn't call her cluster. Neko pre-empted most of her attempts to monitor the radio via interface. And Ganesh – well, Ganesh was no help. Sometimes when she interfaced she found the bridge and the bricks, but unlike the witch-doctor projection of herself, she could not penetrate these objects to discover the math that made them. She cursed herself for not being clever enough to help Ganesh; yet she was also afraid of it. Sometimes the AI gave her only darkness, yet from all around the sound and smell of the bull, breathing. This terrified her.

It was easier not to think about what was happening to her. Once in a while, like a plant turning toward light, her thoughts would lean wistfully toward the past; First; her cluster.

This hurt.

She stopped doing it.

Every day was the same. She woke up, put on her suit and checked all its fittings and levels, and went out on the hull to collect. Usually she was looking for a flagellate called MLB-6. These fed off a particular subsystem over the heart of a particular well, where the major source of chemical energy was generated by a moldlike colonial prokaryote whose fibrous colonies grew on sulphur crystals in high concentrations of sulphuric acid. MLB-6 died as soon as they were removed from their temperature zone; on the first day, by the time Kalypso had isolated even a finger-sized collection from the surrounding System, they were all dead. This was unacceptable to Neko.

'How can the subs build the luma if they're defunct? You have to monitor the temperature of your collection fil more carefully. Pay attention to what you're doing.'

Neko refused to give her food until she'd gotten it right. Hunger improved Kalypso's concentration no end. She brought the live samples back to Neko, who introduced them to a meter-long section of tame luma she was growing in a storage basin in the hull, then gave Kalypso her air and food rations. Most days, Kalypso's suit alone could not keep up with her oxygen needs.

The well that Neko harvested was usually quiescent, but sometimes the luma around it quivered with vibrations sent from deep beneath the sea floor. Luma formed stacks at whiles in certain 'hot zones' around the well; Neko tried to explain to her about the particular relationship between some of the subs resident in these sections of luma which caused it to solidify, but Kalypso was as dumb as if Liet were speaking to her.

'The System knows how best to exploit each niche,' was all she could really absorb. Which didn't provide much insight; but then again she wasn't really focused on gathering insights.

At night they would curl up in the hollow of Neko's boat to save resources, and she would be expected to address the Earth Archives and try to fix them. Kalypso didn't think she came across as a very convincing witch doctor, but then she reminded herself that witch doctoring as she knew it hadn't existed in the time Neko was living in the interstellar, since Ganesh had only started to use the luma after the Dead were infected. The AI had needed a lot less management in those days, for it still relied mostly on its Core for guidance.

She had begun to avoid Dreaming, but she told Neko that she was making progress.

In the rare intervals of radio contact, she heard much quarreling over boats, heat converters, food, and oxygen. But she never caught the voices of her own cluster.

Every morning, Kalypso would rise to check the cultures. Overnight, the luma bloomed with a colonial prokaryote unrelated to MLB-6. Neko had a method of collecting and storing this, too, which she neither demonstrated to Kalypso nor explained. She merely continued managing the tame chunk of luma and navigating. The latter took up a good deal of her time, for the constant flux of heat from the wells not only created dangerous conditions, but also made for very weird, extremely localized weather.

'It doesn't help,' Neko remarked several times as they were beset by yellow fogs that clogged their air filters insidiously, 'that there are so many airbornes to contend with around here. You probably don't want to think too much about what you're breathing.'

Then she sent the terrified Kalypso up above to collect, one irrational hand over her nose and mouth despite the protection of the faceplate, as she contemplated the consequences of inhaling a bunch of airborne subs. It was bad enough that Neko seemed to be able to *eat* not only the native algaics, but also one or two other subs produced *en masse* by the Wild luma. Actually, she drank them, in a kind of tea. She didn't offer Kalypso any. 'Your metabolism couldn't handle it,' she explained.

Kalypso was never sure what else Neko was up to while she was out on the hull collecting minute amounts of MLB-6, but it had something to do with the precious piece of tame luma that Neko kept. Kalypso's visual examinations of the micro-System never gave her much of a clue as to what was happening inside it, but she was sure Neko was using it as a processing factory, similar to the Works. But the Works were constructed of Earthmade materials and were operated by Ganesh. There was no AI operating Neko's luma, and in any case the subs involved produced such tiny quantities of chemicals that it was hard to see what value the project could have. Yet it was the primary focus of Neko's considerable energy.

Days passed. In the seamless cloth of T'nane's surface, Kalypso began to notice details of design. They passed through a colony of oxygen-producing thermal algaics a mile across. Neko checked the CO counters, found the air safe, and the two of them stood breathing for several minutes until the wind changed. A day later, they came back the other way, and the colony was scored through with faint yellow lines. The algaics were dying: not randomly, but in well-ordered blocks. Looking back into the water cleared by their passage, Kalypso could see the glow of the luma beneath, lit up by various subsystems. Her experience of luma had only ever been in the transit tubes, where, held rigid by Ganesh's electromagnetic signals, it had behaved like a passive material, slave to the AI's instructions. Now, in the Wild, luma began to acquire a personality . . . except, Kalypso thought, there was nothing person-like about it at all. It formed architectural shapes at times, glimpsed in the depths or occasionally breaking the surface; at other times it lay inert, a jelly. In places it seemed absent altogether and the boat cut the water cleanly. Yet the luma was always there, a huge, tacit presence.

Two or three nights running she was unable to face with Ganesh for even a moment.

'Atmospheric interference,' Neko said when she complained about it, passing her a bowl of food. 'This is a problem. We don't have much time.'

'Time for what?' Kalypso's eyes stung with weariness. She ate like an animal.

Neko's hands flashed before her. 'Don't you ever think about where your food comes from?'

Kalypso paused and swallowed, studying the rice as if she'd never seen it before.

'I do think,' she answered slowly. 'I wonder about a lot of things. It's just that nothing makes any sense, so after a while you just stop questioning. You figure you won't understand the answer anyway.'

'Think about it now.'

'Well, you might have set up a farm out here, I guess. Don't know where you'd get enough light to grow rice, though, and you'd need some kind of agro baffles. See what I mean? I may be eating it, but I'm damned if I know where it comes from. Unless – ' she laughed, ' – well, obviously unless it comes from First.'

No sooner had the words left her hands than Kalypso remembered Jianni's complaints of supplies gone missing.

'I see!' she exclaimed. '*You've* been given the spare heat shields, haven't you? And maybe other things as well. The Mothers *haven't* abandoned you.' This cheered her, for some reason. Anything that made her feel she was still connected to First, probably, was a good thing.

'There is trade,' Neko allowed cautiously.

'Trade? For *what*?'

'Soon,' Neko said, 'you'll see for yourself. I hope for your sake that the Archives are almost ready to be used.'

Once again the fact that Kalypso could willfully ignore the contents of her own head served her well. She closed her eyes, pretended Neko wasn't signing at her, and chewed her food.

picasso's blues

Neko's craft slit the water, a weapon gliding home over glowing skin. It was morning, and Kalypso had been allowed to sleep until she woke on her own. She stood almost straight, maybe not actually revived, but not wasted, either. They had travelled all night, carried by a fortuitous current parallel to the Rift. Ahead she could see other boats, each one illumined as if by flames. The clouds were blacker than ever and the sun somewhere behind them a dim lost seed blown across the sky. It gave just enough light for Kalypso to make out Neko's profile.

'It's cold here,' Neko said. 'You could take off your suit. If you want.'

Kalypso was sick of wearing the thing and complied, retaining only the hood with its breathing gear. It was actually very hot by Kalypso's standards, and she was soon sweating fiercely, but the wind was dry and she didn't mind. Flecks of pale gray ash lodged in her pores.

'The one in front is the funeral boat,' Neko told her, and for a second Kalypso got the notion that she was inhaling the ashes of the dead instead of volcanic tuff. A cylindrical enclosure, evidently made of luma, rose from the deck. It was from the top of this structure that the fire rose, brilliant and smokeless.

'I don't understand,' Kalypso signed, 'how you can spare a craft for dead bodies. It seems sentimental.'

Neko smiled. 'Wait. See.'

The funeral boat was the first to arrive. Its pilot hooked Neko's boat, pulling it close, and talked with Neko in the sign dialect Kalypso didn't understand; then Neko signed to Kalypso, 'This is

Teres. She will be doing the negotiating with your Mothers.'

'Negotiating?'

Teres showed a huge smile. She reached across the gap between the boats and rubbed her hand along Kalypso's collarbone and down one arm with a familiarity that set Kalypso's teeth on edge.

'Not plump,' she signed broadly. 'But not all dried out either. I am pleased.'

'Negotiating for what?' Kalypso demanded.

Teres smiled again, looking happier all the time. Something Kalypso couldn't read passed from her to Neko.

'Quickly,' Neko indicated, holding up a sheath of fluid. Kalypso recognized it as the product culled from Neko's tame luma. 'I have the catalyst. Let's feed her.'

For a moment Kalypso was afraid they were going to make her ingest the stuff, but despite Neko's words, Kalypso was ignored. The two Dead went to the stern of the funeral boat, where tame luma formed a wide cylinder about as tall as Neko, resembling a smokestack. The 'fire' was actually a mass of steaming phosphorescence within the upper segment of the stack, from which issued sheets of glowing gas that rose and vanished in the atmosphere. Synthetic capillaries clung to the sides of the luma; a braid of them extended along the hull and was lost among Teres' equipment. And a single line flowed to a tall vial, less than half full with a substance whose color changed slowly but constantly through a sequence of rich, fluorescent hues.

Neko saw her staring and commented, 'That's precious fluid. The MLB-6 you gathered provided one of the catalytic molecules we'll introduce to this luma to make the compound that will end up in that vial.'

Kalypso watched Neko climb to the top of the luma stack with their stock of the sub she'd called a catalyst in one hand, which she thrust within the gaseous emission. Teres, below, appeared to be interfaced, yet she signalled rapidly to Neko. Most of her signs were in code; Kalypso didn't know what she was saying, but clearly she was directing whatever Neko was doing up there. She caught the words, 'No, the liver will be better,' and 'Check cerebrospinal field'. At length Neko came down, took a pipette and drew off a small amount of the sparkling fluid from the vial attached to the luma stack. The temperature of the air had risen significantly, and Kalypso began to cast about for her suit.

'So what is that stuff?' she asked, to distract herself.

'This is the substance we use to produce our cash crop.'

'What are you talking about?'

'Picasso's Blue, of course. You asked what we traded to get our food and supplies. Picasso's Blue can't be synthesized in the Works. It's a biological agent, and we are the only ones who can make it.'

Kalypso shivered. 'I thought the Mothers made it. They were looking for a natural resource that they could use to motivate Earth to send ships, but Picasso's Blue is their only result, and it's not good enough.'

Teres only laughed. 'Even the biggest lies are mostly truth. *We* were looking for such an agent. Picasso's Blue was *not* our only result. These things we have done to our bodies are a continuation of the work Sieng began. We are our own experimental subjects when it comes to infectious agents that can increase our viability in the Wild. This work has proved more fruitful than the mythical Oxygen Problem, and it has created an economic niche for us.'

Relief stole into Kalypso. 'They *have* helped you.'

'Yes, of course: they've provided us with supplies. They have to. They need Picasso's Blue.'

'What do you mean, they *need* it?'

Neko gave her a piercing look. 'Have you never used it?'

Picasso's Blue was a privilege the Earthborn reserved for themselves; but to Kalypso every restriction constituted a challenge, and the proscription of Picasso's Blue was no different. She admitted shyly, 'When I was very young . . . with someone else.' Tehar. Once. And the feeling ever after of having exchanged jigsaw-puzzle pieces of herself with the fledgling witch doctor, lingering after the effects had subsided. Only she'd never been sure whether he felt it, too. 'I've always wished I could do it again, but the Mothers are so secretive.'

'Now you know. We make it. We sell it in exchange for everything we have. We have caused them to be addicted to it. This was necessary for our survival.'

Kalypso couldn't really process this series of cool assertions, which stood too many of her most basic assumptions about the Mothers on their heads. But it was easy to keep asking questions.

'But the stuff in that vial doesn't look like Picasso's Blue.'

'It's not. I told you – we make it. That's why we need Earth Archives so badly.'

'Picasso's Blue,' Teres cut in, 'contains a viroid which has a treacherous effect on its users. The first time you are infected, your body can't repel it and you succumb to a gorgeous fever. While you are sick, time and space are re-ordered for you. You become like one of Picasso's subjects, recomposed according to essence. Your perceptual math is made over from without. Enormous depths open before you. Great heights appear. Unspeakably beautiful connections between things become evident. You transcend yourself and even the world.'

'Yes,' Kalypso breathed, remembering.

'Words,' Neko added, 'become real. If someone speaks to you while they paint you with Picasso's Blue, their words come true for you. It's very powerful stuff.'

'Once you recover, all you want to do is go back. In fact, your body craves a return to the infected state, because certain of your neural tissues have been stimulated by the waste products of the virus and they will tell you, in no uncertain cognitive terms, that you want more. So you take more, if you can. And the effects of language will continue to work for you: you remain suggestible, able to experience the sensations invoked by words. But the time-space shift of Picasso's Blue is a receding model of the universe. Every time you return, it becomes slightly less vivid, for your body is clever enough to develop immunity. Yet the craving only grows stronger. Eventually, it becomes so that you paint yourself with Picasso's Blue, and instead of taking itself apart and mixing with the cosmic dance, your body just gives a slight phase-twitch in time and returns to normal. You can remember how it used to be, but you can never get back there. It must be terrible.'

There was no malice in Teres' manner, but no sympathy either. Looking at her, Kalypso felt even more so than with Neko that Teres was no kindred to her. Ganesh, Kalypso thought, feels more human than this on a good day. This led to an odd thought.

'Wait a sec. What do you mean, *you* make it?'

'That,' Teres whispered in her ear, 'is what you're about to witness.'

It was the first voice other than her own that she'd heard in days, and stripped of tonality, it made her shiver. Kalypso shrank away.

Other boats were converging on them out of the mist. Kalypso counted five beside Neko and Teres. The Dead were a motley collection. Everything about them looked scavenged. The other pilots were also female, but most of them were slightly less thin than Neko. They all had white hair, but each of their headpieces had a unique design. Most obscured their faces.

There was a period of general confusion while the Dead were reunited with one another. The boat was jammed full: Kalypso had been long accustomed to having people's hands and bodies pressing against her, but she felt claustrophobic now and on the verge of panicking. She got loose and pushed her way to the stern. Teres was still there.

'You were interfaced,' Kalypso said to her.

'And so will you be, once we get things under way.'

'Are you saying Ganesh knows about this? About Picasso's Blue?'

'That's what I'm saying. We keep all our Sieng data in the Earth Archives. It's too complicated for a simple navigation computer to swallow.'

'Sieng data?'

Teres nodded in the direction of the luma, as if it ought to be obvious.

Kalypso inspected the luma more carefully, and this time noticed a large mass suspended inside the translucent cylinder. 'It looks like a cocoon,' she said, taking out her u-tool and switching on the handlight.

What she was looking at had once been a human being, curled in the fetal position. Now the body bloomed with colonial unicellulars.

She staggered back. Hands curled around her, smoothed her skin; she turned in their grasp, shaking them off only to feel them replaced by several other sets of hands. She had suddenly become the focus of attention, and the Dead passed her around among them, like a pack of dogs, examining her. Every bit of space in the boat was full: there was nowhere to hide. Finally Kalypso crumpled to the bottom of the boat and huddled there, hiding her face. Then, just as quickly as they'd shown an interest in her, they left her alone. An attitude of ritual had set in. Working with coordination worthy of a well-integrated cluster, the Dead began altering the configuration of the boat. Up went the scaffolding and the weatherstained plastic canopy with its faint growths of luminous indigenes. A mad system of vents and hoses went into operation, drawing out poison and bringing in purified air from each of the tethered boats. The whole structure shook and rattled in the wind, but apparently did not leak.

Kalypso crawled once again to the stern and pressed against the warm luma. It held a static charge and her fingertips sparked when she touched it.

The Dead took off their masks and hoods and other hybrid contraptions and seated themselves, their mingled bodies fitting together like machinery. The sight and feel of this menage of limbs was not in itself orgiastic. But there was something extraordinary happening to their faces. What had been blank and still as granite now melted to flesh and skin: lips parted, throats exposed themselves and eyelids lay heavy and dark. Each face changed, the staircase of its own history winding down behind it to reveal the complex personality behind the anonymous tough bastard. This wasn't exactly sexy, but it was something to see.

And it made no sense how – drifting low in this boat with its macabre burden under a black sky on a yellow sea – how they all reeked of Earth.

Tense and slightly sick to her stomach, Kalypso watched Neko draw still more fluid from the vial attached to Sieng's luma. She poured it carefully on to a thin, concave disk.

'You will have to interface now, Kalypso,' she said. 'This is a painful process for us. We need the Earth Archives to hold our awareness.'

Dread-laden anticipation hummed through the funeral boat. Kalypso tried to assimilate the fact that she was expected to be able to dish up Earth Archives as a kind of anesthetic, and couldn't. But she accepted the sedative Neko gave her, because there was nothing else she could do.

'We know our way around the Archives,' Neko added. 'Keep out the noise for us, at least. If there are places we can't go because of the damage, we can accept that. But we must have a clean immersion in Earth. It's essential.'

Kalypso felt herself nodding. This was insane. She hadn't repaired anything. She could shotgun them, of course – but where? They might not even be able to interface. Yet she did nothing to express this.

In the very bottom of the boat Teres sat, head bowed, arms clasped about her knees. Her shoulder blades and spine were sharp with hunger. Neko gave her the fluid-laden disk and a very fine paint brush. Teres looked at them, slipped a temperature gauge into the fluid, waited.

Meanwhile, the Dead were passing something around: a box roughly the size of one of Azamat's spread hands. When it reached Kalypso she saw that it was battered and grubby, despite the reverence they showed it. It was Earthmade.

'We brought them to celebrate with,' Neko signed at her. 'Cuban. When the first of you was born, we were going to smoke them. By that time there would be a surplus of oxygen.'

Kalypso looked at the neatly packed oblongs, touched the wrappers and closed the box.

'A fabulous waste of air,' she signed, yawning. 'What decadence.'

'Yes,' Neko replied. 'What folly.'

Kalypso passed the box on. They all touched it reverently, eyes closed. Their breathing grew slow and regular. Kalypso yawned again, feeling heavy.

Teres stood up.

'You must interface now,' Neko signed. Teres approached Neko first. Kalypso had begun blinking slowly, but she did not interface yet. She wanted to see what was going to happen. Teres put the brush into the fluid.

'Interface,' Neko signed again. Kalypso saw that her feet were trembling and jumping spasmodically. The others began to shift in place.

Teres bent over Neko and traced the brush over her ribs. Kalypso suppressed another yawn as Neko's eyes squeezed shut and she convulsed. Her left hand flashed the sign for 'interface'.

Kalypso didn't want to see any more. She let go and fell into Ganesh.

The first things she encountered were Liet's hands with their purple nail-polish. She wanted to ask Liet to help her get access to Earth Archives, but Liet was busy massaging a female corpse. The corpse consisted of a mass of statistics. Tendrils of Diriangen functions swirled from the decaying flesh. Numbers and graphs jockeyed for position in the seethe that had been a person.

'Look closer and you go inside and are lost,' Liet said. 'Comprehension is danger.'

But Kalypso wasn't interested in riddles and tried to ignore Liet. *Earth Archives*. She held to the thought like a buoy, building the Core suitcase in her mind. The Dead would be in here somewhere too, blaming her if they couldn't get a piece of their favorite desert island or whatever it was they each wanted to use as anesthesia. She saw the suitcase in all its detail, ran her hands over it, tested its weight. Of course she remembered the hole through which the jazz vine had passed – couldn't *not* recall it – and suddenly she found herself inside the original Ganesh, the interstellar ship before it had been dismantled.

WELCOME TO EARTH ARCHIVES.

Lucky stars, thank you.

The interior of the ship was close and warm and Earthmade,

which boosted Kalypso's spirits. She roamed through the bridge to the passenger section, where Lassare was lying in a Dreamtank. Kalypso looked down at her face. She had never been pretty, but she had once been thin, and her face in repose still looked young, despite the years of the Crossing. Ganesh had slept her deep and true.

NOT HER. THEY WANT THEMSELVES.

Kalypso drifted down the rows of tanks, gazing on each of the Earthborn. Mari. Robere. Teres? The woman had looked very different *before*. When she passed Teres, the sleeping body smiled and Teres verbed, 'Thank you. I am going home.'

Teres climbed out of the tank and stretched. A door appeared in the air in front of her, the kind that divided in half like a stall door; muffled voices came from within. Teres was wearing a long coat and gloves, and she pushed the door open. Kalypso caught the scent of cinnamon, the shuffle of children's feet on the tiled kitchen floor and blown snow – then pulled away to the interstellar. She had six more Dead to dispense with. She continued down the line. Jianni. Stash, Rasheeda. Neko.

'Make the pain go,' Neko verbed. 'It devours.'

ME, TOO.

Neko was weak, and Kalypso had to lead her to her destination. It was somewhere in Asia – Taipei, possibly. She felt Neko rising to the idea of a crowd. Streets jammed with people. Noise, humanity, bumping into strangers – ah, yes. Strangers. A remote and alluring concept. Kalypso was seduced by it: the idea of vanishing into a crowd of people who had never known you and never would, this was alien and thrilling, and come to think of it she couldn't understand the language either, so she was really lost. She fought the urge to stay and left Neko arguing with a rickshaw driver.

By now she'd begun to nurture a tiny hope that the witch doctors had repaired the damage of the crash and all would soon be well. The interstellar was holding its integrity for her: the Dream was working. She continued walking among the tanks bearing the Earthborn, looking for the remainder of the Dead.

Korynne. Azamat. *Sieng*.

She looked into Sieng's tank. Sieng was not there. Where she had been was a handwritten note on a piece of paper. It said:

To:	The Dead
From:	Sieng
Re:	The Oxygen Problem

Thanks for the memories.

Love always,
Azamat

After she read it, the note auto-combusted and she found herself up to her neck in cement.

A small boy with a trowel was nearby. His eyes were white and irisless, and he wore a red cape. He was laying bricks around her. Nearby was a wheelbarrow filled with mortar.

'Stop that!' Kalypso cried. 'I'm trapped in here. Help me get out.'

'I am a Grunt,' he said in a deep voice. 'I don't think. I build things.'

He placed a brick beside her right ear, tapped it into place with his trowel.

IT HURTS. KILLING ME.

'You're not a Grunt,' she wheedled. 'You're just a kid. I'll teach you a bunch of stuff if you let me out.'

'Wow!' the boy exclaimed suddenly. 'Lookee what's in there!'

AH THE PAIN. WHY DO YOU CALL ME UP ONLY TO MURDER ME?

The sightless kid turned the trowel toward her and in the cement she could see many people with blindfolds. They were walking across a high structure over water. They carried all their possessions and dropped most of them as they went. The boy grinned behind his white eyes.

'OK, I'll let you out,' he sang. She was free. There were bees everywhere. She kept seeing color charts.

I'M LEAVING. I'M GOING

The boy waved his red cape at her, which was no longer red. 'See these colors that only bees can see.'

The Color was Blue. It was everywhere. Blue Everything. She could taste it. A guitar chopped up in pieces played the sound of a trumpet. She was on a desert highway and a sign read: SIENG. 217 MILES.

Everything dissolved into code. Kalypso was tossed in a maelstrom of bad math. Once she thought she felt Tehar brush past her and clutched blindly at the place he might have been. Nothing was there but the Dead and their agony. The Dead were furious. The Dead were pissed off. If the Dead could have annihilated her, they would have already done so. Twice. Even as they became code they manifested their displeasure in sharp, hostile, sense-cutting functions.

The return was slow and insidious. Gradually the funeral boat and the Dead and the rattling canopy and the darkness crept over her, until the fact of consciousness could no longer be denied and she found herself with open eyes, in the boat, surrounded. Teres was passing among the Dead with a conical sack. From the torso of each of her compatriots she scraped blue ooze, which slowly desiccated in the hot air to become Picasso's Blue. Her body was bent almost double with exhaustion and strain.

Seams appeared in the single flesh of the Dead and its parts went their separate ways. Later they were all sick. The tent had to be taken down so everyone could retch violently over the sides. No one could speak or sign. They crawled and staggered and waveringly fell into their respective boats, until it was only Kalypso and Neko and Sieng, who probably was in better shape than either of her living relatives.

And Teres. Livid.

'You aren't worth the air you breathe,' she accused. 'Let's kill her, Neko, and mate her to Sieng. She would be a good source of fresh tissue.'

Neko turned on her as well. 'What kind of witch doctor allows such chaos to overcome a node? Have I not given you days of interfacing to clear up these problems in the code? Explain yourself.'

Kalypso stammered and quaked for a bit before she got the words out. 'I don't know what I'm doing, OK? I admit it. I'm not a witch doctor. Not even close. Azamat lied to you. I thought if I told you, you would kill me.'

Teres turned to her. The bright skin. The invisible eyes. Kalypso cowered.

'He has *stolen* all our data on Sieng. How dare he?'

Neko said quickly, 'Don't hurt her, Teres.'

'Ah,' said one of the others. 'So he steals the theory behind our livelihood, ruins our only pleasure in the world, and offers us a child who is not even a witch doctor as a consolation prize. Will we sit back and let ourselves be disenfranchised?'

There were angry signs passing among the others.

'You may be right, Charl,' Neko agreed. 'We have let them fumble along with their mission plans for long enough. If this goes on, we could lose the Archives completely, and then we'd have nothing of Earth.'

That this was unbearable to contemplate was obvious from their postures, whether or not Kalypso could understand the specific signage of their faces.

'I'm going to call Lassare,' Teres said. 'Find out the meaning of this.'

'Ganesh won't give you a reliable interface,' one of the others reminded her.

Teres went to the radio. 'We'll try this.'

'They'll never hear you.' Yet the Dead all switched their interfaces to radio. Teres adjusted frequencies and whispered into the pickup. No sound came through the console: the speakers had probably been scavenged for some other use.

It took some time before Kalypso turned her interface to the frequency they were using. The first thing she heard was Rasheeda's voice.

'Halloooo? This is a reserved frequency. Jubellek, if that's you being cute, pick another channel.'

'Rasheeda, it is Teres.' Kalypso could just make out the sibilant phrases.

'It's not Halloween,' said Rasheeda in a strained voice. 'Are you ready to talk terms?'

'I want Lassare.'

'I can barely hear you.'

'Then get me a com channel through Ganesh.'

'Very funny. You know we can't do that. Look, just tell us what you want. You insult us by resorting to terrorism. We can work this out.'

'You need the Blue, don't you?' Teres said with relish. 'I can tell from your voice.'

'That's a sick negotiating tactic,' Rasheeda answered. 'You know we need it. We have done our best by you. There's no cause for you to be so vicious.'

'Vicious? Marcsson has stolen our data and destroyed our territory within Ganesh. Do you expect us to sit still for it? If you think to get control of Picasso's Blue yourselves, you're in for an unpleasant surprise. You need *us* for that.'

Lassare came on the channel. 'Calm down, Teres. We're working on getting Marcsson back to First and repairing the AI. If you'll name your terms, I'm sure – '

'Terms? Terms? We're coming back: those are our terms. There will be no more Picasso's Blue for you. Your policies have come to ruin. Earth Archives are under threat. What have you done for your children but let them be weak and ignorant, like this one?'

'You have one of our children?'

'Only a small one.'

'Which one? You have no right – '

'Kalypso. She claimed to be a witch doctor but she's useless for anything except tissue harvesting.'

Kalypso couldn't take any more. She flung herself at the console and screamed, 'Lassare, save me! They're insane. Don't let them infect me – '

Neko seized her and pulled her aside. Kalypso fell down, tears streaming from beneath her interface. She lost the frequency for a second.

' – act of war. We had an agreement. You can't simply come in and take over.'

'Watch us.'

'Teres. This is foolish. We must trust each other. Perhaps we jumped to conclusions in accusing you. We accept that maybe Marcsson was operating on his own. Or maybe it wasn't sabotage at all. Or even if you are behind the crash, we can come to terms so long as you give us Picasso's Blue. We must have something. We're losing control of the kids.'

Teres turned to the others and signed, 'Weak-willed bats. What should we do?'

'Don't give them any Blue,' Charl warned. 'Find out the status of Earth Archives.'

We're losing control of the kids. What the hell did that mean? Kalypso heard herself snuffling in the nomansland between laughing and crying.

'The witch doctors are insisting we not jam Marcsson's interface or try to take him by force,' Lassare replied when Teres passed on the question. 'They believe Ganesh can be repaired but they haven't given us any details about individual nodes.'

'Where is Marcsson now? What's he up to?'

'He's been in the clayfields, but the witch doctors say he must not be upset. We are monitoring him.'

'A lot of good that will do. Give us his present location.'

'No. Absolutely not.'

'Then you must not need Picasso's Blue as badly as you say.'

There was a long pause.

The Dead exchanged facial expressions. Kalypso sighed.

Rasheeda came on the line and read out coordinates.

'We will deliver the Blue shortly. You can pick it up at First.'

'But we're at Oxygen 2 – '

Teres cut the link. 'What shall we do to Azamat?' she asked.

'I don't think we should do anything to him,' one of the others signed. 'We don't know his reasons, but neither do they. Nothing will be accomplished by taking revenge on Azamat for damage to Earth Archives.'

'We can stop him from doing more damage,' said Teres. 'He can't make things any worse if he's dead.'

'But things are not worse. We have some access to Earth Archives. Yes, he was impertinent to take the Sieng data – ' Neko had to stop signing when Teres grabbed her hands and slapped them down imperiously.

'Impertinent? Is that what you call it? We could use that data to find new psychoactive agents. Something better than Picasso's Blue. That's the only way we'll ever get Earth's attention.'

'Everything Marcsson is doing is happening by interface,' Kalypso said. They all jumped at the sound of her voice. 'You can attack him physically, but the only way you'll ever solve anything is through Ganesh. I may not be a witch doctor but I *know* he's working the interface.'

'She only says this because she wants to return to First, and she hopes we'll take her there.'

'That doesn't make it any less true,' Kalypso said. She had been able to follow the conversation because they'd been using standard Sign; but as soon as she'd spoken, some of them reverted to their private language to exchange secret signs.

'The value of Sieng's data is questionable,' Charl said. 'We've been doing studies on her body for years, but Picasso's Blue is the best agent we've found. The idea that Marcsson can come along and steal our invention and sell it to Earth or something like that – it's ridiculous. If it did happen, we should applaud him, anyway. Who cares who makes the discovery, provided we get Earth's attention?'

Their gestures indicated they found the idea of Marcsson making a great discovery laughable.

'Whereas Sieng's body,' Teres added thoughtfully, 'is absolutely essential. Yes: as long as we have these tissues, we are in power. As long as we can make Picasso's Blue, nothing else can truly threaten us.'

'I don't know about you, Teres,' one of the others remarked, 'but I don't want to make any more Blue without the Archives. I don't think I could take another extraction like this one.'

Signs of agreement.

'We should get ourselves some real witch doctors,' Neko said. 'It's time to go back to First.'

Charl nodded support. 'If they can't save Earth Archives, we can always take the station anyway. Get as much hardware as possible. If necessary, we'll take the Core of the AI and start over.'

Kalypso made a choking noise.

'You,' Teres said, pointing at her, 'will wait here. Neko, stay with Sieng and the child. We will deliver the Blue as we promised, and then go to First. It's been too long since we were there.'

Once the decision had been made, everything happened fast. Teres would take Neko's boat and leave Kalypso and Neko in the funeral boat.

'I could be highly useful to you,' Kalypso said eagerly, dogging Teres's every movement. 'I know First like the back of my hand. My closest friend is a witch doctor. I don't want to stay here – '

Teres ignored her for some time, then suddenly turned and cuffed her across the face. 'According to Neko, you're lazy, you're sneaky, you can't take care of yourself, and you're a liar. Stay with Neko and be glad you're alive.'

Kalypso took the hint. Before she knew it, the Dead had moved off in ragged formation up a broad luma channel. She and Neko were alone again.

'Teres likes you,' Neko said.

who owns the air

Kalypso was in a deep sleep when something thudded into the hull. It had taken her hours to finally rest: the Dream had overstimulated her neurally, and the discussions of the Dead afterward had only made things worse. The flashing hands of their fateful speech haunted her when she closed her eyes.

When the noise woke her, she rolled over sluggishly, disoriented, and bumped into the glowing column of Sieng's luma. Her eyes opened when she realized something had struck the boat. Another vessel had come alongside and hooked them with a magnet. A tall figure was silhouetted against the gray and red clouds that reflected the light of the System.

Marcsson stepped across the gap just as Neko lurched to her feet. Kalypso scooted as far away as possible, half-asleep and confused. Marcsson towered over the Dead woman, yet his manner was appealing, almost childlike. Not everything they said to each other made sense. Marcsson's signing was fast and manic. He punctuated his gestures with the polyrhythmic body-tapping she'd seen him do before.

She caught enough of the exchange to begin to worry.

'I'm almost there. I have processed all the studies. Now I must apply them. She will be the last thing.'

'No. Absolutely not.'

Marcsson outweighed Neko by about forty kilos, Kalypso wagered.

'This is more important than Picasso's Blue. It's more important than you or any of your comrades. I'll have it, Neko.'

He moved fast, and the boat shuddered, unsteady because the

magnetism binding the two boats had repelled the luma and left thin water beneath. Kalypso grabbed a piece of Sieng's equipment for balance as he reached the stern, where Sieng was, and the boat tipped wildly. Neko was rummaging in a storage area.

Marcsson took his u-tool and began degaussing the luma.

'Don't cross me,' he said. 'She belongs to me now.'

Neko had found a navigating pole and now pointed it at Marcsson. He grabbed the tip and shoved it aside, only to be smacked across the shoulders with it as it rebounded. The u-tool fell and skidded along the deck; Neko seized it and came at him, extending the blade. He stepped aside as if holding a door open for her and grabbed her arm to control the weapon, but the u-tool slashed into the luma column. Murky fluid gushed out.

Neko stood still, her hand going to her mouth in shock. The luma stack wavered, its integrity compromised by the combination of disturbed magnetism and the physical cut. Marcsson reached through the slit and a gelatinous mass spilled into his arms. It was still recognizably human, despite the growing things that had made a home of its structure. Sieng's body was carnival-bright.

When Marcsson turned, his face transfigured by awe, Neko raised the u-tool again. He dropped the corpse, which sprawled gleaming and horrible on the deck. Kalypso couldn't take her eyes off it.

She felt the boat shift and wobble. When she looked away from Sieng, Marcsson had knocked Neko down. He knelt on her chest, tugged away the air hoses, ripped away the collection bag and filters for good measure, and threw her mask aside. Neko's bare face met the light, eyes wide with panic.

Marcsson didn't have to do much. He held her arms down easily. Neko's twisting grew feebler.

Kalypso did nothing. A little tune ricocheted from one side of her head to the other. After a while she identified it as 'Equinox'. She looked at the corpse again.

Marcsson sat back, distracted. He turned and studied the scattered pieces of tubing and hardware from the luma that had held Sieng.

'That's too bad,' he muttered. 'Shouldn't have done that. Stupid. Stupid.'

He stood up and crossed back to his own boat. Kalypso crawled to Neko and put the mask back on her head. She couldn't tell whether Neko was still breathing. Her guess would have been no.

Marcsson came back carrying hardware and collection equipment. He set it down, picked up Neko, and conveyed her to the other boat. When he returned, he went to the helm and Sieng's boat began moving. He then devoted his attention to Sieng's body, talking to Kalypso without looking at her. He continued to interface.

'Are you all right? I have a great deal of work to do but if you're injured in any way you must tell me. We have some medical supplies.' He paused for her answer, panting slightly in his efforts to confine the corpse beneath the helm.

She looked at his hands on the brilliantly colored dead forearms, which oozed.

'You seem healthy enough,' he said eventually. 'I will have to ration your air. It's nothing personal. I want you to understand that if you can.'

Kalypso couldn't respond. Sieng's intestines were bound in an indigenous daffodil-yellow cobweb; this didn't prevent them from inching steadily across the bottom of the boat as it vibrated with motion. The keel glided in syrup, penetrating the forms that scrolled and pivoted beneath, the life and death of things without apparent center. Kalypso watched the sky roll into itself behind Marcsson's head. She could see his mouth but not his eyes. His mouth was slightly open. She was stuck. There was nothing she could do. She had lost the conviction needed to lift even one finger.

She saw the illuminated helm with its radio. She was probably looking at it the way Neko had looked at her.

The landscape seeps into the mind and makes maps in its own image. Kalypso knows this all too well: in a Dream you project your mind outwardly, but this, now, is just the other end of the same process. The world seeps in and tells you what and how to think, to be. Everything you do is a response to it.

But this is a world derived on different principles than anything your body knows. You haven't evolved with this place. You are not of it, nor it of you. How deep into structure do you have to go to arrive at a common ground? For there is no membrane here keeping you away from *It*. There is no Ganesh to run interference, no Works, no cluster. There's only a sculpted curve of plastic sourced deep in Earth's history and formed by your species' habits of mind. There's only this boat, itself partly indigenous and therefore suspect, keeping you from falling far far far from yourself, to a place where nothing understands you and you are so far out of context as not even to qualify as flotsam.

It was possible that she was in a state of shock, Kalypso observed. She was exhausted: that much was certain. Animal instinct must be taking over, because she made no attempt to do anything. She curled up amidst the ruined luma, some of which stuck to the outside of her suit, and allowed the hum of the boat's engines to lull her to sleep.

She woke with a jerk when Marcsson kicked her. Nearby he slouched slack-jawed, his suit barely registering respiration. He was deep in interface, trapped in a fugue of some kind. His body twitched violently.

Kalypso's skin felt slick, and there was a strange smell. The canopy was up and the bottom of the boat was flooded with spilled luma. Sieng's body itself had been removed.

She realized she wasn't wearing her suit. It was nowhere to be seen.

Her hand went to her bare throat.

She looked for it everywhere. It was gone. She looked again. Gone.

The luma disgusted her; she tried to get it off herself, plagued with a sudden bout of psychosomatic itching. She thought about what was touching her and nearly retched.

Marcsson sat up, suddenly alert. Kalypso collected herself; made herself breathe regularly; focused. This was important. She positioned herself across from the Grunt and looked him in the interface.

'Tell me what you did to my suit.' She kept her voice level and reasonable, as if they were sitting over bowls of hot cereal at breakfast in rem2ram after a long night of work, he putting her to sleep with a description of the antics of his subs, she wondering how he could not notice. As if they weren't sitting on brilliant orange water, dragged by a thermal current, in a boat that muttered and sang with every temperature change as it self-adjusted. The sky moved fast and flat, dark in some places and darker in others.

Marcsson stretched and yawned. She pressed her face against her knees. Her skin was disgusting. Her own smell offended her.

'Please can I have my suit back. There's nowhere I can go. I can't breathe on my own. I don't even really know where we are.'

'I'm sorry. I can't give it back. I couldn't have used Neko; she would be a dead end. I need your skin.'

There's nothing to say to this, is there?

'Sieng is using your suit,' he added after a while. 'There isn't enough room in the cockpit for all three of us, because I'm going to need to spread out my gel sheets to finish compiling. So I had to put her out on deck, and without the suit she'll become contaminated. I can't afford that. Besides, I don't trust you.'

'You don't trust *me*?'

'I don't like the way you're looking at me. I think the Wild may be getting to you. Possibly you're a danger to yourself and others. You'll be perfectly safe as long as you stay under the canopy.'

She couldn't answer this. It was 90 degrees away from making sense.

'Why can't we go back to First?' Kalypso pleaded with him. 'All anybody wants is to get Ganesh running again. It can't work, staying out here. No one will punish you, and sooner or later you'll have to return, anyway.'

But he paid her no attention, such that she began to wonder if she was there. On a rational level, she knew he was profoundly disturbed – damaged in some way. Yet his will was stronger than hers. He was so forceful, so convinced of himself, that it was easier to go along with him than to maintain a posture of detachment. She began to accept his behavior.

She told herself that although she was physically his captive, her mind was her own. She instructed herself that she could be strong; could retain a sense of herself.

This of course was untrue.

Somebody had changed the rules out from under her. They never warn you when they're going to do this; it just happens and you have to unravel it for yourself.

Time moved slowly in the Wild. She was unable to interface, though she never stopped trying. Marcsson stayed with Kalypso under the canopy for three days while he taught her the procedures she was to use in processing the data he was collecting from Sieng's body.

'I need you to be my eyes,' he said. 'I have a defect in my vision at close range. It's uncorrectable. You will be doing the fine detail work.'

She became inured to his constant presence. He made her memorize the chemical ratios associated with a whole slew of subspecies. He taught her counting techniques and categorization; he taught her how to plug data into various formulas he'd devised. Sometimes he talked theory, most of which she didn't understand, so she nodded a lot and tried to stay awake. She only remembered the bits that didn't make sense. They stuck in her mind and chafed like sand in an oyster.

'There's a language in disease,' he instructed her. 'When a bacterial agent infects you, it takes apart your structure and replaces it with its own. To do this successfully, it must understand and be able to exploit your unique features; it must know you. It must know how to speak to you, to give the instructions that will benefit it, and destroy you.'

'Understand? Know? Language?' Indignation roused her from a chronic semi-stupor. 'Azamat, we're talking about prokaryotes here.'

166

'That doesn't mean they can't have language, which is simply a way of codifying history, recombining and recalling it. You're thinking in terms of organisms again. You know why I took data from the clayfields? Because there's fossilized evidence there going back millions of years. Understanding how the System organizes itself can only occur by looking across time. To see how this co-evolution developed. We don't witness this exchange of genetic material in terrestrial ecosystems. We don't see the blurring of the concept of species, and we need to find out how it could arise. It couldn't have always been this complex. It must have once been simpler. And I must . . . ' he had begun to breathe hard, although as he spoke he was doing nothing more strenuous than administering tiny amounts of tracer to luma cells under the microscope. '. . . I must know my enemy. Here. Look at that and tell me exactly what you see.'

His face was flushed. She thought of Sieng's corpse, looked into the microscope, and began reading off counts. After a while she tried again.

'So . . . when you compile all this information. How long will this take?'

'I've been working on the problem for twenty years. I'm not close to being finished. But I'm starting to get inklings.'

'What will you do with it all?'

'I'll be in a position,' Azamat said, 'to infect the System. I'm learning its chemical language. So I can instruct it to do as I say.'

'To make oxygen, you mean? To balance the atmosphere?'

'I'll hunt it down,' he said dreamily. His fingers and legs twitched rhythmically.

'What happened in Alien Life, Azamat? You were in the Core. I remember some of it, but I couldn't – I couldn't understand it, I couldn't *stand* it, actually. What were you doing?'

'Recite for me the exact sequence of procedures for isolating dipirolinic acid from *flagrare* sub 19 at a temperature of 113.'

It was as clear a change of subject as could be. Kalypso tried to summon her scattered concentration to answer the question.

'You're making me into a walking technical manual,' she griped.

'You have a long way to go before that happens,' he said with a faint smile.

She had begun to get the feeling that he liked her. She found herself trying harder to be smart. This disturbed her, but she couldn't seem to stop. Without appearing to try, he was crafting her to his will.

When it finally came, the prospect of being left alone in the boat caught her unprepared. Marcsson said, 'I am going outside to be with Sieng. Touch my supplies at your own risk. Touch the helm and I'll know about it. Touch my work and it will mean your life. Understand?'

'I understand.'

'Who owns the air?'

'You do,' she said fervently.

'Good. It's more true than you know.'

After that, he began spending some time every day on deck. While he was gone, he left work for her to do, recording population statistics. While he was inside, he ordered her around like a galley slave, but the airmix in the canopy kept her alive, and when she did well he sometimes sat and talked to her. When he checked her work, his hands and eyes moved robotically over the studies. He was never out of interface, and he was never farther than six inches from the inert radio. Kalypso kept her eyes averted, but she coveted it.

She learned how to use certain chemicals to attract and repel various strains of *v. flagrare*; this got to be kind of fun once she had the hang of it, and sometimes when he wasn't around she played with the colony samples he had collected and was growing in proto-luma. Most of them could be easily differentiated by color and texture, and she learned to make abstract, moving paintings with them, using different additives to move each color where she wanted it. There was a good chance that lightheadedness caused by impure airmix contributed to the amusement factor of this activity. Or maybe it was just a little piece of her old self asserting its survival, revelling in insubordination. Sometimes she couldn't remember the procedures. Sometimes she made mistakes and fudged the results.

There were also times when Marcsson hovered over her and watched everything she did. She tried hard to draw on her memory of Liet's subconscious to help her not fuck up. In her mind's eye she could see Liet bent over a tray of gel, aligning an irregular grid of green light over the fluid. She had the idea that Liet was establishing migration patterns for a helper series, whatever that was exactly. There were some equations vaguely associated with what Liet was doing, but Kalypso hadn't been able to absorb them at the time of the Dream and certainly couldn't recall them now. She had a thin sense of Liet's mental process, though: it was familiar and comforting. Liet could think like a snake: pure economy of movement, devastating simplicity. Speed.

Think like Liet. Think like Liet.

Easier said than done. But either she got this work done right, or she didn't breathe. She steadied her hand and began to suck up the gel. Very. Very. Carefully.

On this occasion, she got it wrong. Marcsson could get mean at times like this, but never in a straightforward way.

'If I bend your hand back like this – ' he demonstrated, and she cried out ' – I can discover by your reaction that it wasn't meant to bend that way. I can try to teach it to bend that way – ' he did it again, harder ' – by repeating this action – and again – but in the end I'll just break the joint.'

She was hissing and sobbing with pain. There was no malice in him, which frightened her.

'Just shut up! Stop talking! Let me go.'

'Yes,' he said. He read her face and nodded thoughtfully. 'That's exactly how it is. Only worse. This is what I go through every moment of every day. Now you understand why I fuck you up, and will continue to fuck you up for as long as you persist in being unable or unwilling to correctly catalog the diagonal disinfinity loop of the sub 19 *v. flagrare*. It is very simple. See? Use the Diriangen function, enter the gel sheet readings line by line, plot the time, and store.'

His blue stare raked her to see whether she accepted what he was saying. She learned to nod rapidly and make eye contact. It was easier that way.

During this time she focused all her efforts on getting to the radio. She was able to monitor the channels with her interface, so she knew that the Dead had reached First and were in discussions with the witch doctors; that the Grunts were impatient; and that the Mothers had not gotten their Picasso's Blue after all. Not yet anyway. But hearing all this only created frustration when she was unable to transmit: she couldn't do this via interface, and she was afraid Marcsson would hear her if she used the boat's radio. The first couple of times he left her alone she didn't dare do anything other than follow instructions. After all, he was only a few meters away, prone to returning unexpectedly – and she'd seen his easy violence. Eventually, though, the radio grew in her mind until it occupied almost everything and it was all she could see or think about, even when it was behind her back and she was in the middle of some other activity.

It was daylight outside. She could see a reddish color in the water outside, but nothing more definite. She had not been out of the canopy in days. Marcsson left. Kalypso had entered a heightened state of awareness. She felt unbalanced and tingly.

The wavering outline of his figure up above. She inched toward the helm, convinced Marcsson could somehow see and feel her disobedience. He was working away pretending not to notice her, but he knew. He *knew*. She touched the console, its casing as pristine as if it had just come from the terran factory.

Be rational, she told herself.

She activated the radio. He was out of sight.

What am I doing. He'll see. He'll know.

She caught herself. *Be rational*, she said again. He would be deep in his studies by now. She placed a call to Oxygen 2. It was easy.

'*Who is this? Identify yourself.*' She recognized the Grunt's voice instantly. Emotion closed her throat.

'Kessel?' she croaked.

'*Is that little Kalypso?*'

'Yes! Yeah, it's me.'

'*Where are you? Tehar has been driving us crazy asking about you.*'

'Tehar? He's OK? Can I speak to him?'

'He's stuck in First. Hold on. Let me get Ahmed for you.'

Stuck? What she wouldn't give to be stuck in First.

Ahmed came on. *'Kalypso, do you still have Marcsson?'*

She swallowed unwelcome tears. Who gave a fuck about Marcsson? What about her?

'Yeah. I still have Marcsson. But I – '

'Take very good care of him, Kalypso. Listen to me. Tehar says the only chance for Ganesh is to get Marcsson's data. His work is rewriting Ganesh's processing facilities. You need to bring Marcsson in to First.'

'I can't. I don't know where I am. I don't even have a suit.'

Pause. *'No suit? How . . . uh, how is it that you're alive, Kalypso?'*

'It's a long story. I don't have much time. He might come back any minute. Ahmed, it's not exactly fun out here. Can't you come get me?'

Static. He was conferring with the others.

'Look, we can't leave Oxygen 2.'

'Why the fuck not?'

'The Grunts have taken over. They've confiscated all of the tentkits and boats and – '

'What?' Her feelings about her own oppression by the Dead and Marcsson spilled over into aggression. 'You don't have to take that! We outnumber the Grunts. Don't pay any attention! Don't let them kill Ganesh!'

It was as if she hadn't spoken. *'Kalypso, be careful. Tehar says Ganesh is turning wild. Tehar says – '*

'Shut up about Tehar a minute,' she snapped. 'You have no idea what I'm dealing with here. I need help. It's . . . ' She should have prepared her words ahead of time, and now fumbled to explain. 'He's hard to handle, you don't know the half of it, and I really can't – '

'You have to. The situation here isn't good either. First is . . . ' there was a kind of choking noise and the line went quiet for a second. Then she could hear him breathing. *'Look, First seems to be . . . I don't know how to say this. Disappearing. It's very – '*

'Yeah, I know, it's the Dead. Ask the Mothers about Sieng's team and you'll see some first class squirming. Listen, I can – '

Ahmed spoke over her. *'Whatever happens, take care of Marcsson. As soon as I can figure a way to come get you, or get you back here, I'll let you know.'*

'You can't! You can't call me here, Ahmed. He'll – '

'All right. You call me, then.'

'Can I talk to the others?'

'No. There's a distress call coming in. I have to go. They're all right. Take care of – '

– Marcsson, she finished for him, and the link went dead. She was shaking with frustration; she was hot, disappointed, confused. They were supposed to reassure her; they were supposed to support her. But Ahmed sounded hyperextended, which she'd have thought impossible. She wanted to crawl among them and be comforted. At least they had each other. What did she have?

She wrapped her arms around her knees and rocked. What had ever made her think she was interested in the Wild? What had ever made anyone think it was a good idea to put people on other planets, where they had to live in oxygen tents such that, if Marcsson wanted to for example, he could throw her outside and kill her anytime? Or if she stayed with him, could do anything at all to her. Anything he wanted.

What had ever made people think it would be a good idea to create children from stored gametes and bring them up on this farm in the middle of nowhere, inculcate into their minds the idea that they were living a good life, feed them on Dreams that could turn savage, just as Marcsson's had done?

She hadn't asked to be born. Was she supposed to be grateful to be alive, when her very life itself had turned out to be somebody's idea of an experiment?

When you are small and not all that terribly bright – especially considering your parentage and the expectation it carries for you to be brilliant – when you are small you've got to be tough. You've got to be strong. You have to wear your strength like a badge, and whatever happens, you have to say, I can take it. Kalypso, huddled beneath the canopy among the specimens she had to process before Azamat got back, suddenly couldn't stand the thought of being strong. It made her feel physically sick.

She thought: If I start to crack, I won't be able to stop.

Would that be such a bad thing? Just let go and not stop? Cry until . . . until what? Until someone came to rescue her?

No – too ineffective. Still, the idea of hysteria was appealing. It was no longer a deterrent, this not-being-able-to-stop extremity of feeling. It was, if anything, an inducement. Maybe she just wanted the rush.

She took off her interface and peered out through the canopy. She could see the muted colors of the Wild; on the deck she could see her own surface suit, lying still. Filled with Sieng.

Tehar, she thought and wounded herself with his name. *Tehar, I need you.*

The *v. flagrare* left a smell that the tent's filters didn't catch. She kept waiting to get used to it but it went away sometimes, destroying her immunity, and then came back to assault her all over again. There was a brownish condensation on the canopy, dripping and drying and slowly slowly slowly blotting out the light.

She had to reach Tehar. And that meant Dreaming. But Marcsson didn't let her sleep in natural patterns. In fact, he didn't let her sleep at all; he kept her awake ruthlessly, and she had to catch what rest she could while he was in the fugue states. These came unexpectedly and stayed for anywhere from seconds to hours. She never knew whether he was conscious or not. One in particular was singular in that he stood up in the middle of it, left the canopy like a sleepwalker – she had to hold the seals shut with her bare hands to protect herself from the atmosphere – and returned with Sieng in his arms. He brought the body into the canopy and laid it out among the gel studies. Kalypso assumed a position as far as possible from Sieng. Marcsson subsided into stillness, but he watched the corpse with watery, fragile eyes. With tiny, precise movements his two eyes scanned the body. They were assembling information: but to what purpose? Behind Marcsson's collection of behaviors, what was going on? What principle was generating his actions? Did he still think in words? Why did he sometimes speak, sometimes stay silent? What did he want? What pieces of him had been broken or re-arranged?

He watched Sieng. Dumb. Inanimate.

'I'm supposed to help you, Azamat,' she told him although he was still fuguing. Felt her lip curling. 'Everyone says you're the thing. I'd better devote myself to you. That's what they say.'

He started from the fugue and gaped at her, a look of sudden realization spreading comically across his face.

'I've made an error. How could I be so stupid?'

His brows crawled with anxiety. Kalypso felt the urge to laugh, hard on the heels of which came fear. Some people, when they went crazy, rotted from the inside out. They appeared perfectly plausible on the surface and went for years without inconveniencing anyone before they finally snapped. Why couldn't he be one of those?

Or, more to the point – why couldn't she?

The tray of gel resting on Azamat's knees shivered.

She thought of the rest of her cluster as if reaching out to steady herself. She thought of Tehar. It didn't seem to help any more.

'I'm perfectly fine,' he said. His eyes searched her face. 'There's nothing wrong with me. You don't need to look at me that way. You're making a mistake.'

He put the tray away and stood up. With the measured care that characterized everything he did, he checked over his suit, gathered his collection materials.

'Algaics,' he said. 'We've been overlooking their impact on the lower levels. Don't you think?'

'Could be,' Kalypso answered cautiously.

'You know, in New Guinea these ants called *irodomyrmex cordatus* have co-evolved with the *M. tuberosa* plant which features a specialized cell-structure that suits its ant inhabitants as if it had been designed for them. The body extends itself across species and generations. Case in point.'

He turned his back to do something and she made a face at it. He had started doing the rhythm-thing again with his hands, which she'd forgotten about but now that it was back, it seemed worse than ever. The helm was extremely active, indicating probable thermal activity in their vicinity. He stood interfaced at the helm for long stretches, snapping polyrhythms across the fabric of his own suit but never speaking to her or acknowledging her presence. Sieng's body in her suit was squashed against Kalypso's thighs where she sat surrounded by sample trays. The body was soft and warm thanks to the currents heating the boat.

She closed her eyes.

When the Dream formed she was running a paintbrush across a large, dark surface. Instead of applying paint, though, she seemed to be revealing something that lay beneath, for with each stroke of the brush appeared another piece of brooding T'nane sky: lowering crimson clouds reflecting the unseen surface. On the handle of the brush were burned the marks: SIENG. 141 MILES.

She kept painting, but something had changed. She was painting Picasso's Blue across somebody's body.

Tehar?

No such luck. It was Lassare, the young and skinny Lassare, and when the blue dust touched her skin she gasped and cried out in a high voice.

'It's a vision of time but I'll never get there Kalypso. The harder I try the farther it will retreat, but I can't stop trying. It's deadly. Quicksand. Paint me. I'll give you anything. Please.'

'Tell me what Azamat's doing with Sieng.'

'How should I know?' Lassare moaned, writhing. 'You're the one who talks to Ganesh.'

'You *are* Ganesh,' Kalypso said. 'You're only pretending to be Lassare. Why do you keep making puns about Miles and Sieng? Where's the jazz vine? What are you up to?'

ANYTHING THAT COMES HERE, I EAT. NO EXCEPTIONS. YOU WILL BE NICE WITH SALSA. GO TO SLEEP.

But instead she woke, hot and drooling, feeling no more rested than before. The sound of the wind outside was high and constant, and she found herself stopping her ears, wincing. Marcsson was busy at the helm. She was pretty sure they were moving to avoid a thermal. He was taking them into an alkaline zone where there was virtually no oxygen in the water, so they relied on stores to aerate the canopy. Marcsson had an oxygen canister with a mask which he used from time to time to top up his suit's levels, but he didn't give any to Kalypso, who soon felt sick. The airmix was always too weak, and seemed to slowly get weaker. She began to think about her body in terms of its cells. How many were dying every minute? Which ones died when, and why? She couldn't feel any of it; she could only feel the wash of chemicals bathing her brain in weariness. Her eyes simmered.

Then she realized her interface was missing.

'Where's my interface?'

Marcsson drummed and patted himself. The gel trays shook gently.

'Marcsson. Where's my interface?'

He didn't answer. He was fuguing.

She didn't feel well enough to do anything but curl up and go back to sleep.

Time, anyway, proved to be the dictator. She made the mistake of hoping that something would change. She told herself, if I can just get through this hour/afternoon/day, then something will give. Sooner or later, I'll be saved. This works for a while; but eventually no matter how stupid you are it dawns on you that you have no control. Nothing you do matters in the slightest. Maybe you'll be saved. Maybe you won't. You just have to wait.

And time carves you into the shapes of its choosing while you wait for something to happen.

You sit fighting it. Pull your knees close to your body, clutch your shins in both hands, rock slightly from side to side. There's a calculus of adversity and its differentials have taken up residence in your very organs, inhabiting your limbic system and decorating you with feelings you'd be better off without. You neither know nor care where these feelings come from, but they're hanging upside down from your rafters in droves.

Don't speak. You'll waste what little air you have. Don't even look at Marcsson 'cause it only upsets you. Even if he's sitting right there, practically touching you, don't look at him.

'And if I feel,' she said slowly, each word seeming to take several seconds to come out. 'An emotion for you, why do I always. Glimpse. Its other side out. Of the corner of my eye?'

His voice came so fast after hers, matched her pitch so closely, she thought it was an echo at first.

'It all happens so slowly,' Marcsson whispered. He paused to breathe from the cylinder. Her spine ached with desire for his air. 'Like a tree cracking stone. You observe the microtubules within luma. Aha – you say – ' He inhaled. 'Structure!'

'Why can't. I feel one thing.' They were talking at each other and he was winning – she knew this but couldn't stop. 'Why can't I just. Hate you.'

'You look at the organization of each species, some vertical, some clustered, some randomized or so you think. The chemistry is deceptively simple. Sulphur, phosphorous, methane – it looks so terrestrial. So ideal. No wonder the probes were fooled. The volcanic activity of course – '

'Shut up!' she cried, frustrated at how little sound she was able to generate. 'Listen to me. Hear me. I am here.'

She had pressed forward into his space, aggressive, gasping. His expression shifted but she didn't know if he registered her presence. The air was gray. She could smell the dread on her own skin.

'What the fuck is with you? See me. Azamat!'

He had drawn back, taking the cylinder with him. He covered his face with the mask as if to hide. Condensation ran down the walls like mice.

'No more of this,' she rasped. 'Let me live. Don't let me die here.'

He brought himself to bear on her face without appearing to recognize her. She saw the blue loco disease in his eyes, just like in Unit 5. Just like in the Gardens. Just like attacking Neko.

This is it, she thought. One blow, and I'm dead. He can easily do it. He will.

The poison wind screamed across the Wild.

He tossed her the mask.

It covered her whole face. She inhaled. This was the closest thing she'd had to an orgasm in recent memory.

He had averted his eyes.

skin

The thermal passed them at some distance. It obscured the volcanoes and brought a glimpse of sunlight in the form of a white veil sheering into the water nearby. The System roiled and adjusted, their oxygen supply stabilized, and Marcsson worked. He never got tired of it. Kalypso seemed to have been forgotten. For hours on end she had to watch him delicately transferring minute amounts of fluid from one gel tray to another; administering light, heat, chemicals; measuring, recording, pondering. She was no longer on edge. If anything, observing his methods put her in a kind of trance. She continued to do the detail work to save his eyes, grateful at least to be kept occupied even if the work was tedious.

She hadn't spoken to anyone but him in days. She had put an automatic SOS on the radio and hoped he wouldn't notice it. Without the interface, she learned how it felt to be stalked by the Wild.

You can feel it. One minute you're beneath the canopy, safely absorbed in some work, convinced of your self. The next it's encroaching on you, consuming you with its emptiness. Beneath the glass of its waters you can feel the neverness, the impossibility of understanding what it is. Your body fails to respond: there is no fear in your body because your body has no programming, no immune response to this brand of terror. If it were a vast height, or a conflagration, or a devouring beast, your body would know how to react. But it is all abstract: it's all built by you. So that when you look at the System and its mysterious colors, or the shape of Marcsson's sleeping mouth and the folds that lie to either side, shadowy with new hair, all you can feel is a horror that will never find expression – not unless you finally manage to touch this feeling with your bare hands. And you don't want that at all.

He began spending more and more time doing things with Sieng's body, to which he was unnaturally attached. He'd begun to systematically collect samples of the intra-Sieng luma, on which he ran various tests. Sometimes he just probed through the tissue with an analysis stick, a surgeon-cum-frontier-explorer deep in the jungle.

That's what he was doing late one night when she was startled by the chime of the radio announcing receipt of a signal. Marcsson was fuguing and didn't react; at length, Kalypso stood and went to the helm. She put the call on speakers.

'Kalypso, it's Tehar.'

She made an inarticulate noise.

'Are you there?'

'Yes. I'm – ' she looked at Marcsson, searched for words. She took so long that Tehar began talking.

'I need to speak to Marcsson.'

'You can't.'

'Don't be funny, Kalypso. I don't want him treated like a criminal. Let me speak to him.'

'It's not like that. He's crazy, Tehar. I don't want him to know we're talking.'

'This is very important. It's the most important thing you've ever done. Just let me talk to him.'

'It wouldn't do any good, Tehar. Trust me.'

'Damn you, Kalypso. How can I help you if you won't cooperate. Get Marcsson, make him come to the radio, and let me speak to him. Do it.'

She continued to protest; while they were arguing, Marcsson popped out of fugue.

'I told you to keep your hands off things,' he said, getting to his feet.

'One of the witch doctors wants to talk to you. From First.'

This flustered him. Kalypso edged away from the radio.

'*Azamat? Azamat, it's Tehar,*' squawked the radio. '*Come and talk. Come on, please.*'

Marcsson stood there for long moments while Tehar patiently repeated his exhortations. Finally he stepped up to the console.

'Marcsson here.'

'*Thank you. Thank you. All right, can you tell me what you were using to encrypt your data, Azamat? There seems to be a logic bug in the Core.*'

'It's too soon to discuss this,' Marcsson said. 'I'm not ready.'

He sounded so normal. Kalypso fumed, realizing Tehar must be thinking she was the crazy one.

'*We don't have much time,*' Tehar said. '*Whatever work you're doing out there, you're going to need Ganesh to interpret it for you, and Ganesh is in big trouble. You don't want to be stuck, I'm sure.*'

'I don't have to tell you that there's no such thing as information. It isn't passive.'

'*Yes, we're seeing that now. The luma –* '

Azamat chuckled. 'The luma. They said, "Oh, Ganesh can use the luma as a storage system. The root directives won't change, because the luma will just be storage, like a big data warehouse." Right? Isn't that what they said? Ah, I forget you're too young to remember.'

'*We can see there's activity in the luma,*' Tehar conceded.

'You know what she did, don't you? Trust Sieng to notice that the Wild was reacting to the slops we threw into it. So she started playing around with her own shit. It's true. Her first series was done with *e. coli*. She kept introducing them to the luma until something stuck. After a while, she got an RNA exchange between *e. coli* and the indigenous subs in the luma. A nice hybrid. Nothing tricky, but she started making population studies of the way the luma worked, started playing around with temperature and magnetism. She had a gift for playing. Nothing deliberate about Sieng, I can tell you. You could never see her logic, and there was never any formal evidence of her thinking.'

'*As fascinating as this is,*' Tehar cut in, '*right now we're preoccupied with a critical –* '

'So it was kind of like Fleming's apocryphyal sneeze. Some got cells got mixed up with some of the samples and were subsumed in the luma as well. This was the first interaction of eukaryotes and the indigenes. And something really interesting happened. The hybrid began to construct lattices around the gut cells, making homes for them in the luma chambers. And the luma itself started firing electrical and magnetic signals at the gut cells. The mechanism behind this was unknown to Sieng. She kept saying, "What if it's a DNA scavenger? What if it's a homeostatic system with no DNA of its own, which somehow, by virtue of its effectiveness in supporting its members, always manages to get reproduced and built *anyway*?"'

'*I don't follow you,*' Tehar said in a strained voice.

'A system of heat and chemo-receptive membranes regulated non-centrally. Thousands of biogenic contributors who can be sporulated at intolerable temperatures, who can spur each other on in a metabolic battle. It's a whole ecosystem, but it plays by different rules. Rules we'll never understand.'

'*System theory is all very well, but –* '

'What nobody appreciated is that Sieng never took never for an answer. She was going to rub up against this thing no matter what. She kept looking for intermediates – something that wasn't an organism independent of the System, but still able to predictably interact with terrestrial organisms. She knew that the basic chemical rules are the same here as on Earth, she knew her physics and her statistics, so it was a question of finding a common ground in the genetics. The thing she failed to take into account was the predacious nature of all sophisticated life. Or maybe she knew. Maybe she knew that the mix she was making was bound to explode.'

His eyes went to Sieng.

'*Marcsson, are you telling me you've been trying to repeat Sieng's work?*'

The Grunt shook himself slightly. His hands stopped drumming.

'No. Not repeat. Organize. She was sloppy. That's why she died. What kind of scientist experiments on herself? A mad one, that's what. All I ever wanted to do was take her work and make it usable.'

Tehar said, *'Was it her data you pulled from the Earth Archives?'*

Marcsson snapped his fingers. 'Bingo. The Dead hid it there. They knew the secret for creating tissues that generate Picasso's Blue was in there somewhere, and they didn't want the Mothers getting hold of that.'

'Um . . .'

'I know, human nature's fucked, right? Self-destructive on a larger scale. You kids are all we have.'

Kalypso, listening to all this, began to feel more and more peeved. Marcsson *was* capable of making sense. Why did she let him get away with this behavior? He was making an effort for Tehar. But maybe this was because Tehar was clearly able to follow what he was saying and respond in kind.

'Azamat? The thing is, you're hitting the nail right on the head when you talk about predation. What I don't think you realize is that Sieng's stuff is eating Ganesh. Now that's destructive. If I could just get some code, some way to make sense of what's happening, don't you see? I need you to help me understand the changes in Ganesh. We could do it through the Dreamer if that's easier for you. I know you've been Dreaming because you leave traces behind.'

There was a long silence. Kalypso held her breath.

'Ganesh has a fever. It's burning,' said Marcsson. 'I am Dreaming in smoke. You touch the fire and you're dead. It's that simple. No, I don't think I can do anything for you at this time. If I were you I'd get out of First.'

He cut the signal. He sank to the deck, slack-jawed, glassy.

'I can't go on much longer,' he murmured. 'Don't know if I can keep a hold.'

He fugued before she could answer.

After this, Marcsson was too quiet. It had been some time since he'd done her any injury, or threatened her. Or even noticed her. It was getting harder and harder to know when he was conscious and when he was interfacing and when he was in a fugue. Once he started interfacing in the middle of a procedure. He froze with one hand reaching for a collection fil. For several minutes he didn't move.

Kalypso covertly turned up the oxygen in the airmix. He played statue.

She breathed deep. Got to her feet. Stepped over Sieng's body. Reached into his pocket. Slipped the interface away from him. Went as far away from him as the confines of the boat would permit.

She put on her face.

She wasn't sleepy and had to use a long, complicated counting sequence to induce herself. At the beginning of the Dream she felt a flash of hope because Ganesh seemed better. She had been sent straight to her home beach. Alien Life was obscured by black, putrid fog. It was hot.

Ganesh are you there? Don't tease me. Don't play me. I have to know.

Silence. Scattered across the sand was a collection of objects, none of them drawn to scale. A huge, dead moth lay like a kite on the wet shore, waves turning its wings to tissue, while nearby a tiny replica of the Taj Mahal sat fist-sized and perfect, gleaming. She recognized the objects from Tehar's subconscious: they were his symbols. She felt a pang, looking at them.

How did they get on her beach, though?

His was an ordered world. She picked up a primitive wooden and metal vice grip, a thing reeking of Earth. If she opened it and went inside, she would touch something of Tehar's worldview. In Tehar's belief, things could be explained if you looked long and hard enough, broke them down far enough, persisted in hurling yourself against them. Faith in your own symmetry gave you the power to break the asymmetries of the world.

She knew instinctively that if she touched Tehar now, in this way, she would end up hurting him. The realization came as a shock. Although they were the same age, he had always acted older. He had always assumed a certain superior position. He was always one step ahead of her, impossible to surprise. It had never before occurred to her that she was capable of doing anything much to affect Tehar; now, suddenly, she perceived him as perishable. She'd gotten in the habit of looking to him for rescue: that was ostensibly why she was in the Dreamer, trying to make contact. But now that she was here, she realized she no longer was acting on Tehar's orders, or even with the cluster's goals in mind. She didn't know why she was doing what she did. Since she'd left First behind, she no longer grasped the causality behind her own actions.

The tide was going out. She opened the vice grip and Ganesh obligingly reeled out the primitive Dream the witch doctor had coded for her. All Kalypso could think was that it must have taken him days to build this. She was touched.

Tehar was whispering against her scalp. His lips nudged her bare temple. Pictures formed when he spoke.

'They're taking First apart. If you sit at the top of the Dome at night, you can see them clearest. Their boats carve dark paths through the glowing algaics; they cast lines on to the feet and swarm up the legs. For the first few nights, you observe no noticeable effects of their pilfering. You figure that they're seeking nourishment, supplies, materials for survival: they're doing what is necessary.

'But then you start to notice that entire panels of luma are missing. Hardware units from the original ship disappear from the conceptual map when you are working in Ganesh. They're dismantling the station. And they seem to know exactly what they're doing.

'It's a big place, and it's not going to go down overnight; but you find yourself wondering what's going on, that all this is happening and the Mothers do nothing to stop it. We can't last long if we scavenge our own station.

'You haven't heard from the Mothers in a long time. You don't have time to monitor the radios for more than a couple of hours a day, because you're in Ganesh most of the time, or sleeping except sleep doesn't seem to help. You watch them night after night, and one night you notice there's something strange about their boats. And the way they move doesn't look quite right.

'Then you start noticing all kinds of details, and when you put them together you realize they can't be any cluster you know. You've never seen these people before. And it scares you. Kalypso, I don't know if I can trust what I see. Ganesh berked Marcsson. I think it might berk me, too. All I do is study code. I don't Dream. I'm not that stupid. But I think I might be berking. Who are these people dismantling the station? Are they metaphorical?

'You're trying to hold too many things in your head. Sometimes you think you hear Ganesh whispering to you; but that must be the solitude. There are half a dozen other witch doctors spread around First, but you seldom contact them except in the form of abstractions through the interface. You're not used to being alone. Never thought it would bother you, but it does.

'They found Jianni's body. His suit had been taken. What's going on here? Sometimes Ganesh shuts down radio and you can't even get through to Oxygen 2. Have they all gone mad? Are you still there, Kalypso? You don't sound like yourself any more. When we spoke I . . .

'Kalypso, the taste of you. It's not fair to think that, but there's no controlling it.'

She cried out, rolled to try to touch him, but there were no more tactile suggestions – he must have run out of energy. The words continued.

'I can only hope you'll be able to interface and get this message. Ganesh has kept most of your node alive. I don't know why. Maybe it just likes you. We've lost so much; it's all encrypting at an unbelievable rate. The structure's starting to break down. I don't know how much longer we can stay. Sooner or later the Mothers are going to lose control of the Grunts and they'll come shut down the reflexes. Or another thermal could come. Please, Kalypso. You've got to get Marcsson in here. I know he interfaces because I've seen his footprints, but I can't catch him. He's too quick and nocturnal. He has ways of getting into Earth Archives that we can't follow.

'We're running out of time. Be careful Dreaming.'

He was gone. Her subconscious vainly tried to shape the memory of him into a natural dream, to give herself the sensation of his body against hers, his breathing marking time; but every time she almost had a piece of him he turned into the Dead with their hard-supple skin and she finally jerked awake, revulsed.

Marcsson was holding her interface. Absentmindedly he put it in a utility pocket of his suit. He said, 'It's time to begin. Give me your wrist.'

He moved to straddle her, grasping her left arm where she lay and wedging it between his knees. She was too sleepy to protest, and he was talking for a little while before she really took in what was happening.

As he spoke, he swabbed her arm with local anesthetic. He didn't talk to her face, but to her skin. He held her arm right up to his eyes as if trying to examine it minutely, but kept blinking and shaking his head.

'Damned eyes. Ruined my career. Well, I'm going to start with what's handy, and once we build the luma, we can alter the subs to our choosing. So your skin can be an oxygen factory if you want. Or you can make Picasso's Blue, or any number of other things, with the correct stimulation. The Dead are programmed only for Picasso's Blue, but that's because Sieng was only getting started then. She's much more evolved now. As I read you and she reads me we're really going to have a ball game here.'

He paused and grasped the scalpel.

'No! Wait, I'm sorry, OK? I'll stay out of interface. I promise. I swear. Put the knife away!'

'The first step, of course, will be building the luma. This is the critical stage.'

'You're not cutting me!' she blurted. 'Hey. Get off.'

She began squirming and found herself neatly restrained.

'Don't wreck this,' he said sternly. 'It's very important. I've spent a long time preparing for it. Be still, or I'll hurt you. Badly.'

She went limp. She looked at the knife and thought she was likely to get hurt, badly, anyway; but when it cut her she felt nothing. Marcsson incised a wavering rectangle in the skin of the inside of her forearm. Under the black there was a brightness of blood. She sat with her right hand clamped around her arm while he dangled the rectangle from a pair of tweezers and transferred it to an empty gel sheet. Then he sprayed the pink patch where her skin had been with fluid from a small atomizer.

'Good,' he said. 'When the anesthetic wears off, it's going to sting.'

Then he turned to the gel trays and began working on the skin he'd cut off her. She watched him for a long time. Then the fever set in. It didn't take long at all. Soon her teeth were chattering. He gave her water and nodded approval. Then returned to work.

'Azamat,' she said abruptly. 'Azamat please talk to me. Say anything. Please.'

He said, 'You get a sky color based on blue-green algae and all it implies. Somewhere under the earth there are roots and nitrogen nodules. This is a special interaction, a kind of ecological linchpin. We can simulate it here but it's unlikely ever to catch on. The sun isn't important enough.'

'Never mind,' she said. 'You're depressing me.'

He looked over his shoulder, surprised. 'Why?'

Kalypso licked her lips. His expression was almost normal, as if they were simply doing labwork and talking. As if he were still dull old Marcsson.

'I don't know,' she answered hesitantly.

'Because of the sun,' he said, holding a tiny blob of Sieng's lung up to a white lamp. 'The sun you'll never see. What's the matter?'

She couldn't speak it. She shook her head.

'None of them would ever believe this,' he said, nodding hard as if this would make his words true. 'My teachers, my colleagues. "But he was so quiet!" they'd say. "Who ever would have thought?" You, too, Sieng. You never even saw me. I might have been a janitor at the opera house and you the diva.'

'Please,' Kalypso signed, saving oxygen. 'I don't want to know this – '

His voice was calm and quiet. 'They weren't wrong, either. I was everything they thought. But now. I don't know what I am now.'

He was looking at her directly. All the questions she had wanted to ask; all her attempts to understand, back at First when he'd begun this berk – she couldn't ask them any more. In fact, she now

188

actively didn't want to know the answers. She turned away.

Later he fugued. She'd grown bold after this display of vulnerability on his part. She stole back her interface.

Bricks again. More of them. The structure was starting to look like an aqueduct or bridge; it had been built high and arching, and the foundations vanished in a luma soup that shifted if you tried to look at it directly. She didn't.

Though she was Dreaming, she was simultaneously conscious of lying in Neko's boat, and when she set foot on the unfinished bridge, her toes and then her feet became the sound on the witch doctor radio channel. The sound progressed up her ankles and calves as Kalypso set out across the partially completed span. It bewitched her and bent her senses. For a moment she became convinced it wasn't sound, it was heat: thermals that moved in her body, and made her skin change color. She looked down and saw the wheelbarrow far below, submerged in the luma. Floating on the surface was a rusted sign. it said: SIENG 2 MILES. There were bodies down there, too: bright bodies floating like Sieng's, like insects in amber. From deep in the luma came light. Marcsson's talk of sun must be affecting her.

Light flooded the Dream. Bare sun the likes of which she'd never seen lanced and subdued her eyes. She heard birdsong.

But it was only Marcsson, shining a penlight in her pupils.

'The fever has you, too,' he said. 'I can see it in the interface.'

She didn't know what he meant by that, but she was grateful that he merely pocketed her interface without comment – or violence. He went back to the fugue soon afterward, and she made herself stand and go to the radio. She was getting pretty good at the controls now: she congratulated herself for having figured out how to lower the volume. She set her ear to the speaker and listened to a fuzzy voice.

It was Ashki, a witch doctor.

'. . . a thermal a few hours ago. A small one, but enough to erode parts of the legs. The structure has been vulnerable, thanks to the vandals, and Ganesh still can't control its extremities. Now the luma's melting in places. For lack of a better word. It's returning to its gel state. Taking *our history with it. I keep thinking of the fires of Alexandria. What might have been different about history if the library hadn't burned.'*

Naomi was talking faster than usual. *'Darling, you need to keep the Earth Archives intact at all costs. We're under tremendous pressure from the Dead.'*

'If you'll let me talk to them, maybe I can convince them that shutting down the reflexes won't save the Archives. They need to understand that. If only they would cooperate.'

Lassare cut in. *'The Dead have been cooperating for a long time. It's possible they've finally snapped.'*

'Save Earth Archives, no matter what, Ashki!' Rasheeda, in ringing tones, like a prophet or a goddess.

'We can't get near Earth Archives. They're not in the Core any more. We don't know where they are. We can't get a code in there, we can't read them, we can't even get a shotgun induced. They're not Dreamable.'

'Reconfigure them, then. Translate them. Do something.'

'Reconfiguring Earth Archives at this stage would be like – well, to use an analogy I know you'll understand, it'd be like playing a piano concerto on a couple of rocks and a rubber band. I just can't do it yet.'

'Watch yourselves. The Dead are going to take you out if they sense you're not accomplishing anything. We're doing everything we can to negotiate.'

'Yeah, we noticed that half the heat shields are gone and most of the food stores. I gather this is the result of your negotiations. When are we getting Marcsson?'

'Don't give us trouble, Ashki,' Lassare's voice warned. *'You'll do better under us than the Grunts, who don't understand the Dead at all. Give us the bottom line and we'll do what we can.'*

'Structurally we won't have a collapse as long as First remains unoccupied. But the looting is becoming severe. The Dome was ruptured yesterday, and there are several breaches in the gardens. You can see algae and weeds already creeping out on to the surface. Don't like to think what will happen to them when the next thermal comes.'

Kalypso began to shiver again and lose her ability to concentrate. Her arm had taken to burning ferociously and she had to hold it at an odd angle to keep the wound from touching any other part of her body. She fumbled with the controls to transmit, but the boat must be low on power. She couldn't get the signal strength she needed. Then Tehar came on the line.

'I've been living in the transit tubes, monitoring the luma. It takes a lot of energy just to keep up with all the shifts in temperature and magnetism. All of us are at it full time and we're exhausted. We've been very lucky with thermal stability but that may not last. I've absorbed so much code I feel like my fingerprints are made of it now. Don't understand it, though, and Ganesh won't cooperate. Doing the smallest job is like trying to perform surgery with a salad fork. But reality as such is worse. The silence. The boredom. Bare time. Time on its own will make you crazy.'

Kalypso let out a strangled cry.

Long silence.

'Tehar,' Lassare said at length. *'We're trying to get Marcsson. We've only gotten one boat over the Rift, and they can't find a clear channel in the luma to reach him. We don't have many resources – '*

'I can't tell you what to do,' he said in a thick voice. *'If you can't bring Marcsson in, I won't blame you.'*

It was as if he was speaking to her.

That's right, she thought, her insides jumping with nervousness. Because I can't take it. Nobody should expect me to. Wait till he hears about this skin business –

'But Lassare I'm going down. I'm headed for the bottom.'

How could she tell him? *What* could she tell him?

'OK, Tehar,' Lassare said hurriedly. *'We're on it. We're on the situation.'*

Weak with fever, Kalypso sank to her knees and clutched her head in her hands. Fuck fuck fuck.

Robere's voice was saying, *'For the last time, the Mothers have no control over any of the equipment, boats, or supplies. So when I come on this channel I expect to be taken seriously. All of you are going to be very sorry when you realize you've placed your faith in a bunch of drug addicts. Stop damaging the station and talk to us.'*

Some hissing noises followed. Possibly Teres; the sound was not recognizably human.

'*We will use force against you if necessary. Let us speak to the hostages.*'

Hostages?

'*Robere?*' It was the voice of Lila, a botanist and the only person on the station smaller than Kalypso. '*Robere, don't worry. I'm all right. It's –* '

Marcsson slipped out of fugue and actually *smiled*. She cut the radio. 'We're integrating,' he announced. His affect was so positive she felt creeped out. 'We're doing a happy data merge. Come. Sit still.'

She was docile by now. She didn't move when he anesthetized her thigh. She watched him cut and remove a patch of skin and carefully atomize the wound as before. He took the skin and turned back to his work. The anesthetic wore off quickly and her leg felt hot. She was sucking her lower lip unconsciously and had begun to whine softly like an animal.

He noticed this and slapped her across the face. 'Didn't you hear what I said? How dare you look at me like you blame me. You're a part of it too. It's just as much your fault.'

She cringed and hid her face.

'I could take you apart bone by bone, one organ at a time. I could make you Sieng. You'd be less trouble that way. It's only skin! It's skin. You should thank me.'

There was a long, strange pause.

'You're so big,' he said. 'You'll never feel it.'

She wiped tears off her cheeks, resentful that she had to show weakness although it was absurd to be self-conscious round someone like him. He went to the ship's system. She could see him fooling with the radio.

'What do you know about the System, anyway?' he asked in a suddenly casual, mundane voice. 'You're the most notoriously ignorant member of your generation. Do you truly have no knowledge of the translation of ecology to mathematics?'

'I know about it from the statistical end,' she said. 'Well. Sort of. I know what a Diriangen function is, and a reducing spiral, and the Stassler Cycle, and – '

'Those are just names. Do you know what they mean?'

'Look. I'm a shotgun. I don't do reality.'

He sighed and looked out through the blurred canopy. The fires of the native subs played in his eyes.

'It's going to flow over you,' he said softly. 'And you won't understand it. You'll be the one it flows over, but they'll be the ones explaining it. None of you will get it.'

Later that day, Siri came on the radio and announced that neither the Grunts nor the Mothers were in power, so anybody from the Dead who wanted to talk should use this channel to speak to the *real* leaders, the youth of T'nane. She ended with an idealistic appeal to common goals and history. Kalypso almost gagged.

The second fever made time move very fast. She was seldom more than one-quarter conscious. When it subsided at last, she crawled around the boat, randomly seeking water, and realized Marcsson was in a deep fugue. She forgot about the water and went for her interface.

The bridge was the only place she could access any more. At the unfinished edge of it worked a builder who had, instead of eyes, a large miner's lamp strapped across his forehead like a huge interface. He was on his hands and knees, humming 'Good Old Stockholm' as he worked. He was wearing an abbreviated cape.

'Are you the matador?' she asked. 'You saved me . . . '

Something – blood? – was running down his limbs. She looked closer and saw long trails of ants.

'You must stop coming here. That's for you,' he said, pointing to a spot on the bridge. 'Take it.'

Lying on the bricks nearby was a jewel. She picked it up. At first she thought it was another message from Tehar; but it was too beautifully designed, too perfect, to be made by a person. Witch doctors didn't make Dreams: they were notoriously analytical, not creative. She ran her hands over it, her tongue, pressed it to her chest so she could feel its resonance against her bones.

Could it be from Ganesh? Had the AI recovered?

Her heart filled up.

It was a simple thing, but elegant: a haiku of Dreams. It whispered its title to her as it launched. *Tiera del Fuego: a lullaby.* She slid into it like silk.

> *Ocean, its flung extremities lashing the sky. Night. Salt on bare skin and ice wind filling throat. Arms aching as the paddle fights the waves.*
>
> *Struggling. Alive on the fraying seam of things.*
>
> *Here, on the water in the wild: no garment, no shelter, no companion.*
>
> *Here, in the canoe, a fire burning: unlikely and real as gravity.*
>
> *Here, with you: fire.*

It was all she could do to slip the interface back into Marcsson's pocket after this. She found the water she'd been seeking and sipped.

Something good was happening. Somewhere.

Or so she wanted to believe.

Now that Sieng wasn't around, she slightly missed the recomposing body. She felt lonely without it. Sieng might be dead, but she was treated with great reverence by Marcsson, whose size did not prevent him from being delicate and refined when he wanted to be.

He was not delicate and refined toward Kalypso, except during those rare moments of attention after he had begun to do microscopic work to her skin – or, rather, to the flesh that was under it. That only happened later, though. For days in which there were no other events for Kalypso, he farmed her skin.

'Communicate,' he would say. 'Yield over.'

One of his hands could cover her face, and did. His fingers and palm molded to her bone, shut out light from her eyes, gripped her skull. Dirt made his skin bitter. In the Dreamer you surrender to a distant level of consciousness because your senses are removed from you; you turn inward. But this was not a turning-inward, it was a turning-inside-out. He would remove her interface so that his hands took her senses almost all of them at once and she froze like a kitten in its mother's grip. She froze and left her self. She transferred her self outside to the flat uncoiling of color on the endless water surface.

At first this was very bad. Then she learned to let it be a kind of relief. When he engaged with her body she was spared the need to think or act because all control belonged to him. She watched her skin disappear and witnessed her own violation: the act was tangible and somehow reassuring because it could be measured.

It was the rest of the time that ate at her sanity. He sat for hours, motionless, and she mimicked him, unable to act on her own behalf – but all the while she was still thinking. Frantically. How can I escape. It took great effort to keep the breathing quiet – not to let a sudden thought register physically. Not to move her lips or eyes.

And then he would stand, stretch, and say, 'I think I'll check met. We're about due for a thermal.'

Regularly he watered Sieng through the suit's air intakes. Also he dangled her in the luma, suit and all, to heat her System. She was like a favored pet. When she was fevered, Kalypso was treated similarly, which she enjoyed despite herself.

Oh for a chance to redo that botched zzz.

He retreated into fugue. But the next day it got worse.

He began to re-apply Kalypso's removed skin to the healing patches of her body. Only now her skin was thick and translucent and bright with indigenes, just like Sieng. She choked and retched.

'What the fuck are you doing, Azamat?'

'Talking. I must talk. I must touch. I must know.'

'You can't. It killed Sieng. You think it won't kill you, too? Or me? Fuck you, Azamat, you won't kill me. Not this way.'

'To be perceived,' he said. 'In every detail. Every – ' he closed his eyes; his hands roved over his own body. Drumming.

Not this again.

His skill level had increased in the interval of time since he'd started this behavior before delivering her to Neko. Now he was like a cross between a Senegalese street child and a self-infatuated cabaret queen. He played himself. ' – moment. I'm going to have to restrain you now. It will be better that way.'

He reached for her in the half-hearted way people reach for their clothes in the morning while they're still half-asleep and thinking of something else.

Kalypso, for some reason instead of sooner, or later, or never, berked now. There was no rational component. She simply moved. She eluded his grasp and scurried toward the canopy seal. Her fingers ripped it open and she slithered out. One of his hands closed on her ankle. She held her breath and wrenched. The boat tipped hard to port, threatening to roll. Hot, fluid luma surged up and smacked her in the face; then she had no choice but to inhale because she was screaming. The air tasted like nightmares.

Marcsson had let go of her ankle. Everything tore and hurt when she moved, but she dragged herself across the hull. If she had any kind of idea in her head at all, it probably had to do with getting her suit back from Sieng, because she flung herself toward the corpse and began to undo the suit fastenings. Marcsson was coming toward her rather slowly, like a monster in a horror film: the embodiment of mindlessness. She'd begun to cough and pant.

There was nowhere to run. She leaned toward an interface that wasn't there.

Then she must have passed out.

Marcsson had her jaw in one of his hands. His lips covered her nose and mouth. He was blowing air into her lungs. She twitched spasmodically, coughed; he backed away. They were under the canopy of Neko's boat.

He had her interface in his hands. He looked at it and said, 'Give yourself up. I don't accept your distance. I don't recognize your boundaries, or your flags. Direct contact only. That's the way it has to be. What I wish for in the middle of the night. What I wake up gasping for, crying out for. I'll never never get it.'

All she could see was her one means of escape, held in his hands.

'Please give it back. Give me my interface.'

'No. Not you! I don't want to touch you.'

'Of course not,' Kalypso heard herself rail at him. 'You want to touch her. Always her her her. *I'm* alive. Please – ' What was she saying? She was *not* jealous of Sieng. She was not that fucked-up, not yet anyway. She steadied herself.

He clutched her interface in one hand. She thought for a second he would break it, and heard herself gasping as if he held one of her living bones. He put it in his suit, out of her reach. He was back inside himself. Marcsson could retreat beneath the folds of his own madness; but she was stuck being sane.

'It hurts,' she said. 'You're hurting me. Azamat. I need the interface. I need it.'

'I can't count the vortices,' he said. 'It makes me dizzy. Where was I? Ah, restraining you. Lie down flat.'

He moved some of the trays out of the way to make room for her. He said, 'I have to do this because the pain will cause you to thrash. It's possible you'll knock yourself out if you hit your head against this casing. I'm sorry about that. But I can't have a sedative in your bloodstream. It could compromise the result.'

'Don't tie me. Please don't. I'll hold still. I swear.'

She was disgusted with herself that she should still be capable of tears and pleading, but there it was. You never knew how low the lowest common denominator of yourself was going to be until you got down there.

He gave her a look that was very close to kindness.

'Well . . . ' he said.

'Please, Azamat. I'll be good. I'll be quiet.'

'I guess we can try it that way,' he said awkwardly. 'Turn over, then. We'll start with your back today.'

Kalypso wished hard for unconsciousness but didn't get it. Not enough of it, anyway. For a time that felt like years, she was feverish, but Marcsson kept giving her water and talking to her, and this made her stay awake.

And surely the fever warped her judgement, for she thought she heard emotion in his words; thought she heard lucidity. She didn't want to listen to his discursive speeches but couldn't really help it. His tone was cadenced and oddly soothing.

'Paradox can only exist inside a person. Math can only exist inside a person. Poetry. Sadness. One person no matter how irritating, boring, dumb or sick embodies it all. That's why you can never see or touch people. They're too big to see, no matter what the distance. Your sensing of them will always be indirect, compiled in your mind according to your mind's shape.

'All your life people pass through you. Some you don't notice. Some leave things behind. Some, collectively, erode you so slowly you don't realize it's happening. Some take souvenirs. Like collecting rocks from a nature reserve – no one thinks the missing item will matter. But one day you look up and you see that so many pieces of you have been picked up and carted off in all directions. You now live in other people whose movements you can't track, much less experience.

'It's possible to go your whole life without knowing this is happening. Instead just feeling a vague lack, a general whiff of entropy or loss. But if one person comes and picks up your favorite rock and walks away with it, suddenly you feel it. An invisible connection binds you to them. If you're really unlucky you've got something of theirs in the bargain, but you couldn't give it back even if you wanted to, nor can they, not even if your rock is kryptonite to them, destined to destroy.

'This is how understanding, aka love, takes you apart.'

He fell silent. She heard herself let out a sigh. Things that were said, things that happened – she had lost all ability to respond to them. She could only receive. The need to escape pain and disorder rose, stayed steady for awhile, and then rose some more; and just when she thought it had gone as high as it could, it went a little higher. But it never diminished.

She couldn't move, or he would tie her and she couldn't stand that. She didn't know what to do other than survive. All that was ever needed was more. More. More. Because it's never going to be enough. You catch yourself up every so often, thinking, surely I can't go any further. It's crazy to press on.

But where are you? In a grayness that will have you, make you become like it, if you stay too long in one place. So you draw on the dregs of yourself, resigned to disappointment as you are constantly reminded of how fucking little you've really got going for yourself. How limited are your resources.

But they never seem to quite run out, either, which prevents you from giving up. You scrape along, teeth clenched, devoid of finesse, but alive.

Things too small to see eat your cells. You accomplish nothing, but refuse to die.

And the pain, at last, begins to abate.

Marcsson says, 'The next stage. Good. We're making progress.' He opens Sieng's bag and reverently touches a dead hand. 'Sieng. Sieng. If only you knew what you are.'

That's when you decide: if you're dying anyway, you might as well kill him.

The logic's slightly dodgy, but under the cirx you can't really be blamed for that, can you?

eskimo for snow

'Why won't you give my interface back?'

She said it for the hundredth time, no longer expecting a response.

It was just another moment in a rotting pile of moments, none of them offering any hope of relief. For twenty minutes, through a gap in the cloud cover, the night was clear. Stars arrived. They were sitting back-to-back in the cockpit, the canopy lowered to reveal a view of the sky; he passed her his mask every so often so she could breathe. Parts of her body had become windows that let in bright color; but she just pretended she was wearing clothes.

She felt his voice rumbling through her ribs. She was no longer perturbed when his responses failed to relate to anything she'd said.

'Language determines the size and shape of reality. We have words for the things we consider important. The case could be made that, if there's no word for it, it doesn't exist for us.'

Pedantic, pedantic, pedantic. With the stars in the sky, even. Still: better that than the scalpel.

'The Inuit have dozens of words for snow. We have only one for love.'

Not so pedantic. She made herself smaller.

After a while he said, 'Kalypso.'

The stars receded. She couldn't sleep.

i'll be your kryptonite

Marcsson had stopped cutting her body open. He'd made her into a sampler of geometric shapes: parallelograms across her thighs, a triangle on her belly and a couple of diamonds on her back. Some of these flaps of skin floated in luma, still dark but beginning to be luminous. Others had been reintroduced to their former locations.

She had survived the fever and the wounds didn't hurt any more, but they itched. They were growing over with something that was not skin. It didn't resemble Neko's carapace, nor anything she'd seen among the Dead. The colors were the same colors that dominated Sieng's corpse; it wasn't difficult to conclude that Marcsson was trying to 'cross' her in some weird way with Sieng. She wondered if this meant she was going to die. But Sieng couldn't be infectious, or Marcsson wouldn't handle her so casually. Would he? Anyway, the infection that killed Sieng was not the same as the agent that had been used to produce Picasso's Blue.

Would she, too, become a farm for some agent? Marcsson studied her under the microscope for hours on end. He was still processing data.

'It's a microcosm,' he said. 'We have a match. We're really getting somewhere at last.'

He didn't actually seem malevolent at this point. In fact, life in the Wild began to get better. He treated her as a plant or other valuable, non-sentient resource. So she couldn't say he drove her to it in any of the obvious ways.

Most likely the loss of her interface was at the root of her violence. She had been afraid of it while she had it, but it was an escape of sorts, as well as a link to something other than Marcsson. She stayed awake waiting for an opportunity to overcome him; this wakefulness in turn translated into an increased hatred and irrationality, an increased determination to destroy. She had nothing else to focus on, so she trained herself to remain awake deep in the night, and to listen for his breathing. In this way she learned to tell the difference between his fugue states and real, organic sleep. She knew that disturbing him from the fugue state was dangerous; but if she tried to kill him in his sleep and he woke up, she might be able to make some excuse that would placate him.

There were times when she passed into a haze of thought, which resembled sleep but provided none of its restorative properties that Kalypso could ever detect. She emerged from one such interlude with the apricot dawnlight smiling all over the tentkit, the stones, the boat. The dull fire of it, defining Marcsson and the edges of her own skin, seemed macabre: or was that just her intention speaking to her eyes? He lay there like a human being, breathing as if he had a right to. She hated him. It would not be sufficient to disable him, or even to kill him. It would be necessary to annihilate him utterly.

She checked met. The temperatures outside were low enough to let her exit the boat without a suit. They were in almost neutral pH, with little current; the water itself was even within human tolerances. Perfect.

He had removed his suit and set it to charge for the night. She folded it stealthily, and then hid it.

She had given much thought to weapons. There were none. The air itself was all she had. She let it out of the seals slowly, admitting airmix from the surface. There was a small store of oxygen in an emergency bladder – enough for several minutes' careful use. She rigged this around her neck, sipping from it sparingly, and set about the task of getting her suit back.

Sieng was heavy, and hot, and repulsive to all sensibilities. The inside of the suit was stained with her and her limbs sprawled over Marcsson where he slept.

But Marcsson kept breathing, and breathing. Maybe he would stay this way forever; maybe he wouldn't die at all. The air indicators outside showed lethal levels of CO. How could he not be succumbing?

Paranoia crammed itself upside down and sideways into every second until she was bursting with it. She had to do something. She sealed the slime-coated suit around herself and began setting it to process oxygen, still breathing from the emergency bladder. Halfway through this process she became urgently convinced that Sieng had to go. Now.

She grasped the transformed tissues as best she could and dragged the corpse to the side of the boat, heaving it up and over the edge. It did not go easily. The boat shifted as Sieng's body slipped into the luma.

Marcsson jerked and sat up.

'Something's wrong,' he said. He wavered to his feet and fell against the console. 'A leak . . . ' He reached for his suit, saw it wasn't where he'd left it, and then turned numbing eyes on Kalypso. 'Where's Sieng?'

Kalypso pointed to the open seal. She wanted to see his face. She wanted him to suffer, and know she had done this to him. And then die. Nothing could ever give her pleasure, but this.

He reeled and caught the rim of the canopy as the edges of her vision started shrinking and she felt weak. She was running out of oxygen. Her suit was still programmed for Sieng.

With a resiliency he had no business having, Marcsson pulled himself against the console and powered the boat. It turned slowly and began going back the way it had come. He put a hand to his eyes.

'My suit.'

He'd never find it in time. They looked at each other. She could almost read his mind: he was rapidly weighing possible actions, seeking the economy of decision that would save his life.

Only it wouldn't save his life.

'You want contact?' she taunted, taking another breath of the planet's naked air. It smelled slightly odd but not deadly. 'You want the big love? Yeah. OK, I'll do that for you. I'll be your finale. I'll be your kryptonite.'

She shouldn't have spoken; now she had to reach for the oxygen bladder to draw a breath and he saw her do it. In a second he would take it from her and the tables would be turned – all because she had to gloat.

The boat accelerated. Act first –

Kalypso sprang up and threw herself at his knees. He fell back into the aperture of the seal, caught her hand and pulled her to the edge. She bit him. He let go and she slithered backward into the cockpit. The boat, which had been plowing through developing luma, now reached clear water, jerked, and surged ahead. Marcsson, half outside and half in, scrambled for a grip on the hull; failed. As he went down there was no emotion on his face – just a sharp, farouche concentration. Luma closed around him.

She could hear his screams dopplering into the distance as the moving vessel left him behind.

She reassembled the canopy with numb fingers. Monkey voices chattered in her head: she was not all right. Everything seemed dark, as if the day wouldn't get any brighter no matter how much time passed. She got the suit working and lay still, utterly absorbed in the act of breathing. When at last her vision cleared, the sky was full of rare yellow light, like a Van Gogh.

He had left the helm open. She changed course to retrace her route. She opened the canopy a crack and looked out.

It was a long time before she spotted the body. He was floating on his back like a seal. He had barely drifted. Sieng was only a few meters away.

She waited a long time. It was not as satisfying as she had expected. How would she know when he was dead? And would the bodies sink?

She went back inside and pulled off the hood, shuddering. She could still smell him inside the boat. The air had been completely drained and replaced and she could still smell him, as if his essence permeated the very substance of the boat and now oozed out again, to fill it, just as if he remained.

There was a pain in her side. Her eyes stung. She couldn't see Marcsson through the canopy, but she knew he was still there. He was watching, with dead eyes, dead breath.

Noises. A high-pitched squeaking, like a rabbit being tortured by a cat. It was coming from her diaphragm and throat.

The boat barely drifted. The colonial organisms in the water shifted and turned. Clouds moved. His body floated into view, slowly coming closer to the boat.

She opened the canopy again to look more closely. His face was blue. Violet algaics had attached themselves to his hair. She touched him. The suit told her his skin was hot, but she couldn't feel for herself.

How much time? She had lost all sense of this, had not even thought to check. By now she was crying so hard the hood fogged. She grabbed his foot and pulled. He bumped against the hull.

What are you doing. What. Don't.

She attached a line to his foot, and then to a collection winch. She began turning the winch.

Don't do this. Let it go. Let it.

Marcsson came back over the side. The boat yawed and bobbed. She had to fold his body with her bare hands to get him through the seal. He lay in a pool of viscous fluid at the bottom of the cockpit.

She sat down and put the breathing mask over his face.

She couldn't tell whether or not he was dead. She couldn't know whether or not she wanted him to be. Her throat ached with sobbing. Objects around her began to move and stretch. Her hands and feet pulsed. She put the mask over her nose again and panted into it.

Radio sounded on her interface. A minute voice said, 'This is Nocturne. *We're picking up your SOS. If there's anybody out there, please identify yourselves.*'

This meant something. She wasn't sure quite what, but decided to stay still.

She was still crouching and sucking at the mask when her boat was boarded. People she once had known wrapped her up and carried her to another boat. She didn't remember their names at first, and when they tried to feed her she was sick.

'Marcsson's in respiratory failure,' she heard one of them say. 'Get him oxygen immediately. Start resuscitation. Looks like atmosphere poisoning.'

'Kalypso? Can you hear me? We'll call your cluster immediately. They've been insane with worry over you.'

She couldn't speak.

'Her affect is very flat,' one of them said to the other. She remembered his name now. Van. Medical specialist.

'What happened to her? And where did that body come from?'

'Shh.'

They turned away and spoke in whispers. As if what they said could upset her.

deep-fried calamari

'I'm afraid.'

'You're safe now. You're with us.'

Words: but they didn't mean anything, not the way words could when they rose out of what was truly happening. Not the way the sky had meaning, or the sweep of the endless sea, or Marcsson's stilled hands after he had been rendered unconscious and lost the ability to move them. She should do something. Speak. Move. Bring herself around.

'I can't move.'

'You don't have to do anything.' Sharia was holding Kalypso's head in her lap. Kalypso's eyes were closed but her body had made itself rigid and would not soften. As a result, the motion of the boat jolted her. She felt inanimate.

'You don't have to do anything at all,' Sharia repeated. 'We'll take care of everything.'

Sharia loved this. Kalypso didn't mind if her misery was the source of Sharia's fulfillment: Sharia couldn't help it if she needed to feel important. If she was in her glory, then more power to her, Kalypso thought.

They had bandaged her damaged skin. It struck her as a stupid gesture on their part and she wondered if they were afraid of contamination. Sharia had not hesitated to touch her. Sharia, in fact, was doing all she could to put her at ease. But Kalypso was beginning to feel that this paralysis wasn't temporary. What if she could never move again? What if she could never ever bring herself to do anything? It was a possibility. She might rest, and lie still, and later continue to be unable to act. It could go on theoretically forever.

She pulled away from Sharia and stood up, bleary, uncertain. Clutching the frame of the canopy, she looked out across the Wild. She wasn't being rescued at all. It was simply that Sharia and X had been teleported into her nightmare and now they, too, were doomed. She started to say something to them about this, to apologize, when she saw something that was not Wild. She saw something made by humans.

Oxygen 2 was several miles from First, removed from the worst turbulence of the Rift but still within the major current of heat that wound away from the volcanoes. It had been constructed out of an engine of Ganesh, a tall shell standing on end with its base submerged and a scribble of glowing Works enveloping its exterior as if the red ink of T'nane's waters had reached up and tried to cross it out.

An agro baffle surrounded the factory at a radius of about 100 meters, acting as an effective thermal shield from the rocks below and a gas barrier from the air and water. Closer to the volcanoes than First, Oxygen 2 was in a more stable temperature zone than the station, and consequently the waters beneath the shield were green with life. Outside the baffle, though, the luma was highly developed: its pull on the hull of the boat was like the grip of a hand. As he steered toward the oxygen plant, Xiaxiang consulted a multitude of charts showing distribution of solidified luma, which had been known to damage boats on collision. It was rare for solid luma to push its way to the surface, but in shallower areas like this one, it sometimes actually formed structures reaching above the water. Kalypso saw the first of these in the gloaming of early morning: a translucent, amorphous mass rising from the glossy sea. It looked like a tumor. It looked like it might begin crawling around at any moment. It looked – in a diseased way – like a piece of First.

The waters around the factory were crowded with moored boats strung in a line outside the gate in the agro baffle.

'We have to go in by ferry,' Sharia said. 'There isn't room inside for so many boats; it's all used for intensive farming.'

Kalypso nodded, which was all she had been able to do, other than sit still, since *Nocturne* had transferred her to the boat of her own cluster. Instinctively, even Sharia knew it was best to talk simply, and of pragmatic things.

'We've been really lucky with thermals so far, being away from the Rift.'

'That's why we've been low on power,' X offered. 'We've had enough tempflux to get by, but we've needed to run the Works on maximum to get enough air and since all the adjustments have to be made by hand, nothing's very efficient.'

Kalypso tried to picture this: human beings sitting in stations in the Works of Oxygen 2, talking to each other and looking at dials, throwing switches, spinning valve-wheels – clumsily trying to imitate the coordinated homeostatic response Ganesh's demons could effect so easily.

'Remember Maxwell's?' X said wryly, reading her mind. 'Looks like we're the demons now. What a joke. Although . . . the good news is, not all of Ganesh's higher functions are down. Yet.'

Sharia amended hastily, 'Look, the higher functions aren't really higher. We just call them that because of the way our cognition's structured. Ganesh isn't layered hierarchically that way.'

'Yeah, fair enough. But the point is, the witch doctors can talk to it, a little.'

Sharia shot X an admonitory look. 'Don't get your hopes up, Kalypso. They still have no control over environmental, but the last we heard from him, Tehar seemed to be getting some contact linguistically.'

'Tehar? When?'

'We haven't actually had contact for a few days. But I'm sure he's OK. He's probably interfacing with the code.'

Marcsson was not on board. He must be dead. She shied away from thinking about him.

'The Dead,' Kalypso said. 'Have you seen them? Tehar said they were looting the station.'

'They've been keeping us busy,' X said. 'We've had to trade for food with them. They withhold Picasso's Blue from the Mothers, which makes life pretty hard.'

'Did they tell you how they make it?'

'Yes.' X's grim expression softened suddenly. 'They told us you're a lousy witch doctor, too. I have to admit to admiring them. They don't have a gram of shame. They take pieces of First and then try to sell them back to us in exchange for whatever portable stuff we've got.'

Kalypso smiled. 'They'll take you for all you're worth.'

'There was a fight. Between Jarold and this Dead woman called Charl. I thought Jarold was going to be killed. But they left him alone. They took Jarold's boat.' Sharia shuddered. 'They're so strange and vicious. I'm afraid of them.'

'Have they been inside Oxygen 2?'

Sharia looked at her as if she was mad.

'Of course not! They've been horrible to us, Kalypso. They kidnapped Lila – you know, cute little Lila, one of the youngest – '

'Yeah, they like us young and cute,' Kalypso said. 'Tastier that way.'

X turned and knotted his eyebrows at her.

'Well, they took her and it wasn't easy getting her back. There were about five or six Grunts plus Ahmed and Grendal and Tomimasa, and they almost didn't succeed.'

'Is there one called Neko?'

'Dunno. Look, we're just about here. Do you think you'll be able to walk, or should we bring a sling or something?'

But Kalypso was staring at a boat she recognized, cruising just beyond the baffle.

'Was that Malik? And Genn? What are they doing with Teres?'

'Them.' Sharia slitted her eyes. 'They can't be trusted any more. The Dead stole them with Picasso's Blue. They've lured that whole cluster away from Oxygen 2. They claim they can teach you to live in the Wild.'

'That's true,' Kalypso said absently. 'But – ' she was going to say something like, why weren't the clusters simply talking to the Dead? But Sharia cut her off.

'Don't think about it, Kalypso. It's not healthy for you.'

'They're sirens,' X chimed in with a leer, 'luring men to their deaths.'

'Oh, shut up. The Dead can't help being ugly. Anyway, so far we've lost only the one cluster. Conditions at Oxygen 2 are bad, but not bad enough to drive people into the Wild. What's disturbing is that those who have gone are helping to take Ganesh apart. I can't understand how they could be so faithless.'

Sharia would always be loyal to the Mothers. Her fundamental appreciation for order would prevail no matter what.

'Give me your paw, Kalypso,' X said. 'Let me show you into my parlor.'

The interior of the factory was largely given over to storage of the chemicals it produced: oxygen, nitrogen, and various polymers in small quantities. Oxygen 2 did not possess the refrigeration facilities that First did, even though its location was cooler: therefore, no liquid storage of gases was possible. Only two or three minor nodes of Ganesh regulated the entire factory, dependent on radio link to the rest of the AI. There was no luma. There were no windows, no Dreamtanks, no amenities worth mentioning. The small percentage of the interior devoted to human occupancy was not divided into cells. It consisted of the open space within the base of the gutted engine tube, threaded throughout by dozens of pipes and tubes like a giant cat's cradle. It was here that the refugees had been obliged to set up housekeeping. They had wasted no time in making a ghetto of the place.

Tents had been assembled high up in the piping; empty surface suits hung like scarecrows from twists in the tubes; barrels of water stood at intervals, surrounded by heaps of soiled clothing and dishes. Crates had been piled to create haphazard walls, and empty oxygen tanks turned on end made seats and tables. There were people everywhere. The air stank richly and the noise was reminiscent of a seagull colony at hatching time.

To Kalypso, it was the pleasure dome of Kubla Khan.

During her initial hours there, she was aware of the activity around her only peripherally. The sense of crisis had not relaxed since she'd left First, only now everyone was crammed into the same space instead of existing in separate, Ganesh-linked sections. The effect was chaotic and probably would have upset her in the old days; now it was welcome. She didn't even notice what it was everyone was running around doing; it was unlikely, she thought, to matter what they did.

Sharia took her to Van, the medical specialist from *Nocturne*. Kalypso lay on a crate while he made an assessment of her condition. Sharia brought out Marcsson's studies of Kalypso's missing skin and offered them for inspection.

Van took out a lightstick and examined her closely for long, silent minutes. He looked at each of the damaged areas in turn without saying anything, his expression emotionless and utterly involved at once.

'There are T'nani cultures. Looking at your bloodwork, I'd say you have been fighting these things off for some time. The damage to you is negligible, but there's no doubt that your tissue is no longer normal. These new layers that look like skin aren't skin at all. The epidermal cells are non-nuclear and they're assembled in matrixes.'

'Matrixes? You mean like luma.'

'Yeah, that's what I mean. There are tiny subs in there. No magnetosomes, but definitely an array of phenotypes. Some of these are so small and mobile they may have migrated to other parts of the body. They may be dormant. Without Ganesh, I can't tell you much, except to say that your body is no longer reacting as if threatened. What's interesting is the cells themselves. I'm going to take samples so I can look at the genetic material, but morphologically they look like a hybrid of human epidermal cells and, if memory serves, some member of the subclass *M. gemino*. It's not clear to me how the macro-structure is regulated.'

'Let me see.' Liet pushed past the others and sat shoulder to shoulder with Van, peering intently at Kalypso's left thigh. 'Yes! To be more specific, it looks like *gemino* 3 or 7. Those subs are exclusive to RV-11. Marcsson must have introduced them deliberately. We can't culture these in the Works because we can't figure out how they react at high temperatures . . . you say he used Sieng's tissues as a source for these cultures, Kalypso?'

'Yeah.'

'I've had a quick look at Sieng. I'd like to compare her cells with yours.' Liet turned her attention to Kalypso's skin samples preserved in gel.

Van said, 'That's easy. We'll get a sample and work this up. You can go, Kalypso.'

'That's it? I can go?'

Van smiled an apology. 'Look. I don't think this thing's going to kill you. However, it doesn't look like you're going to kill it, either.'

'Will I become like them? Like the Dead?'

His look was cautious. 'In what sense?'

'Will I make . . . things?'

'Picasso's Blue, you mean? Not unless the agents used to develop your skin are the same as those that infected the Dead.'

'We know that they're not,' Liet said. 'Kalypso has several different indigent systems operating. The ones on her back are not the same as the ones on her legs, for example.'

'I was an experiment.' She knew her tone sounded clipped.

'Your skin might be used as a factory for other agents,' Liet said.

Van was studying Kalypso's face closely. 'Time will tell,' he said. 'You shouldn't concern yourself with any of that now.'

Sharia murmured something in the medic's ear, and Van turned and conferred quietly with her. Kalypso heard Marcsson's name and tensed.

'He's alive?' she said. Her voice shook. 'Where is he.'

'He's not here,' Sharia said, too quickly, and Kalypso knew she was lying. But she accepted Sharia's words, her reassuring hands. 'Kalypso, you look weak. Do you want something to eat?'

She knew she was being coddled and didn't care. She nodded. Van went off to look at Sieng's body and Sharia went to fetch food, but Kalypso stayed where she was. Liet was lost in study of the skin samples, ripping her fingernails off one by one until she'd damaged the cuticles; then she would idly put a bleeding finger into her mouth and suck it. One foot tapped with no real rhythm and the muscles in her jaw could be seen working.

It was a familiar sight. Liet was thinking, and as trying as it was to observe, it might lead to some good. So Kalypso waited, and ate what Sharia and X brought. And waited longer.

'OK. Uh, Kalypso.' Finally Liet looked up and brushed loose strands of hair away from her eyes, which darted without finding focus. She fumbled with her words. 'Your skin. Sieng. For twenty years her body has been an interface. The Dead, they think of her only as a factory for the sub they use to trigger the Picasso's Blue viroid in the skin of the Dead. Just like we think of the System as a factory for oxygen. But Sieng's more than that now. The infectious agents that killed her have been battling over her tissues for years. She was submerged in luma all that time – god, I wish we had the luma fluid because it would be a record of every interaction, we could see the history like a movie but it's no use crying over spilled milk I guess – anyway when she was submerged a whole micro-System grew in her. Evolved. And her body became a translator between human biochemistry and the System. We're seeing forms in her that don't exist anywhere else.'

'Human biochemistry?' Sharia sounded incredulous. 'Sieng's dead. What kind of human metabolism can be happening?'

'She might not be metabolizing, but structurally, her body's being transformed. Her DNA's being reconstructed, broken down and made into something else, something sustainable. Sieng may be dead, but she's still running against the grain of entropy. Anyway, Kalypso's not dead and that's what counts. The cells that were grown in Sieng also attacked Kalypso, but they were repelled. Why? Probably because they were more comprehensible to Kalypso's immune system than the original indigenous subs were comprehensible to Sieng's body. Suggesting that a kind of path is being made between us and . . . and . . . well, and them.'

'*Them?*' X could be seen restraining himself from making a wisecrack.

'The only way to find out is to do more studies.'

'I don't want to be eaten,' Kalypso protested. 'Will it affect my mind? Will I become like Azamat? Is this why he's crazy?'

Liet looked startled.

'I don't know. I don't *think* so. I mean, we're talking about skin so far, not brain tissue . . .'

'That's what *he* said. It's only skin. I'm so big I'll never feel it.'

'You? Big?' X chortled.

'I'm not sure he was talking about me, though. He never looked straight at me.'

Liet's eyes had gone fuzzy. 'How do you spell epidermis?' she asked.

Someone told her. She put on her interface and wrote the word in the air. 'Uh . . . Tehar?'

'Let her be,' X said to the others. 'She's got an idea again. She'll be no use.'

'Is she talking to Tehar? Liet, are you talking to Tehar?'

Liet lifted the interface and shone a crooked, rather asinine smile on Kalypso.

'No, I can't seem to reach him. Um . . . I'm starving. Anybody else wanna eat?'

'Yeah,' X said. 'Good idea. Enough of this speculation for now.'

Again she had the distinct sense she was being insulated from reality, and again she did not protest.

Despite the best efforts of her nestmates, the Mothers resumed harassing Kalypso within a day. They were convinced Marcsson had told her his secrets. She'd begun to figure out that the current friction between the Grunts and the Mothers had to do with the idea of effecting an assault on First to shut down the reflex points. The Grunts continued to insist that, since the Dead had already started taking First apart, it was better to salvage anything that could be saved of the station. This would improve the chances of survival for the clusters, who were in turn beginning to venture out into the clayfields with tentkits to escape the confines and deprivations of life at Oxygen 2. Furious that the Dead had been allowed to manipulate the Mothers and make off with critical supplies, the Grunts began mustering support for a raid on First.

'They want to shut down the reflex points and try to take control of the Gardens and the Works, which are crucial for our survival. They say they don't give a fuck about the Earth Archives and I guess they have a point,' Ahmed explained reluctantly to Kalypso. 'But the witch doctors won't leave. Tehar says the station can't be run manually, anyway. It's too big and complicated.'

'The Grunts will attack anyway, sooner or later,' Sharia said. 'It makes sense. Tehar is being noble, but I think he's berking in there. Its time to cut our losses and move on,.'

The Dead guarded the reflex points and traded pieces of the station back to the infuriated Grunts in exchange for whatever goods they desired from Oxygen 2. They were far outnumbered, but no one had wanted to mess with them because the witch doctors said that if the reflex points went down, all would be lost. Meanwhile, the witch doctors tried to convince the Dead that the only way to protect Earth Archives was to keep Ganesh running.

The Grunts maintained the supply lines and said very little. Grunts never did anything in a hurry, and they were probably weighing their options and waiting for developments from the witch doctors within First. But no one had heard from the witch doctors since Marcsson had been brought back.

They avoided talking about Marcsson in Kalypso's presence. She understood that he was still in a coma, but interfaced. Liet had been going over his data and sending things to First. Yet Witchdoctor Radio, as Kalypso had come to think of it, remained silent.

When they learned Kalypso was back within their province, the Mothers wasted no time in pumping her for information she found herself reluctant to give. There was no ideological reason for her reticence; she simply felt too weak to speak about the Wild.

'It's simple,' Naomi declared. 'Just give us an account of what has been happening to you. We don't need you to interpret or theorize. Just the facts.'

Kalypso lowered her eyes halfway and looked aside in distaste.

'Don't hold out on us, Kalypso,' Lassare said. She looked haggard, if this were possible. 'You'll have the last laugh.'

Kalypso twisted her arms around herself and grasped her shoulder blades in either hand. Her clean skin felt slippery.

Sharia touched her head. 'Kalypso?'

'You wouldn't understand.' Her voice sounded like a man's. 'Couldn't I just have some music please. I can't do anything right now.'

'We just need you to talk. Sharia, don't baby her. She can take it.'

Sharia answered in a very low, calm voice, her fingertips grazing Kalypso's scalp. 'Lassare, in about five seconds I'm going to take Kalypso away and you'll never see her again. Don't tell me what she can take. We don't know what happened to her out there. Look at her body.'

'That's not like you Sharia,' Kalypso said wonderingly. Again the touch on her head. She closed her eyes.

Lassare said, 'Was Marcsson in communication with the other Grunts? What was their plan? When did it start to go wrong?'

Kalypso let out a long sigh. Not this sabotage thing again. 'He was doing his research. There was no conspiracy. He wanted to solve the Oxygen Problem and he fucked up. You knew what he was doing. You must have. You authorized him to work in that region. Did you think this wouldn't happen?'

Sharia said, 'Kalypso you don't have to talk about this.'

'You should have been stronger,' Kalypso said. 'You're addicted to Picasso's Blue and you're liars. You're damn liars, all of you, and you're weak.'

'Strong isn't enough,' Lassare said. 'I came to that conclusion a long time ago. I am strong; we are all strong who came here. We're stronger than anything we left behind. And it wasn't enough. You think we're weak because of the addiction. But addiction isn't a weakness. It's strength. It's a reaching out – '

'For some lousy hits of Picasso's Blue you kept them out there for *years*,' she said in a ragged voice. 'All the time I was growing up and you were applying your cluster psychology and Ganesh was imprinting our heads, they were out there. Farming their own bodies. Your colleagues. So you could feel strong when you weren't strong.'

'What would you have done, Kalypso Deed? Do you want to be unborn? Do you wish we had let you perish as an embryo?'

'They were the ones who could have solved the Oxygen Problem. They had the skills. If anyone could have done it, they could.'

'Sieng had already perished. They were all infected. We didn't know what we were dealing with. We still don't.'

'Give me music,' Kalypso said. 'I'm not talking without it.'

It was fun giving ultimatums instead of receiving them; it was fun doing this when your life wasn't at stake. Well, maybe it wasn't fun. But it was preferable to the conversations she'd had with Marcsson in the Wild.

And it got her what she wanted.

The next morning Ahmed came up behind her and slipped her interface over her.

'Music,' she cried, springing to her feet. 'How? How?'

'Tehar got the music node back a while ago. Said it was the easiest way into Ganesh. Something to do with your special pathway into the Dreamer. He's using it as a channel to Ganesh. Or whatever's left of Ganesh. I've downloaded and vetted it for you, so don't bother trying to get into the System because you can't. You're offline.'

She kissed him and then pushed him away, wrapping her hands around the face. She knew they were staring at her as she closed her eyes and paced back and forth in the narrow passage between supply crates. Through a gap in the containers she could just see a sliver of bright water beyond Oxygen 2. All she had to do was lean into the interface, and she could have music again. Every night and every day she'd craved it, and now. She could have it. She stood still.

Direct contact, Azamat said. *I'll never get it.*

She took off the interface and looked at the floor.

It didn't make sense. She had been rescued. Saved. This was the time for fulfillment, relief, recovery. In the Wild with Marcsson she had felt she would never need anything again, as long as she could get away.

She took a deep breath. Put the interface back on. Well, she needed this.

It was Bartok. Hour after hour, she let it take her over. It elevated her and convinced her she was caught up in something tragic, which was absurd but what else was there? The cluster, orphaned from Ganesh, sitting around looking at each other – how could she help but find them stupid, for they didn't know what she knew. Kalypso didn't know what she knew, either, or couldn't express it. She went in and out of the music, alternately seeking and rejecting numbness.

They watched her closely. They watched her as if she were a rabid animal. Just as they had been conditioned all their lives to do, the clusters hung together in family groups, isolated by piles of equipment and conduits; something in their poses made her think of bats in a cave and this made her think of Ganesh which made her sad but that wasn't the problem, she didn't mind that not really. What she minded were the looks on the faces of her cluster as she came out from under the music interface. Herself reflected in their collective demeanour.

She smiled and felt her cheeks stiffen with disuse. She shifted position to sit closer to them, next to Xiaxiang, and cast about for something to do. Her eyes fell on a makeshift pack of cards someone had made from used food storage containers.

'Hey,' she said. 'Anybody up for a little five-card stud?'

Her voice sounded really deep. She cleared her throat and started to shuffle. She could feel everybody staring at her but all her concentration went into the rhythm of moving the cards, the slip of them and the ease with which her fingers remembered what to do. She had a kind of sense of holding something back, but she didn't know what it was until Xiaxiang put his hand on the back of her neck and she was crying. Ridiculously, uselessly, pointlessly; but she couldn't stop.

Of course it was too late, now. It meant nothing.

She kept seeing Marcsson floating among the algaics. His peaceful face, like Ophelia in the flowers . . .

Eventually Sharia found some zzz and pressed it against her forearm. She swam in and out of consciousness, aware of the buzz of activity around her, rising and falling as crises came and went. They settled her in an unoccupied space among storage crates, where she slumped idly studying the muscles of her legs, which seemed to have atrophied some since leaving First. As the day went by, at least one member of the cluster was always with her, no matter what. She couldn't speak, of course, but from time to time her head cleared enough to admit an understanding of the conversations around her. There were frequent meetings, some involving only a few people, and others, it seemed, attended by virtually the whole colony.

Rumors had begun to circulate among the clusters. She heard them as through a veil.

'Ganesh has probably murdered the witch doctors.'

'An AI that sophisticated was bound to develop cognitive problems. Jacovitz predicted it on Earth ten years before Ganesh was even designed.'

'The Dead are just waiting for their chance to infect us.'

'Yeah, did you see Kalypso?'

'Shh, don't – '

'Robere's plotting something. I think the Grunts have made up their minds.'

'The Mothers have run out of Picasso's Blue.'

'The Mothers are stoned senseless on alcohol, Siri. It's up to us to make a move. We can't rely on them any more.'

At length the sedatives wore off and no one remembered to dose her again, so she sat in some rigging several feet above the floor of the common space, which was littered with puddles, and watched the action unfold. Her imagination had been captured by the doings of her comrades, as if she were watching a play.

Word had gotten out that a strike was being planned against the Dead; suddenly the atmosphere was galvanized. The difference between the Grunts and the Mothers was that the Grunts never engaged in histrionics. They never even discussed what they were going to do: they thought for a long time, quietly, and then just acted with a minimum of fuss. All of a sudden, things were happening fast. A knot of bodies had formed in the largest open floor space. The alpha-types of each cluster had gotten themselves down with the action, and the balance of the younger generation hung around the fringes, listening. The Grunts could scarcely conceal their euphoria at the idea of leading a knock-down-drag-out with the Dead.

'All right.' Robere raised his hands and addressed the group just as if he were announcing a drill or exam. 'We've formed a team which will be leaving at dawn for the station. Repairs need to be made to the Gardens, and we'll be harvesting as much as we can carry. If you're on the team, I've already spoken with you about your objectives. If you're not on the team, I'm about to give you the chance to get a piece of this.'

He paused.

'What about the Dead?' someone from Siri's cluster shouted.

'I'm coming to that. As some of you will have heard by now, we've just had an incident with the Dead this morning. Lassare contacted them and informed them that we have control of the corpse of Sieng. She offered to return it to them and to admit them to the colony with full powers if they would stop attacking the station and provide Picasso's Blue.' He paused, and his expression spoke volumes about what he thought of the second condition.

'They refused.'

Murmurs.

'In fact, they threatened to shut down reflexes if Sieng's body is not supplied immediately. They believe we intend to use it for some nefarious purpose of Marcsson's. They don't believe he's in a coma.'

'Haven't the witch doctors gotten through to them?' asked Siri. 'Don't they understand that if they shut down the reflexes, they'll ruin any chance for Ganesh to recover?'

'I believe,' Robere answered, 'that they figure if they can't play, we can't play. That's why we have to take them out.'

'You mean fight?' Whoever had said it sounded incredulous.

'If they force a confrontation, yes. There are only seven of them. They can't stand up to us. I don't think anyone here advocates violence, but the Dead have gone too far. What I'm looking for now are about five or six people to act as protection for the expedition tomorrow. Kessel will be leading the repair and recovery squad, and I'll be leading security. You need to be strong, aggressive, and not afraid of the Dead. I already have some of you in mind, but I'm going to make this announcement openly so nobody can say afterward that I was part of some kind of conspiracy. None of us – ' he gestured to the other Grunts ' – are trying to coerce anybody into doing anything. So. A show of hands?'

Kalypso couldn't help but laugh as a thicket of hands went up. Who wouldn't want a chance to act after being stuck here all this time?

Ahmed stepped forward.

'Robere, why are we fighting over Sieng's body? If they want it so badly – and, you have to admit, they probably have a right to it – why not just give it to them?'

Noise. Everybody talking at once. The echoes shot up the sides of the enclosure; partials flew among the piping like butterflies. Kalypso stopped her ears.

Robere held up a hand again and waited for quiet.

'Because it wouldn't end there. They have not offered us any terms. They have merely made demands. If we give them Sieng's body, they will control everything. And they will be able to make as much Picasso's Blue as they want, which means that the Mothers will play right into their hands.'

'They're sitting on the reflex points, Robere. You think they're bluffing?'

'Wait for the witch doctors!' the small botanist called Lila interrupted in a weak soprano.

'Wait for the witch doctors?' countered Siri in a withering tone. 'We haven't heard shit from the witch doctors for days. For all we know they're dead. It's time to go in and get the Dead away from First before there's another thermal. If they shut down Ganesh, we'll knock them out and boot it back up again. At least that will give us some control of manual emergency systems.'

'Jianni was supposed to have done this,' someone else put in. 'He was going to turn off the nerves.'

'Jianni died trying,' Robere said. 'Look, we can't all talk at once. Let me make a proposal without interruptions, and then we can fight about it. All right?'

Silence.

'Now. What Siri says is correct. We've avoided risking a shutdown of Ganesh, but given that the witch doctors have not succeeded in getting the station up and running again, the risk no longer seems so great in comparison with the chances that the Dead will permanently disable the station with their vandalism – or that there will be heat damage to the farms and Gardens. We've been lucky so far, but luck doesn't last for ever. I know that the witch doctors have got a few nodes back on their feet, but they aren't the essential functions we need. And some of the nodes have suffered a second crash. Obviously there's a problem with com, or we'd be able to get Tehar on the line and let him have his say. We simply haven't had contact, and we can't just sit here and do nothing. We're going to recover everything we can. We'll get the bridge of the ship shielded and secured before the reflex points come down. So – you want to debate? Go ahead. I'm taking volunteers, though, because we don't have time to make a decision by committee.'

'Speaking of which,' Ahmed said wryly, 'what do the Mothers say? Why aren't they speaking?'

Everyone looked around. The Mothers had removed themselves from the scene and were scattered around in odd corners of Oxygen 2. At length, Rasheeda stood up.

'We don't support this action,' she said. She opened her mouth as if to add more, closed it, and sat down with a drunken air of dignity.

Kalypso happened to be looking at Kessel; his expression was homicidal, and for a second she flashed a memory of Jianni and wondered what would be different if he were here now.

Robere said, 'We leave at dawn. Those who want to have a debate, I don't need you. I need people who can contribute. I'll assemble a team just inside the main doors.'

He turned and pushed through the crowd. As hell began breaking loose, Kalypso's cluster retreated to the space they had established in the shadows beside some water barrels, leading Kalypso softly by the hand. She could feel them thinking around her, but they seemed impenetrable to her now. The cluster had finally become a unit: the plans created for them long ago on Earth had been fulfilled. They were a single thing that groped around itself, a whole made of pieces that had fused over time thanks to proximity and good psychology. Now they were limping toward something with each other: some understanding that would make them powerful.

But they couldn't understand the Wild, no matter how they tried. And she couldn't understand them – not any more. She had been scrubbed too close to the bone, shaped into something that no longer fit among people.

She regarded them each. Xiaxiang. The giver. He couldn't help it – his generosity was compulsive. You wanted to make him stop but then you'd realize that without him you would implode under the weight of your own self-absorption. So you'd try to penetrate his focus on you and turn it back on him, to find out what he was *really thinking* underneath that kindness and goodwill. And you'd find out he was like that all the way through.

Liet, who always seemed to have misplaced her own head until you asked her something she knew, and then you found out she knew *everything* and would tell you. Sharia: alpha female and Class A worrywort. Sharia would never drop the ball. Each of them registered inside Kalypso almost as an archetype; but she saw them now from outside the circle.

Ahmed, who could always be counted on to be direct.

He appeared from out of the crowd and said, 'We have to make a decision. Either we back the decision to invade, or we throw our lot in with the Mothers.'

Tehar. No way of knowing what to think about him.

And Kalypso.

'Decision? What decision?' Sharia was flushed with emotion. 'Did you see the Mothers? They're . . . they're . . . they've finally – '

'Loco,' Liet put in. 'Deep-fried calamari.'

X said, 'We need to get Tehar out of First. It bugs me that we haven't heard from him.'

'Ganesh,' Kalypso heard herself say.

Ahmed touched her face and made her look at him. 'We know you tried to kill Marcsson. What we want to know from you is why.'

'Is he going to live?'

'Last I saw, he was in a coma. His interface was still functioning, but they have no idea whether he'll regain consciousness. He was taken to First at Tehar's insistence. Kessel had to smuggle him in when the Dead were distracted dealing with Lila and her cluster.'

Kalypso nodded.

'Tell us why you did it.'

'It must have been terrible,' Liet offered, her melting eyes following Kalypso. 'To make you do it.'

Kalypso drew a breath and found herself saying, 'No, there's nothing gut-wrenching at all about destroying another person if you're convinced it's either you or him. It's like a switch.'

Kalypso could hear herself breathing, fast and loud, as if she were climbing hard in First; doing a big, fast climb before a big, fast joy. The old days.

Liet pursed her perfect red lips and said, 'Could you be more specific.'

'Killing's a form of bondage. I still wish I'd done it. I want to be bound. Held down. Pressed to the ground. It would give me something to be, somewhere to go. I could be a killer.'

She knew what she meant but even in her own ears she sounded berkers. They were all staring at her.

'What? *What?* Why do you stare?' She realized she had signed it when she could continue to hear her own rasping breaths as the words came out. She couldn't seem to stop breathing. The more she did it, the more she had to do it. Things went pale and fuzzy.

Sharia grabbed her hand and slapped her face.

Kalypso snarled, seized Sharia by the hair and threw herself at her cluster-sister, biting and scratching. Sharia screamed and doubled over, Kalypso was picked up bodily and dragged away, still writhing, spittle flying.

'Enough,' Xiaxiang was saying repeatedly in her ear. She was screaming, throat on fire, as they tied her up. She kept thrashing until everything hurt and she couldn't breathe. Then she subsided into something like catatonia.

'You didn't hurt her, did you?' Liet asked.

'She's a danger to herself, and to us,' X replied. 'She needs to be quiet. Let her alone. Maybe she'll sleep.'

Tears oozed across her face.

'Don't get upset,' she heard Ahmed say to Liet. 'She's just a little berky. She'll come out of it.'

'He's right,' Sharia said, recovering.

'Did you read that in the manual?' X snapped. Then: 'Sorry. It's just a little unnerving when someone loses it like that.'

'See what happens if you touch her now.'

'Leave her.'

'No. It's not safe to leave her. She's been traumatized. She needs contact.'

'You touch her.'

Ahmed's hand on her back. Tears. His arms encircling her; his heat.

'Sharia, come here,' Ahmed commanded.

Sharia, trembling, sitting close and putting a finger on Kalypso's wrist. Kalypso lifted her head and put it on Sharia's lap. Sharia held her.

a priori fucked

They gave her the greatest gift they had. They immersed her in Earth – whatever had been salvaged from Ganesh and stored in their interfaces. Model airplanes and wooden furniture; lampshades and slowly spinning ceiling fans; bowls of grapes and silk-covered boxes; the sound of thousands of birds settling in the tops of oaks on their way north, blackening the sky (no, no – no black skies please) adobe and sage and empty plastic bottles and tire tracks.

Teres said, *none of it's yours.*

What was real then? The lines cut straight and true by Marcsson's knife. The burn of bilgewater riding along her tensing thigh. Wind shuddering the canopy. Futility.

No one's going to hurt you.

It will be all right.

Take care of Marcsson.

The ability to withstand paradox is over-rated. It would be better to collapse and forever after eat with a spoon. Sometimes it's good to be angry but at times like this it's better to be quiet.

They had decided to back Robere. Ahmed, in fact, was going to be on the security team. No one mentioned Ganesh. No one said much of anything. It was going to be a long night. Liet occupied herself with her interface, probably still studying Sieng's tissue. Sharia dozed off. Kalypso shivered but thought nothing.

X crooked his finger at her. 'C'mere, Kalypso. Your body temperature's all messed up. I'm going to give you a bath.'

There was no shortage of hot water, and the cluster had a barrel they used for washing. X made her get in. He handed her a piece of soap, which she examined dispassionately.

'You could pretend it's a rubber ducky.'

'Go away X.'

He started humming 'Take the A Train'.

'This is stupid. It's a waste of water.'

He plucked the soap out of the water and started scrubbing.

'The way I see it, Kalypso, is Better You Than Me. If you're crazy, you're crazy. But if I'm crazy, I can't tell whether you're sane anyway, and I probably don't care, being too self-absorbed to notice even if you paint yourself a new color. No offense.' He poked gently at the yellow patch on her back.

'I am not insane.' Her voice vibrated oddly as he was rubbing her back hard. 'I'm perfectly capable of washing.'

'Maybe I want to do this. Maybe it's a grooming ritual left over from when we were pack animals and I was the pack leader and you were just some insignificant beta female.'

'We were never pack animals. This whole cluster thing is artificial.'

'Please. I can't believe you don't remember. You were Lassie and I was Rin Tin Tin. You were Snoopy and I was Scooby-Doo.'

'Snoopy was male.'

'Ah! But did you ever *see* his genitals? Time to rinse.' He planted his hand on top of her head and forced her under. She came up choking, eyes tearing.

'This is not a way to get clean.'

'I prefer you dirty. This is all just an excuse to tell you about my theory.' He began slowly massaging her scalp; she closed her eyes. Pleasure.

'Are you ready? Because I've been waiting and waiting to tell you this and I need your full attention.'

She didn't respond.

'OK. So. My theory is, the starting point for the decay, decline and ultimate dissimulation of rock and roll into the more generic sea of industrial commerce is located in George Martin, the Beatles' producer. He was a frustrated musician. Plus, he had ideas. Lousy combination. With him bringing his stuff to the material, the locus of power had shifted from the performer, whose job it was to be childlike and sexy, to the producer, whose job it was to be in control. Now, as soon as you take the power away from the primal source of creativity, you have to invent terms such as "creative control" to take its place. As soon as you remove the reality, you have to invent the word for it, in other words, so as to explain what's missing. Take "Baby You Can Drive My Car". Can you honestly tell me that's a better song thanks to that rinky-dink piano riff in the chorus? Of course not! It's cheez whiz. That riff subverts the natural, unadulterated hipness of the tune in the name of being cute. What I'm saying, Kalypso, is that because of the meddling of George Martin you ended up, decades later, with the concept of the dance remix, and then the radical reinvention of the familiar by rap and the art of the rip-off – yes, I know, you could argue rehashing is intrinsic to musical history, it's just like jazz but Kalypso, I've been thinking about this a lot and the fact is that it had become intellectual by then, it had to. No matter how pretentious *Yes* were, at least they were sincere. They had to be. Nobody knew any better in those days. So – my ultimate point? Here it comes. What I'm saying is, the essence of helpfulness is decay and destruction. It starts with sneaking in an unnecessary piano riff and it seems harmless enough, it even seems profitable. But it's bad news for daylight, it's the coming of the big darkness. Now, go ahead. Tell me I'm wrong. Say, "X, you're so wrong and here are all the reasons why."'

'X you're so wrong.'

'Why? Why? Give me one good reason. How can you possibly refute my obviously clearheaded rationale?'

'Because technology was going to make all those things happen anyway. George Martin, all he did was fuck up some songs.'

'Well. That could possibly be true. But Kalypso the consequences. The consequences of even *one* fucked-up-by-George-Martin song.'

'The consequences are one fucked-up song.'

'And that's the saddest thing of all,' he intoned significantly.

'If you're finished with my therapy for now, I'd like to get out of this water. It's getting cold.'

'By all means, by all means. But I've helped you. I know I've helped you. See? That was a pissed-off look you just gave me.'

'No, it wasn't.'

'I helped you! I helped you!'

'The essence of helpfulness is decay and destruction.'

'Ah, you *were* paying attention! But that was just bullshit. Fine. You want to pretend to be unreachable? Go ahead. I won't tell anyone. But you and me both know – '

'X don't say it. You'll make me sick.'

But he had already begun, wringing his hands for effect as he spoke: 'Even one little, small, runt-like fucked-up song is one too many. Don't be fucked up Kalypso. Don't let it happen.'

'Can I go now.'

There had been a time when Kalypso couldn't see the point of sleeping without Dreaming – without Ganesh. By now, though, the behavioral conditioning of her youth had been overrun by the primitive and powerful instinct to retreat into unconsciousness when bored, overwhelmed, depressed, or sick. She had embodied most of the above conditions in varying combinations ever since being rescued from the Wild; so this was how she'd been spending her time. Day and night didn't much matter on T'nane, but it was not long after dawn, and the departure of the assault team, when Tehar's voice shocked her awake.

He wasn't actually present, she realized groggily. It was a transmission of his voice from First. All other activity had stopped. Lassare was on the radio, but someone had rigged amplification and their conversation blasted throughout the factory.

Tehar was saying, *'We have a situation on our hands.'*

'You wanna tell us something we don't already know, baby?'

'I mean,' Tehar resumed, *'that what happened to Ganesh is a little less obvious than we hoped. There was no sabotage. There was no accident.'*

'Are you saying Ganesh did this to itself?'

'No.' Pause. 'It's a little worse than that.'

'Well?'

Tehar's voice wasn't all that clear over the air, but Kalypso felt empathy as if he were right up against her in Ganesh. She could hear his consternation.

'It's got to do with Azamat Marcsson.'

'I told you, Tehar – he's in a coma. You can't depend on getting anything from him.'

Static. Lassare made an impatient gesture at the speaker, but of course Tehar couldn't see her.

'Marcsson's data is – well, it's singular, to say the least. We've been looking at the material he's compiled on the boat's storage facilities; it's had all of us occupied all of the time. That's why we haven't been able to communicate with you. We think we have re-created the incident that started all this. It began when Ganesh first interacted with Marcsson's data in the Alien Life sim. Something woke up.'

'Something woke up.' Lassare at her most deadpan.

'I can't think of any other way to put it. There's a form of life loose in Ganesh.'

'A virus? A sub-personality? What do you mean?'

'The data on the Oxygen Problem were interpreted statistically by Ganesh, and that interpretation either necessitated or resulted in or caused – it depends how you look at it really – let's say it caused a form of mathematical thinking which triggered a reaction in the station's luma, causing the crash. The AI infected itself with an unknown – for lack of a better term – cognitive paradigm. It started thinking . . . different. That's the source of the unreadable code, the noise, the crash.

'Come again?'

'Look, we already know the System on this planet is alive and could be treated as an organism in its own right. Evolving. Adaptable. What we're seeing now is intelligent behavior. Maybe even some kind of consciousness.'

'Intelligent?' Lassare's incredulous tone.

'By applying intelligence to the System, we can extract intelligence from it. If we can learn its language, we can communicate with it. Maybe. But the more immediate problem is what to do about Ganesh.'

'Yo, back up. How can the System be intelligent? Yeah, it's complicated; we recognize that or we'd have solved the Oxygen Problem long ago. But it has no CNS. No senses.'

Liet said, 'Don't be silly. You don't need a CNS and senses to have intelligence. That's just a crutch.'

'Liet, be quiet. Tehar is talking.'

'Well, you have a point, Lassare. I'm describing what I'm seeing, but to tell you the truth I'm not sure how to get around the lack of CNS . . . '

'Tehar, it's simple,' Liet scolded. 'The CNS and the senses, this apparent dichotomy between inside and outside, abstraction and reality: these are a consequence of our special evolution. Each of us is a turned-inward bubble, a curious piece of the world's topography. The universe communicates with itself via you. But you can't empathize with a thing whose structure is founded on different principles. You must rely on counterintuitive means. You must rely on the rational, and of course the rational is based on the physical as you know it – kind of a Gordian knot. Ganesh doesn't have this problem. It can find meaning in statistics that your senses can't grasp and your mind can't organize, because Ganesh has only one sense: a reaching toward the abstract, a math-sense. And it translates this into our five senses – but Ganesh is more than human and it can learn paradigms that are physically impossible for us.'

Everyone was gawking at Liet. Several people looked annoyed.

Naomi broke in. 'Are you saying there's an *alien intelligence* on this planet?'

'I don't know,' Tehar admitted. *'I mean, that's a question of terminology. But there's something here which can't be explained away by our presence.'*

'I'll need to see physical evidence.'

'What do you consider physical? Lassare, by its very nature this thing I'm talking about, this alien, exists only in thought, in Plato's realm of the Ideal if you will.'

This sounded familiar to Kalypso. She had the uneasy sense that Tehar had been listening to Marcsson; but that was impossible. Marcsson was catatonic.

'If I will? No, I won't, thank you very much. Plato? Give me a break. If it isn't actual, then how can we perceive it?'

'Because Ganesh acts as a lens for us to see into structure. Ganesh makes mathematical concepts real.'

'Mathematical concepts are not intelligence qua intelligence.'

'This one is. What I mean is, this form of mathematical thinking is behaving like a living organism. It's a pattern that breaks itself in order to grow. It's showing strategic behavior and it's shown, I believe, signs of self-consciousness via Marcsson.'

'Marcsson was in a coma.'

'He still is. But you should see the readouts I'm getting off him. Lassare, he's still interfacing.'

Kalypso pricked up her ears. She felt an occupational itch to witness what Tehar was describing.

Lassare brushed this aside.

'I fail to see how a bunch of prokaryotes could demonstrate intelligence even by the most liberal definition.'

'Look,' Tehar persisted. *'It's not that the* flagrare *are intelligent in themselves. They can't even live independent of the luma system. That's why Ganesh would never let us call them organisms, remember? I'm not saying there's anything resembling a neural system here.'*

'Then how can they think? What you're talking about, it implies thinking. It depends on thinking.'

'It only depends on your thinking,' Tehar replied, his voice rising in frustration. 'You can't understand what you can't understand. You want to extract something from a phenomenon and hold it up to the light, see it in your terms. But it can't be seen by you. Ganesh can see something you can't see.'

'Where's your evidence?' Lassare demanded. 'Where are you getting all this?'

'The evidence is inside Ganesh. Look, I don't care if you call it an alien, I don't care whether you think it arises from the System or just materialized out of nothingness, but there's stuff happening in Ganesh that is not mathematically comprehensible to me or to anyone else who has looked at it. It's not human thought. It's something Ganesh has synthesized by studying the information Marcsson fed it. And, possibly, by using the information in his subconscious to guide it.'

'You think Marcsson understands it?'

'I don't know what Marcsson does or doesn't understand. I don't know what capacity he may have to communicate. I don't know how much of what has happened to him is available to his conscious mind – if he still has one. But he was in the Dreamer when he entered that data. It passed across him, and to a lesser degree it passed across Kalypso Deed.'

'No it didn't,' Kalypso said, but no one heard her. 'I don't understand math.'

'Since that time, his behavior changed radically. I don't know if what happened to him is the equivalent of what happened to Ganesh. I don't know why he's in a coma.'

'Oxygen deprivation, according to those who examined him.'

Liet looked at Kalypso. Kalypso looked away.

'Well. In any case, I simply don't know. I can see from the code that Ganesh is being rewritten and I know it's not a simple thing, like a virus. It's not just rewriting information. It's rewiring the way of thinking. Do you understand the distinction? Eighty per cent of Ganesh is luma storage. But the twenty per cent that's core is what determines our ability to interface with Ganesh. It's a tragedy to lose data, especially the material from Earth that we all see as precious. Yet what I'm saying is that we're going to lose more than data. We're going to lose Ganesh entirely. Ganesh's entire way of thinking is threatened. It's going to cease to be able to communicate with us, unless we can find a way to communicate with it. Do you understand?'

'What are you going to do about it? Sit back and watch it happen?'

'I'm trying to communicate with Marcsson via the face. All I can hope is to use his knowledge, his understanding, his perspective, to establish control.'

'Are you getting anywhere?'

'Not yet. But I know he's Dreaming.'

'Tehar, we're gonna talk about this our end,' Lassare said. 'Give us a little time.'

'Right. I've got my hands full here anyway. I'm out.'

Static. Then silence.

No one said anything at first. Then X laughed.

'Alien? Alien? It *can't* be an alien. There are no SFX.'

'He's got a point,' Sharia said. 'We can't even see it. How do we know it's there?'

Lassare was back on form. Her voice was clear and full of conviction.

'It's not bad news at all. It doesn't have to be. Listen: the ecosystem has an intelligence; it speaks a language. We're going to learn it, exploit it, make it work for us. We'll teach it to think the way we tell it to think, and it will produce oxygen, and cease to produce carbon monoxide, and we'll transform the atmosphere and turn our attention away from the Oxygen Problem, so we can begin harnessing the thermals and using this planet's energy sources to serve us.'

This was the Lassare Kalypso had always known, glimpsed through a parting in the alcohol.

A tentative voice: Lila, the small one who'd been kidnapped by the Dead. 'But what about *it*? What about the so-called intelligence?'

'There is no "it",' Naomi put in abruptly. '*It* is an abstraction existing within Ganesh.'

'The data came from the planet.'

'Let's not panic. There's no alien out there, kids. It has no existence independent of the neural structure it finds itself within – in this case, Ganesh.'

'Neither do we, actually,' X said mildly.

'Yeah, what does that have to do with anything?' Siri put in. 'You're talking about raping its mind. You're talking about – '

'Surviving,' said one of the Grunts who'd stayed behind to keep an eye on things. 'Lassare is talking about surviving.'

Kalypso had forgotten to be traumatized. She stood up.

'But is there an alien or not? Is there something behind this paradigm or logic or whatever you want to call it? I mean, Marcsson is more than his language. He's the thing that speaks, not the speech itself. We don't know who – what – is speaking when he opens his mouth. Or used to.'

'All of that's debatable.'

Which debate had already started, severally.

'Does there have to be a separation. Couldn't there be a thing that exists, lives, only as an abstraction?'

'Isn't that what Ganesh is?'

'No; Ganesh has a size, and a shape. And we made it. We know what it is.'

'We used to.'

'This is going to be something different. A different way of being.'

'But how was it made, and what of? Evolution . . .'

'No. No.' Rasheeda waved her hands. 'I can't think any more. All of you figure it out. I can't.'

'Anyway,' X said thoughtfully, 'we're not seeing or touching it, except through Ganesh. Or through Azamat, in theory. We're getting a glimpse, not even a glimpse, just a reflection.'

'For that matter, it only takes form through the statistical manipulation used by Azamat,' Liet said. 'He massaged it into being. So it only exists through our math.'

'Math is the same everywhere.'

'There's no way to prove that.'

'Enough!'

X said: 'What would it mean to solve the Oxygen Problem now?'

'Marcsson talked about language,' Kalypso murmured. 'He talked about giving instructions to the System.'

'He can't talk now. Oxygen deprivation.'

Kalypso felt her hands clench into fists. X put his arms around her.

'Like I said.' Lassare raised her voice over the discussion, which was intersecting itself and losing coherence. 'Here's the point. We talk to it, we get it to stop fucking with Ganesh maybe. Or better yet we find out how it works. How the System works. How to tell it to stop producing CO and start producing oxygen. This Crash is an opportunity to change everything.'

Liet stood up, stumbled over someone's outstretched legs, and raised her hand, waving it around even though everyone was looking at her and waiting for her to speak.

'What is it, Liet? What do you have to say?'

'Uh . . . ' Liet saw that she was in the center of attention and flushed. 'Um, if it has no existence independent of Ganesh, and the Dead shut down the reflex points, then . . . what will happen to the alien?'

There was a sudden change in the mood even before anyone spoke. A deadening. The boats had left for First. The mission was under way.

'Does anyone know? What will happen?'

Ahmed put his hands over his face and scrubbed.

'Not good,' he said. 'The reflex system – it'll wipe whatever's there. Everything but the root programming in the Core. I'm pretty sure. Call Tehar and ask him.'

'Goddamn it all.' Naomi's mouth had become a kind of short-hand, like the sewn indication of absence peculiar to rag dolls. 'What kind of idiocy is this? What are we trying to save?'

'Is it too late? What are we doing? Does anyone have the faintest idea?'

Panic is virulently contagious. Suddenly everyone seemed unable to cope. The younger generation fell silent in the face of the Mothers' emotion.

Lassare put her hands across her face as if to ward off the words, turning one cheek as she cried, 'Don't don't don't don't turn that way. Just don't. We can't help but go on. We'll paint by numbers over this planet's ecology if we have to. We'll make it ours.'

'*Après moi, le déluge*, homegirl,' said Rasheeda in a sister-amen tone.

'Guilt will consume you.'

'It's not about guilt,' Rasheeda said.

'Why don't we just overwrite our own programming? Wouldn't that be easier? Write in suicide instructions and end it neatly.'

'Who cares about neat endings if everybody's dead?'

'You must remember this: a kiss is still a kiss.'

'If Neko couldn't convince herself to die, what makes you think we can? Or the children? They won't – '

237

'They won't survive without Ganesh,' Naomi persisted. 'Look what happened to the little one. Kalypso.'

'Everything we do is destructive. We can't help that. It's our nature to destroy things but we might as well have pleasure in the bargain.'

Siri got in between Lassare and the radio. Her voice rang out through the amps.

'Tehar, there's a team coming out there to get the Dead out of First before they can ruin it completely. Is that going to endanger you?'

'Get the Dead out? The Dead are sitting on the reflex points like they're trying to hatch eggs.'

'Yeah, well, it might mean a temporary shutdown but since you say Ganesh is in trouble anyway – '

'No! Siri, don't let them. You can't shut it down now. We'll lose the whole thing. We don't even know what it is, or what it's in the process of doing to the Core. It wouldn't be safe to lose power.'

'Catch-22,' Siri answered. 'What are you gonna do when the next thermal comes?'

'I need time,' Tehar said. *'Look, let me talk to the others. Call off this attack on the Dead though. Please. I'm going out now.'*

Ahmed sighed. 'That's what I thought.'

'The itsy bitsy spider went up the water spout.'

'The Myth of Siphilus, is that what you're trying to say?'

'Maybe they'd do better without Ganesh,' Rasheeda said. 'Maybe they need to make their own myths.'

'Make them out of what?'

'It's a relief in a way,' Lassare said. 'We can take our hands off now. Doesn't matter what we do.'

'It's not my fault,' Naomi shouted. 'I was just doing what I could do. I won't accept blame.'

The next thing everybody knew, Naomi was ripping off her clothes and kicking them in random directions. She began to howl and eventually collapsed in the fetal position, sobbing.

'I should be so lucky,' Lassare said. 'Couldn't we be more original, Naomi? That's a textbook berk you're indulging in.'

Rasheeda stood looking down on Naomi.

'Why you little animal,' she said.

'Should we help her?'

'I can't be bothered.'

'Is there more booze somewhere?'

'No,' Siri said. 'You've all had enough.'

'Is it true that you're disenfranchising us then?'

'I'm afraid so,' Siri answered. 'You have nothing useful to contribute.'

'Suicide is looking kind of spunky.'

'I didn't push out seven babies just to commit suicide over a little. A little. You know. Whatever.'

'It would be an anticlimax.'

'Everything's an anticlimax. Life is just *this happened* and then *that happened* and then *nothing much happened* and then *something else happened*. We never smoked our cigars. We never got our moment of glory.'

'What percentage of the station has actually been removed or ruined?'

'That's scarcely an argument for suicide.'

'About fifteen per cent I guess.'

'You don't *need* an argument for suicide. Arguments are irrelevant – *therefore* suicide. Not even therefore. You don't have to involve logic at all. Just do it.'

'You go first.'

'I had no idea it was that bad. How long can the Works function?'

'And what are they doing with the parts?'

'The Works need Ganesh.'

'Some of that fifteen per cent has got to be melted luma. Attrition from the well.'

'I'm not saying I want to. I'm just thinking out loud.'

'Well, don't.'

'I hate these meetings. We never get anything done. Can I go now?'

'Go where?'

'Oh yeah.'

'I want to play.'

'Ants don't play. Azamat told me that.'

'Altruism only makes sense for haploid organisms.'

'Sssshhh – the O word.'

'Organism? Organism organism organism. Eco-fucking non-sense I'll use the word if I want to. System bollix. Ants are organisms and so are we.'

'Ants are cuter.'

'Would it help if they were our kids.'

'If they looked and smelled like us you mean? DNA.'

'I doubt it.'

'Well social obedience can be carried too far.'

The noise of someone vomiting broke up the conversation.

'Earth is gone forever.'

'It is safe to say that.'

'Better gone forever than present but unreachable.'

'I disagree.'

'Semantics.'

'I am overflowing wih love and joy,' Rasheeda said. 'My heart yawns wide and includes you all. I am not threatened. I am not broken.'

The vomiting stopped abruptly.

'I heal,' Rasheeda cried. 'I am the light.'

'OK, suicide could be an option after all. But only if it's violent.'

'That's enough,' Siri shouted. 'All of you shut up. We're going to get on the radio and stop Kessel. It's that simple.'

'They're maintaining radio silence. So the Dead won't detect them.'

'Then we'll go after them.'

People started to move; instinctively, the strong ones among Kalypso's peers edged away from the Mothers, avoiding the scene of their breakdown. The conversation turned to practical matters. How to recall the two boats that had left. Who should go. What to do instead of attacking the Dead.

Kalypso sat down next to Lassare. At first she didn't think the Mother even noticed her presence, but after a moment she began to talk quietly. The conversation rattled on, but Kalypso and Lassare sat in a bubble of mutual attention.

'You children talk of Dreamer deprivation; you talk of missing Ganesh. You want your environment, your context: it makes you yourself. You'd deprive us of our paradigm, just as we're about to deprive this planet of its logic if we can. We were meant for Earth. Why do you think we use Picasso's Blue? It gives us back what we lost. It brings our old memories closer, our hopes, and it pushes the nearby stuff away. We can tell the stories we want to hear about life on this planet; and Picasso's Blue ratifies them. It's – '

'Institutionalized delusionry,' Kalypso intercut.

'It's what's made us believe. Without it we couldn't have gone on with taking care of you. We needed to believe what we were doing was right.'

'So you believed it by telling it to yourselves, with the aid of a drug. But it was all lies. Everything was a fiction created by you.'

'If you can maintain a fiction long enough, and well enough, it becomes a truth.'

'So that's it? That's your lesson to me? What about love?'

'Love? What makes you think I should care about you? I brought you into a world I can't control and I knew it. It was and is my responsibility. If I let myself care about you, I have to take you on, and you're doomed. The grief of your life.'

'You're supposed to be a mother to us. That's what you've always purported to be. If you loved us, you would tell us the truth.'

'I am a mother, insofar as it's possible to be under the circumstances. But mothers are not capable of love, not in the way you want to believe; and especially not on this planet. Men can love because none of this is really their fault. It's out of their hands as far as they can tell because they have the capacity to stand once removed from the reality of existence. Men are at liberty and luxury to love. They stand bemused before the universe and wonder about it and feel love. Not us. Not a Mother.'

'You're not making any sense,' Kalypso said, but she didn't especially mind. 'Just like Marcsson.'

'Poor Azamat never stood a chance. I remember him so well. We were practically kids, not even thirty when we were selected. He was picked for the team because his career was in ruins. He'd had an accident and ruined his eyesight. He couldn't do close detail work any more; had to start over.'

'His eyes are no good.' She remembered this much.

'He used to be a myrmecologist. Studied ants. That's what brought ants to my mind just now; he never got enough of talking about them. You think he could put you to sleep talking about the System? You should have heard him talking about formicine ants. You could sleep for a year on his lectures.'

'How could he get so excited about such tiny little things?'

'Some people believe life's in the details,' said Lassare. 'Not you, of course. You like it big.'

'Ganesh was big. And if it's ruined by this, what can replace it?'

'Your imagination fails you, Kalypso. The Wild of this planet is the biggest thing. The witch doctors are forming a bridge with an alien way of mind, a paradigm we've never known, but we'll know it now, thanks to Ganesh. Thanks to abstraction, language, translation. Thanks to Marcsson, if he succeeds. This is the biggest thing you'll ever know.'

'No,' Kalypso said suddenly. She could feel herself about to become stubborn and irrational. 'You're wrong. The biggest thing is a human being. We're so big we can't even be seen.'

Lassare stared at her. She gave a laugh that was half-scorn, half-uneasiness.

'We're *nothing*, Kalypso. Haven't you learned? Don't you see how easily we're shattered?'

Kalypso studied the lines and softnesses of Lassare's face. 'What's going to happen to Azamat? This alien of yours has been eating his mind. What's going to become of him?'

'He could be a hero, if Tehar uses him well. He's going to teach Ganesh the meaning of the language that is rewriting it. And when Ganesh understands, we'll be able to solve the Oxygen Problem.'

'What about Marcsson. Do you think this alien thing can rewrite his mind and he can still survive?'

Lassare wavered. 'He should survive long enough to provide Ganesh with the correct associatons. That's what we've got to hope for.'

'But he'll be destroyed. And the thing that's eating him – it will die, won't it? Because it will have killed its host. They'll both be destroyed.'

'He's already infected. It's only a matter of time.'

'A priori fucked. Just like all of us. And you stand by.'

'Kalypso! After what he did to you. After the narrow escape you had. What are you saying? You should be glad it's going to be over. You hate him.'

'Yeah.' She leaped up. 'How many words for snow, Lassare?'

'On this planet? We don't even *have* snow. Where are you going?'

home
sweet
home

Sharia was having the time of her life telling people what to do. Kalypso tapped her on the shoulder.

'Get me into contact with the Dead,' she said. 'Now. If Teres understands that the Earth Archives are in danger, she'll never shut down the reflexes.'

'The witch doctors have been trying to tell her this all along. The Dead don't want to listen.'

'They'll listen to me.'

Sharia, flushed with excitement, plainly was grabbing at any excuse she could find to deny Kalypso's demand. 'Your interface has been programmed to lock you out of everything but music.'

'Well, reprogram it.'

'Kalypso, it's not that simple. We're in a crash. What do you want?'

'Never mind,' Kalypso said. 'I need the Dreamer anyway. Do you understand? I need to get Teres and then I need the Dreamer. Sharia. Get me in. You have to get me in.'

X felt her forehead.

'Cut it out,' she said. 'I'm not sick, and I'm not joking. I have to get into Ganesh. Don't you see this changes everything?'

'All right,' Sharia said. 'Calm down. Let me see what I can do.' She stepped up on a storage barrel and whistled for attention. They were all well-trained to respond to such prompts, and they gazed up at her as if she were a conductor.

'We need to buy the witch doctors some time,' Sharia said. 'Look: Tehar's getting a handle on this *thing* whatever it is in the System. It's only a matter of time before he can work with the new code as well as the old code. We're talking about solving the Oxygen Problem here, but more immediately we're talking about returning Ganesh's sovereignty. Once Ganesh has regained consciousness, it will be able to defend itself from the Dead and the weather and anything else this planet can throw at it.'

Listening to the conviction in her ringing tones, Kalypso couldn't help thinking Sharia was going to make a hell of a Mother one day. If.

Van spoke up. 'We don't have time. Kessel and Robere are going to get in there and mix it up with the Dead. Sooner or later somebody's going to hit the reflex points and whatever the witch doctors are doing is gonna get trashed. Whatever Robere says about diplomacy, we all know how it's going to be.'

'Then we have to stop them,' Sharia said. 'And save Ganesh.'

'Save Ganesh. You make it sound so simple.'

'It is simple,' Kalypso said. Her voice, lower and richer than the others', cut through the talk. 'Let me talk to the Dead. I know how their minds work. I need to reach them.'

She had by now acquired a certain mystique as a result of having been lost in the Wild and having subsequently berked off in-definitely to Some Other Place. The whites of their eyes showed when they looked at her.

There were a few inconclusive murmurs.

Sharia said, 'OK, enough talk. It's settled. We're going to stop Kessel and Robere. We'll figure out how as we go along. Now. Who's in this with me?'

Another reshuffling of bodies as the clusters prepared for action. Kalypso stood in place while the tide of people moved around her. Someone was breathing on the top of her head. She glanced up. Liet was picking her lip and humming. She looked puzzled and a little dazed; not unusual.

'Kalypso, do you really think you can convince Teres?'

'I doubt it,' Kalypso whispered. 'But I'm not going to sit back and let them blow the reflex points now. Liet, can you bring all the work you've done on Sieng and me?'

'You want *me* to come?' Liet looked terrified.

'Please.'

Liet's eyes rolled up beneath her brows as she thought. 'I've got lots of good stuff,' she said. 'I've got everything I took from the boat.'

'Bring it all. It could be useful.'

Sharia brushed past, shouting instructions. She drew a quick breath and muttered, 'I hope you know what you're doing, Kalypso.'

Liet and Kalypso exchanged glances. Liet read Kalypso and sprouted a little smile.

'It's OK,' she said softly. 'I don't usually know what I'm doing, either.'

She was back on a boat, one as crowded as the funeral boat where the Dead had made Picasso's Blue. Only the mood was distinctly upbeat: Kalypso's peers still approached the Wild with the can-do attitude promulgated by the Earthborn, and Ganesh. They didn't know any better. In a way, this made it easier for her, since otherwise all of the trauma she now associated with boats and the Wild would have surely undermined her confidence.

And she was – suddenly, unreasoningly, inordinately – confident. She felt almost reckless.

She was going back into Ganesh at last. Vows to stop Dreaming notwithstanding, it was all she knew how to do. The closer they drew to First, the stronger she felt. Several boats ranged across the water: no one had really wanted to stay behind, now that something was finally being done.

'I feel like a Viking,' Xiaxiang said. 'All I need's a blond wig.'

By some miracle, the Gardens were still alive. They radiated the dim cloudlight, the emerald heart of a dead or dying city. Even from here she could see that enormous sections of luma were missing. The better parts of two legs were gone entirely, crippling the architecture: where they had been there was nothing now but steam.

Rain cascaded off the Works. If they were operating, they did so at a low level. As for power: all lights were out. It wasn't a good sign, but it didn't necessarily mean that the reflex points had been shut down yet, and when Siri interfaced she said there was still action on the System. She just didn't know how to interact with it.

The boats of Robere's team could be seen drifting at the base of the structure: they had probably entered through the Gardens. As for the boats of the Dead: one of these floated near a damaged leg. It was too distant for Kalypso to identify its occupant.

They conferred about the locations of reflex points and discussed the infiltration plans of Robere's team. What would be the best way to get in communication? Could they attempt to negotiate with the Dead themselves, rather than simply botching what Kessel and Robere were trying to do?

The caldera had been ripped open and rain poured in. Sulphuric acid would be eating into the Earthmade structures, but sliding off the luma unscathing. Memories of Earth were being consumed, but the native substances would survive.

'I'm taking us in,' Sharia said. 'We're going to have to work our way through the station until we find our people. Still no response on radio, Van?'

'Not from our people. I think they've powered down. They'd be telling us to shut up, otherwise. I can hear the Dead transmitting, though.'

'How?' Kalypso said. 'They can't speak.'

'They tap in code.'

'You haven't sent any messages explaining why we're here, have you?'

'Of course not. All we need is the Dead getting into the Dreamer ahead of us. They might mean no harm; then again, we don't want to find out the hard way.'

'I'm going for leg seven,' Sharia said. 'We can break in that way. Kalypso – '

'I'm going up the outside of the caldera,' Kalypso said. 'I hope somebody thought to bring climbing equipment.'

'It would be a lot safer to climb inside,' Van said levelly. 'There's no need to create extra danger.'

'Kalypso's right,' Siri contradicted. 'We have no way of knowing what's happening in there. There are no coms inside, it's dark, and the vandalism may have made the transit tubes weak.'

X caught her eye and held it. 'But Kalypso. You haven't climbed anything for weeks. Be careful. Save the heroics for the Dreamer.'

She said, 'There aren't going to be any heroics.'

The other boats had gone directly to the Gardens. Liet and Kalypso snailed up the side of the leg, using ropes to satisfy Liet's safety bug even though the surface suits themselves could grip the luma. The movement of the boats on the water beneath was silent and slow. Everything, in fact, seemed to be happening in slow motion, and the fact that there was no visible evidence of events within the station lent an air of menace to these long, wearying minutes.

X was right. She was soon exhausted. Liet took the lead, her longer limbs propelling her faster; she stopped several times to wait for Kalypso. Unit 5 was just below the caldera, which was now an entry point since it had been damaged. She did not expect it to be guarded. When Liet halted, splayed across the broken dome, Kalypso was too winded to speak, so she crawled up behind and gave Liet's ass a shove to get her attention.

Liet turned her head and signed, 'There's someone in there. Maybe they expected gliders.'

Kalypso panted for a while before she went to the edge of the gap and looked down.

It was Teres.

Kalypso signaled for Liet to stay put. All her life she'd wished to be bigger, but never more so than now. She really wanted to knock Teres down and hurt her. With that in mind, she climbed into the caldera and let herself drop.

Teres looked startled, then amused.

'My chickadee,' she signed eloquently. 'So happy to see you here. What are you doing?'

Kalypso got to her feet, rubbing a bruised hip.

'I have to talk to you. About the Earth Archives.'

'Ah, you mean the archives you got lost in? When you were pretending to be a witch doctor. Those archives?'

'Yes. Teres – '

'Your people have brought this on themselves. You betrayed us. You betrayed Sieng. I should kill you where you stand, only it's against everything I've ever known.'

Liet said, 'Kalypso can't help it if Marcsson overpowered her. You should see what he did to her. She'll look like you one day.'

Kalypso waved at Liet, hoping to silence her. It didn't work.

'Anyway, Sieng's more valuable as a source of ecological data than as a mine for Picasso's Blue. There's a whole mathematical system to be inferred from the System via Sieng and now, Kalypso. That's what's caused Ganesh to berk, and that's what the witch doctors are working on. But it can't survive if you shut down the reflex points.'

Teres was looking unusually vicious. 'All we care about are Earth Archives. It's too late in the day to be thinking of new mathematical systems.'

Liet said, 'If you shut down the reflexes, Earth Archives may or may not be preserved, but without the mind of Ganesh to process them for you, they'll be of no use.'

'The Core will remain unchanged from the day Ganesh was built.'

'No it won't,' Liet sang, oblivious to the fact that Teres looked ready to kill. 'The Core's been breached, infiltrated with the new paradigm. You take down the reflexes and everything goes down. Nothing comes back.'

'That's impossible. How can you know such a thing.'

'I've seen it,' Kalypso said. 'I've seen the condition of the Core. I'll show it to you. Come into the Dreamer and I'll show you everything. I'll show you there's still something left in there, even if we don't know how to talk to it. Then you decide whether you want to keep provoking the Grunts. They're here to destroy you, you know. They don't care about the reflexes. They don't even care about Earth Archives. They want survival hardware so we can scrape by in tentkits.'

Teres engaged in a long exchange of tapping across the radio. Finally she said, 'What is it the witch doctors think they can do?'

'They hope to communicate with whatever's in Ganesh. They hope to learn its language.'

'I'm suspicious of this ploy to get me in the Dreamer.'

'I'll make you a bet,' Kalypso said. 'You come into the Dreamer, and if it turns out that I'm lying, that what I've said isn't true, then I'll be your slave for life.'

'And what is it you want from me?'

Kalypso said, 'If you see for yourself that the Core is no longer impervious to outside influence, then I know you won't shut down the reflexes, which is all I want.'

'I won't promise that,' Teres said. 'It might be a trick.'

'Fine,' Kalypso said. 'Be that way – I don't give a fuck. If I win, I want the cigars.'

Teres threw back her head and emitted a rattlesnake laugh.

'All right, my little slave.'

Kalypso had occasionally bent the rules at poker, but she'd never hedged a bet.

Well, there's a first time for everything.

'You're on,' said Teres.

They shook on it, hand to claw.

'Call off your people, then,' Kalypso said.

'Call off yours.'

Liet was already on the radio to Robere.

'We have the station surrounded,' he said. 'Nobody gets in or out without my knowing about it. How much time do you need?'

'Dunno,' Liet said. 'Couple hours, I guess.'

'I'll give you an hour, then I'm calling you. I need results by then, otherwise I'm moving in while I've got oxygen.'

Liet looked at Teres. 'One hour,' she said. 'We'll take your word for it that you're telling your people to keep the reflexes up for that time.'

Teres was tapping away. 'My word is good,' she signed. 'I will meet you at – where was it, Kalypso? Unit 5?'

Kalypso was already standing on the edge of the transit tube. 'Yeah. Rem2ram, Unit 5. Bring the cigars, Teres.'

Teres smiled. 'You will make a lovely slave.'

'Come on, Liet,' Kalypso called. 'Jump.'

It was not a joy that took them to Tehar; it was a dark and bleak rush down transit tubes that showed no neural activity. Liet had determined Tehar's location, and she led the way with the ease of a lifetime's familiarity with the crawls. The hatch to the cell in question was closed and sealed; they pried at it with their fingers to get it open. Then Tehar was grabbing their hands, pulling them into the cell where he'd been holed up all this time. He closed the seal and stood back. Liet flung herself at him. They embraced. Tehar looked at Kalypso over Liet's shoulder even as his hands stroked her back.

'It's a jungle in here,' Kalypso said, pushing aside fronds of high-oxygen plants. The cell was stuffed with supplies, gas canisters, and other gear. There was little room to move. Tehar had released Liet and was studying Kalypso. She returned his gaze levelly.

'I thought we would fall into each other's arms,' he said. 'But . . .'

He looked exactly the same. It was as if nothing had happened. But everything had happened. She played with the leaves of a plant, at a loss.

'Yes,' she said. '*But.*'

Liet was unaffected by this exchange, which was far from unusual. She poked among the equipment.

He shook himself slightly. 'We don't have much time. I'd better take you up to rem2ram. It's not going to be like you remember. Think you can handle it?'

She looked at the floor. 'Yeah. I can handle it.'

Liet said, 'Come on, then. It's downhill from here, Kalypso. You can rest when you get in the tank.'

She clambered out of the seal. Kalypso began to follow but Tehar stopped her. He reached out and tugged her hood away. His hands touched her bare head. Then his lips.

'This is going to be over, Kalypso. Then. After. You and me.'

She repeated, 'This is going to be over.'

They slid through inert luma toward Unit 5. Kalypso's courage had headed south some time during the moments in Tehar's cell. Seeing him had brought something back to her which she'd been tougher without. Somehow through all these trials she'd held on to the belief – however deeply buried, however illogical – that Ganesh would always be there. The AI was a stable collection of reference points, a blueprint for how and what to think. Kalypso's ability to take conceptual risks had always depended, whether she acknowledged it or not, on the trust that there would be a home base to touch. A place to come back to.

But it was different now. Everything was. The station lay in ruins. Somewhere in here was code; electromagnetic fingerprints; physical evidence of the ideas that gave her and her people their identity in this world. Was Ganesh there, too? What if it wasn't?

Where would she turn?

When they got to Unit 5, Liet did the preliminary checks on the Dreamer while Tehar took her to the tank she was to use.

'Marcsson has been interfacing for days,' Tehar said. 'I haven't been able to get to him. I don't know what you're going to find.'

'I'll be all right.' The atmosphere in the room had been well-maintained by the witch doctors. Kalypso peeled off her suit.

He didn't look convinced. 'Ganesh is dead. You need to understand that before you go charging inside. There is no more Ganesh,.'

'But how do you know? It was never technically alive in the first place, so how can it be dead?'

'You'll have to take my word for it.'

'But I don't.'

'Kalypso. I've seen the code.'

'Then how did Ganesh and I communicate all that time I was in the Wild? How did you and I interface? How can the tanks be functioning?'

'They aren't. Whatever is going through the processors now, it's not Ganesh.'

'Just like whatever's going through Marcsson isn't Azamat, is that what you're saying? But it is. He's still in there somewhere.'

'Semantics, children,' Liet sang. 'Kalypso, I need your body over here. I'm putting you in the smaller auxiliary tank. Not as luxurious, but you're small enough not to mind.'

Teres came through the hatch. She approached the Dreamtank from which Marcsson had made his last, fateful run, gliding a horny fist along its smooth side. 'It's been many years since last I Dreamed,' she whispered. 'Since the Crossing. What a sleep that was.' She climbed into the tank and Liet attached the connection points.

At length, Kalypso got in her own tank. Tehar was pacing, his body visibly shaking.

'Kalypso. Don't think you can get friendly with the interface. You can insist on calling it Ganesh as long as you want, but it doesn't know you and it isn't your friend.'

She tossed her head. Her strength must be coming back after all, because she said, 'No one knows me. No one's my friend. I'll be fine. Move over. I'm gunning Teres, and you're gunning me. Make it good. I don't have much patience for amateurs.'

Another bullshit sandwich, Kalypso, and Tehar will see it for what it is as soon as he starts looking at your vitals. Heart racing, trembling, legs going taut. But Tehar was apparently busy just maintaining the face; she hoped he'd have the skill to see her through this. Liet adjusted the points and smiled at her.

'Right now we need to get to the Core, show it to Teres in terms she can accept, and then get out before we hit trouble,' Tehar said. 'Can you suggest a path?'

'Where's Marcsson? Can you detect him?'

'I haven't been able to catch him, and you certainly shouldn't try. Keep your mind on what you're doing. Teres is an inexperienced Dreamer and you've got to give her clear signals.'

Teres's whisper was amplified by the acoustics of the Dreamer unit.

'Azamat is there? Take me to him. If he is to blame, then let him explain what he has done to the Archives, and the Core.'

'That's not a good idea,' Kalypso said. 'He's dangerous and so is Ganesh. Let me take you on a little tour and you can see the Core.'

'Stop talking to me like I'm some kind of idiot.'

'You talked to me that way in the Wild.'

'You *were* an idiot.'

'And you're an idiot here, so shut up.'

'I'm not doing this your way, Kalypso Deed. Take me to Marcsson, or the bet's off.'

Tehar said, 'I'm taking you on the same path you used for your music. Only it's not going to sound much like you remember.'

'Take me to my home node,' she said, and closed her eyes. The lid of the tank came down and her senses left her. 'Home sweet home.'

fire

She didn't know where she was, or where Teres was in relation to her, or if anyone else knew where either of them was; but she was so relieved to be Dreaming that she forgot about the Dead woman almost immediately.

I am inducing you. Let your thoughts go free.

Surrounded by fluid, semi-conscious, feeling vaporous; argentine bubbles rushed past her face, swelling and breaking on her skin. A chaos of water.

Statistics.

You could carve the math of water in stone and make it stand still. Not a problem for the likes of Ganesh.

Keep thinking. Don't verb yet. Almost there.

Simulate a simple operation in a dynamic system such that a person, using five senses, can pick out its salient mathematical features. You can do it easily if you know what you're looking for. But to make the data speak when it seems you've got nothing but interference. To learn a language without knowing what any of the words refer to, and to begin speaking it . . .

You'd sound crazier than Marcsson. At least he had syntax. At least –

Shit. Was that what had been happening to Marcsson all this time?

She verbed, 'Tehar? Language. It's about language, and what language refers to.'

Yes, that thought had crossed my mind.

Teres was generating images of the ship's bridge as seen from inside. Through the viewport was darkness punctured by stars.

'Take me to the Core,' Teres verbed clumsily.

I don't know how to get there any more, Tehar verbed in response to Kalypso's request.

'Where's Azamat?'

Last time we tracked him, he was in the Core. But nothing's where it's supposed to be any more.

'Can you get me into Alien Life?'

Maybe. Hey, maybe you could lure him there. Then he might lead you back to the Core.

'Sounds sketchy.'

You got a better idea?

'No, I don't have any ideas, good or bad. What do you mean, lure him? Lure him with what?'

She was already back in something resembling her home node, but the sand was made of static. The water wasn't water, it was the smell of decaying fruit.

Liet's giving me some of the data she collected from Sieng. He won't have seen it. Maybe you can use it as bait.

Fishing in Alien Life. How appropriate. Teres had appeared. She was near the shed, looking at the ruins of the rescue craft and laughing. The data started appearing all over the place, stylishly gift-wrapped.

'Hello, Sieng,' Kalypso said. She began gathering up the presents. Watch out. Something's coming.

A cormorant popped up from beneath Alien Life and bobbed around. Marcsson parted its head from within and crawled out. He took the boxes away from her and dropped them in the pockets of his lab coat, whence they were assimilated.

'You can't do that!'

But of course he just had. Things had changed in these parts if a doze could count coup on a shotgun and not the other way around.

'Don't come here,' he said. 'I took your interface. Now you're back. Don't you ever learn?'

'No,' she said. 'I never learn.'

'You want to understand. But if you understand, it will take you over.'

Keep it steady. We're getting some good stuff here. Azamat is definitely displaying some of the same cognitive signatures as Ganesh. This is fass.

'Take me over like it's taken you over? I'm here to help you.'

'Then give me Sieng. I need Sieng.'

Teres came up beside her and asked her who she was talking to. Kalypso ignored her.

'They're going to shut you down. The Dead think they can still save Earth Archives. They think they can get what they need from the remains of Ganesh.'

'I am Ganesh now.'

Whoa! What was that? Kalypso I'm cutting stimulation. Your body's going apeshit up here.

As well it should. 'If you're Ganesh, then you'd better start paying attention to your perimeter because you're being invaded.' It was true. Things were flying out of Alien Life, attaching themselves to Azamat's body, and melting into him.

Don't forget about Teres. The point is to show her what's happening.

Kalypso had the inexplicable urge to touch Marcsson in the Dream. She resisted. 'What's happening to you, Marcsson? Why were you so cruel to me?'

Teres is getting bored. Don't fuck this up, Kalypso.

'You tried to kill me,' he said. 'But you didn't. Why.'

Teres stirred impatiently. 'Kalypso, I don't see anything. I don't feel anything. Where's this proof of yours?'

'I don't know,' Kalypso said to Marcsson. She began walking into the water. 'I really have no idea.'

Damn. Robere's on the line. Our hour's up. Kalypso, make something happen.

Teres grabbed hold of Kalypso's hand. 'Where are we going?'

Don't go into Alien Life, Kalypso. You're losing Teres.

'Come on, Teres,' Kalypso said. 'Be brave. It's only Dreaming.'

Kalypso, cut it out. Keep hold of Teres. I've told Robere we can -

'This isn't Alien Life any more,' Marcsson informed her, although she'd already guessed. 'It's the Core.'

'Too late, Tehar. We're already there. At least, it smells like an old suitcase.'

Hey Columbus this don't look like India. Where are the elephants?

She didn't know who said that but addressed Marcsson.

'That's enough, Azamat. You're on my turf now and I'm not having this from you.'

Kalypso, Teres just woke up. She's pissed off. What the fuck do you think you're doing?

The Core of Ganesh felt very much as it had during Azamat's ill-fated Dream run, but Kalypso herself must have become inured to sensory trauma because she no longer allowed the puree of concepts to distract her from existing.

'This is everything in Earth Archives, isn't it?' she said incredulously, beginning now to understand. All kinds of stuff was flying by at high speed; some of it slid off, some of it tried to tangle her.

She swatted at a swarm of data as it tickled her eyes, and it pulled her into the midst of a camel train: flies everywhere and everybody was dressed in black and she was . . . what *was* she?

Beneath the robes and the sweat and the smell and the heat, below the embodiment, a kind of sound or other less obvious sense. Inside the bones: a resonance. It called her and her own structure began to sympathetically throb and then soften, liquefy. Mute.

I'm not a thing any more. I'm a function whose tail lashes its face, a parasite that kills the host and itself. I don't belong here.

His vacant and sexual gaze. Preying. That stumbling in the gait which signifies illness, nearness to death.

On the ground. Now. You shouldn't be doing this, but are. The pleasure of distance. You cannot know what is being experienced in those aching, blackened teeth. I'll teach it to excite you.

He said: I'm only close enough to scare you. If I were any farther away you wouldn't see me at all – but I would still be there, eating you. The metabolism of my existence involves the devouring and reconstituting of you.

Kalypso we've just had half a node come up! Whatever it is you're doing, keep doing it.

Shit. She didn't know what she was doing.

'Azamat, are you ever going to speak to me in terms I can grasp? I think you owe me. What's the purpose of this? What's it got to do with the Oxygen Problem?'

Sensory deprivation

We were looking for order and we found it. Or it found us. What is my purpose? It has no purpose, it just tries to live despite being beaten for no reason. There's no purpose to me. Something has me in its grip and I try to live. That's all. I'm not big enough to hold it. You like big things, Kalypso. You don't want anything to do with me or any other human being. I can teach Ganesh how to solve the Oxygen Problem. I can finish the Dream we started.

She can feel pressure in her ears, big water being held back by some invisible force. The rate of flow is increasing. Earth Archives will spill over into the only empty space left: her. Unless she does something. First day of Shotgunning 101: change the imagery, and you control the Dream.

'We are on a submarine,' Kalypso suggested. 'Earth Archives are outside in the water. The hull is strong.'

And they were. Or rather, she was. He remained annoyingly discorporeal.

Kalypso what are you doing? You can't just start building stuff. Teres has just ordered an attack on the Grunts. We don't have time to play games.

'Marcsson, I said we're in a submarine. Get in here. Quit hiding.'

He sat at the periscope.

'Very nice,' he said. 'Let's be cordial about this. Why not? There's nothing else left.'

'Can you teach us to understand the System? Is it something we can communicate with?'

'That depends on Ganesh. Right now Ganesh can't understand you and you can't understand it.'

We have trouble at reflex point 4. Kalypso, you're going to have to come out.

'Case in point,' Marcsson said. 'I don't want this thing shut down any more than you do. I live here now.'

'How? How? I don't understand.'

'I don't want you to understand. Just go on being stupid, Kalypso, or it will get you, too.'

'You're using Sieng's data. How.'

'It's part of a bridge. I'm learning the chemical sequences to engage the planetary System on its most basic level. So that when I give it a command, it must obey.'

'It commanded Sieng,' Kalypso said. 'You tried to tell me but I didn't get it. The System commanded Sieng and she died.'

'I thought you were Sieng but you turned out to be much larger. I can infect the System. It will make oxygen.'

Outside the submarine, the ocean is shaking. Outside is everything that history is made of. It's invisible to Kalypso because she has constructed a steel hull to save herself from its volume. But something else is lunching on it.

The devouring and reconstituting of you.

'And then what?'

'I infect the System and in so doing I infect myself. You understand?'

'No.'

'I am the action of the System reforming itself.'

'But *I'm* infected, not you.'

'You're just a music. You're just a piece of time, an anti-silence.'

Play me again. Put me in your ears.

The situation outside is not looking good. The Grunts

260

have Reflex 4. I don't know what this will do to the Core but be ready for anything. Are you coming out or not?

Marcsson was doing things to the controls of the submarine.

'Hey,' she said. 'I didn't write anything in there. You better not try to dive because it's not programmed.'

'Watch me. Periscope down.'

Kessel and Charl are engaged in a standoff at Reflex 1. Teres is making her way toward the Core.

The soft parts always hide themselves adjacent to the vicious parts. It's a form of psychic camouflage. But you'll inevitably find them if you refuse to lose.

Liet says three witch doctors have escaped. The Dead still have every reflex point except 4.

'We're going to the bridge,' Azamat told her. 'It's not safe for you anywhere else.'

The submarine was no more, and Marcsson was invisible. Kalypso could see that the bridge was almost finished, yet she could not make out what was on the other side. The luma below was full of bodies and objects.

'You're standing on me,' he said. 'Ganesh is Wild now.'

Oh, I could go into it. A falling. I'm stretched across an abyss, a discontinuity I'm reaching into something I don't know, bridging or trying to. Sometimes I think I'm there but it's impossible for this to occur. Presenting a conundrum.

Maybe there is no other side. It's like a fault line I'm on, a shift between paradigms. On the other side everything's different. The rules change.

So the only way. The only way I can be a bridge is to fall. I'm afraid, but I jumped or was pushed already and I don't even know it. There's no one here to answer me when I call. You come as close as anyone has, but I know you don't hear.

'Azamat,' she said.

'It won't be here tomorrow. It won't stick around to get nailed down. Nothing alive does. You and your Miles Davis.'

'What?'

'Never mind. Don't bother to analyse. You'll want to. They'll want to. Don't bother.'

> 'Stop sounding like you just
> came down from the mountain.'
> 'I want a last cigarette.'

Azamat was sitting on her beach, which had been parceled off into geometric shapes containing running streams of tiny black creatures. He was wearing a red cape, which he snapped and flourished at her.

'Olé!' he said without much conviction.

Kalypso, what are you doing in there?

'Who the fuck do you think you are?' she said viciously. 'This is my Dreamer. Don't you come in here and move shit around. What's that – an ant farm? Get it out of here.' She wasn't sure why she was so angry. It wasn't the same emotion that had made her try to kill him before; it was the kind of anger you feel at people who mean something to you, and the fact that she felt it made her angrier still. She felt royally hoodwinked although she couldn't have said why.

He drew a line in the sand. 'I dare you.'

She stepped across it. The ants stung her foot; she hopped away, incensed.

'See? You're just the same as you ever were. Kalypso.' He was shaking his head and laughing.

Each of the six Dead, sitting on a reflex point.

'What are you doing in here? You can't *be* here. This is my place. I don't just mean, you're not allowed. I mean, you can't. This interface we're having. It's impossible.'

'Not for me. Not any more.'

'Who the fuck do you think you are?'

Genn on a reflex point.

'You already said that,' he laughed.

'I have a right to know. After what you did to me.'

Malik on a reflex point.

He climbed up into the lifeguard chair.

'Hey! Get the fuck down. That's my chair.'

'I've taken everything else that's yours. Why not this?'

All reflex points covered.

She reached through the interface, intending to come up with something to blow him away with. A bazooka, maybe, or a medium-sized cannon. Or a bolt of lightning, although she didn't think he really deserved anything that biblical.

Nothing happened.

Seething, she climbed the side of the chair and tried to physically push him down. It was no easier in the Dreamer than it would have been in real life.

'How dare you do this to Ganesh?'

'What are you going to do to me?' He laughed.

'I'll destroy you,' she hissed. 'I'll bring you down, I'll make you as if you never were.'

'Yes,' he said. 'You will.'

And suddenly they weren't at her node any more. They were standing on the bridge. It made a high arch out into darkness. Luma sparked below. At his feet was an open cigar box, ten times the size it should be.

```
Kalypso, respond. I can't find you.
```

'I want,' he said, 'to be capable of love and silence. I want to.'

In the box was a kitten.

'Please,' she said, and the futility of her words was obvious even before she spoke them. 'Just let me take over this interface now. Just let me. Just.'

```
Come, Kalypso. It's too late. It's too late. Come on.
```

'This creature has no place here. It has needs but no ability to pursue them. It must be provided for.'

He bent down. She noticed that he was emaciated, as if he'd not eaten for weeks. He reached into the box and stroked the kitten's back. It arched against his finger.

'That's why we love it. We are attracted to its vulnerability. It reminds us of our own children.'

'Let it go, please.' She could feel that something bad was going to happen. Who was making it happen? Ganesh? Azamat? Or was it she herself? Why couldn't she get control? She reached through the interface and came up empty.

He picked up the kitten. It sat in the palm of one of his hands, purring.

'It doesn't love me back, of course. If it were bigger, it would eat me. And then it wouldn't be vulnerable; I would. It's all a question of scale.'

'It's hungry,' Kalypso said.

Teres snarling at Robere.

'Yes. It needs its mother. They don't know how to chew at this age.'

'Don't do this.'

Robere snarling back.

'Do what? You think I mean this creature harm?' Suddenly he threw the animal back into the box. It cowered for a moment, claws extended, trying to right itself. Azamat shook the box fiercely. The kitten flipped over, rolled, recovered.

'Cats are nicely flexible, especially when they're young like this. It's not easy to break their bones. However . . . ' He produced a curving knife of the type used to gut fish.

'Azamat, don't. Don't. This is an abuse of the Dreamer.'

'The Dreamer's extinct. There will never be another Dreamer.'

He pinned the kitten down and cut off half its tail. The sound it made was an injection of pain and horror.

'Stop it now.'

She flung herself at him but he simply displaced himself to another location. Like a magician. That's my kind of move, Kalypso thought. But she couldn't get at the interface. She couldn't make anything happen. She could only witness.

Kalypso, are you there?

The kitten was trying to lick the bleeding stump of tail. Marcsson looked grave.

'Fuck you,' Kalypso shouted. 'You can't get to me this way. It's a Dream. I don't care what you do.'

'I'm not crazy,' he said. Looking at him now she was inclined to believe him. His face was steady, consistent. And if he was controlling this Dream, he had resources of a kind she couldn't begin to approach. 'You're being distracted by emotion. Cruelty has a function. You just don't know what it is.'

Kalypso?

She felt Tehar making rapidfire adjustments to her body temperature. In the Dream spittle flew from her lips and she felt her veins stand out in anger.

'Don't you philosophize at me! No. I won't look.'

But she did. It was a Dream and she had no choice. He'd let the kitten out of the box. It scuttled belly down, hackles up, leaving bloody footprints on the new bridge. The knife in Azamat's hand became a club.

'We're going to get to the bottom of you. We're going to decode you.' He stepped after the kitten and raised the club thoughtfully, carefully, like a golfer preparing to putt.

She tried to close her eyes but couldn't. She had to see what he/it/they wanted her to see. She needed indifference, badly, but couldn't find any. She tried to fake it.

Lassare's voice on the radio, going, 'We can master the System. Come to your senses, you fools!'

'Go ahead. I don't care.'

He brought the club down. It caught the cat in the pelvis. Again the sound, worse than before, and more prolonged. The kitten tried to get away, dragging its useless back half.

'There,' he said with satisfaction to the kitten. 'How does that feel?' He turned to her. 'How does that feel, Kalypso? Are you feeling it? Is it big enough for you? Is it wild enough for you?'

There was a time, not long ago, when she would have bristled at his sarcasm; it would have hurt her. Not any more.

'I've been on the receiving end of it all. You broke me. You broke me Azamat and you can only do that once. Now you'll have to deal with the shards.'

The kitten was keening, a sound that reached into some old part of Kalypso's brain and thrashed. For an instant she flashed that she was the animal, got a taste of its senses – just enough to shake her up. Her vitals and waves went crazy; Tehar fumbled and stabilized her.

A view of First from one of the robot stations on the farm cells. The surface of the luma moving toward First like water toward a drain.

She found herself curled up on the ground. Azamat was on his knees beside her. His hand cupped the back of her head and he drew her against his body.

'Shards?' he said softly. 'I don't feel anything sharp.' He was running his hands down her back. Just as he said, her body had gone soft. While among her cluster, she had sobbed and thrashed and struck out to no relief; now, in one gesture, he had reduced her to a state of total release. She felt as dim and relaxed as a plant.

'Yes,' Azamat said. 'That's better.'

'I hate you.'

He had enveloped her entire body with his limbs. There was a look of tenderness on his face. This is awful, she told herself. It's terrible. But she was quiescent; she had given herself over without ever making a choice. She could still hear the animal. It was making some progress, wheezing softly.

Only it's not sinking. It's not going down.

How do I know this sound? Kalypso thought. I've never been anywhere near a cat.

It's climbing.

'I hate you,' she said again. 'You killed Ganesh.'

'It was mutual, or will be. Go to sleep.'

'No. What are you going to do.'

'Sleep now,' he said gently. 'I will take care of you.'

But Ganesh knew what a cat sounded like.

Ganesh. Ganesh was still here. She gathered herself.

'I came here to save you,' she said. 'I don't know why I want to save you but I do. Whatever is happening here, it doesn't have to happen.'

'Yes it does.'

'You're in a coma. You don't even know what's going on.'

'You can't help,' he whispered. 'You can't save me. Go to sleep.'

'No.'

'I'll torture the kitten again. I'll take it apart bone by bone.'

'I don't care.'

'It's a real kitten to you here. You can't pretend to me that it isn't because I know that it is. Just like this is real. My lips on your hand are real.'

'I know,' she said. He was holding her hand lightly against his mouth. She could have easily withdrawn it but she didn't. He kissed her fingertips.

'So go to sleep. You don't want to see this.'

'I've seen you kill before.'

'And don't pretend to be jaded.' He smiled. 'I'm nothing, Kalypso. I never was anything. You know that. I know that. You think I don't know what people think of me? Good old Azamat. Gets the job done. Not much of a spark; not much of an imagination; not much of anything. But can be counted on to do what's needed. That was my function on this mission; it always has been and it always will be.'

'What's happening to you? Tell me.'

'I'm the bridge-builder. I'm the bricks. I'm the bridge. I'm the guy who jumps off.'

'Azamat, we're in the Dreamer. Are you aware of that? This isn't real.'

'Oh yes it is. Tell me how a Dream works.'

'Ganesh digs a bank of associations and references for you. Sensory. Cognitive. When it feeds you data, it translates them into your subconscious, which in turn rules your senses. So you can touch the abstract.'

'The System only exists in the mind that can understand it. I'm teaching Ganesh to understand the System, and the System to understand Ganesh. What we did to your body? I'm turning that into pure thought. I'm turning that into language.'

'But *I'm* the bridge. It's my body you used for a bridge. Me and Sieng. Why am I not going crazy like you and Ganesh?'

'Because you don't understand. You don't grasp the abstraction. Your ignorance of the math saves you, Kalypso.'

'Irony of ironies.'

A picture of Charl with her hand deep inside a panel in the luma. A picture of Kessel, talking to her.

'Go to sleep now. Change is coming. I need you out of here.'

'The Mothers have done this to you,' she railed at random. 'How many sacrificial lambs have they made?'

'If it weren't for the Mothers,' he said, 'none of us would be here. I would have remained on Earth for lack of funding, and you would never have been born.'

'That doesn't give them the right – '

'It gives them what it gives them. I'm bigger than you. That doesn't give me any rights either.'

'But you carved up my body.'

'Exactly.'

'And I hate you for it.'

'I know.' And he smiled again and she smiled back, the moron that she was.

'What is this?' she said. 'Why do I feel this way? Are you doing this to me?'

'I don't know. Go to sleep.'

'If you say that one more time, I'll – '

'You'll what?'

Tehar verbed her: she felt it coming in, but she couldn't decipher it. The message had been scrambled inside Ganesh.

'There are 1001 ways to take a man's life,' Azamat said. 'You're the only thing I have left. I want you to go now.'

I'm not doing as he says, Kalypso thought. Tehar had verbed her for a reason. Maybe he'd found some way to help her. She had to try harder. Azamat was becoming emotional; that meant he was distracted. Maybe he could be distracted more.

'Will you kill that cat?' she demanded. 'It's suffering. Why don't you just kill it?'

He stood up, still holding her in his arms. She liked this, and thought again of the rush she'd gotten, the first time he'd knocked her down, in the Dreamer unit. He walked over to where the kitten lay, unmoving except for its labored breathing, eyes glassy but still alive.

'Do you recognize it?' he said. 'You kill it.'

He put her down. Produced the club again.

'Hit it hard,' he said. 'You don't want to risk having it live to feel the blow.'

We're getting more nodes come up. Kalypso, hurry. Whatever you're doing, can you do it faster? Teres is about to blow.

She took the club. There were two obvious choices. Hit Azamat with the club. Or try to run across the bridge. Or both.

Too obvious. She put the club down and stooped. The kitten was beyond saving. Half its body was a stinking, crushed mess. The other half appeared to be in shock. She curled her hands around it and picked it up; it yielded oddly in her grasp and she winced, fighting disgust and horror and pity. She brought it to her chest and held it there in one hand. Azamat was shaking his head.

'You can't do that,' he said. 'That isn't fair and it won't work.'

'Why not? Explain why.'

'I'm going across the bridge,' he said defensively. 'You can't make me stay.'

The kitten's heartbeat was fast. Its breathing was fast. How could it still be alive? How could it withstand such punishment?

Kalypso began to run out across the bridge. The luma below was bright.

That's good. That's good. Hurry please. Teres –

She glanced down and saw Sieng's blue spine, miles long. Sieng's magic organs, blurred within the luma. Kalypso's body tingled all over. The luma discharged violently; she stumbled. Vast ecstasy opened in her skull. She lay on the bricks, covered in feline blood and fur, unable to stop herself looking over the brink and into the System below. After a while she noticed Azamat had caught up with her and was laying a few bricks at the ragged edge, meditatively. *Sound of Witchdoctor Radio starting to untangle itself.*

'Don't mind me,' he said. 'Looking at you now, I'm noticing a few more details I could add. Your subs are progressing nicely. They'll serve you well, when all this is gone.'

The luma below had begun a siren-song: 'All Blues' by Miles of course.

'You hear it taking me apart?'

The devouring and reconstituting of you.

'That's peach sorbet,' he said. 'That's my first girlfriend's dog. That's the way it felt to score a goal in the playoffs against Stuttgart. That's a really bad case of poison ivy I got in America. That's – '

'No!' she cried. 'Enough!'

Picture of the reflex points all being pulled simultaneously. If Ganesh had a back, it would be broken.

The Earth Archives were vaporizing into System noise. Marcsson's life poured through her on its way to dissolving.

'I thought being a bridge would be static,' he said, scraping the excess mortar squashed between two bricks. 'Architecture doesn't move, and that's all I am, a piece of architecture in the new System. But I don't feel static. I feel like I'm falling. I'm falling and always will be. Is perpetual motion the same as stillness? What did Isaac Newton say?'

'Isaac and everything from Earth are gone,' she sobbed. 'Don't do it. Don't do it.'

Kalypso, there's nothing I can do. The reflexes have come down. You have to get out of there.

Azamat Marcsson and his bug collection and his perfectly neat lab reports and his timed bicycle route to work in the morning (17.6 minutes unless it was raining) and his family all sitting around the table saying virtually nothing and chewing their food thoroughly and his observation of social decay in formicine colonies from the detailed analysis of their kitchen midden and the ritual of flossing the teeth always starting from the back right and the bored summer he spent, aged fifteen, calculating pi to thousands of decimal places and the Swedish girl he fell in love with over the net only to meet her and, although she was half-cute and funny and did really want to come to his room and see his ant farms her physical presence proved too distracting and he begged to go back to a phosphor-bounded relationship –

'Please Azamat,' she said impulsively. 'Let me go. Let me be with Ganesh. This isn't for you.'

You can't sleep with one eye open

'I've tried to protect you. That's all I ever tried to do. Even when you were Sieng.'

Luma piling on itself at impossible speeds. Surface temperature plummeting.

'I was never Sieng.'

'You always will be, now. There are many more levels. The thermals go very deep. I'm going to be falling for a long time.'

Picture of Liet crouched over the remains of Kalypso's workstation in Unit 5.

'You'll leave the Dreamer, you'll fight with Tehar, you'll go have something to eat – and I'll be falling. You'll get back to Oxygen 2, find someome to make love with, and I'll be falling. I'll still be falling and you'll be explaining to the Mothers why you did what you did. Why you let me do what I'm about to do. You'll be talking for all you're worth, Kalypso Deed.'

Picture of Sieng's data as encoded for human consumption.

'After a while they'll get tired of you. You'll wear them down and they'll throw up their hands and drink. While you're sleeping, I'll be falling. You'll gather up some scraps of music – yes, I'm going to try to save you some music, but if I can't you'll play it yourself, you'll play it from memory on that lousy joke of an instrument you call a bass guitar because you don't know any better, you'll find a way.'

Picture of nothing because it's all going down.

'You'll be reunited with that fucking Miles Davis I've had reconfiguring my soul all this time thanks to you, and you'll sit there with your eyes closed, grooooving. I can see you Kalypso. And I'll still be falling.'

So where are you?

'Days and weeks will go by. You'll tell yourself you want no part of the Wild. You'll stay resolutely behind. You'll refuse to have any part of anything. You'll be a complete pain in the ass to everyone. All this time, I'll be falling.'

Where are you?

'And then, one day – '

Where are you?

'I don't know when, but one day you'll change. And all this will cease to be the thing that takes you over. It will go away and leave you free. And you'll decide you need a boat but you'll have no skills to barter and no one will want to do you any favors because of your attitude, so you'll have to cheat some poor sucker out of his boat in a poker game – Yeah, I know you cheat, don't bother to deny it. And I'll . . . '

'You'll still be falling?'

'I don't know. I don't know how long it will be.'

'What will be at the bottom?'

'I don't know that either. I won't ever be able to tell you.'

She struggled with this a while. Finally: 'Don't.'

'Thank you,' Azamat said, 'for saying that. Now ask Liet for the final data she collected from your skin.'

'Why?'

Ahmed shouting on the radio, 'It's not what you think! It's not what you think! The reflex points don't work.'

'You know I can't answer that.'

'But – '

'*Kalypso.*'

He looked her full in the face then, for what seemed like the first time ever. She didn't know what passed between them. It was after all only a Dream. That was how she explained it to herself afterward, anyway.

Don't work?

Don't work?

'Tehar,' Kalypso verbed. 'Ask Liet to please feed me whatever else she has. Don't worry. I can handle it.'

Kalypso where are you?

'Please. Do it,' she said to Tehar with Azamat standing still and watching her.

'I'm afraid.' That was the last thing he ever said to her.

We're sending now.

She didn't feel the statistics come through but she felt the last winds of Azamat's memory, the complexity of light and smell in grass and the drag of a razor across his jaw and the way it felt to solve a quadratic equation for the first time and many things of this nature which were of Earth and ought to be alien to her but now they weren't and never would be again.

Kalypso?

Kalypso's body was changing colors in the places where she had been cut. Mysterious and tiny events were occurring in her skin but she couldn't perceive them. Below the bridge, the luma began to move. Her eye fixed itself on the mutilated kitten. It squirmed, stiffened as if about to expire, and exploded into a horse-sized Bengal tiger with hot breath and a voice pitched as deep as a bomb. The tiger sprang at Marcsson, who dropped the trowel and jumped off the unfinished end of the bridge. Everything broke down.

Kalypso?

Kalypso didn't have the faintest fucking idea what happened to her after that.

You won't find yourself in the aftermath. No one can, because being human you don't bend that way. It's not in the cards for you.

You can't get there. You can't imagine what it's like, or try. You can strain and wish. You can make its analogies dance and sing but you can't get on the back of it and ride. The anatomy of distance has no hand by which you can touch and hold that which you desire. You lived in an ever-enlarging reality that now won't stretch another millimeter. It snaps back in your face. This is the end of language. If you go, you won't return; something else will. That's why you can't go and neither can anyone else.

Except Azamat. Azamat is going on. He can go where no one else goes.

Kalypso was back in the ur-system, familiar territory, lights of the Works spinning outside, caressing the station – only you know now it can't last. Above, the radical ocean-sky that she used to think she was so smart to have Dreamed.

Below, Marcsson sleeping in the Dreamtank.

His face shone like beaten metal. She put her fingers through the water. Touched. Skin and flesh yielded; then bone. Behind the interface his eyes were closed.

The feeling was like a storm, a developing thermal whose colors would not define themselves: not for her or for anyone. It was too late.

Kalypso come back now.

Her flesh was numb. What a useless, ungainly sack of shit did all her arms and legs make, wedged and folded protectively over her torso, exposing her curled spine. None of it belonged here any more.

'Come on. That's it. Wake up.'

Take me to the slaughter, she thought at Tehar. She knew she hadn't spoken aloud, yet she was mildly surprised when he didn't hear her. So this wasn't still the Dreamer. Probably.

I've had enough. This is the end now. Anything more would be in bad taste. I'm not going to ever wake from Dreaming again. Never. I won't have this isolation. I won't have this waking-from-sleep-to-be-alone. No.

He disengaged contact points. She half-lidded her eyes. Mustn't react too much or the anger would come and then she would lose this equilibrium.

'Kalypso we have to leave now. We can't stay here. I've already sent Liet away. Kalypso.'

I never wanted to know, she screamed. She screamed it inside, where she was empty. Where no one could hear her. I never wanted to see a human being. Not that way. I didn't ask to see.

'They've shut down the reflex points.'

She'd miscalculated about one thing: anger wasn't possible. She was far beyond the orbit of anger. Tehar was agitated and trying not to show it. He had seen the System begin to come up as Marcsson built the bridge. He had seen for a moment the alien, or whatever it was, that had taken over Ganesh and Azamat and maybe even her. Now it was gone.

'I'm sorry.' Tehar was holding her hand, stroking her fingers.

Tears would be equally irrelevant.

'Let's go,' he said and she could hear the earth and its leaves and sparrows in his voice.

No. But she stood up. It was easier than she wanted it to be.

They left Unit 5.

one eye open

' – out! Everybody out! *Reflexes are all down. Get ready for the heat.'*
Robere was in such a panic his voice stretched to the alto range and
snapped.

Liet was waiting in the transit tube. Tehar yelled at her for not
leaving and she yelled back, then started pushing and shoving at
Kalypso.

'What's happening? What's happening?' Kalypso heard herself
repeating in a blurry, childish tone.

'Don't think, Kalypso. Move!' Liet commanded. Normally Kalypso
would be doing anything but thinking at a time like this: thinking
was dangerous, troublesome, painful. Moving was easy. Yet here was
Liet acting like Kalypso and Kalypso acting like Liet. How apropos,
Kalypso thought, still failing to move with anything resembling
speed or coordination. Everything's changing places. Nothing's like
it was. *Dance, dance. Declassify yourself.* No. Shut up, Marcsson.

They climbed toward the caldera, Tehar pulling her and Liet
pushing. The confusion on radio was torrential.

' – *trying but it's melting* – '

Ahmed: *'Robere, believe me, it's not what you thin* – '

'You stupid bastard Grunts you made us do it,' Teres whispered.
Manic tapping filled the channel and was cut off.

' – *coming round to your heading, just* – '

*'Don't fight us, Teres. We'll help you get out but there must be no
viol* – '

A magnetic shock passed through the transit tube. She felt it in
her hands and legs where they touched the side of the crawl. Liet
stopped pushing. 'Tehar, d'you feel that?'

'Yeah. Kalypso, did you feel it?'

Kalypso said, 'Columbus, I don't think we're in India any more. Let's know each other. Toto, that's some flying elephant. The devouring and reconstituting of you. Azamat, don't jump please. Together they do a kind of flamenco.'

'Keep going,' Liet said. 'Be quiet, Kalypso.'

' – to Oxygen 2 as fast as you can. I don't care – '

'Robere, the channel's blocked. The luma is sporulating way too fast.'

'Cut it if you have to.'

'It's almost up over our heads. Shit – '

'OK, calm down everybody. The heat isn't as bad as I thought. I wonder where it's all going.'

'I've been trying to tell you it's going into the goddamn luma is where it's going,' Ahmed's voice said. 'We can see Landings 3 and 4 from here and they're being blocked. The luma's rising. You better mo – '

Tehar gave a shout.

'It happened again.' He scrambled frantically up the tube, went to a sensor point, and put his hands on it.

Liet said, 'Tehar I don't think that's a good id – '

L'IDEE, said a soft Ganesh voice on Kalypso's interface. She glanced at Liet, who was wide-eyed and trembling. CECI N'EST PAS UNE PIPE.

Kalypso surged up the tube and flung herself spreadeagled on the sensor point. She didn't dare say it, but Tehar did.

'Ganesh?'

I AM NOT HERE. I AM STILL SLEEPING.

'I'm talking to you. You're moving through the station.'

I ALWAYS SLEEP WITH ONE EYE OPEN.

Loud, horrible, overwhelming sound filled the interface. Kalypso ripped off her hardware and clung to the side of the tube, breathing hard. She reeled from the physical blow of the noise. Her ears rang. She saw Liet's lips move but couldn't hear her voice. Liet, too, was staring at her interface in shock.

'What was that?' Liet said again.

Tehar took his interface off. He was pale. 'Elephants,' he said. 'Let's get out of here.'

They gained the caldera and ran slipping along the wet, curving surface, avoiding transit chutes, until they reached the exposed edge of the station. They could see the luma creeping up the nearest leg. Out near the farm cells, vertical stacks of luma were rising from the surface as if conveyed by elevators. First sat in the epicenter of a slow-turning kaleidoscope, with luma in all colors migrating like iron filings, attaching itself to the station. They could see one of the boats of the Dead, trapped by the quickly solidifying luma. As they watched it was raised up and carried along like a stone by a glacier.

'This can't be happening,' Tehar said. 'Set your faces for radio.'

' – you people need help?' It was Lassare at her most cantankerous. 'I'm sending out a rescue party.'

' – ck off Lassare, I can handle it!'

'Ahmed, tell Kessel to take his head out of his ass and give me coordinates for a rendezvous. There's a cool zone two miles west of Landing 6. I don't think you'll have sporulation there no matter what. There's a natural – '

'Come on. Move it. Both of you.' Liet led the way over the side. They watched dumbly while she descended along the skin of the station, toward the moving fire of the well.

' – detouring to the southwest. There's a pillar here at least ten boatlengths and growing – '

' – medical supplies? Burns among the Grunts.'

'Send Van if you can. Charl bit Kessel and he's convinced it's infected with the – '

Tehar pulled Kalypso's interface off and took it away. Then he pulled her over the edge.

Their boat wasn't yet trapped, but the channel of navigable fluid leading from the place they'd moored it was narrow and tortuous. Liet was talking on the radio when they arrived; no sooner had Tehar set foot on the deck than she gunned the engine and for the second time in her life, Kalypso found herself fleeing First with only moments to spare.

'We have to pick up Robere and some of his people. They took one of the Dead's boats and got stranded on the luma. Here, Tehar. You take over. This isn't my area.'

Liet left Tehar at the nav console and dropped to the back of the cockpit, where Kalypso was sitting with her chin resting on her folded hands, staring flabbergasted at the metamorphosis of the landscape around them. The channel in the luma grew deeper and deeper, so that translucent, glowing walls rose above them to either side. Lucent veils of colonials could be seen lying in planes within. Light also flared below, and streams of orange and yellow subs sledded in streams down the walls of the luma culvert.

'*Clearly we need to take control again,*' Naomi was saying on the boat's radio speaker. '*Teres, we will only be too happy to come to terms, but after the crisis, so if you could leave the heat converters and get the hell out of there with as many people as you can, I think you'll be doing everybody a big favor.*'

Wind eddied and roared.

'Is it a thermal?' Kalypso asked timidly.

Liet grabbed herself by the shoulders and squeezed as if to hold on to herself. 'I . . . don't think so. I never imagined it could move so much power around in such a coordinated way . . . I mean, we know the power's there, with all that heat. But I always figured we were talking about a data storage system, not an *engine* . . . '

'What's an engine?' asked Tehar, turning from the console for a second.

'The System, apparently.'

'Yeah,' Tehar laughed, steering to avoid a moving berg of luma. 'No shit. There they are!'

Robere and his team were running along the top of the luma, slipping and sliding. They tumbled into the boat and Liet fell sobbing on Ahmed for a while, which he clearly enjoyed. He grabbed Kalypso by the ear and pulled her against him. Tehar made for clear water, out beyond the agro baffles. There was so much bickering on the radio that he turned it off.

'I guess you missed some of the reflexes,' Tehar said to Robere, who looked shellshocked.

'No,' Ahmed said, his voice vibrating through his ribs and into Kalypso's skull. 'I was there. We looked outside and all this was already starting to happen. Teres had somebody sitting on each reflex point – including Genn and Malik and all that lot. They pulled them all at the same time, and for a minute everything went down. Even radio. Then radio came back up, and the luma just kept moving. The sensor points came up spouting garbage. I opened up an access panel and the Earthmade circuitry had been eaten away. Replaced by luma.'

'I don't believe you,' Kalypso heard herself saying. She buried her face against his body, wishing she could feel his heat but they were both wearing surface suits.

'You don't have to believe me. Just open your eyes.'

Kalypso opened one eye. In the spaces between and around her fellow humans, it saw brilliant luma. She closed it again.

have a cigar

The night was loud. Clouds skated across the luma, driven by the screaming storm winds of atmospheric tempflux. Two seasons after the Integration of Ganesh with the System, gales continued to batter the colony as the luma altered its relationship with the planet's inner fires, changing the gas balance, temperature, and pressure. Thermals continued to happen, but they seemed minor events in comparison with the continual met upsets that tested the colonists to their limits. No one dared complain, however: T'nane's skies were cooling, and sometimes they even cleared. Tonight, Kalypso counted four stars.

'Put your finger there,' Ahmed instructed. She did, and the substance of the rope felt greasy against her finger as he pulled the knot taut. 'There. Nice polymer, eh, Kalypso?'

They were drifting slowly along the edge of the Rift current, surrounded by stacks and arches of displaced luma, which had built themselves into uncanny parodies of Earth architecture. The fluid beneath the boat fizzed with rising oxygen, and migrating colonies of subs snaked across the current in colored bands according to their pH. In a gloved hand Ahmed held one end of a purple rope that he had just fastened to the boat. The other end dragged in the luma behind them for fifty meters and counting, its terminus gradually extending itself: it was being synthesized as they travelled, drawn from the luma according to some biological algorithm Ganesh had planted in the System.

Ahmed had Dreamed it into being.

'I want to ask you something,' he said now, and she glanced up at him expectantly. The wind blew his hair into a black V and his exposed face was actually flushed with cold. Hardship over these many weeks had robbed his face of its softer flesh: he didn't look like the boy she knew. 'Is it possible . . . that is, do you think . . . do you think *it* gets into us. When we Dream.'

A needle and thread of anxiety went to work in Kalypso's stomach. 'I don't know.'

He frowned. 'Tehar thinks it does. He says the translation works both ways. He says we can't master the System without its also mastering us.'

'I don't know,' she said again, woodenly. She didn't want to be reminded of Tehar. For days on end after the initial Integration, they had been in one another's presence constantly. Once it was possible to return to First, Tehar had insisted on taking her back into the Dreamer to establish a basis of communication with the Integrated Ganesh so that recovery of the scrambled Earth Archives could begin.

The Dead's plundering of the station had turned out to be fortuitous for everyone: most Earthmade components present in First during the Integration had been subsumed in the luma and were unrecoverable. When Tehar patched Kalypso a visual link between the Dreamer and Oxygen 2, the latter looked like a wrecking yard, with the Dead and the Grunts haggling over scraps of Earth. Kalypso had watched it all through the Dreamer. She'd had no conversations with Ganesh, no confirmation of its presence; but when she Dreamed, her senses had extended throughout the luma as if she were seeing through Ganesh's new & improved senses. She watched the first of the deep pockets of buried oxygen as they were released by the luma into the atmosphere. The fact that they must have been present all the time, buried in the depths of the luma, stimulated excited speculation about the events by which the planet's gas balance had changed so rapidly in the first place. ('We still haven't solved the Oxygen Problem,' Naomi said darkly. 'Now it's merely solving *us*.')

Through the Dreamer Kalypso observed the development of hybrid subs, neither terran nor native T'nane, in the Wild. She listened to the sound on Witchdoctor Radio – to her and no one else, it was beginning to resemble music. Ganesh itself seemed small by comparison to the changes it had unleashed on the planet. It was in keeping with the decentralized nature of the System that the station sometimes seemed to have become not the CNS of the planet, but merely the point from which its human inhabitants were able to communicate with the System: its mouth, perhaps.

But to take such a view might be underestimating Ganesh, Kalypso thought. She missed the old AI. Her Dreams were quiet. Maybe too quiet.

Nothing else was quiet at all. Together Kalypso and Tehar listened to the radio exchanges, the negotiations and squabbles and eventual pulling-together of the Grunts, the Dead, the Mothers and the kids; the luma gave nobody any choice but to co-operate. Physically, all of the factions had become inter-mingled, with everyone popping in and out of First, Oxygen 2, and the Wild at need. Every day there was some kind of emergency, and inevitably the emergencies were not of such a nature as the Earthborn had trained their offspring to deal with, so all the old rules broke down and got reinvented, quick. Philosophically, the colonists were becoming polarized according to those who believed the System had a mind, and those who believed the only mind in question belonged to Ganesh, with everything else being pure data. The social strata separating each faction of T'nane society lost all integrity with respect to this question, so that Tehar and Kalypso found themselves in the disconcerting position of being perched up in rem2ram Unit 4 surrounded by slow-morphing luma transforming the station, while on the radio Robere and Siri and Charl argued fiercely against Sharia and Stash, with every so often Liet putting in her two cents on either side. Their society had become as unrecogniz-able as their planet.

'It doesn't matter,' Kalypso muttered one time, bored with the debate. 'You'll never see it. You'll never touch it.'

Tehar reached over and rested his palm on her leg, which was viridian streaked with purple at the moment.

'No,' she responded to his tacit question. 'I haven't seen it, either. It's in my body and I can't touch it. I can't know it.'

'*There's something out there,*' Sharia railed, and they both smiled. '*Look around you. How can this all be Ganesh?*'

'*How can it be anything other than Ganesh if it's coming* through Ganesh?'

Tehar sighed and switched off his interface. 'Why can't they worry about where their next meal's coming from? Why do they waste so much energy on this question?'

Kalypso said nothing for a long moment. 'Some things are easier to think about than others,' she answered at last. She thought she was saying something profound but Tehar only laughed, so apparently she wasn't.

They shared food and air and body heat while the planet reconfigured itself around them. At heart they had ceased to know one another, probably because Kalypso was deeply fucked up and unable to articulate how or why. Tehar didn't understand why she avoided all but the most superficial contact with him, and with everyone. Maybe he put it down to trauma. He just didn't get it and she couldn't blame him, since she didn't really get it either.

They made love once. Kalypso cried. She let him think this meant she was surrendering her emotions to him at last, but she was only mourning the fact that she couldn't. She tried to memorize him. His dimensions and movements. And the way he used time in sex. And all of the small imperfections of his skin and frame, and the condensation of his breath on her forehead, and the weight of his thumb on her lower lip and how he wouldn't look at her when he was going to come: these things somehow accrued into Tehar so that when he rolled away in the end, finished with her, she felt bereft; he said, 'I forgot how small you are.'

She could feel it starting already, a slight ripping that would eventually become something else, some cousin of pain. She made herself smile, but his mouth was unexpectedly somber. Maybe he was getting it after all.

'Don't look so sad,' she said. 'Everything's going to be different now. No more claustrophobia. No more following instructions.'

He seized on this. 'You're happy, then?'

'Yeah. Definitely,' she lied brightly.

Soon afterward, she stole a boat.

She was standing on Landing 2, supposedly helping Ahmed and Kessel maneuver a piece of hardware into a waiting boat. She had her surface suit on, but had pulled the hood down and was taking every other breath through her open mouth. The CO consumers which the System had begun to produce had taken hold quickly in the waters around the station, and her suit informed her that it was safe to breathe. Occasionally.

'It's just a bunch of engineering problems now,' she heard Kessel say from within the transit tube. There was a sound of bumping and heaving. 'It's concrete. We can work with that.'

Ahmed's deeper voice reached her even through the seal.

'Can we stop calling it the Oxygen Problem, then?' he said.

'Fuck yeah,' said Kessel, and then got stuck in the hatch seal. His head came through, then one shoulder, and he managed to grab a piece of wall on Kalypso's side of the seal. He huffed and wriggled, but the hardware was jammed between his body and the edge of the hatch.

Kalypso stifled a giggle.

'Hey, Deed! Give us a hand here.'

More masculine groans and curses. Kalypso started forward to help, but at the last second she burst out laughing, spun on one heel, and threw herself into the boat.

'Don't be a wiseguy, Deed,' Kessel warned. 'I'll use you for a basketball if you don't behave.'

Still laughing, she cut the line and gunned the boat away from the dock. When she looked back, Kessel and Ahmed had both gotten through the hatch and were standing on the pier, waving their arms at her. She waved back and fled.

The agro baffles had long since come down. There were only a handful of passable channels in the luma, and it took her half an hour to get past the supersurface luma and into a region that resembled the Wild she had grown to know so well. The storm winds were so strong that she had to crouch behind the dash like a racecar driver, and she was glad she had no hair. Precipitation flew sideways, spattering on the hull of her boat. There were subs in the water, using the weather to seed themselves from one region of the System to another.

It was still a bleak planet. The volcanoes still glowered over the Rift, and the colors of the luma might never be friendly, Earth colors. She would never belong here.

But . . .

It took over three hours' journey into the Wild before Kalypso realized she didn't have to go back. She could become a thief and scavenger, like the Dead. Or, like the Dead, she could learn to live off the luma. At least now she might have a chance of teaching it to grow something compatible with her physiology: terran-type hybrids were cropping up all over the place, lately.

She thought up all kinds of ideas. She cruised through developing luma with the clouds flying past her and the dark sky and lucent surface reflecting one another, and she began to feel powerful.

Then Teres caught up with her.

This put her in a bad mood. It spoiled her fun. She tried to outrun the Dead thing, but Teres found a better current and cut her off.

'Leave me alone!' she shouted as soon as Teres got close. 'I'm not coming back.'

She sounded like a four-year-old and she knew it. At least this was Teres, not Lassare.

'They want you back.'

'Too damn bad.'

Teres drew her boat alongside and hooked Kalypso's. Kalypso picked up the hook and tossed it off. Teres signed, 'You're thicker than I thought. Why do you leave your people? You are no outcast. They love you.'

'I can't be with them,' Kalypso said. 'I don't know what I am. Look at me!'

As soon as she said it, she knew Teres would laugh. But the Dead woman's face went still.

'They have told you that you will die of these agents?'

'Well . . . no. Van says I'm still human. He wants to study me, though. He says the work is only beginning. But I don't care.' She put her hands on her hips the way Sharia would, and tossed her head.

Teres signed, 'You are the most important person in the colony. You are in the best possible bargaining position. I am sterile, used-up, unwanted. You have given birth to a world.'

Kalypso stared. She had never thought of it this way.

'Here,' Teres gestured. She turned and rummaged among her supplies. Carelessly, she tossed a rectangular object at Kalypso. When she caught it, Kalypso gasped.

'You won the bet,' Teres said in a hoarse whisper. 'They're yours. Go play.'

And Kalypso, shocked that Teres had handled them so casually, clutched the cigars to her breast. The Dead one powered her boat and left without another word or sign.

After Teres had left her, Kalypso turned her boat about and glided back toward First in a daze. She passed a boat with Naomi and two Grunts and Van, who waved at her shyly. Sober, Naomi looked frail and somber. She was counting collection fils and didn't see Kalypso.

She entered a luma canyon and passed tentkits dotting the supersurface luma like splotches of paint. Translucent blocks of luma fluoresced in the coming night, keened softly in the wind. Very slowly, they were changing shape. She passed someone walking across one of these blocks, picking a slippery path, head down against the wind and rain.

Kalypso flexed her thigh muscles, thought about walking, and then about running, and then about roads, and then about bus stations. Vermillion fingers of some version of *v.aa* travelled down the sides of the canyon like squadrons of . . . Damn. Like squadrons of Marcsson's ants.

She got to First and dragged herself back to Unit 4, preparing herself for a scolding by Tehar. But he wasn't alone: they were all sitting there, sharing a meal. Sharia leaped to her feet when Kalypso came in and grabbed her hand.

'Where were you? We were so worried . . .'

Kalypso ignored her, as usual.

'I need a favor,' she said, looking at Ahmed. He glared at her for a long moment, reaching over to cuff X, who was giggling and poking him in the ribs. He narrowed his eyes suspiciously.

'*What?*'

So here she was, with Ahmed.

'Are you sure you want to go through with this?' he asked her.

'No,' she said. She helped him draw in the rope and coil it on the bottom of the boat. 'I Dreamed one time that I was having tea with my projections. It was a little house, with stuffed armchairs. Outside the windows you could see all this,' she gestured to the Wild, 'reforming itself. In the room were all these little tables with those white lace things on them, what d'you call them – '

'Doilies, I think.'

'Yeah. So we're all drinking tea and my projections are talking way over my head about a lot of stuff, and I know they're explaining what's going on outside the windows but I can't make sense of it. So I'm looking around for something else to do and I see this roly-poly cat sitting on the back of a couch, making little chattery noises and staring at this brass birdcage in the corner. There's a parrot inside. Too big for the cage, really. And the parrot is scat-singing. I go, "Nigel?" and the parrot stops singing and says in a very correct tone, "Azamat". Then it starts singing again. And the whole time, the cat is just sitting there, watching, and the tip of its tail is twitching.'

She paused. Ahmed was giving her a blank look.

'Doesn't matter,' she said. 'Are we there yet?'

He pointed off to starboard, and she saw the other boat. One person was standing in it, the other sitting.

'I wonder what it's been like for Neko,' Ahmed mused. 'To be out here alone with him all these months.'

Kalypso had not seen Neko since the day Marcsson had stolen her from the Dead woman. Initially Tehar had smuggled Marcsson away from Oxygen 2 as a means to prevent anybody from disturbing the development of the Ganesh System, as he called it – for the brouhaha over resources and rights had continued for many days before settling down to a dull roar as the transformation of First began to dictate everybody's actions. Neko had turned up some time later and offered to relieve the T'nane-born caretakers who had been assigned to protect Marcsson. It was a job they had been only too glad to relinquish.

Neko must have spotted their boat as well. Her low vessel turned in its own channel and began to come toward them, slicing through the gelatinous luma. Ahmed squeezed Kalypso's shoulders and accelerated slightly. Kalypso didn't respond to him. She was thinking about the luma System and wondering whether bits of Ganesh-logic had travelled this far yet; whether that accounted for the increased growth of algaics here. In the wake of her boat she could see the disturbed liquid swirling, revealing every now and then a snatch of light generated by the *flagrare* far below. If Ganesh had been colonized by the System, the System had also been colonized by Ganesh. Down there, deep in the luma's structure, Earth logic was mating with System logic. Maybe someday she would truly interface with the Wild.

She recalled the tiger chasing Marcsson off the end of the bridge and thought warily: then again, maybe not.

Ahmed had quickly grown fluent in the special Sign of the Dead. Kalypso waited while he explained to Neko, trying not to look into Neko's eyes as the Dead woman stepped across into their boat. Instead Kalypso addressed Ahmed.

'I need time,' she said anxiously. 'But not too much time. You know what I'm saying?'

'Yeah,' said Ahmed. Kalypso crossed into Neko's boat. Suddenly she lost her resolve and glanced at Neko.

'He is what they used to call a "vegetable",' Neko signed to her. The luminous Wild silhouetted every gesture as the two boats glided in tandem along a broad channel of cooled luma. 'He cannot attend to even his most basic physical needs. He is as passive as Sieng, and about as good company.'

Marcsson was sitting in the very spot where Teres had kept Sieng in the luma tank. He looked harmless and dull. He was interfaced, of course. He didn't look up.

'Does he never speak?' she asked.

'Does a vegetable speak?' Neko said. 'No.'

Kalypso coughed nervously, trying to hide her disappointment. She gestured for them to go, and Ahmed turned his craft and drew off to some distance; but he didn't leave altogether.

They're afraid for me, she thought. *Of* me.

She blinked in the ashen wind, which was finally dying down. They were floating in the same super-colony of photosynthetic algaics where she and Neko had paused briefly to inhale the bare air of T'nane, that day during her captivity, so long ago. The colony had grown exponentially since then. Green cells flared with the light generated by the *flagrare* below; the glow reached even into the mahogany sky. The air smelled sulphurous, but it was breathable. She took Marcsson's breathing gear off for him as well, so that she could see his face.

If you counted the time he'd spent sleeping during the Crossing, Azamat would be in his eighties by now, just like all the Earthborn. She'd never thought he looked old before now. Maybe it was the interface shielding his eyes which made the rest of his face seem grave. The lines to either side of his mouth were slightly deeper, the cheekbones more pronounced. Otherwise, he appeared unchanged. He gave no indication that he noticed her presence, which was a reassuringly familiar kind of behavior. His statement to her in the Dreamer, *I am Ganesh now*, seemed a little absurd. This was also reassuring. She began to relax.

'I brought you something,' she said. 'I won a bet against the Dead, but it's really thanks to you, so . . . ' She unwrapped a cigar and put it in his blunt hand, which did not react. She passed it under his nose.

'*Mmm*. Cuban, Azamat. They have ants in Cuba? Oh, that was Costa Rica, right? Whatever.'

It took three tries before she managed to light his cigar. She put it between his lips and it fell out right away, burning his bare thigh. He didn't flinch. She picked it up.

'Come on, now. You can do this.'

In the end she prised his jaws open, slid the cigar between his teeth, and sat back. She lit her own and waited, wondering if there would be any reaction.

After a couple of seconds he inhaled slightly. His lips closed around the cigar, which blazed as he took a long pull. The interface continued to flicker with activity, uninterrupted.

Kalypso smiled anyway and took an inaugural puff of her own. She thought about the distance the cigar had travelled and what it was supposed to mean, and for a second she tried to imagine Cuba – but only for a second. She closed her eyes as the smoke filled her senses.

They both started coughing at the same time.

Thank you . . .

Ella Fitzgerald
Peter Gabriel
Miles
Meredith Monk
Paganini
Me'shell Ndegeocello
Dmitri S. and Keith Jarrett
Midnight Oil
Radiohead
Bela Bartok
Public Enemy
György Ligeti
Soundgarden Soundgarden Soundgarden

and John Grado, who made the headphones.